A BLIND EYE

By

Howard E. Strickley

Copyright © Howard E. Strickley 2016
This book is sold subject to the condition that it shall not, by way of trade or otherwise, be lent, resold, hired out, or otherwise circulated without the publisher's prior consent in any form of binding or cover other than that in which it is published and without a similar condition including this condition being imposed on the subsequent publisher.
The moral right of Howard E. Strickley has been asserted.
ISBN-13: 978-1532888533
ISBN-10: 1532888538

For Ashley Nunn – 1966-2015

My consummate supporter, friend, and critic whom I miss profoundly.

And of course Frances, Ethan, and Ruben.

CONTENTS

Prologue	*1*
One	*7*
Two	*53*
Three	*89*
Four	*105*
Five	*129*
Six	*140*
Seven	*164*
Eight	*175*
Nine	*189*
Ten	*209*
Eleven	*224*
Twelve	*233*
Thirteen	*266*
Fourteen	*294*
Fifteen	*335*
Sixteen	*385*
Seventeen	*388*
Eighteen	*415*
Epilogue	*423*

This is a work of fiction. Names, characters, businesses, organizations, places, events and incidents either are the product of the author's imagination or are used fictitiously. Any resemblance to actual persons, living or dead, events, or locales is entirely coincidental.

PROLOGUE

October 6th 1997

Samuel Parker switched off the television. He should have been pleased with what he just saw; the police had questioned the wrong men and it seemed that, although the job had not gone as originally planned, the outcome was better than any of them could have hoped for. Parker was not comforted by this. Ever since the job, he'd had a sense of overwhelming dread.

Life wasn't going to be like this for much longer though. In two days he would be in the tropical sun and clean air; never to return to the country he had loved so much but now suffocated. Parker's world had not been the same since the job and he was desperate to find some sense of normality as well as a place *they* would not find him. In the meantime, it was sit tight. So far – so good. They had not come calling.

While preparing coffee, he looked out of the window. The last of the sun was sinking behind the estate, leaving streaks, like open wounds across the sky. He stared up fearfully, when the doorbell startled him.

For a moment, Parker could do nothing.

Walking the hall, Parker hoped it would just be the postman delivering more exotic brochures to faraway lands where he would be certain to spend the rest of a life in safety. He paused for a moment, and then opened the door.

Not the postman.

It was *them*.

"Sam, how the devil are you?" asked the attractive woman.

"Nice to see you again, Sam," said the tall man by her side.

Parker gave them both a weak smile. "Nathan, Carla." He nodded politely. "You'd better come in."

Parker led the couple through to the sitting room and offered them both a seat. Parker sat down opposite them, putting his hands together to stop them shaking. The couple he'd known for five years were dressed immaculately as always, both in dark Armani suits with the faintest of chalk stripe. Each had jet-black hair, Nathan's short and slicked back, and Carla's long and shiny, tapering to the middle of her back.

However, Parker didn't know them anymore. They were once inseparable, scruffy rebels, hell-bent on shaking up their tiny worlds. Things were very different now. His friends had become polished killers, basking in money and power their benefactor gave them in equal measure. Parker had loved them once, felt safe around them, like one might around family. Now he viewed them like strangers and they scared the hell out of him.

"Is everything all right?" he asked. "I thought we weren't supposed to meet for another week."

"Relax," replied Nathan. "Everything's fine. You've seen the news, just a terrible accident. It couldn't have turned out better."

Parker looked at the man he'd once called a friend. Nathan's smugness made him feel nauseous.

Carla noticed the holiday brochures strewn over the coffee table. "Going away, Sam?" she asked, sifting through them.

Parker just nodded. He was aware of the smell of coffee coming from the percolator in the kitchen. The aroma, for some reason, was almost overwhelming.

Nathan unbuttoned his jacket, sat back, and crossed his legs. "You did a good job, Sam," he congratulated him. "The boss is pleased with how it all went. Turned out better than we could have hoped."

"So you keep saying. We could have both been killed! You risked everything."

Nathan shook his head and sighed. "For fuck's sake, relax."

"Relax!" snapped Parker. "You weren't supposed to do what you did. We were meant to follow them, that's all. I was just meant to drive and you would take care of the rest. You weren't supposed to do what you did!"

"I did what I had to do," replied Nathan, patiently. "We've been through all this before. I saw an opportunity and took it. You know as well as I do that it couldn't have turned out better. No one is ever going to be looking for us. They don't suspect a thing."

Carla was bored with the squabbling. She faked a yawn and picked up a brochure from the coffee table. "Have you been to Barbados before, Sam?"

"Why don't we just cut the crap?" Parker said, suddenly. "What do you want?"

"Okay," replied Carla. "Fuck it, Sam, what are you thinking? Where do you think you're going, eh?"

"I want out," began Parker. "Is that so hard for you to understand? Listen, Carla, I've done my bit and I don't want any more of it. I didn't join up for all this. It's too heavy for me. I'm out."

Carla sighed. "You don't just get out, Sam. You knew that all along." She gave Parker a cold stare. "You don't just fuckin' leave when you feel like it. This isn't the Cub Scouts!"

"Please," Parker implored. "Don't I mean anything to you anymore? What about our time in the NLA? Doesn't that mean anything to you two? This is not what we're about. For God's sake, we killed someone!"

"Things are different now, Sam," replied Nathan. "We all knew it would be. We've joined something bigger and better than the NLA. The Family is the future now."

"The Family's out of control," Parker replied. "We're in way over our heads. Do you realise what we've done? We're never going to get away with it. Jesus, I'm not even sure why it had to happen in the first place."

"You know perfectly well why it had to happen, Sam," said Carla, removing a hair from her jacket sleeve. "There's a bigger picture now. Finally, we have the power to change things. And let me remind you that, thanks to Nathan, we *have* got away with it."

"This isn't how it was meant to be, Carla," Parker went on. "We're puppets for God's sake! And the person pulling our strings is fuckin' crazy."

"He's been good to us, Sam," replied Carla. "And to you! Let me remind you of the substantial pay-out you just got for this one."

"Listen, Sam," began Nathan. "We don't want to fall out over—"

"Fuck you, Nathan!" snapped Parker. He immediately regretted his words. "I'm sorry, Nathan. I didn't mean that. It's just too much. I can't live like this anymore. I'm scared."

Nathan took a deep breath and let it out slowly. "I understand how you feel, Sam. Really I do," he said, with his eyes closed.

Parker held his hands out. "I just want to go. You can trust me, you know that. I'll be far away from here. You won't have to worry about a thing." He sat forward on his seat. "Why don't you come with me? We have lots of money. We could all start a new life, a fresh start. It will be just like the old days."

Silence hung for a long moment. Parker grew embarrassed.

"Stop worrying," replied Nathan, holding up his hands. "We didn't come here to fight. In fact, quite the contrary. Carla has something to show you. Go on, show him, Carla. Show him what you've got."

Parker sat bemused as Carla stood up. She walked up to where he was sitting and wiggled her way between his legs. She smiled wickedly down at him. Parker watched as her skirt gradually rose over the tops of her thighs, and then inched up to the bottom of her panties. White lace was the last thing Parker ever saw. Parker never saw it coming, never heard the dull thud of the gunshot or witnessed his own blood splatter the tops of Carla's thighs and front of her blouse.

Before Carla had a chance to pull her skirt back down, her husband was behind her. He wrapped his arms around her then tucked his hands down the front of her underwear. Carla gasped with pleasure as her lover caressed her; pleasure heightened by the fact that Samuel Parker watched them, his dead eyes open in astonishment.

ONE

Jeramiah Stone relaxed into the taxi seat and lit his first cigarette of the day. Taking a long drag, he looked out of the window. The grey morning streets didn't help with his sleepy, miserable mood. But, then, nothing would have this particular morning. Today was the worst anniversary of his life. Milly had been dead two years to the day.

Feeling chilled, Stone asked the driver, rather bluntly, to share some of the hot air warming his cosy driving cubicle. The driver scowled at him in the rear-view mirror but did as his passenger requested. The heater fans wined and warmth rushed through the rear vents, carrying the stench of roasted dust. The sudden burst of air sent the ash from Stone's cigarette all around the cab.

"Fuck it!" he cursed, brushing ash from his trousers.

"I told you, mate. No smoking," scolded the driver over the intercom.

Stone glared at him as he caught a flash of humour in the driver's eye. Doing as he was told, he threw the cigarette out of the window.

Sitting back again, Stone contemplated why he was being brought in on a Saturday. His articles were always ready by at least Friday for the Sunday edition of The Informer, so this summons had to be over a rare issue of legality.

His Sunday column was one that could wreck a career or, at the very least, make someone's life extremely difficult. This wasn't because what he wrote was nearly always damaging for some misfortunate member of the famous and elite, but because Stone was right. The Informer had rarely been sued over any of its allegations fronted by Stone's infamous column, which sent out a very clear and worrying message to anyone that happened to be at the end of his poison-tipped pen. Sunday's article would be no exception. Thanks to Jeramiah Stone, come Monday morning a career could be as good over and a reputation in tatters.

His taxi turned onto Fleet Street, which seemed like mid-afternoon with the amount of people already on the streets. Saturday was the busiest day for the Sunday editions of all the tabloids and broadsheets. Conversations were being held on the side of the street accompanied by mobile breakfasts eaten between the mouthfuls of last minute information before it was sent to print.

The taxi drew up outside The Informer's offices and Stone got out. As he waited for the driver to make change, he perused the building where he had worked for the last eighteen months.

The Informer's offices dominated Fleet Street with the arrogant demure of a New York governmental office building. Sharp, reflective windows adorned its seven floors. A steeple roof gave an almost religious presence. Two gargoyles flanked either side of the seventh floor, hunched defiantly on marble altars. The gothic tone added menace to its exterior boldness, leaving any admirer believing Gotham City had once existed where London now stood. 'The Informer' arched in gold polished letters over the main entrance.

The Informer, besides being one of the oldest tabloids, boasts one of the highest readerships in the country. This, in turn, means it is one of the most powerful institutions in the land. Failing a war or overseas conflict, its pages are, more often than not, devoted to the new celebrity phenomena or, more to the point, the potential scandals surrounding them. Those in the public eye, or indeed in its office, treat the workings of The Informer with the greatest of respect. With a population demanding an almost angelic quality from the celebrities and politicians influencing their lives, The Informer makes sure these heroes are dutiful of those demands.

The Informer is, as are most of the tabloids in England, a paper committed to gossip and scandal rather than real news; claiming this is what readers want. The Informer thrives on the appetite of a public obsessed, not just with the rich and famous, but with their failings. With politicians now falling into that bracket, The Informer has an endless supply of material to satisfy that appetite.

Stone spun his way through the revolving doors

and into the lobby. Of course he couldn't have known it then, but it would be the last time that he would ever enter the building.

"Morning, Mister Stone," said the smartly dressed receptionist sat behind a horseshoe desk with 'Informer' along the front.

Stone stepped up to the desk and smiled. "What time do you get in, Karen?" he asked.

The receptionist wet her lips. "I start at seven-thirty, Mister Stone."

Stone observed her flirting. Karen's breasts tried to escape her tight blouse as she inhaled.

"There should be a law against that," he said, witnessing the attempted breakout.

"Against what, Mister Stone?" asked the receptionist, with her best 'doe-eyed' look.

Stone winked at her. "Getting up at seven-thirty." He made his way to the elevators.

A lift arrived, offering Stone a life-size reflection of himself on the opposite wall as he got in. He pressed button number seven and the lift quietly started towards the registered destination.

Stone looked at himself in the mirror. He seemed older this morning, or maybe it was just a different mirror on Saturdays; one that reflected the truth. He was still attractive. At thirty-eight, he wasn't in danger of losing it all to middle age just yet. His dark hair wasn't thinning and the grey still spared him. Some might have been pleased with what they saw, but there was something Stone didn't quite recognise about himself anymore. The hurt he harboured inside had seeped out. And while he was still capable of deceiving his reflection with a smile or even laughter, the eyes he looked back at would never let him forget.

Outdone by the mirror's findings, Stone scanned the walls where honours and distinctions in the newspaper's history were mounted in glass-fronted cabinets. This journey was never easy for Stone, reminding him what he had become. He once had an illustrious career working for a broadsheet where he was arguably one of the best foreign correspondents in the business. Now, it was reduced to a Sunday column called, 'Blood from a Stone'.

Every week, Stone gave his readers an investigative report into a member of the social elite, government or business community. The article would invariably be cruel and damaging. Once Stone had despised the paper he now worked for and the kind of journalist he had become. Like many things in his life, it didn't matter anymore. Now there was another agenda. A man in the public eye, who because of his political status went unpunished, had killed his wife suddenly and unjustly. Stone's column was his way of making sure that never happened again.

His eyes fell on the news article he recently had written concerning the death of the Princess of Wales. His report of the tragedy made The Informer the highest selling daily, earning respect from his colleagues and, more importantly, job security. The praise, however, was somewhat ironic. Sure, like most journalists, he was covering the Princess's new romance with Dodi Al-Fayed, son of Harrods owner, Mohammed Al-Fayed, but Stone hadn't been in Paris where they were killed. Years of industrious journalism gained Stone a rank of informants and friends in the business. A freelancer by the name of Louis Guilett, who *had* been in Paris at the time, gave the details of the story to Stone. The French media were not going to pay Guilett anywhere near what he knew his friend's paper across the water would. The Informer paid Guilett for the details concerning the crash and Stone signed away his friend's work with his own name. He wrote a heart-rending account of the tragedy followed by an appropriate obituary of the princess's life, which had won him the respect of an adoring public.

Now, exactly one month after the funeral, the public mood was still gloomy. Most of the dailies still carried stories on the circumstances surrounding Diana's death and what she had achieved during her short life. The press were keen to appease the mood of the nation. The brief of all of the national tabloids and broadsheets was to make sure that nothing derogatory was written about her. Any reporter who *did* could be in very real danger of being lynched. Because of this, hypocrisy was rife. Two months ago, The Informer had nothing good to say about the princess; desperate to uncover faults that would shatter the fairy tale pretence of her life and work. Now things were different. The princess was a 'candle in the wind' that should never have been extinguished.

Stone wondered how one human being could ever have that much effect on so many people's lives. For Stone, the country's mood seemed faked. He had hoped her death would bring change but it hadn't. Nothing really changed. Even the work the princess had been heavily involved in concerning the ban of landmines was still falling on deaf ears. Even America (who had loved her like their own) was refusing to sign a treaty banning their use, which ninety other countries had.

The media, anxious as ever to capitalise on the mood, took charge of the public. The oppressive agenda of the British press was to make sure that the country grieved the princess until they said otherwise. There was no other news, nothing else as important as her death; no one else's life as important as hers. Mother Theresa, the nun who devoted her life in India to helping the sick and poor, died just a day before the princess's funeral. The press didn't consider her life and work of such importance as to warrant being given anywhere near the amount of parchment that they gave the princess.

Other news was still bad, and it seemed what Diana's death might have heralded by way of uniting the nation and the start of a better, kinder, more charitable Britain was short lived, unachievable, and for the most part, uninspiring. Life seemed to be going on as before, with or without her. In time, Diana would be remembered as just another celebrity, killed tragically young, mourned briefly by a country that seemed all too familiar with grief.

Other cuttings behind the reflective glass were of Stone accepting awards when his career had been flourishing. Columnist of the Year and Reporter of the Year for The Global. All from a time long ago where he had once been dedicated to his profession, working for a reputable paper. Once he had reported on the continuing conflicts in Afghanistan to the warring factions in the Middle East as an overseas correspondent. At the same time he was one of the most popular journalists on Fleet Street with an enviable career ahead of him. Most of his colleagues were adamant that Stone would naturally make the transition into television with his experience, not to mention good looks, to carry him there. But it was all at a time when he was happy; a time when Milly had been alive.

Following his wife's death, a shattered Stone slowly sunk into depression, unable to give his work the commitment it demanded. Too much time off work and not being able to meet his obligations to overseas news, meant his last employer, The Global, had to sack him.

After a year in retreat, Stone emerged able to face work again, though in a smaller capacity and with a very different agenda. The Informer was happy to take him on and gave him his own column; uncovering the failings and misgivings of the intellectual elite. Stone was not in the news business anymore; he was now in the sleaze business. Tragically, Stone had become everything he said he wouldn't after losing everything he thought he couldn't.

Eventually, the lift bell declared his arrival at the newsroom.

The open-plan office of the newsroom was a hive of activity. Desks were laid out in long, regimental rows, each with a computer terminal throbbing with the same urgency as the newsroom itself. Telephones rang constantly, fingers tapped at keyboards with vigorous efficiency. It was the very heart of the paper. And the room was beating loud and fast.

Stone made for the drinks machine. He lit another cigarette and waited for a strong, sweet coffee to be dispensed. The sugar tempered his mood. He headed for his section of the newsroom and snuck up behind his assistant.

Rachel Martin had been Stone's researcher for his column since he had joined the paper. She was just about the only person he liked or cared about in the industry these days. Their relationship was a good one, despite the fact they had recently ended a brief romance. Rachel had been the only woman Stone had been emotionally linked with since the death of his wife. The affair had been uncomplicated, as Stone seemed temporarily incapable of the intimacy he'd once had. For that reason their personal relationship ended. Rachel had her own demons to deal with and no intentions of taking on anyone else's.

Stone perused the article on the screen that Rachel was editing. The headline for his Sunday column couldn't have been bolder.

"Shillingway's Secret Trips to Euston Prostitute."

Royston Shillingway was a wealthy political figure. He had been a member of the House for the last twenty years and was popular among his Labour colleagues on the back bench and with the public at large. Shillingway was sixty-nine, a big man with a permanent smile nestled within a white beard that almost spread the circumference of his cherry-red face. He was, in fact, the quintessential Santa Claus lookalike. Professionally, Shillingway had always been an outspoken politician on many issues; most that appealed to the far left of the population. Not least, were his career-long views on the legitimacy of the monarchy in a modern democracy, and the taxpayer's money maintaining it.

Recently, his views had struck a chord with the young, increasingly disillusioned voter. He was a new Labour annoyance that not only had influence in his own party but also attracted certain sympathies from the right political camps. His birthright and vast sums of inherited wealth didn't seem to bother a public that was becoming increasing intolerant of politicians. The public liked his refreshing honesty, fun-loving manner, and animated appearance. Regardless of these appealing qualities, Royston Shillingway was the same as everyone else, inherently flawed. Shillingway's weakness was that he had a fondness for a certain young prostitute he frequented near London's Euston station.

Stone's editor had given him the tip about Shillingway and the story. A man had approached Stone anonymously on the end of a telephone, asking him to meet in a pub. Stone had gone to the meeting where he traded information with a doctor from Harley Street. The consultant had acquaintances with the very specialist that was Shillingway's and had access to some very private information concerning his health. In short, Shillingway had caught a venereal disease and wanted it kept under wraps.

Stone had arranged for the doctor to receive twenty-five thousand pounds for that information. Stone's editor had then given him the resources to track down the prostitute that had given Shillingway the disease. Tracking her down had been the easy part and a substantial fee had her running in off the street. Stone had met the bleached blonde in a cafe near her home and got the gore. The transaction had been simple enough but the story which followed was, for those involved, catastrophic. Of course, due to disclosure laws, the doctor's affidavit had been irrelevant. That didn't matter. The prostitute's story would ruin a man's life, his forty-year marriage, and his political reputation.

Stone announced his presence by tapping Rachel on the shoulder.

Rachel flinched. "Oh, it's you. What are you doing in the office today?"

Stone rolled his eyes. "I thought you'd be pleased to see me?" he said, looking past her and reading the screen. Next to the story was a picture of the prostitute Shillingway had been visiting, and a photograph of his wife. Stone glanced at it then quickly looked away as if he felt the gaze of Mrs Shillingway all over him.

Rachel squinted at the screen. "This is good," she declared, whilst correcting a spelling mistake. "Is it true?"

"Is what true?" replied Stone, stubbing his cigarette into the full ashtray on her desk.

"Shillingway. The prostitute?"

Stone frowned at her. "Of course."

Rachel sighed. "You'd better have something to back this up when it comes out tomorrow, Stoney, or the shit is going to hit the front of this building and leave us all stinking for a thousand years."

Stone laughed and helped himself to the rest of

Rachel's bacon sandwich.

"Seriously, Stoney, do you have this one backed up? Not exactly a good time to be making waves in high places. I'm surprised Marcus is letting you ride with this one."

Stone sighed. "It was our glorious leader who gave me the story in the first place. Shillingway's been a very naughty boy. As soon as he denies it, we bring out the ace card. Margaret Plummer." Stone laughed. "Or, Miss Scarlet, as she's affectionately known under the arches."

Rachel sat up straight in her seat and stretched her arms, pushing her breasts tightly against the front of her jumper. As planned, it didn't go unnoticed. "This is going to piss a lot of people off, Stoney. Poor bastard. Just think of his wife."

"Careful Rach, you'll have me in tears."

Rachel smiled weakly in response and Stone noted it. "What's the matter with you, Rach? You don't actually feel sorry for this guy, do you?"

"No. It's *us* I feel sorry for. Is there any good news out there?"

"No," replied Stone. "And who'd read it if there was?"

Stone was right of course, but Rachel felt sorry that he thought like that. She went back to work. "Anyway, what *are* you doing here?"

"The boss wants to see me."

"What about? Oh, let me guess. He has another story for you? Jesus, Stoney, you're about the only journalist I know that has stories delivered to their desk straight from the editor. I reckon he likes you." With a glancing wink towards the editor's office she said, "Either that or it's personal."

Stone couldn't help wondering about the last remark. He had successfully brought down a large portfolio of people in the public eye, all handed to him on a plate from their mutual boss. For a brief moment, the reason intrigued him.

"Well?" Rachel waited. "What you in for?"

"That's what I'm going to find out. He's probably getting jittery about the story." Stone took his leave after a lingering look at his ex-lover.

As always, the banter with Rachel had raised his mood to one that might be appropriate when seeing the editor. Stone knew he was working here because it was good for the paper to have a journalist that was once highly respected writing for it. But Stone's devotion and enthusiasm for the business was wavering and it wasn't going unnoticed. In truth, his column would never get written if it weren't for Rachel. She carried him and his editor fed him stories. Stone knew only too well that he couldn't keep up the pretence much longer. He knew that if the editor didn't want to discuss the Shillingway bombshell, it was probably going to be one of those motivational chats he liked to give to a journalist who wasn't keeping pace.

Before he had a chance to knock, the editor's door was flung open. Standing with a large smile on his chubby face was editor in chief, Marcus Becker. "You lucky bastard, Stone," he boomed, and ushered the reporter into his office.

"Why am I a lucky bastard?" asked Stone, as he sat down.

Becker grinned all the way to his seat. He was dressed in a grubby, un-ironed shirt, with the cuffs held away from his wrists by means of silver shirt bands. He wore bright blue braces, which held up trousers that were far too tight for his large build. Stone thought all he needed was a fat cigar jammed in the side of his mouth and Becker would have looked like any of the news men depicted in a movie from the golden era of Hollywood.

"Good story on Shillingway," he began. "You'll be pleased to know I'm giving it front page. Make sure that tart's waiting in the wings when the shit hits. It's going to be one hell of a mess when this comes out."

Stone nodded wearily. His boss was happy with the story, which meant only one thing. Sitting upright, he prepared himself for the motivational speech.

As he watched Becker open a new packet of cigarettes, Stone noted that his boss looked much older this morning. Becker was fifty-nine, retiring in a year's time. He probably could go on forever if it weren't for his doctors indicating that if he didn't pack it in soon, he wouldn't see three years of his retirement. Becker's heart no longer had the same enthusiasm for journalism as did his brain.

Stone, like most at The Informer, knew very little about Becker. He was single, never married, and kept himself to himself. Whether this was because he was an intensely private man or he had a professional ethic of never mixing with the people he worked with, no one was sure. Fact was, he never did. This didn't seem to bother anyone, especially Stone, as he had no desire to spend any more time in Becker's company than absolutely necessary.

Stone became impatient. If he was in for a dressing down, he wanted to get on with it. "Marcus, did you call me in on a Saturday to discuss my article, or to show me your beautifully decorated office?"

Becker belched, quickly putting his hand to his mouth as if it were never meant to happen. "You know, I've got to start eating properly," he said, lighting a cigarette. He flashed the packet at Stone, who didn't stand a chance in the split second he was given to accept, and then sat heavily back in his chair.

"What would be the story of the decade?" he asked, and then dragged on his cigarette so hard Stone thought he might burn it to the end. "What would be the scoop of the century?"

"Don't know?" replied Stone. "I thought the Shillingway story was pretty close."

Becker sat forward in his chair and smiled greedily. "Not even halfway... Who's the most famous fucker in the world?"

Stone couldn't be bothered with twenty questions, not this morning. "John Holmes," he replied, referring to the well-hung porn star of the seventies.

Becker ran his hand through his heavily greying hair. "Very funny. Who's never given an interview to anyone?"

Stone shrugged.

"Who's potentially one of the richest men in the world?"

Becker waited again.

"Who's one of the most influential and powerful figures in the art world? The same person who sold one of his paintings for twenty-five million pounds to some Japanese guy last week?"

Stone got it. "Abraham Conty," he replied, wondering where the conversation was going.

"At last," Becker cheered, and flopped back into his tall leather chair. "Abraham Conty."

"So?" asked Stone.

"Like I said, Stone, you're a lucky bastard. The great Abraham Conty wants *you* to do an interview."

Stone was genuinely surprised. "Me? Why me?"

Becker shrugged. "Fucked if I know? Got an invitation in writing from him this morning. He wants *you*, my boy."

"You're joking?"

Becker smiled and shook his head. "You know I never joke about a scoop, Stone."

"Come on, Marcus, why me? I'm no art critic and I certainly don't do interviews. We have an arts division to take care of this kind of thing."

Becker waved his hand in front of his face. "Apparently he doesn't want all that." Becker took the invitation from the envelope and read it aloud. "He says that to coincide with his forthcoming exhibition at the Tate, he would like to give an interview. He doesn't want to conduct this with any art critics whatsoever and suggests that Jeramiah Stone conduct the interview, whose work he has admired to date." Becker held the letter up. "He is quite specific, and very clear about who he wants to do it. If this is what Abraham Conty wants, then this what he's going to fuckin' get.

"I'm serious, Stone," Becker went on, "this could be the big one. This one you need, Jeramiah. It's an opportunity of a lifetime. Something like this doesn't come around that often."

Stone looked up at Becker. He knew what his editor meant by him *needing* this one. "When's he coming in?"

Becker smiled. This morning he was king of treats. "He's not. You're going to him."

Stone frowned. "Where is he?"

Becker had obviously rehearsed their meeting. He pulled a drawer open and heaved a large atlas onto the desk, already open with a marked page. "There," he puffed, pointing to the map.

Stone's gaze traced Becker's cigarette-stained finger, pointing to a small green dot of land just off the southern coast of Spain.

"An island?"

"Not any old island. That's the famous Conty Island. You're going there, to stay, by invitation of the man himself."

Stone sat back in his chair. This wasn't what he was expecting. "Shit."

"Yep," said Becker, smugly. "That's just how the other papers are going to feel when they hear that we've bagged this one. They're going to go nuts!" He thumped the top of the atlas with a powerful fist.

"They won't fucking believe it!"

"Yeah, but what do I get? Like I said, what do I know about the art world?"

The truth was that Stone did know a little about the art world. His wife was a leading art critic and journalist, which is how they'd met. She'd been working for a highly regarded art magazine called The Gallery before her premature death. He recalled that Milly had always wanted to meet the great man herself. Sadly ironic that he was going to get the chance instead.

"Let me just remind you, Stone, of how important this is," Becker began. "This man is a very big fish. He knows nearly all heads of state and numerous celebrities, actors, rock stars. He's world famous to the point that his art is, and will be even more so when he dies, the most celebrated works the world has seen. This guy's bigger than Picasso for God's sake. Now everyone's talking about Conty again because of this exhibition. Also, he's recently married so everyone wants a slice of the famous couple. Everybody loves the guy, or at least, his work. He's patron of just about every art institution there is and currently the most influential figure in the art world. He donates substantial amounts to good causes." Becker paused abruptly with a shrug. "Apart from this, no one knows anything about him. That's why it's so important. He's never uttered a word to the media about anything *ever* before. They don't get much more private than Conty."

Becker lit another cigarette. "He's an eccentric. The man's almost a recluse." Becker exhaled a steady stream of smoke in the direction of the ceiling.

"You're going to find out about this guy and get some shit on him."

Stone just stared at his editor. "What?"

"Get something on him. This paper isn't an art magazine. We want the juicy stuff. Find out who he *really* is. What does he do in his spare time? Find out about his wife while you're there. What are they like as a couple? Is she in it for the money? Does he drink? Does she? Does he smoke? Take drugs? Both? Is he gay and the marriage a farce? You know, get the *juicy* stuff."

With a muffled belch, Becker turned back to Stone. "Whatever, find it out. You know the score, Stone. You do a good job on this and it could be the one that gets you back up there. You do remember where *up there* is, Jeramiah?"

Stone nodded wearily. There was a time when it had not been like this. There was a time when he hadn't had an editor like this either.

"What happens if there's nothing to find out?"

Becker screwed his face up. "You'll be in Spain, so get a little Spanish kid and put him in Conty's fuckin' bed for all I care, Jeramiah. Just get some shit on this guy." Becker belched again. "Jesus, what have I been eating? Look, everyone knows he's great, boring! No one goes to the lengths he has to keep the rest of the world away without wanting to hide something. Now there has to be something, so find it out. Try and remember that's what sells, Stone."

"I know what sells," replied Stone, patiently, "but surely this will be a good enough scoop without having to—"

Listen, Jeramiah," Becker interrupted, "try and remember who you work for now. I have bosses as well, and my bosses want to sell more papers than anyone else. Our readers are not fuckin' art lovers, okay. Our readers like scandal. They like gossip. Scandal and gossip is what this paper gives them. That's why we sell more papers than anyone else and I intend, no, correction, I *have* to make sure that it stays that way."

Stone didn't see any point in pursuing the moral line with his boss. Becker was right. The Informer was not that kind of newspaper. "When do I go?" he asked, softly.

"You go Monday morning. He even had a first class ticket sent out for you. One-way, mind. He's going to bring you back on his private plane. I reckon this guy likes to be in the driving seat, don't you?"

"Monday!"

"Calm down." Becker fanned his hands. "I've got some people working on his history from the arts supplement and what we know about him. It will be e-mailed to you as soon as they get it, which won't take long because there's fuck all on the guy. Best thing you can do is enjoy the rest of your weekend, pack, and then think about how you're going to conduct your investigations, I mean your interview." Becker laughed. "Anything else you're working on at the moment can wait.

"We'll handle the Shillingway story when it breaks. You've done what you needed on that one. You take as long as you like to bag this one. It's an open invitation. No timescale. We're not letting an opportunity like this pass us by. Now, his exhibition will be opening soon at the Tate. I've arranged a tour to get you familiarised with his work." Becker handed Stone a piece of paper. "That's who you will need to ask for," he said, pointing at the name on the paper. "He's the curator of the exhibition and will be expecting you this afternoon."

"You say that no one has ever got a word out of this guy?"

Becker shook his head vigorously, reminding Stone, for some reason, of a Labrador. "Nothing, he's a fuckin' enigma. You bring this one home and you could be on for your third award. This time for *us*."

Stone thought it wise to look enthusiastic at that point. His relationship with Becker had always been tolerable ever since he joined The Informer. Becker gave Stone the freedom he needed to get a story and Stone brought the paper good articles, which in turn brought readers. The problem now was Stone no longer believed in what he did and Becker knew it. Ultimately, Becker was all too aware that Stone was only with The Informer because of his own agenda and didn't really like working for the paper. That fact annoyed Becker. He knew that Stone and the rest of Fleet Street considered The Informer to be a second-rate tabloid compared to the heavy presses. Eighteen months ago, Becker was pleased that he was able to bag a journalist who was considered to be the best in the business. Trouble was, Stone wasn't at his best anymore.

Truth was, Becker wouldn't have even considered Stone for such an important story if it weren't for the fact that Conty had specifically asked for him. After all, Becker had his own boss to answer to.

"Any other questions?" asked Becker, looking out of the window to the newsroom.

Stone shook his head. "No, I guess not."

"Good. Here's your ticket. You arrive in Malaga Monday morning at nine, their time. He's arranged for a driver to pick you up from the airport."

Stone took the ticket wallet and stood up.

"Good luck," said Becker, going to the door and opening it to the noise of the newsroom. "You're a lucky bastard, Stone. Interview in Spain with the most famous man on the planet. Shit, you get a scoop and a break all at the same time." Becker leant forward. "Just keep this to yourself until you get back. Not a word to anyone, Jeramiah." He held a chubby finger to his lips.

Stone smiled and shook Becker's hand, sticky with excitement, or so he hoped. "Leave it to me," he said, then made his way back to his desk.

Rachel was still editing the Shillingway story. "How did it go?" she asked, on seeing him.

"Good. I'm off to Spain."

Rachel smiled. "You lucky bastard!"

"So everyone keeps telling me," replied Stone, reading over Rachel's corrections on his story.

"What are you going there for?" she asked, slapping Stone's hand as he tried to press one of the keys.

"You'll see."

"Rachel ran her tongue over her bottom lip. "Need someone to go with you?"

Stone looked at her and for a moment seriously contemplating her offer. "I need you here when this story breaks. Maybe we could go out when I get back and I'll tell you all about it."

Rachel swung her chair round to face the screen. "I'll think about it."

"You do that."

"Have a good trip anyway."

"I'll bring you back something nice," Stone promised, then started to make his way towards the lift.

"Say hello to Mister Conty for me," Rachel said, within earshot.

Stone turned to see Rachel with a wry smile on her face. He glanced suspiciously towards Becker's office, and then made his way out.

Once the doors had closed and the lift descended toward the ground floor, Stone leaned heavily against the wall. He had just been given the story of the year and should have been excited, but was far from that. The meeting with Becker had left him deflated.

Stone's contemplation of his next assignment ended when a black cab pulled up alongside him. He got in and instructed the driver to head for St. John the Baptist Church Cemetery, Chelsea.

The driver of this cab was much more amiable than the last and even allowed Stone to smoke. The heavens opened as they left Fleet Street and the driver decided he would cheer his passenger up by discussing the Louise Woodward trial.

Louise Woodward was a nineteen-year-old nanny from Cheshire, England, working out in America, Massachusetts, and accused of killing an American family's baby, Matthew Eappen, while in her care in February 1996. If found guilty, she would face the death penalty. The driver obviously thought it was a miscarriage of justice and shameful to put a young girl through the rigors of an adult court on such a serious charge, and let Stone know that the only sensible course of action available was to send the SAS immediately to Massachusetts and, "'Ave 'er out!" as he firmly put it.

Stone wasn't asked for his reaction to the case, though he had to admit the driver's opinion was arguably the best one. Stone was once an outspoken critic of the American justice system while working for The Global, especially concerning the death penalty. He had written some very contentious articles on the American overseas policy, accusing the American government of being hypocritical when policing other governments around the world for humanitarian crimes, when their own criminals, convicted of murder, were subject to the death penalty in thirty-eight states. This was one of the many things that he had once campaigned against – a time when he was passionate about his work. Now, Stone was indifferent.

Ironically, Stone wanted to follow the Woodward story but Becker, in his wisdom, decided there might be a conflict of interest because of his well-known views about the case. Stone didn't actually have to worry about his non-involvement. The Informer was more ruthless than he ever would have been. They asked all their readers who were about to go on holiday to the States to send their tickets into The Informer. Tickets had arrived in the thousands. The Informer then sent the tickets to the American Embassy in London as a national protest. The donors received a Free Louise Woodward T-shirt for their support and an alternative holiday destination.

Just as the driver's deliberations were in danger of becoming the ramblings of a lunatic, they arrived outside the church. Stone asked the driver to wait.

Stone pulled his coat around himself. He made the painful journey up the path through the cemetery. By the time he reached his wife's grave the rain was thrashing down.

Stone knelt close to the graveside so that his wife could hear him over the downpour. There were fresh flowers on her grave as usual. Stone paid the church groundsman to make sure that fresh flowers were put down every morning. Tenderly, he straightened them, making sure that the flower heads faced towards the headstone. As always, he read the epitaph.

Here lies Milly & Jessica Stone.
Died together on October 6th 1995.
Rest in eternal peace.

Stone stared at the grave and as always reflected on that fateful day, never wanting to forget the pain; as if he did, he would somehow forget them. Now he remembered vividly the young officers that had come to their flat that day. Never would he forget the expression on the male officer's face. Of all the officer could have dealt with during his time as a policeman, Stone knew it was the worst thing he had ever done in his short career or probably ever would. Stone shut his eyes and remembered the words that he would hear for the rest of his life.

"I'm afraid I have the most dreadful news for you, Mister Stone..."

Stone remembered how he'd held up his hand to the police officer's mouth. He didn't know how, but he knew what he was going to say; he just couldn't let him say it. But he couldn't stop the words that came from the young man's colleague, the words that he never expected.

"I'm so sorry to ask you this, Mister Stone. Did you know your wife was pregnant?"

Stone opened his eyes and stared at the grave. Rain splashed on the marble, flattening the delicate petals of his wife's favourite flowers. He propped the poppies against the headstone to shield them.

For the first six months following her death, Stone hadn't been able to come where his wife and child lay. Now it was different. Now he had to come. Being beside his wife's grave was the only place that he felt anywhere near related to the man he once was.

For some, the cemetery was a place where the bereaved could find an understanding – to be able to heal. A place to learn to accept a life lost for reasons known only by a god torn to love far fiercer than could be understood. Stone mourned, but he did not heal. As far as understanding why Milly and Jessica had to be taken, that was something he avoided contemplating. For Stone, to understand it all by resigning himself that this was God's work was simply beyond his capacity.

"I'm going to interview Abraham Conty," he whispered, voice trembling. "I know you would be pleased. I know how much you admired his work."

Stone touched his wife's name, feeling the engraved letters with his fingers. He traced the letters of the name of their child that he, and he alone, had named. Milly would have liked the name Jessica. They had spoken about names for children before as both dearly wanted them. Stone had no idea and only found out later that Milly was on her way back from the doctor's to tell him that they would be expecting their first child. Tragically, she never made it. Milly Stone was run down an hour after finding out she was pregnant, fifteen minutes away from telling the man that now grieved over her.

"I'll try and do the best I can. I will try harder. I promise."

Stone felt ashamed as he always did when he promised Milly something. He didn't know if he could try harder. Her death had broken him and he felt he didn't even want to try, let alone work hard at anything anymore. Once, he had believed. He had believed once in everything he did, everything he wrote. But how could he now?

After a long look at the epitaph, he kissed the tip of his fingers and pressed them against his wife's name. Then he rose and headed back to the cab, just as he had every day for the last year.

Several minutes passed before the taxi driver asked

where Stone wanted to go. He could see that his passenger was upset and waited patiently for him to give instructions. Eventually, a more composed Stone told the driver to take him to the Tate.

As Stone was driven to the gallery, he read Saturday's copy of The Informer.

The front page had been devoted to a woman who had just delivered Siamese twins. Unfortunately the twins shared a heart and doctors had said that if one of the twins were not terminated, both would die. Below the headline was a heart-wrenching account of the mother's ordeal in being asked to choose between the lives of her children. The Informer, to help with this troubling time, gave a premium rate number for their readers to call to give either a 'yes' or 'no' as to whether the mother should terminate. For those readers who found there wasn't enough information written about the procedure, there was a diagram suggesting the various operation techniques the doctors could use in separating the two.

The second page was actual world news. Most of the page, however, was domestic, detailing the fact that the Prime Minister, Tony Blair, was the first leader since 1921 to have a face-to-face meeting with the leaders of the political wing of the IRA, *Sinn Feinn*. The meeting was to press Sinn Feinn to finally give up their arms following the Good Friday agreement. The Informer was against any dialogue with Sinn Feinn and reminded the readers of how many innocent people had been killed by the IRA. The point was made even clearer by demonstrating the numbers with little silhouettes of adults and children.

Stone then read an article concerning a man allegedly addicted to biros that he habitually chewed at work. He was said to have consumed fifty biros a week for the last five years. The Informer insisted the stresses of work made him do it and asked its readers to donate biros as the man's employer was seriously contemplating charging him if he ate any more.

Several pages were given to Princess Diana and, among other things, a row concerning what they were going to do with all the flowers left by mourners outside her home. The country was still at odds as to the legitimacy of the monarchy following her death and The Informer, given its pro-royalist stance, gave a full page reminding the country what it was that the monarchy had and *did* do for the nation.

Stone took the time to read an amusing letter sent to Mary Clement-Homebridge, The Informer's agony aunt, from a man that claimed he had two penises. This meant he had trouble keeping a girlfriend as they found it to be rather repulsive. Mary had suggested that he cheer up as, given his extra appendage, he was probably one of the most intelligent men in the world.

The arts column was the only interesting article Stone could be bothered to read in detail. It was a relatively large story about the exhibition by the reclusive Abraham Conty about to open at the Tate – the largest exhibition of Conty's work ever seen in one place. The Informer's readers had a chance to win free entry if they sent in a self-portrait to be judged. At the top of the story was a faded black and white photograph of the artist. Stone squinted at the picture of the great man. He thought it odd that he was to soon to look at that face for real.

Eventually, they arrived. Smartening himself up and making sure his hair was neat, Stone made his way down the steps to one of the most famous galleries in the world. Once inside, he headed straight for the information desk. A lady in uniform smiled at him as he approached.

"Good morning, sir. How may I help you?"

Stone reached into his back pocket and pulled out the piece of paper Becker had given him. "I'm Jeramiah Stone of The Informer," he replied. "I'm here to see a... Mister Vincent."

"Yes of course," replied the woman, picking up the phone on her desk. "Mister Vincent, I have Mister Stone from The Informer to see you... Thank you, I'll tell him." She put the phone down. "He's coming right down."

"That's very kind of you. I'll wait over here."

The woman nodded politely, and then turned her attentions to the next visitor.

Stone sat down under a poster advertising a Matisse exhibition at the end of the year. He didn't have to wait long. A tall, bespectacled man with barely enough weight to fill his pinstripe suit announced his presence.

"Mister Stone?" he asked.

Stone got up. "Yes. Mister Vincent?"

"That's right," replied Vincent in a well-groomed voice, and shook Stone's hand. "I understand you're doing some research on Abraham Conty?"

"That's right," replied Stone. "I understand he's on show here."

"Will be. We're preparing as we speak. Conty will be on exhibit for the next ten weeks from Monday. Causing quite a stir. Quite extraordinary, Mister Stone. Are you a fan of his work?"

"I must confess I know more of his reputation than his art."

"Well, good you came early. This place is going to be pretty busy next week when the exhibit opens."

"I can imagine. Thank you for your time. I know you must be very busy."

Vincent frowned. "I don't wish to sound rude, Mister Stone, but I usually deal with Michael Frowd from the arts division of The Informer."

"Well, we're doing a special feature on the exhibition and Michael's asked me to cover it," lied Stone.

"Of course." Vincent gave Stone a grave look. "May I take this opportunity to offer my belated condolences. Milly was a great friend of everyone at the Tate and we all miss her very much."

"Thank you," Stone replied, immediately fond of the man before him.

"Milly was a great fan of Conty and was an invaluable consultant on his work." A brief, uncomfortable silence hung between them. "Well, do follow me," said Vincent.

Stone was led up to the east wing of the museum, where the contemporary artists were housed. They passed through many halls of recognisable art.

Schoolchildren sat on the floor in front of the masterpieces, busy sketching crude reproductions of what they saw. Most of the well-known artists' works shared a single room, Hockney, Hodgkin, Peter Blake, but Vincent didn't seem to show them any regard. Stone was aware that Vincent was as eager to see Conty's work as he was.

They came to the entrance of a large hall with 'Conty Exhibition' over the top of a decorative arch. A security guard stood by the doorway.

"Here we are," declared Vincent, excitedly. "By Conty's instruction we've kindly been donated works from galleries all over the world, enabling us to house the most comprehensive collection of his work ever. We're delighted that Conty decided to do this in Britain, especially at the Tate.

"Conty is displayed in four rooms which include his masterpieces over approximately the last ten years. We've even reduced our collections of other artists to accommodate the Conty collection. When the Tate Modern is completed, we'll be able send other works to them and house much more of his work here."

Stone got his notebook out and followed Vincent's lead. Staff wearing surgical gloves were still in the process of mounting some of the works in the large room.

"Well, this is the first," Vincent began, pointing to a large canvas situated behind some red rope. "This one is called, 'Cleansed.'"

Stone stood in front of the painting which showed a picture of a woman standing in a river, holding a child in one arm and pouring water over the child's head with the other from a golden urn. The painting was shocking in a sense – the top half of the child's body was horribly disfigured, as if burned. Where the water had been washed over the child's face, it seemed to have repaired miraculously that part of the deformity.

"Quite wonderful," Vincent remarked, keeping his eyes adoringly on the painting. "He has a masterful eye for the human body."

"The picture has a lot of anguish," remarked Stone, as he studied the faces of the subjects.

"Oh, yes indeed," replied Vincent, his voice resounding around the empty hall. "The expression on the mother's face, as that is whom we are led to believe it is, is quite pained. She knows she is healing her child with what is arguably holy water, but at the same time there is great sacrifice in her face, as though she takes personal responsibility for the child's disfigurement."

"How do you know she's the mother?"

"Good question," replied Vincent. "The breasts give it away. The woman's breast being uncovered is Conty's way of indicating the maternal relationship between the two subjects."

Stone looked at the painting carefully, studying the intricate detailing in the work.

"The mother's bodily proportions are perfect, and she is quite charming," Vincent went on. "This is done to emphasise the child's deformities. You see where the child is being cleansed and healed," he pointed at the picture, "well you'll notice that the repaired features, if you like, are as divine as the mother's. A wonderful piece of work."

Stone made notes – grotesque, deformed, beautiful, cleansed.

Vincent turned to him. "Anything you'd like to know?"

Stone looked back at the painting. "When was this done?"

Vincent screwed his thin face in such a way Stone could visibly see his cheekbones. "Ten years ago," replied Vincent, holding his glasses up and squinting at the date on the canvas under Conty's signature.

"I don't know what it is," Stone said, thoughtfully, as he perused the work, "but it seems familiar in some way."

"Indeed," agreed Vincent. "Like all of Conty's work, there are always influences in the works from the great masters. He's never done anything modern, no sculptures, nothing like that. I suppose this reflects his traditional nature. You see, what's fascinating about Conty's success is that he's not what you would call a revolutionary artist. I mean he doesn't challenge art the way Picasso or Matisse did. What makes him extraordinary is the sheer power of his work, the sheer depth of the painting. Another thing, which is quite remarkable about Conty, is the fact that what you see is what Conty originally intended you to see. That is to say, there are absolutely no mistakes. We know this because we've had a lot of his work x-rayed. It also revealed something quite extraordinary."

"Which is?" asked Stone, eagerly.

"He doesn't sketch or prepare. The paint goes

from the pallet to the brush to the canvas. No initial sketch, nothing. Some artists like to use blue brush water to allow them to see the basic outline of the work they want to do. Not Conty. He literally paints straight onto canvas. Absolutely no pre-preparation."

"Is that rare?"

"Not unheard of, but paintings of this quality, Mister Stone, well you would expect the artist to put a rough sketch down first. This picture always reminds of the 'Madonna and Child' by Albertinelli. Yes, the masters are clearly an important influence for Conty." Vincent leant to Stone's ear. "Except, he's better in my opinion," he whispered, with a qualified smile.

Stone noted Vincent's enthusiasm for Conty's work and had to admit that it was infectious. He was starting to get mildly interested in this great man's work.

"Has he come here himself?"

"He has, but I can count the occasions on one hand. I've met him only once. He is a very private man. Though the few times he has been here, it's very exciting, as I'm sure you can imagine. His wife handles the arrangements concerning his exhibitions."

"What's he like?" asked Stone.

"As I say, I've only met him briefly on few occasions, but I'll never forget it. The man equals his reputation." Vincent smiled. "I knew very well I was in the presence of greatness."

Stone felt the hairs on the back of his neck stand up.

Vincent led him in front of the next piece of work. "'Time', he calls this one."

Stone stared at the large canvas, measuring around five foot in length by two. Painted on it was a naked man viewed from behind, his arms stretched out, reaching for a furious sky. He was painted as if floating in mid-air. Once again, the top half of the man was perfect in its representation of the male form. From the waist down, the rest of the man's body seemed to be melting away, his lower body dripping onto a large stone epitaph sticking out of a muddied ground below.

Stone was quite taken aback by the sheer force of the picture, especially the detail of the hair of the man, waving in an imaginary breeze. The sky was absorbing and boiled above the man, painted with a passionate and seemingly unrestrained use of red and orange. Stone stepped closer and the detail of the painting unfolded as he gazed upon it. He could see clearly the veins in the man's arm. Every muscle fibre and every sinew of the man's back was so intricately painted he was sure of movement – of life. Even the hair on the man's head seemed individually painted, each its own unique shade of brown. Sweat clung to the man's back, each droplet with its own shape and density.

Stone couldn't help but be moved by the work. There was something in the despair of the individual that he couldn't help but relate to.

Vincent echoed Stone's thoughts with a whisper. "Truly magnificent! The man is reaching for the sky with such urgency, you can see the muscles in his arms and back being stretched to their limits towards this savage sky, which at any minute you think will come raging down. A religious piece, we believe. See how the body is falling to what is presumed to be the man's grave. See how desperately he tries to flee his own demise. I would suggest influences from the High Renaissance here. Michelangelo himself could have painted this. Bold statement I know, but the quality is astounding as you can see."

Stone nodded. Vincent lost him at times, but he still got the point. More than anything at that moment he wanted Milly by his side so that he could share it with her. Although Vincent was an informed chaperone, it fell short of the experience Stone needed.

"There's a lot of anguish in this one as well," he remarked, and added the same information to his notes.

"Maybe Conty fears his own demise in some way. Maybe it's a fear of God. Who knows? He never comments on his work."

"Why not?"

"Too easy maybe," Vincent considered. "He's in the business of painting the works, not explaining them. Truth be known, he probably doesn't know himself. Gifted people like Conty are not always able to understand what they have done or indeed why."

"How much do you think this painting would be worth?" asked Stone, getting down to the nitty gritty.

"Priceless already," Vincent replied. "Conty donated this work to the Tate. It's not for sale."

"Does he sell much of his work?"

"Not many when you consider how prolific he is."

"But if this piece were to sell, how much?"

Vincent shrugged, his bony shoulders pushing the shoulder pads in his jacket up then down. "It's a fine piece. I don't know, based on what he's sold already, say, ten million."

"Ten million!" gasped Stone.

Vincent nodded nonchalantly.

"Why is he worth so much?" asked Stone, having made a note of the price.

"Because he's brilliant," replied Vincent, without hesitation. "A genius. He has to be the most important painter the world has seen since any of the masters. He shows more detail in his works than Holbein, better use of light than Turner. I could go on and on. Plus the fact of course, he rarely sells his works. Because of that, when he does sell any of his paintings, they fetch enormous sums at auction. I believe from our records that he has sold no more than twenty paintings to date. However, their combined value is quite extraordinary."

Stone stared back at the painting. "And when he dies?"

Vincent pushed his spectacles back to the top of his hooked nose. "Well Conty's not old; I think about sixty-five. I believe he's in good health. To answer your question though, it would be an unhappy day when he does die. We would lose perhaps the best there has ever been. And I do mean *ever*."

"I meant the price," replied Stone carefully.

Vincent sighed. "Priceless for a lot of the pieces. The rest would be worth a fortune. You see, Mister Stone, art is good currency nowadays. The people that mainly buy, or should I say, can afford these paintings, are usually wealthy businessmen. You can't rely on gold or currency given the fickle markets, so they have taken to investing in art. Works by Conty and indeed many other great artists will, at the very least, hold their price and at best should make their owners a great profit. *Especially* when the artist dies."

"And you say he paints a lot."

"Oh yes, he's prolific. Come, I'll show you the one that he's just sold. Bought by a Japanese collector. I'm afraid it goes overseas at the end of the week. No doubt you read about it in the papers?"

Stone followed Vincent into the adjacent room. On the whole of the south wall was the largest canvas in the entire gallery; a piece, which measured ten feet wide and five feet in height. Standing next to the exhibit was a security officer dressed in a black uniform.

"What do you think of that?" asked Vincent, proudly gesturing to the grand masterpiece. "A Blind Eye."

Stone was truly taken aback. The picture was a scene by a lake. Many people sat or walked by the riverbank under a cloudless blue sky. Lovers kissed, the elderly nattered about them. People were lying on the banks laughing, small children dangled their legs in the water and played with toy boats. Kites were high in the breeze, dogs running after their masters or a thrown ball. Picnics were laid out on chequered tablecloths, bathers lay drying out under the sun. Just a typical day by the lake; nothing seemed to be out of the ordinary.

Stone scanned the painting, picking out the wonderful detail of the crowded bank. As he marvelled at the reality of the work, he was suddenly captivated by what was going on in the centre of the painting. In the middle of the lake, oblivious to anyone else, was a person drowning. The man's face was one of terror, his arms flaying, desperately trying to attract the attention to the hordes on the bank.

Stone was suddenly overwhelmed. He wanted to shout at the painting. He wanted to shout at the people on the bank oblivious to the plight of the poor man. "My god!" he whispered to himself.

"This is a master at work," declared Vincent, adamantly.

Stone was happy to hear his voice. All he could do was nod.

"The most powerful picture I've ever witnessed in the twenty years I've worked here," Vincent went on. "Do you see the way he's painted this? The only person that seems to want to help this man is the only person not actually in the painting – us, the viewer."

Stone just stared.

"I personally think he's playing games. Conty knows what one is thinking when they view this painting. The viewer is challenged as opposed to any of the abstaining onlookers. But with all that, Conty gives us more. Look at the people on the bank. He's painted their expressions in such a way that it leads you to believe that they know the man is drowning. Look at the priest strolling with the two ladies. He almost wants to look up, but why doesn't he? Surely they must be able to hear him at least? Look at the children playing with the boats at the edge of the water. They *must* be able to see him. Why don't they call to their parents? Why is everyone ignoring him? Wonderful piece. Although much more detailed, it reminds me a little of 'Bathers and Asnieres' by Seurat," he said, thoughtfully.

Although Stone didn't have a clue as to the painting Vincent referred to when comparing Conty's work with Seurat, he scribbled in shorthand what the curator said.

"Is this piece something to do with community spirit?" he said. "The way society ignores those in trouble?"

Vincent shrugged, much to Stone's disappointment. "I really don't know. I've asked myself the same question a thousand times. Maybe the man is an outcast? Why is it the priest cannot bring himself to look?"

"How much was this sold for?"

Vincent sighed. "It goes next week to a wealthy Japanese collector by the name of Hoishi. It went at auction for twenty-five million."

"Are you sad that it's going?" asked Stone, though he knew the answer by the expression on Vincent's face.

Vincent nodded. "A wonderful British artist going overseas. Yes, I'm sad."

"It seems that Conty has no loyalty to this country. Surely he would have liked the work to stay here?"

Vincent smiled. "Conty has made it clear that he is just an artist. He has no intention of getting wrapped up in international feuds over his work. He has been quoted as saying, 'I do the work, you can all argue about the rest!'"

Stone noted the quote. "Do you know any more about him?"

Vincent shook his head. "Not much. As we all know, he is very private. Causes a bit of fuss wherever he goes. Lives on an island in Spain with his second wife. Of course he's worth a fortune, but donates huge amounts of money to charities. We don't know much of his early career, I'm afraid."

Vincent looked at his watch. "Mister Stone, I don't wish to be rude, but I really have to be getting on with the preparations. If you want to see more I could find another member of staff to show you around."

"That won't be necessary. Thank you for your help. You go and attend to what you have to."

As Stone said his goodbyes, he noticed a couple of Tate staff wheel in a large canvas on a trolley. Both he and Vincent stepped out of the way to let them by, watching as the staff uncovered the painting. Stone was intrigued as the painting started to reveal itself and stepped closer.

Vincent came alongside him. "Arrh, one of my favourites," he said, fondly.

Stone knelt in front of the painting. In the left hand side of the canvas, a chair was by a window with light streaming through it. An easel was set in front of the chair with a tiny unfinished painting mounted on it. Someone was sitting in the chair, one arm held out towards the easel. They had a brush in their hand, the bristles just touching the canvas. It was all that could be seen of the anonymous artist. To the right was another figure, sitting on a stool with their face in their hands, elbows resting on knees. Their features were not that distinguishable as the light from the window flooded in, making them seem almost translucent, as if the figure itself was made of mere light. They seemed to be smiling as they sat watching the artist paint.

"What do you think?" asked Vincent, with a whisper, as if aware that too much noise might spoil the moment.

"It's remarkable," replied Stone, honestly, studying the detail of the work.

As Stone looked closer he noticed what he hadn't initially. The figure sitting on the stool, leaning slightly forward, revealed themselves. Just on the floor behind them, draped around the leg of the stool, was the tip of a wing. Stone moved closer to the picture.

This was not a wing of a bird, that is to say it wasn't like any wing that Stone associated birds with. The almost translucent wing-tip caught the light in the quills, so it seemed almost fizzing with a golden glow. The feathers were so intricately painted that Stone wondered if he could actually see them flutter, as they might from a gentle breeze that came through the painted window.

"It's a wing," he marvelled, pointing to what he thought was his own unique discovery.

Vincent smiled. "An angel," he replied. "I didn't see it at first either."

"What does it mean?"

"I guess the person in front of the easel is Conty himself, and the angel is his way of acknowledging that he has a divine gift. As if someone is watching over him. I think it represents Conty's faith. At first I thought the angel was sitting for the artist, but then, on inspection, I realised if that was the case, the angel would be looking to the side or out of the window while being painted."

Vincent knelt at Stone's side and pointed. "You see here, the look on the angel's face. He's actually staring at the artist. He's not sitting. He's watching him."

Stone squinted at Vincent's findings. "It's incredible," said Stone. "I think it's beautiful."

Vincent nodded. "There's more."

Stone turned to him. "More?"

"Have you noticed anything else about it?"

Stone squinted back at the picture. "Like what?"

Vincent was almost childlike in his enthusiasm. "Look at the tiny picture you can see Conty is painting on the easel."

Stone leaned closer to the canvas, tracing the tiny brush that was raised to the easel. Then he saw it. "He's painting A Blind Eye," he said. "I can see the tiny figures by the lake."

Vincent clapped his hands together excitedly. "Absolutely. He plays with us all the time. Conty is painting A Blind Eye while an angel watches over him. One of my favourites!"

Stone shook his head and smiled as he turned back to the painting. He then added one word to his notes

– faith.

"What's this one called?"

"It's untitled," replied Vincent. "Now I really must get going," he said. "Are you sure I can't get anyone else to show you round?"

"No, I'm fine," replied Stone, reluctant to take himself away from the masterpiece.

"Very good," Vincent acknowledged and shook the reporter's hand. "It's been a pleasure meeting you, Mister Stone. Milly spoke a great deal about you."

"Call me Jeramiah. And, thank you. Thank you so much."

Vincent gave him a warm smile, and then hurried off. Stone turned back to the painting. He stared at it some more, inspecting the intricate detail of Conty's work. As he perused the masterpiece, he was aware of someone by his side. He turned, expecting to see a member of staff, but there was no one there. A chill went over him. He was sure he felt someone.

After ten minutes, he decided it was time to go home and try to collate the information he'd gathered, and see what had arrival by e-mail from the office. He started to make his way to the entrance, when he noticed a group of Japanese children surrounding a picture. As he came towards them, they thankfully dispersed and allowed him a private view. The photograph was of a man shaking hands with Vincent. Surrounding them was a swarm of people mostly with cameras. Stone read the words printed at the bottom of the framed photo, which read:

"Abraham Conty donating 'Cleansed' to the Tate

museum, 5th February 1995."

Stone stared at the photograph, but more importantly at the man who was Conty. He had seen pictures before but never really paid the man much attention. He knew him to be around sixty but the photograph portrayed him younger. By his side was his second wife, Jennifer. She was extraordinarily beautiful, with long dark hair and Mediterranean features. She was at least thirty years her husband's junior and that itself intrigued Stone into thinking what kind of marriage they had; though he guessed it probably had something to do with money. She, like her husband, was relatively unknown. The world, along with Stone, could only speculate as to the type of relationship they had in private.

Once outside, Stone flagged a passing cab that swung in for its ride. He got in and gave the driver the destination. His thoughts turned to the pictures in the gallery, then to the woman in the photograph. Stone realised he was beginning to get excited about interviewing Conty. In fact, he was actually looking forward to meeting the man behind the paintings with great anticipation.

Stone couldn't have known it then, but it was to be a meeting that would change his life forever.

TWO

Stone arrived, paid the driver, and then headed up the steps to the entrance of his flat. He dialled his security code into the silver box and iron security gates opened with a gentle click. Picking up his mail from his allocated container, he casually sorted through it as he made his way down the hall.

The first thing he noticed when he got inside was his laptop. An envelope icon was flashing in the corner of the screen indicating that he had e-mail. Stone ignored it and went to the fridge to get a soda. He sat at his desk and took a long swig. A picture of his wife, alone on the mantle, drew his gaze. Once again he was reminded of the day that he had spent two years trying to get over. He found himself getting angry as he was reminded of the past, so he turned to the window overlooking the park across the street.

The park was a busy thoroughfare during the day for most people who lived in the borough, all flocking for a place of solitude from the demanding pace of their day-to-day lives. Though at night it had a very different reputation.

At night the park was a place to be avoided, unless one was a drug addict, in which case it was a meeting place for a fix and somewhere private to lay down while the drug took over the mind. The only thing at night that would attract the masses would be a rock concert or carnival where there would be enough security to convince people of safety. For Stone, the park symbolised what the world was all about, with two ways of life at each end of the day, the good always turning to bad.

He opened the window and a cool breeze refreshed the stuffiness of the room. A couple walked arm in arm along the path opposite. They stopped to kiss until they noticed that he was watching and moved off quickly, laughing either at him, or themselves. For a moment, Stone thought it strange that people could be so happy in a world that was as he knew it to really be. Stone felt sad for the lovers in that moment and wondered if they knew what he knew? Wondered if they understood true love, true love and its consequences? He wondered if they knew that to know true love, you had to know that one day something precious would always be taken from you.

Stone turned his attentions to his laptop. He clicked the flashing icon and went into his e-mail. There was only one. The subject line read, 'Info on Conty' and Stone scanned the limited history of the artist sent by his office.

Abraham Conty, born February 1955 in Norwich.

Father was a carpenter. Mother was a nurse. Both deceased.

Married Louise Matherton in 1960, who died 1988.

1989 – an exhibition of Conty's work was put on at Edinburgh festival, titled "Magnifique" – Critically acclaimed as an exhibition of masterpieces. This was the beginning of his fame.

Told The Times in May 1983 that he did not want to be interviewed which started media hype around him.

First picture sold in 1991 for 7 million pounds. Title, "In the Dumps."

Stone stared at the small picture on the screen. It showed an abstract piece of a man with his face in his hands, elbows resting on his own backside. Stone was reminded of the references that Vincent had made to Conty's works being influenced by the masters. The picture reminded Stone of the works of Lucien Freud.

Remarried in 1996 to Jennifer Cantrose, age 27. Former art student at Seville University. Ceremony was on his private island off the south coast of Spain.

Stone studied the photograph of the couple a moment longer, then read on. The information was irritably limited. There were photographs of Conty with famous people when caught socialising, as well as information on his philanthropy. From the time Conty left school, it seemed he had disappeared off the grid. Reports had him travelling up until the time he was discovered as an artist living in Barcelona, but the gap nevertheless was there, intriguing Stone to suspicion.

He apparently had no children or relatives alive that could potentially shed any light on either the artist's past or any of his friends that were willing to divulge any information about the mysterious genius. That in itself was odd. Stone knew only too well that at least one person should have been bribed out of their loyalty by now.

Stone finished reading the information on his next project with disappointment. No time to investigate Conty further, which is probably why the artist had invited him over at such short notice in the first place. Becker was right – Conty did like being in the driving seat.

That's all we've got I'm afraid, Mr. Stone.
J. Stevens - Informer Librarian.

Stone flicked through the notes taken while at the Tate, comparing them to the information on the screen.

I know nothing about you, he thought to himself.

Eventually the screen suddenly gave way to his favourite screensaver of a three-dimensional cow that would rotate twice then explode in a hail of legs, udders, and horns. After the Friesian body parts evaporated, it would reappear and do exactly the same thing. Stone watched it a couple of times then turned to his address book and flicked through the various numbers of colleagues in the business that might lead him to more information on Conty. After the fifth call, he still hadn't gotten anywhere. Abraham Conty, it seemed, had gone to great lengths to keep his past private.

Stone prepared himself coffee then headed for the spare room. As soon as he opened the door, he could smell her. This was Milly's room, her study where she had written most of her articles. Stone hadn't changed the room in any way, leaving it just as his wife had the morning she died.

For Stone, it was a place he would often go just to sit. A place where, in a strange way, he felt closest to her. The room immediately evoked memories for Stone and he smiled as he remembered their intimate times together. The room was special; a sanctuary they agreed would be the place they shut away the rest of the world. Stone remembered it all. He stared at the two beanbags in the corner and recalled how they used to lay on them, getting high and staring up at the small stars through the skylight. He could hear the music they used to play, the laughter resounding around the small room, the sound of Milly's voice.

Stone sat down and took a sip of his coffee. Books on art lined very available space of the walls. Stone gazed over the top of his coffee mug and scanned the many titles. Almost immediately, his eyes spotted a large book, *The Concise Works of Abraham Conty*.

Stone retrieved the book and sat back at the desk. He lit a cigarette and opened the cover. The insert gave a brief description of the artist and the influence his works had on twentieth-century art. Stone turned the page and scanned the photographs of the artist's masterpieces. He recognised some of the paintings from what he had seen at the Tate; others were more obscure, taken from Conty's earlier career. As Stone turned the pages, he saw notes Milly had jotted under various pictures. They were brief descriptions of the works with personalised interpretations.

Stone read what his wife had written and ran his fingers along the indentations on the page, warming but strange that the life of a person could be proved this way. Otherwise there was no proof that anyone had *really* been, except the memory held by loved ones or a photograph. Stone had hundreds of photographs. To see Milly's handwriting was different. In a profoundly reassuring way, it was as if she had just been sitting at her desk.

As Stone read on, it was clear that Milly had indeed been a real fan of Conty. Nearly all the notes she had written were high praise of the works, with comments such as *brilliant* and *magnificent* scribbled under certain photographs. Milly was right; they were what she said they were. Portraits of various anonymous faces adorned the pages, with such fine detail that Stone could have sworn he saw an eyelid twitch or the faintest of movements at the corner of a mouth. Without doubt, and even without the benefit of a trained eye, Conty was clearly a quite brilliant painter.

As Stone turned more pages it occurred to him that none of the pictures were modern. There was no obscurity in the subject matter of any of the pieces. Most were scenes depicting nature in various forms. Portraits were a large part of the portfolio and landscapes. If obscurity *was* evident, it was only in the meaning behind the subject matter. Pain and suffering were clearly present in many of the works but equally balanced with paintings depicting sheer joy and merriment.

This was not the work in a sense of the revolutionary artist. Conty had not been labelled a genius for that. The title had been earned through the sheer magnificence of the very art itself. Conty was quite simply brilliant at the craft of painting. Milly had made several notes under many of the pages. One defining mention was under a portrait of an elderly woman who posed in front of a lemon tree. Milly had remarked that, "not since Rembrandt had she witnessed a more precise account of what a person had looked like at the time they were painted."

Stone carried on reading whilst the world outside seemed gone for a moment. He was preoccupied and content with just sitting and turning the pages. And with little notes penned neatly by Milly to accompany him, it was indeed a perfect moment.

Stone turned over another and discovered a small piece of paper tucked into the spine. He gently lifted the paper and turned it over. On the back was a small portrait of Milly drawn in pencil. Under it was written, "August is fine."

Stone stared at the sketch that he knew to be Milly. The hair and features were exactly like her. He didn't know what the writing underneath meant, or whom it was from. Stone only knew it wasn't Milly's handwriting and tried to think what she might have done the August before she died. Nothing of any significance about that August or any other August came to mind. Instead of putting it back in the book, Stone folded it once and placed the sketch into his wallet.

Stone rubbed his eyes. *I'm tired*, he thought.

After closing the door, he went through to the sitting room and sat at his desk. He witnessed the cow's gruesome demise several more times, then wandered to his room to lie down. He was asleep in minutes.

He awoke late into the night, dragged himself off his bed and went to make a drink. Entering the front room, he collected up the handful of mail and sifted through the usual bills and demands. The large envelope was probably a phone bill until he realised there was no stamp. The handwritten address intrigued him enough to warrant it being opened.

From inside the envelope, he retrieved two photographs. At first, he didn't know what the hell he was looking at. Then, with sudden horror, he got it.

Stone snatched himself upright and put a hand to his mouth. "Oh my god," he said. Oh my fuckin' god!"

He picked the envelope up again and peered inside. There was something else, something he had missed. He retrieved a small piece of paper, folded once in half. Written in the centre, with the same, neat handwriting that addressed the envelope, read:

I know who killed her.

Go to 27 Berrick Street, SW2 – Sunday at 8p.m.

Do not share this information with anyone.

If you do, your life will be in danger.

Stone stared at the note, trying to decide if what he was seeing was true. He went back to the photographs and studied them.

Opening the drawer, he fumbled frantically for the magnifying glass. Holding the first photograph up to the light, he studied it intently. There it was. The magnifying glass showed it clearly – a gun.

Stone pondered on what was written. 'I', not 'we' was the first obvious clue. 'Who', not 'they', was that another clue? So maybe it was one person? 'Killed', not 'murdered'. Was there anything in that? Stone was doubtful; surely it meant the same thing.

Stone sat back.

He needed to think.

What should he do?

He needed to get help.

For a moment, he contemplated the police but the note had told him not tell no one. Surely 'no one' didn't include the police?

He held the two photographs up to the light again, looking from one to the other. Then he saw it, as if somehow it hadn't been there before. In the top right-hand corner of each photograph, the time and date they were taken.

Stone leapt from his chair. Flinging open the doors of a large pine cabinet, he rummaged through the piles of back papers stacked inside. After a few minutes, he found what he was looking for. He held up the folded edition of The Informer and sat back on the floor. *This can't be happening*, he thought as he scanned the front page. According to the press, the time and date of the accident were more or less the same as in the photographs.

For the next half an hour, Stone paced his flat, glancing every now and then at the pile of evidence on his desk. He needed to tell someone. Christ, he needed to share this with someone!

He looked at his watch. Midnight. Tomorrow, the note had told him. Tomorrow he was to go to Berrick Street.

Who was going to be waiting for him of Berrick Street and what were they going to tell him?

He sat back down and studied the note again, turning the paper repeatedly as if to find a clue that would tell him more.

Do not share this information with anyone.

If you do, your life will be in danger.

Who was this person?

Was it a he or she?

How did they know his address?

The questions were many and he couldn't answer them all.

Stone didn't feel that he could cope with this on his own. Not this, this was too much. Rachel had always... That was it!

Stone quickly gathered everything from the table. He fetched a folder then stuffed it with all the evidence he had. After grabbing his coat, he then left his flat for the home of the only person he thought he could trust.

Stone took forty minutes to arrive at Rachel Martin's house and was glad to see that lights were still on. He paid the taxi driver who raced off, leaving Stone alone on a poorly lit street just off the main road. He knew he was being stupid, but Stone suddenly felt chilled at being left alone.

He turned to look at the opposite side of the road. Trees lined the pavement, rocking gently in the late night breeze, leaves sprinkling shadows across the road as they were caught in the soft beam of the street lamps.

Stone clutched the folder to his chest and hurried up the steps to Rachel's door. He stood for a while, staring at the doorbell. At that moment, he contemplated turning back. He had been warned and by simply pressing the bell could be endangering his life. Stone was so preoccupied with what could happen to him that he didn't think of the danger he might be bringing Rachel.

Stone rang the bell.

It took several minutes before Rachel answered the door. She was dressed in a cream housecoat, her make-up still on but her hair messed up.

"Stoney?" she said, squinting into the gloom.

Stone didn't know where to start. "I need to talk with you, Rachel," he said, as calmly as he could.

Rachel looked behind her and then closed the door a little more. "Can it wait until the morning?" she asked, awkwardly.

"No," replied Stone.

"Well... Err. I've got my mother staying. It's a little

inconvenient."

"This can't wait, Rachel," said Stone, adamantly.

Rachel said nothing for a moment. She stared at Stone. Something clearly spooked him.

"Look, wait here. I'll just make sure she's tucked up, okay?"

Stone nodded, although he didn't particularly want to be left out on the street.

Rachel was not gone long. She returned and ushered Stone inside. "You want something to drink?" she asked, taking his coat.

"No, I'm fine," Stone replied. He then hurried through to the living room and went straight to the window. Carefully, he pulled back the curtain to allow him a small view onto the street. He then sat with the folder clutched to his chest.

"Stoney, what's going on?" asked Rachel. "Who you looking for?"

Stone looked back at her. "I don't know."

"Jeramiah, you're scaring me. What's going on?"

Stone took a deep breath. "Listen to me carefully. I've got something to show you. I received some photographs in the post. What you are about to see you have to keep to yourself, okay?"

Rachel was getting even more spooked. "What are you talking about, Stoney?"

Stone reached into the folder then handed Rachel the envelope. "Here. Take a look."

Rachel took the envelope as if it were a bomb. She

kept her gaze on Stone as she reached inside. Slowly she slid out the two photographs.

At first she didn't know what she was meant to be looking at. The picture was taken obviously while the photographer was mobile as it was slightly out of focus and the whole shot off centre. The photograph was of a small white car, just ahead of whoever had taken it. There were two people in the car and, judging by the quality of film, it was moving quite fast. Ahead of the white car was a dark Mercedes Benz.

Rachel looked at Stone then at the photograph. The second shot was nearly identical to the first one. It was shaky but showed the same white car, this time alongside the Mercedes. The person in the passenger side of the white car pointed at the Mercedes. Rachel looked up to see Stone offering her a magnifying glass. Rachel took it and inspected it closer. The passenger was not pointing. At the end of his extended arm was a pistol.

Rachel stared back at Stone in disbelief. She could feel a small hollow feeling in the pit of her stomach. "Is this what I think it is?"

Stone found it hard to swallow. He nodded.

"This is the car she was killed in? This was taken in Paris?" she asked, holding up one of the photographs.

Stone nodded again.

"It can't be true?"

Stone breathed in deeply. "You worked on the Diana story, right?"

Rachel nodded. "Yeah, you know I did."

"What day was she killed?"

Rachel was still staring at the photographs. "Err, about a month ago. Yeah, thirty-first of August."

Stone rubbed his eyes as he gathered his thoughts. "What time?"

"How should I know?"

"Roughly?"

"I don't know, around one in the morning I think. Yeah, early hours I think."

Stone nodded. "Look at the time and date in the photos."

Rachel hesitated then looked at the top right-hand corner of the first photograph. The date was 31st August 1997. The time was 12.05 a.m. The second photograph was the same date but the time was 12.07 a.m.

Rachel stared blankly at Stone as he retrieved a copy of The Informer dated the next day.

"The first call that the fire brigade in Paris received was from some American tourists," he began, reading from the paper. "The call was made at twelve twenty-seven a.m. precisely, on the thirty-first of August."

Rachel sat beside him. "This can't be true?" she said, processing everything.

"I believe it is," replied Stone. "You know the latest on this story? You know the authorities have been looking for a white Fiat Uno that eyewitnesses said they saw in the tunnel chasing the princess's car?"

Rachel just nodded.

"Look at the white car. A *Fiat Uno*."

Rachel studied the photograph. "Jesus, Stoney?"

"You'll see that the car has no number plate."

Stone was right, there was no licence plate.

"This is what came with the photographs," Stone went on and handed Rachel the note.

Rachel read it. "Who sent it?"

Stone held up his hands. "I don't know. It came in the post today. Hand delivered. You know as much as I do. I've maybe worked out a few things that give me clues though."

Rachel frowned.

"Well," began Stone, examining the note again. "Whoever sent the note is an 'I', not 'we'. So are we to assume that it's one man who knows this, or one woman? My guess is that it was one of the paparazzi that were following the princess that night. I think this was taken by a man on a motorbike."

Rachel shrugged, not really sure if Stone's findings were that important. "You have to go to the police, Jeramiah."

"It says I'm not to. I shouldn't even be telling you."

"So why are you?"

Stone sighed. "Give me a break. Who the fuck *am* I meant to tell?"

"Well, okay then, now you have. So what are you going to do?"

Stone got up and went to the window. He peered into the empty, pitiless night.

"I don't know," he said, sitting again. "I have to

follow it up though. I suppose I have to go to the meeting. That's what they want me to do. I guess I'm going to find out more then."

Rachel got up and poured them both a drink. "Are you going to tell Marcus?" she asked, handing Stone a glass of whisky.

"No," he replied. Stone didn't know why it was so easy to come to that particular conclusion. Somehow he just knew that telling Marcus Becker would not be a good idea. Not yet anyway.

"Jeramiah, the paper can give you support on this one. If you're going after this story, which I guess you will, you're going to need help. You need to let people know what you're doing. It could be dangerous."

"Story?" snapped Stone. "This isn't a fuckin' story! This is serious, Rachel. These photographs are evidence that the Princess of Wales was murdered."

"She couldn't have been," replied Rachel. "There was an autopsy."

Stone stared into his glass. "I don't know, maybe it's another cover-up then."

"Exactly!" said Rachel, urgently. She then realised that their voices were too loud. "That's exactly why you should get some help," she whispered. "If it's not going to be Marcus, then it better be the police."

Stone took a long swig of his whisky. "Listen, Rachel. I've thought about this. If this is true and those pictures are real, then it's murder, right? Or attempted murder, I don't know."

Rachel nodded.

"Well, then whoever murdered her is a powerful

force. I mean this was a calculated, professional job. The police obviously don't suspect anything, right?"

Rachel nodded again.

"And no autopsy discovered any wrongdoing?" Stone went on.

"Right," said Rachel. "There's no way they could cover that up."

Of course they can. "Ok, so, let's assume the man holding the gun fires at the car, I don't know, at the tyre. If that happened for real, then why hasn't it come out? The police must have inspected that car a thousand times. Are you telling me no one found a shot-out tyre? Maybe he didn't shoot at the tyre. Maybe he shot the driver or the princess. If he did, why the hell doesn't the world know about it? Shit, Rachel, this could be a cover-up." Stone stood and took her by the arm. "If there is a cover-up, the police are in on it, which means I can't go to them. Not yet. Not until I know more."

Rachel looked back at the photograph then took a large gulp of her whisky. "Jesus, Stoney, aren't you getting ahead of yourself here?"

Stone glared at her. "Someone's trying to reach out to me. Someone who thinks it serious enough to warn me." Stone picked up the note. "'I'm sorry to have come here,'" he said softly, "'but I didn't know what else to do. I suppose if anything does happen to—'"

"What the hell, Jeramiah? What do you mean if anything *happens*?"

"It's what the note says, Rachel. If these pictures are real, then I could be onto something very big here. Someone's gone to great lengths to cover this up and won't take kindly to a reporter digging around."

"That's exactly why you go to the police," Rachel insisted.

"No, I don't," replied Stone, adamantly. "Not yet."

"Why doesn't whoever sent these go to the police? Why do they want you to know?"

"I don't know," replied Stone, downing the last of his drink. "I'll guess I'll find out on Sunday."

"So you're going to go? You're going to go to this..." Rachel snatched the note out of Stone hands. "This, Berrick Street."

Stone nodded. "Of course, I have to."

"How do you know these aren't fake?" Rachel asked, waving the photographs in Stone's face. "They can do almost anything with computer enhancing, you know that. How do you know this isn't some prank?"

"I don't. And I don't know they're not real either. I know someone who can help with that anyway. I know a photographer who can verify them."

"So you'll involve others?"

Stone looked back at Rachel. She was right. Having them verified would mean getting yet another person involved. "I don't know," he replied, getting up and pouring himself another drink. "I guess I'll wait to see what happens when I meet whoever sent them. Until then, I can't decide what to do."

"I'm coming with you," Rachel insisted.

"Forget it!"

Both were silent for a moment.

"What about the Conty interview?" asked Rachel.

"What about it?"

"You leave Monday morning. How are you going to follow all of this up when you have to be in Spain?"

Stone shrugged. "I guess someone else will have to do it."

"Conty has specifically asked for you, Jeramiah."

"What do you think is more important, Rachel?"

"I know that, but you'll have to tell Marcus what's going on when you tell him you can't go. What the hell are you going to say?"

A weary Stone hadn't thought of that. "I'll cross that bridge when I come to it."

Rachel saw the strain. "Are you going to be okay?"

Stone nodded. "Yeah, I'll be fine. Just keep this to yourself, Rachel. For God's sake don't tell anyone about this until I've found out what's going on."

Rachel stared at her ex-lover. At that moment she felt terribly guilty. She nodded. "I promise," she said, having already broken it. "Just keep me posted on this one, okay? Don't do anything silly."

Stone gathered the photographs and put them back into the folder. He downed his second whisky.

"I'm going to leave these with you," he said, handing Rachel the envelope.

"Why?" replied Rachel. She backed away from the

file as it might explode.

"It's evidence," replied Stone. "I think they would be safer with someone else than me. Just in case."

If Rachel wasn't scared before, she was now. "Just in case of what?" she asked, angrily.

"Please, Rach. Just take them and keep them safe."

Rachel glared at Stone for a moment then reluctantly snatched the file.

"No one's to know, Rachel. You promise me?"

Rachel bowed her head as it was already too late. "Okay, I promise," she replied without looking at Stone directly.

Stone kissed Rachel on the cheek. "Thank you."

She showed him to the door. The cold night air rushed into the hallway, chilling them more than they were already.

"Remember, Stoney," said Rachel, pulling her housecoat around herself. "Don't do anything silly."

Stone gave her a weak nod of assurance then turned out into the world that was now dangerous and unknown. With a cautious look up each end of the street, he left.

Rachel waited until Stone disappeared into the night then closed the door. She leant against it for a while, absorbing what had happened. At that moment she felt ashamed that Stone trusted her enough to bring this to her. She was not worthy of that. He had no idea what she was. She had used him as she had all of the men in her life. Whether it was for money, status, or both, there was always something that she stayed with a man long enough for. Ever since the death of her father, she had used men just as he had used her when she had been a child. At that moment, for the first time since she could remember, she wanted to be trustworthy, and hated herself for being the contrary.

Slowly, Rachel lifted her head up. Standing at the end of the hallway was the man she was presently using, Marcus Becker.

"You heard?" she asked, softly, clutching the file to her chest.

Marcus nodded. "Most of it," he replied. "Enough to know that this sounds pretty serious."

"What the hell are we going to do, Marcus? If these aren't fake, this means she *was* murdered!"

Becker ushered Rachel through to the sitting room and sat her down. After pouring them both a drink, he squeezed beside her. He had to find out exactly what the photographs showed.

"I know him," Rachel said. "I know he'll do this on his own. My god, Marcus. If this is true, then he really could get in terrible trouble."

"I think you better show me the photographs, sweetheart."

Rachel winced at the endearment. This was it. If she handed Becker the envelope, she would betray the only man that had ever really meant anything to her. Rachel took a long swig of her whisky. It was the one that told her she was getting drunk and felt the room slightly kilter.

"I have to see them, baby. If you don't let me in

then I can't help him." Becker boiled with hatred for Stone. The fact that she was reluctant to break her promise to him proved that Rachel was still fond of him.

"He thinks she was murdered?" he asked, coaxing her gently.

Rachel nodded. Her mouth was so dry, her vision cloudy as the whisky took hold. She had drunk too much. "He was sent two photographs and a note."

"I love you, Rachel. I'm trying to help, but you need to tell me everything."

Rachel hated it when Marcus told her that he loved her. Hated it not just because she had never loved him and never would, but because she had been so coldly manipulating to make him believe it. She felt ashamed. It was a game that Becker had fallen for. She wanted out and Marcus had money – it was as simple as that. But now, all of a sudden, she regretted everything.

This was not the time contemplate the life she'd made for herself. What harm could it do to tell Becker? If Marcus could help Stone, then surely she was doing the right thing.

She turned to Becker and took a deep breath. Then she handed him the photographs.

*

Stone made his way down the end of the street, towards the lights of the main road where the taxi rank was situated. He was worried, only this time not without good reason. As he reached the end of the road, he quickly ducked in the shadow of a tree.

There, he waited.

At first he wondered if he was tired and suffering from a fearful imagination. He was nearly about to carry on up the road, when suddenly, he saw his would-be pursuer emerge from the shadows. He was right; there was someone following him.

From within the weeping sanctuary of an old willow, Stone waited. His stalker kept in the seclusion of the trees as he made his way towards him.

Stone's heart and mind were racing. He didn't know what he should do.

Was he to confront the man?

Was he to run?

Was this the man that had sent the photographs or someone more sinister?

The questions bombarded his brain and the fear rose steadily. Whatever he decided to do, it would have to be quick; the stalker was closing in on him. He waited until the man was only a few yards away, preparing himself for confrontation.

After a deep breath, he stepped out in front of his pursuer.

The man jumped at the sudden appearance of Stone and called his dog to his side. A Labrador trotted obediently from the trees and joined his master. The man nodded suspiciously at Stone and hurried past. The panting Labrador circled Stone playfully then followed on after its startled master.

Stone stood for a moment, waiting for his heart to slow down. He felt stupid as he watched the would-be assassin stroll out of sight with his killer Labrador following obediently. He realised then, he might spend a good deal of his time looking over his shoulder from now on.

Clutching the lapels of his jacket together, Stone made his way home under the cover of street lamps.

*

He didn't get much sleep that night and it was now 6 a.m. Stone's mind should of course have been on the Conty interview but it was difficult to concentrate on anything with the meeting that evening looming ever nearer. There was nothing he could do until then. The photographs were safe with Rachel and he was still alive regardless of potential threats.

He made a strong coffee then sat down at his desk. On the top was the ominous note. He picked it up and read it again:

I know who killed her.
Go to 27 Berrick Street, SW2 – Sunday at 8p.m.
Do not share this information with anyone.
If you do, your life will be in danger.

Stone downed his coffee and went to shower. He had a whole day to kill before he had to go to Berrick Street and decided to look up an old friend. No one would know more about the night of Diana's death than Bobby.

Robert Sumpter was an independent photographer with whom Stone had become good friends after working together on an overseas assignment about the

'Palestinian child soldiers' in the Middle East. Now, Sumpter was paparazzi. Bobby had seen enough horror and the fact that tabloids were paying huge sums for exclusive pictures meant that he was happy to leave the dangerous war zones and earn a substantially better living taking less risky pictures of harmless celebrities caught in compromising positions.

Stone knew Bobby was in Paris the night the princess was killed and hoped he would know some of the details leading up to her death. Of course, it meant going against what the note had told him, but it was only Bobby and he wasn't going to tell him anything about the photographs, so what harm could it do?

After showering, Stone rang his friend who agreed to see him. Arriving at Sumpter's he made his way up the steps to the intercom. Looking around to see if anyone had followed him, he then pushed the button and waited for Bobby to answer. A security camera whirled around and levelled itself at him.

Stone held his hand to his face.

"You can't hide that ugly mutt from me," came the voice of Bobby Sumpter over the intercom. "Come on in, buddy."

Stone made his way inside. Bobby Sumpter waited by his door at the end of the hallway.

"Good to see you, Jeramiah," greeted Sumpter, and then he looked at his watch. "Even if it is seven-thirty on a fuckin' Sunday morning. You wet the fuckin' bed or something?"

Stone was reminded of his friend's almost compulsive use of bad language. "Good to see you too, Bobby," he replied. "I'm sorry about the early call, but it's important."

The two men embraced then Sumpter ushered Stone inside.

Sumpter's flat was a mess. Pictures and papers were strewn everywhere, along with half-eaten microwave dinners, pizza boxes, and empty cans of beer. If there was furniture, Stone couldn't see it.

"See you're still keeping busy," remarked Stone, stepping over the mess and trying not to let the musty smell of the flat register on his face.

"I need a good woman," replied Sumpter, clearing a space on the sofa. "Jesus, Stone, I haven't seen you since..."

"It's all right, Bobby," replied Stone, "you can say it."

"Since the funeral," replied Sumpter, sadly. "How you been?"

Stone smiled. "Getting there, you know."

Sumpter nodded. "Now, what can I get you? I know there's some booze around here somewhere."

"It's seven-thirty for God's sake. I'm fine."

Sumpter sat on a stack of photographs opposite Stone. "So, you're back at work."

Stone nodded. "Yeah, back at it."

Sumpter smiled. "You causing some stink at The Informer?"

"Just getting back in the swing of things really."

"I read your article this morning about Shillingway. Looks like you're well in the swing of things."

Stone wasn't flattered. Sumpter had known him when he had been a different journalist to the one he now was. He didn't have to worry though. Sumpter knew the game. After all, he had been a different photographer once. Now, Sumpter took a hundred pictures hoping one of them might be bought by the tabloids. This was the same for both of them; throwing the shit until some of it stuck; not always the shit you wanted to stick and not always in the places you wanted it to stick to, but it was a living and Sumpter, like Stone, was past caring about who ended up stinking.

"What about you, Bobby? Keeping busy?"

Sumpter shrugged. "Have to be careful now, Jeramiah. Everyone's careful what they take, you know, after Diana's death. Seems that photographers aren't the most popular beasts on the planet. Be a while before things die down, then I guess it's back to normal and I can start earning some real money again."

"That's what I want to talk to you about, Bobby," said Stone, leaning forward in his chair. "I need to ask you a few things about the night she died. You were there, right?"

Sumpter nodded. "Yeah, I was there. I wasn't chasing her though. It was chaos, Jeramiah. I didn't get a shot at her."

Stone thought it morbidly ironic that Sumpter should mention the word 'shot'. "You know what happened there?"

Sumpter frowned. "What's this about then, Jeramiah?"

"I'm just doing a piece on the details, that's all."

Sumpter frowned. He'd been in the business too long for bullshit. "Conspiracy theories aren't your style, Jeramiah. Jesus, she's only been dead a month."

Stone faked a smile. "It's nothing like that. Just been asked to do a piece on the build-up, that's all. I just want to find out what it was like for the photographers that were after a picture. Seems they got a rough ride afterwards."

"And there's still an investigation going on you know?" Sumpter remarked.

"I know," said Stone. "I just want to get a few of the facts, see it from all sides. The country's pretty much still blaming the paparazzi."

"Bullshit," replied Sumpter. "I was there to get a picture sure enough, but none of us got anywhere near that fuckin' car before it crashed."

"Why do you say that?"

Sumpter shook his head. "I tell you, Jeramiah, the whole night was a fuck-up – for all of us."

"Why, what happened?" Stone pressed.

"You want a coffee or something?"

"No," replied Stone, wanting to get on with it. "I'm fine."

"Do you know the Ritz?" asked Sumpter, lighting a cigarette. "Where she stayed?"

"I know *of* it."

"The hotel is situated in the Place Vendome," Sumpter began, using a surprisingly polished French accent to describe the area of central Paris. "The Place Vendome is huge. It's like this big square with expensive jewellers and shops all around it. It's the posh end of town. The Ritz is one of the only hotels in the square – plum in the middle. Well, it was the same old story, chaos most of the day. Diana was being followed as soon as she arrived in Paris from Saint Tropez. Eerie really, when I think about it. It was just another day. The usual games were being played on us, you know, hide and seek, decoy cars, that sort of thing. But we knew where she was headed. It wasn't a secret that Diana and Dodi would go to the Ritz after their holiday."

"Were you the only English photographer there?"

Sumpter shook his head. "No, there were about three of us. The rest were out of town – Spanish mainly, some French guys. I guess there were about seven of us waiting that night."

"Did you know what time she was going to leave the Ritz?"

"Didn't have a clue. We waited for fuckin' ages. It was bloody freezing that night as well. Anyway, we waited. And we waited. Then, all of a sudden, a few of the foreign boys rushed off."

"Rushed off?"

"Yeah, they got a tip that she was going out the back, which of course made sense. Most celebrities staying at the Ritz are escorted out the tradesman entrance to avoid photographers. It was pure luck for the rest of us that stayed."

Stone looked confused. "How do you mean?"

"It's like this, Jeramiah. She's been there before and always goes out the back. The usual game is to send a decoy car out front and get us chasing about everywhere. But this time it was different. Weird."

Stone leant forward. "Weird?"

"Yeah," Sumpter continued, thoughtfully. "The others raced off because they get a tip she's going out the back. Well, some us that were left thought, for a moment, to do the same, but then we see a commotion in reception. Now the security won't let us in, but I went up to the revolving doors and peered inside. I couldn't believe it. There they were, her and Dodi, coming down the stairs. They came down but waited in the lobby. Security is everywhere. I guess they were deciding which way they should go. Well, I get back to my bike just as they come out. I couldn't believe it; they just strolled straight out the fuckin' front entrance."

"Then what?"

"Well of course we start snapping away. Her and Dodi get into the back of the Mercedes and drive off. I can tell you they were in a big hurry."

"And you all gave chase?" asked Stone, directly.

Sumpter threw Stone a steady gaze. "Yeah, we did."

"What happened next?"

"The car races off and we get on our bikes. Well, on the back anyway. Most of us have drivers. It's not that easy trying to take a picture when you're steering a bike."

At that point Stone remembered the way the

pictures he had been sent were taken. The camera was obviously unsteady, indicating that the photographer was not riding pillion.

"Bobby, did you see anyone on a bike on their own?"

Sumpter frowned. "Didn't notice any. Is that important?"

"Just wondered," replied Stone.

"Yeah, well, the Place Vendome is full of motorcyclists. It's a place where bikers like to hang out, you know, show off the metal."

Stone was thoughtful. "I'm sorry, Bobby. So the Mercedes speeds off from the hotel and you start to follow."

"That's right," replied Sumpter. "Now, there's two ways out of the Place Vendome. We started to follow the car up the Rue Saint Honaire, that's the east road out of the square. Then we turned into the Rue Saint Florentine, it's a narrow street that comes out onto the Place de la Concord, then onto the Coors La Reine. That's the dual carriageway along the Seine, where she was killed. Now as we pull into the Rue St Florentine, a van pulls out of a side street, straight out in front of us, *that* the press didn't tell you. We were held up for at least four or five minutes because of it. Typical, a bird was driving it. We start shouting at her, so she gets out the van and starts shouting back at us. Strange really."

"Strange?"

"She was English. Feisty bird, and a looker. Anyway, we couldn't have caught that car even if we tried. The van held us up just long enough for the car to get a head start. Now I know why the girl was English. It was a fuckin' clever move."

"Clever?"

"The van. They haven't used that one before."

"I don't understand?"

Sumpter smiled. "We know the decoy tactics with the cars, you know one goes that way and the other goes another way, to confuse us all. But the van pulling in front of us certainly worked. That bitch was a decoy, part of the security. We would never have caught up with their car. Like I said, clever move."

"Are you saying the van pulled out in front of you on purpose?"

Sumpter tutted. "Come on, Jeramiah. A van suddenly pulls out of a side street right out across the road just as their car pulls away. You got to hand it to their security for that one."

Stone stared at a crust of pizza poking out the lip of a pizza box. "Then what happened?"

"Me and my driver think, *Fuck this,* and we don't even bother to go after them. We knew we'd never catch them. Those that did go after them, caught up with the car *after* it had crashed, I can assure you."

"So you're saying that no one could have caught up with them?"

"No way," replied Sumpter, adamantly.

"And you don't believe in a conspiracy?"

Sumpter smiled. "You know the underpass where she was killed?"

"I'm not familiar, no."

"Well, let me give you an insight because I've driven it a lot. That Mercedes was a security car, which means that it would have been heavily armoured, bullet-proof glass, armour plating, that sort of thing. Now a car that big is hard to control at high speed at the best of times, but you don't take that particular corner just under the Alma Bridge at that time of night at nearly ninety miles per hour with a car that weighs that fuckin' much. The driver must have been crazy. I wouldn't have taken that corner at forty. It was a done deal, Jeramiah, and nothing to do with any of us. Plus the fact they reckon the driver was drunk. Fuck me, Jeramiah, to say the odds were against them would be an understatement."

"You sure you didn't see anyone else going after that car?" asked Stone, thoughtfully.

Sumpter shook his head. "That van stopped us all. Came right across the road. To be honest, I can't say what happened in the tunnel, but none of our lot, based on what I've told you, could have got close enough to do them any harm."

"But they were trying to get away from someone," remarked Stone, more to himself than Sumpter.

"I'm not denying they were trying to get away from us, but to blame the paparazzi for the cause of the crash is just not fair."

"I didn't mean it like that, Bobby. I just wonder if one of the paparazzi *did* catch them. Maybe someone you didn't see?"

"Possibly," replied Sumpter. "But we usually all stick together on these deals. That way if one of us knows something, we all do. It's a code. We look out for each other."

"What about the white car the authorities are investigating? The Fiat Uno?"

Sumpter rolled his eyes. "I never saw any white car, Jeramiah. Mind you, there was a lot of commotion at one point. The guys I was with all had bikes or scooters, no white car. As I say, I can't say what happened in the tunnel."

Sumpter got up from his seat and went through to the kitchen. "You want a brew, Jeramiah?" he shouted. "All this talking is making me thirsty."

Stone scanned the flat. "Not for me, Bobby," he replied, then sat back and absorbed the information.

"You sure you won't have a brew?" asked Sumpter, sitting back down.

"No thanks, Bobby," Stone replied. "Let me ask you something?"

"Fire away," replied Sumpter.

"Let's just say there was a cover-up. Let's say for argument's sake that the driver was shot. You think a thing like that could be kept quiet?"

Sumpter shrugged. "I doubt it. If someone wanted her dead, that was a pretty messy way of doing it. I mean, why chase the car? Why not take her out somewhere else? She's was always flanked by security but there were times that I witnessed where, if you wanted to, you could have easily taken a shot. If this is a cover-up, then whoever it was, is some serious shit and working for some very powerful people."

Stone suddenly felt a little nauseous. "Thanks for

your time, Bobby," he said, getting to his feet.

"You want to stay a while? Maybe do some breakfast?"

Given the state of the flat, Stone thought the idea absurd. "No thanks, Bobby. I have to go. I'm off to Spain tomorrow and I need to sort things out."

"All right for some."

"You could say that," replied Stone.

"I'm not surprised. After that Shillingway story, probably best you get as far away from here as possible."

Stone put a hand on his friend's shoulder. "I want to thank you for your time, Bobby. It was good seeing you again."

"No problem, Jeramiah. Don't you go getting carried away with that conspiracy bollocks though."

"I won't," replied Stone thoughtfully.

"And don't leave it so long. No good cooping yourself up away from everyone. It's been a long time now – too long. A lot of people have been asking after you. We all miss you, Jeramiah. Don't be a stranger."

Stone nodded. "I won't."

"You need anything, you let me know. Promise?

"Promise."

Both men hugged each other, and then Sumpter showed Stone out.

As Stone made his way down the steps, he decided that he'd learned two things from his friend. The first was that nothing Sumpter had told him could actually prove the Princess of Wales was murdered. The second was that nothing Sumpter had told him would prove she wasn't.

THREE

8.30 a.m. Having made sure Rachel was back on side, Becker had called his driver and was already being chauffeured to the home of his boss, Edward Murren.

Rachel had been asleep when he'd left. They had spoken at length through the night until Rachel had fallen asleep happy in the knowledge that Becker would be behind Stone all the way and give him any support he needed. Becker knew it was important to let Rachel know he would take care of things and everything would be all right. But things were far from all right. The more he thought about the consequences of what Stone had in his possession, the more he feared their future together. He knew Stone, but more importantly he knew his reputation. If Stone were going to get stuck into a story like this one, he would be a formidable adversary. This was as serious as it could get.

Stone was as good as dead now, he knew that. But

what concerned Becker more than anything was that Rachel could be in serious trouble as well, now that she knew. Actions would have to be taken, investigations started, he knew that, which meant he would have to get Rachel safe. If The Family found out what Rachel knew, they would have her killed too, and Becker could never let that happen. He wouldn't let anyone take her from him.

Becker promised Rachel he wouldn't interfere until Stone was ready, alleviating any fears Rachel had about Stone finding out she had told him. He hated lying to her but, of course, it was for her own good. The photographs were real. Becker knew that. Lying to Rachel would keep her suspicions at bay and ultimately save her life. When Rachel awoke to find him gone, she would find a note that said he had been summoned for an emergency meeting at the office. The sudden departure would be blamed on legalities concerning Stone's story on Shillingway.

Becker was scared. The prospect of meeting his boss with the news he had was daunting to say the least. As owner of The Informer and head of The Family, Edward Murren was an intimidating figure. He was unlike the rest of the members and least of all like Becker. Murren was a well-educated man, born into a long line of wealth, so the financial gain of being part of the organisation was not his motive as it was for the likes of Becker or indeed most of the other members. In fact, none of the monetary or social gains of being a member were of importance to Murren but more about what The Family stood for. The organisation was Murren's baby. One he cherished and defended at all costs.

Becker feared and respected his boss in equal measure. As owner of the largest circulated newspaper in the country, Murren was certainly a powerful force in the British media. Allied to this, he had stakes and interests in hundreds of other companies with significant influence in the marketplace and overseas trade. It was a godlike position to have in life and Becker coveted it. Murren had editors at his instruction, politicians at his mercy, and the country at his word.

Taking a long swig from his hip flask, Becker sat back and shut his eyes. All he could think about was Stone. How dare he! Becker's life was finally in order. Finally he had found the woman of his dreams and within two years he would retire and relax with enough money to keep himself and Rachel in luxury forever. How dare Stone try to take that away from him! Becker consoled himself. Murren would know what to do and, as always, take care of things and protect what Stone was trying to take from him.

The car pulled up to the large security gates of the mansion and came to a stop. Becker stared at the security camera. The gates opened and Becker's car headed up the long gravel drive into the large oval courtyard. As soon as Becker stepped out of the car, the front door opened. A smartly dressed young man came out to meet him.

"Good morning, sir," he said as Becker came up the steps.

"Morning, Michael."

Becker wasn't surprised to see Murren's personal assistant on a Sunday at his home. Michael did most things including answering the door. Becker was one of the few to know that Michael was not just the butler. He was also Murren's lover.

Michael led the way through the impressive lobby of the house into the library. Murren stood in front of the window. He turned as he heard the two men come in.

"I'll leave you to it," said Michael, cordially, and then left. Michael was not a member of The Family and had no business being in the room with the two men.

Murren smiled at him before he left. He did not offer the same gesture to Becker.

"Good morning, Edward," began Becker.

Becker's boss went to the drinks trolley. "Morning Marcus. Not too early for a drink?"

"No, please," replied Becker.

"I want to thank you concerning the Shillingway story, Marcus. The country doesn't need people like that in government. I read the article on the plane this morning. Stone was as ruthless as ever."

"He was," replied Becker. "The reason I'm here concerns the very man."

"Who? Shillingway?" asked Murren.

"No, Edward. It concerns Stone."

"What's the problem?" asked Murren, handing Becker his drink. "If Shillingway is taking legal action, you should have contacted the lawyers."

Becker took a long swig of the Napoleon brandy. "It's nothing like that, Edward. We've got a serious problem."

"Take a seat, Marcus." He ushered Becker to one of the large leather sofas. He sat opposite Becker, watching him intently.

Murren was a handsome man with looks far younger than his sixty years. Whether this was because of surgery or the fact that he had a young lover was open to speculation. His hair was dyed a jet black without a single grey hair to spoil the charade. But it was the man's eyes that left the impression more than any other feature. They were bright green, punctuated by the faintest of pupils, like ink stops. Around his pupils were delicate rings of lighter green that extenuated the eyes, making them seem almost reptilian.

He sat quite still as he waited for his editor. The only movement was his hand gently rolling the brandy glass.

Becker downed his brandy. The first thing he had to do was lie to his boss.

"Stone came to me last night," he began. "I think you better have a look at these, Edward," he said, and handed him the envelope.

As the photographs were retrieved, Becker proceeded to tell his boss what he had overheard Stone telling Rachel.

The news was absorbed with a calmness that unnerved Becker even more. His boss took only one sip of his brandy the whole time Becker was speaking, without a single interruption. When Becker had finished, Murren calmly downed the last of his drink then got up to refresh his glass.

"You say Stone came to your house with these?"

Becker nodded. "Late last night. I took the photographs from him and told him that I would have them verified before taking things further. He doesn't suspect anything, Edward."

Murren looked up sharply. "I should hope not, Marcus."

Murren was then silent as he perused the photographs, shuffling from one to another. Becker could feel the beads of sweat along the top of his forehead.

"When is this meeting going to take place?" he asked, suddenly.

Becker reached into the inside of his jacket, retrieved a piece of paper, and handed it over. "Tonight," he replied, looking up at his boss's reaction as he read what was written on the paper.

Murren fingered the piece of paper whilst warming his brandy glass in the palm of his other hand.

"And Stone has no idea who sent him the photographs?"

Becker shook his head. "No, he hasn't the faintest idea."

"You believe him, Marcus?"

Becker nodded. "Yes, I do. He's expecting the support of the paper," he lied. Now came the questions and Becker would have to be careful. Murren was shrewd and if he suspected that Becker had come about the information third hand and was not telling him, the consequences would be unthinkable.

"What did you tell Stone when he showed you the photographs?"

"I told Stone that he has the support of the paper, naturally. That he should go to the meeting and keep me informed."

"And you have Stone on your side?" Murren questioned. "I mean, Stone is going to return to you and tell you everything that happened at the meeting?"

"I see no reason why he wouldn't. He would need the paper if he wanted to run with the story."

Murren studied Becker. He thought his gaze would be on him forever until Murren went again to the drinks trolley. He held up the brandy decanter to Becker, who politely shook his head.

"Why would anyone try to be reaching out to Stone with this?"

Becker shrugged. "I've thought about that, but can only assume it's because of Stone's former reputation whilst working at The Global."

"How do we know Stone won't go to the police?"

"He thinks it's a conspiracy, Edward. He thinks the princess was shot and that there was a cover-up. Given that, Stone doesn't know whether he can trust the police."

"Well he's right," Murren mused. "The photographs were presumably taken from a motorcycle?" he went on, as he inspected the photographs again. "Are we to assume that whoever took these was part of the paparazzi following the car? Is that who we are looking for? The reason I ask, is I understood, Marcus, all the paparazzi were accounted for that night?"

Becker expected this. "They were, Edward."

"Then can you explain how one of them managed to take some photographs of our operatives?" Murren held up the photographs. "I mean this has clearly been taken by paparazzi on a motorbike who was behind our team, probably the same man who's trying to reach out to Stone. What the fuck happened here, Marcus?"

As Murren finished asking the question Becker was already reaching for his handkerchief, as it was unusual to hear Murren use bad language. He wiped the sweat from his brow. "If Nathan had obeyed orders in the first place, then this mishap might never have happened. He had no business taking matters into his own hands. He took a huge risk in what he did."

Murren reached for the cigar box. He took one of the finest Cubans out, pausing a moment to light it. "His orders were to take them out," he eventually said, letting out a steady stream of smoke. "How he did it is not really the issue. Especially given the outcome. This mishap lies with you, Marcus, not Nathan. The logistics of that job were down to you and no one else."

Becker stared at his boss. He hated the way he defended Nathan like he was some favourite pet that could do no wrong.

"There was something else on the note."

"Go on," said Murren.

"The note warned Stone not to tell anyone and that his life would be in danger if he did. It would suggest that whoever sent the note knows about us, Edward."

"Impossible!"

"Then why the warning?"

"They couldn't possibly know about the organisation or anyone involved in that crash, I can assure you."

"I hope you're right," replied Becker.

The remark seemed to annoy Murren who looked up suddenly. "This is what we do," he said, letting the remark pass. He sat down and leant forward enough on the edge of the seat that Becker could smell the sweet brandy on his breath. "We have to act fast. Stone is to be followed to this meeting. Find out who this photographer is. Where Stone goes, I want him tailed, Marcus. You make sure that Stone is on our side. I want him to believe he's going to get the full co-operation of the paper to help him follow this story up. Understand?"

Becker nodded. "There's something else, Edward," he said, nervously, dreading telling Murren about more complications. "Stone has to leave for Spain on Monday morning."

"What the hell for?" replied Murren.

"I haven't had the chance to tell you yet, Edward. I've had an invitation from Abraham Conty. He has requested an interview."

"*The* Abraham Conty?"

Becker nodded.

"Why?" asked Murren.

"To coincide with his exhibition at the Tate next week. It's pretty big, as you can imagine."

"I know. I've been invited to attend the opening party."

"Conty has personally requested Stone conduct the interview," Becker continued. "He's invited him to go to his island in Spain."

"Why the hell is he asking for Stone?" asked Murren.

"He said that he admired his work."

"Oh, this just gets better!" said Murren, angrily. "Great bloody timing."

"I know, Edward. I'm afraid it doesn't give us much time. Do you want me to pull him from the interview?"

Murren was thoughtful, rolling the cigar through his fingers. "No," he said. "I don't think we will. This doesn't give Stone much time either," he replied, blowing out another long plume of smoke. "No, you let Stone go to Spain. That way if anything happens to him, it will be a Spanish problem." He looked menacingly at Becker. "And something is going to happen to him, Marcus."

Becker nodded. Murren was taking charge and he was starting to feel a little better about the situation.

"This is in our control," said Murren, thoughtfully. "Firstly, we know Stone has been tipped off that the Paris crash was no accident. All the proof Stone has is a photograph of a man in a car pointing a gun at the princess's Mercedes. As for the car, well we know now that the French authorities are looking for a small Fiat. We also know they will never find the car, so no problem there."

"Secondly, he is to meet the person that sent these photographs this evening. So, Stone meets with this person, and then tells you the outcome of the meeting. As soon as we find out who's trying to reach him, then we act accordingly.

"Third, Stone then has to go to Spain to interview the great Abraham Conty, right?

"Right," replied Becker.

"So Stone won't have chance to get his teeth into anything before he goes. When Stone is in Spain, he has an unfortunate accident. The whole thing is stopped before it has time to start. No, don't pull Stone from the interview. You make sure he gets on that plane."

Becker watched Murren take a long, contented drag of his cigar.

"You'll take care of this, Marcus. You don't have much time so get on this quickly. You have the necessary means at your disposal. Do not do *anything* until Stone is off British soil. In the meantime, make arrangements for a man to follow him to the meeting tonight and find out what happens." Murren sat back in his chair. "And I'd appreciate no fuck-ups this time, Marcus."

Becker nodded. "Yes, sir," he replied. "Edward, I want my brother to take care of this."

Murren looked perplexed by the request. "What's your rationale, Marcus? I'm not sure that's wise. We haven't used him in this capacity before. He's only done security or surveillance work for us up to now."

"I trust him, Edward."

"Are you saying you don't trust our other operatives?"

"I'm saying that I trust him more because he's my brother. I trust him to finish this once and for all. Besides, who else is there?"

"You know who else, Marcus and they're bloody good at it."

Becker of course knew the operatives Murren referred to. He had felt uncomfortable about them joining The Family from the start, a decision he was overruled on. Most of the operatives were ex-military, with the occasional ex-police officer, either of whom could be relied on for their discretion. These operatives were different. They were an unusual couple and seemed only to pursue the thrill of action rather than support the cause.

Whatever they were like, Murren said they were in and the chain of command started and ended with him. The husband and wife team were Murren's special recruits into the organisation, of which he was extremely proud. Both originally were members of a group known as the National Libertarian Alliance (NLA), which Murren had heard about. The Family kept an eye on these types of radicals – they served as the perfect recruiting ground for full-time operatives.

The NLA was militant to say the least, and crude in their operations, with nowhere near the capabilities, wealth, or resources available to it as The Family had. However, Murren liked its basic philosophy so he recruited a number of its members, including the husband and wife team that were part of the NLA's command. They were his special operatives, ones that showed great allegiance to the cause and, more importantly, him. Their specialties were covert operations, blackmail, and now, murder. Murren adored them, not least because of the sexual favours Nathan allowed his wife to give their bisexual leader. In return for their loyalty, Murren offered them financial security and an elite club that could protect their wealth, and them. With the backing of Murren, it made them a formidable force within the organisation, one that even made senior members like Becker weary of the membership.

Becker hadn't wanted to use them on the Paris job but was forced to as Murren had insisted his pets be there in what he called an, 'essential capacity.' A mistake, Becker knew it from the start, but the order was not to be disobeyed. The job, although extremely successful, had not gone entirely to plan, with Nathan taking matters into his own hands. Becker had been furious with Nathan's cavalier actions which now seemed to be coming back to haunt him. Although Nathan's fault, it looked like Becker was going to carry the blame for his stupidity. A scary thought. Becker was all too aware of what happened when someone fucked up. After the Paris job, Murren had assigned his pets to take of their old associate from the NLA, Samuel Parker.

Parker's crime was that he was found out to be preparing to leave the country with the quarter of a million pounds he had earned from the job. The Family was a club one didn't just leave; Parker knew that. Because of the long association he'd had with Nathan and Carla, Murren thought it fitting to send the couple to revoke their old friend's membership.

"There's no one better than my brother, Edward," Becker assured him. "He's highly trained, as you know, and can follow orders. I'd think he'd be ideal for this kind of operation. I know he won't fail me."

Murren was thoughtful. "He's made it clear to us before that he doesn't do this kind of work. He refused to have anything to do with the Paris job, a refusal I only allowed because he's *your* brother. What makes you think he's going to want to involve himself in this?"

"He will, if he thinks that I may be in trouble. Besides, I don't want to work with anyone else, Edward. You did say it was my show."

Murren gave the situation some consideration. There was no doubt that Becker's brother was highly trained. He also knew the devotion Becker and his brother had for each other. That would certainly go a long way to guaranteeing the job's success.

"Very well," Murren replied. "You're right; it's your show, Marcus. But, in the meantime, I will organise my choice of operative to assist on the ground. As capable as your brother is, he won't be able to be everywhere at once, so he'll need a little backup. If Stone starts snooping, which we can assume he will, there will have to be a team to tidy up after him. I'll get things moving right away."

Murren got to his feet. "Now, tonight as you know is the half-yearly dinner for all members. We don't want to concern them unnecessarily about these recent events so we won't tell them. I don't want panic setting in over this. As far as they're concerned, the job is a success and the matter closed."

Becker nodded obediently.

"Just make sure your brother's well enough for it, Marcus. You know he was pretty messed up in the war. This has to be put to bed before things start getting out of hand. He is to have no direct contact with any of us until his mission is completed. All information is to be passed to us using the agreed channels. Okay, Marcus?"

"I understand," Becker replied.

"I don't want you worrying about this, Marcus, but we can't take any risks with a determined reporter. That trip to Spain must be one way."

Becker took a large sip from his glass. "Understood," he said, softly.

"When we have some time aside from the dinner tonight, you can tell me what happened at Stone's meeting. Remember, the others must not know about this."

Murren glanced at the large grandfather clock behind Becker. "Now if there's nothing else, Marcus?"

"No, I think that's it, Edward."

Murren showed Becker to the front door just as Michael came out of the adjacent room with Becker's chauffeur.

Once the chauffeur was waiting in the car, Murren shook Becker's hand. "Keep me informed, Marcus, and try not to concern yourself. I fear nothing from this and I want you to have a clear head whilst we get to the bottom of this. You have The Family behind you, remember that."

Becker nodded. How could he forget? "Thank

you, Edward. I'll see you tonight. Goodbye, Michael."

Michael waved. "Goodnight, Marcus. Nice to see you again," he replied and closed the door.

As Becker made his way to the car, Murren came down the steps and called out to him. "One more thing, Marcus."

"Yes, Edward?" Becker replied.

"Tell me, no one else knows about this, do they? I mean Stone wouldn't have gone to anyone else?"

This was it. If Becker were to show the slightest hint that he was lying, it was all over. "Of course not, Edward," he replied evenly. "I've told you everything."

Murren stared for a while, as if looking for some sign of doubt in Becker's face. "Just checking, Marcus," he said eventually. "Safe journey. I'll see you tonight."

Becker wiped his mouth. "Thank you, Edward," he said, then got into his car. His chauffeur drove off. As the car passed through the electronic gates he could feel the hairs on his back settling down. There would be no sleep for Becker tonight; there was much to do and far too much to worry about. A consolation though. The Paris job under his command had glitches, and remarkably he had just left The Family home alive.

FOUR

·-⇾·•-————————-•·⇽-·

John Kirns, that's who he was now, sat quietly at his desk. The last part was ready to be glued and he was contented with the result. When he was sure the parts had been stuck together, he let go of the pieces he was holding, placed the model in its stand and sat back. To anyone else, it would have seemed extraordinary for a man with such big hands to assemble something so intricate.

Kirns was proud with what he had accomplished, and with some little ceremony attached the name of the boat at the base of the galleon. HMS *Victory* had taken him eight months. Stretching after being sat for so long and rolling the stiffness out of his shoulders, he dropped to the floor to do his press-ups.

Kirns's life was one of order. The press-ups were one of the practices he went through every day, beginning at 4 a.m. every morning without fail. Then, after breakfast, he worked on his model for three hours before more exercise. At forty-five, he wanted to make sure he kept fit. But it wasn't just because of his age. Kirns was ill. Fitness, along with medication, seemed to keep it under control, as well as making sure that when he was needed he was in good shape to see the job through. It seemed he was needed now and was glad. Kirns had been through a long and painful summer and he needed something more substantial to occupy his mind than a model boat.

Exercises completed, Kirns then got into the shower. He was feeling good and was looking forward to seeing his brother again. Kirns loved his brother dearly. In fact, his brother was one of the only things he did love. The other was his country. These two precious things in his life, he would willingly die for.

Washing himself gently, the warm water soothed his body. He looked down as he started to wash, ever careful around his genitals. Lifting his penis, he examined the scar tissue underneath.

There was never getting used to what he saw even if there was no feeling anymore, though he had to be careful of the hot water on the sensitive tissue. Hot water might have been a stimulant for others, but not for Kirns. What was left of his manhood remained flaccid and would forever more.

Gently he soaped the scars on his legs. As he bent to his feet, he felt it start to happen. Why then, or any other time, was impossible to tell. There was no defining moment; it just came when it wanted to. Kirns was always frightened of what was coming. Ordinarily he was afraid of nothing, but this terrified him. He knew the dull ache in the back of his head would grow into something obscenely painful. Now, doctors were only able to control the illness with pills and could do nothing to prevent the frequent attacks. Neither could they erase the memory of what had happened, and Kirns was transported back to that fateful day.

Serving with the 22 SAS, Kirns had been a member of one of the first Special Forces to cross into Iraqi enemy lines during the 1990-91 Gulf War. He, along with the rest of the twelve-man team, codenamed Viper 12, was dropped into Saudi Arabia at Tabuk, northwest of Riyadh. From there, they crossed the border into Iraq. Their mission, to locate and identify mobile Scud (Al-Hussein) Missiles. This had been tried before by Bravo Two Zero, but the attempts were relatively unsuccessful, with the majority of the unit captured and tortured by the Iraqis. The head of allied forces, General Rose, assigned Viper 12 to finish the job Bravo Two Zero had started.

With hand-held Global Positioning Systems (GPS) Kirns and his team had relayed the missiles' co-ordinates back to their base. Trouble was, sometimes it took a whole hour before attack aircraft were able to reach the target area so, of course, the missiles were often moved. Given this, matters were often taken into their own hands. Using 'Milan' anti-tank missiles mounted on Land Rovers, Viper 12 had caused havoc for the Iraqi forces by blowing the Scuds up themselves.

As much as Kirns and his colleagues had been trained, they were – Just as Bravo Two Zero were before them – surprised by the freezing conditions they had to endure while retreating from the retaliating Iraqi forces. Four of the team were lost to exposure alone. Out of twelve soldiers, five had returned. Kirns was caught by a blast from a mortar fired by the pursuing forces, injuring him seriously. Luckily, an American Chinook helicopter on reconnaissance was able to rescue the rest of the team and take them to safety back across the border. Kirns lost both testicles in the blast and nearly his life.

Kirns had been discharged from his regiment with a medal of valour having only served two days in the war. He was devastated by what had happened as it meant the end of his army career and his love life. Soon after, Kirns was to find out that a personal war had just started. He was found to have an inoperable tumour on the left-hand side of his brain. The tumour would soon finish off what the Iraqis could not.

With vision blurring, Kirns knew it would be dangerous to remain in the shower, and quickly made for the bedroom. There was never enough warning and he knew it was already too late for medicine to stop what had started. Nevertheless, he grabbed the bottle of medication from the bedroom cabinet and emptied four of the large pink pills into the palm of his hand. Kirns winced and popped the pills, knowing it was too late. He threw the light switch and drew the curtains. His head was on fire. The heat now engulfed him into the world that he alone knew. A world that was all hurt; unforgiving and brutal. He fell on the bed, clutching his head, moaning for the hurt to go away. It wouldn't. Instead it got worse and pounded violently. Curling up into a ball, Kirns clutched at his skull, legs thrashing at sheets. Then, as suddenly as it had started, it was over. Kirns fell unconscious.

*

Becker's chauffeur-driven Lexus arrived outside the North London apartment blocks. He peered out of the window and noticed the curtains were drawn on one of the apartment windows and he feared the worse. He asked his driver to wait and hurried into the building.

Becker hurried to the lift and made for the top floor. As usual, he was apprehensive about seeing his brother. Their meetings brought back bad memories for them both, reminding them both of the systematic abuse inflicted on them by their foster parents. This was their secret. A secret that bonded them like glue.

The Family would not be happy about him using his brother, but what choice did he have? What did they really know about their relationship? Besides, he was owed. Yes, The Family had made sure that his brother was looked after financially after the war, but now they wanted him shut away so he wouldn't be a liability to their operation. Becker knew the rationale behind it, but this was his brother – the only person he could trust to get him out of the current mess he was in.

The lift opened and Becker went to the door adjacent. He put his ear to it but heard nothing. He knocked then waited.

Again, nothing.

Becker stood patiently a few more minutes then let himself in with his spare key. He looked around the small living room and smiled as he perused the walls. They were adorned with photographs of his brother standing proudly next to the soldiers from his regiment; all taken in different war zones from around the world. On his brother's beret was the most precious insignia a soldier could ever have worn on his uniform. Becker moved closer to the photograph and peered at the famous emblem – a dagger, with two wings wrapping themselves around it and the words, 'Who Dares Wins' written underneath. It was the badge of the 22 SAS, the most elite regiment in the British army. Becker was as proud as his brother was.

As Becker perused the many photographs on the wall he was suddenly aware of the faint sound of running water. Moving to the door of the bathroom, he called for his brother. The door was ajar so he peered inside. It was empty. After turning the water off, Becker hurried straight for the bedroom. Peering inside, Becker saw him lying on the bed. Quickly, Becker went to the window and opened the curtains. The morning light speared in, illuminating his naked and motionless sibling.

Becker stared at the scars on his brother's legs and abdomen and was taken back to the time he had spent sitting by his bedside in hospital after he had returned from the Gulf with near fatal injuries; the painful recuperation his beloved had to endure and the months of misery. Becker still couldn't accept that John should have gone through what he had.

He woke his brother with caution. Kirns's eyes flickered. Becker let out an audible sigh of relief and clapped his hands together. Kirns was drowsy, the drugs would have taken effect and with effort he started to come round. He managed a smile on seeing his brother and tried to get up from the bed.

"I'll make you a coffee," said Becker, after making

sure that his brother could sit up on his own.

Becker went to the kitchenette. His brother was not long behind him and entered the kitchen rubbing his face.

"Another attack?" asked Becker. He went to his brother and cupped his face. "You taking the medicine, John?" Becker looked into his brother's tired eyes.

"Yes, course," replied Kirns, struggling to focus on his brother.

"How many attacks this week, John?" asked Becker.

"Just this one," lied Kirns. "Took me by surprise." He never liked to lie to his brother. Becker didn't know about the tumour and Kirns told him that the attacks were just vicious migraines. Truth was, it was the third attack that week. They were getting worse – more intense and painful. Kirns knew he didn't have long.

Becker smiled at his brother then kissed him on the forehead. "Here, get some coffee down you."

Kirns took the mug. "That would be good," he said, wearily. "What time is it?"

"Ten," replied Becker. "I see you finished the ship."

Kirns led his brother through to the sitting room. "Yeah, what do you think?"

Becker examined the boat. "I think it's beautiful." He then sat next to his brother.

Kirns could tell his brother was troubled. When agitated as a young boy, Becker used to pick at the loose skin around the edge of his fingernails, just as he was doing now. "So, Marcus, what's up?"

Becker smiled. "That obvious?"

"You, here on Sunday morning at this time? There has to be something the matter. Besides, you look terrible."

Becker clasped his hands together. "I've got a problem, John," he said, solemnly. "It's serious."

"What's the matter, Marcus?" Kirns hated to see his brother upset.

Becker wondered for a moment where to begin. The last twelve hours were beginning to take its toll on the ageing editor. "A reporter of mine was sent some photographs." He loosened his tie.

Kirns frowned. "What photographs?"

Becker struggled with the hard part. The Paris job was not something that his brother had been an advocate of. "You better have a look at these," he said, and handed his brother the envelope.

Kirns looked at his brother as he retrieved the photographs from inside. He studied them in silence.

"You see the gun?" asked Becker, watching his brother's reaction.

Kirns nodded. "Yeah, I see it."

"This reporter received the photographs anonymously in the post. Because of their content he panicked and showed them to..." Becker paused. He couldn't tell his brother about his relationship with Rachel. In fact, he had never told his brother about any relationships with the opposite sex since his brother's injury. Being with a woman was not something that John Kirns would ever be capable of again, so Becker had always been delicate about the subject of women. "To a reporter friend of mine," he continued.

Becker lit a cigarette. "This is serious, John. This could mean the fuckin' end for me."

Kirns noticed that he was trembling. "Calm down, Marcus."

"The thing is, this reporter got an anonymous note with the photographs. Whoever sent the note told him that they knew who killed her and provided an address, presumably to meet whoever this informer is." Becker handed his brother a piece of paper. "That's the address where he's been asked to go. I guess whoever they are will tell him more then. How they got the picture we don't know. I'm guessing that a paparazzi has slipped through the net, took the fuckin' picture of our men and is trying to cash in somehow."

"Does The Family know about this?" asked Kirns.

Becker nodded. "I've just come from Murren's place. I've fucked up somewhere, John, and I have to put this right. Murren is blaming me for the picture. I thought the paparazzi were all accounted for."

"I told you not to use Nathan. I told you, Marcus."

Kirns was as sceptical as his brother about Murren's head boy. Kirns had met the man in question on various occasions working with him and his wife, Carla, on a covert surveillance operation. Carla had been used to entrap a businessman at a London hotel. Kirns had sat in a car with Nathan for three hours one evening, while his wife had sex with a wealthy pharmaceutical owner. Kirns witnessed the ecstatic look on Nathan's face as he watched his wife on the monitor. He knew then Nathan was seriously deranged and that the relationship he had with his wife was far from normal.

Although Kirns was never meant to know about senior plans in the organisation, Becker told his brother everything. When Kirns found out Nathan was to be used on the Paris job, he had begged his brother not to.

"And I told you Murren insisted," Becker went on. "How was I supposed to know he was going to take the shot then?"

"Then let Nathan take care of the clean-up."

"No way!" replied Becker, adamantly. "I don't want that asshole having anything more to do with this."

Kirns took a deep breath, still trying to clear his head. "What about the car I saw on the news? The one they're looking for?"

"We took care of it. They'll never find it."

"Shit, Marcus, I told you not to get involved in all of this. I knew something would go wrong. The whole fuckin' show's getting out of control. It should never have happened, Marcus. The killing won't stop now, you know that?"

Becker was beginning to feel tired. "We've been through this, John. You know why it had to happen

"Why you though, Marcus? Why didn't you just leave it to them?"

"Because I knew where she would be. I had all the

connections. I'm a senior member, John. When you're asked it means you're being told. That's the rules when you're a senior."

"I still don't understand why you have to take care of this?"

"I told you, because Murren has asked me to. And when he asks, you say yes. Listen, John, as far as Murren's concerned, I've fucked it up and now it's up to me to make it right. Besides, I'm in. You're in, John. We don't just pick and choose what we do; we don't just go home when we've decided we don't want to play anymore. You know the rules, John."

"Why though, Marcus? Why did this have to happen?" Kirns sat forward. "Why did they have to kill her? She has two sons for God's sake!"

"And I suppose you thought about the children of those fathers you killed in the war," snapped Becker.

Kirns bowed his head. He never liked it when his brother shouted at him. "It was different, Marcus. That was war."

"And you think this isn't?"

"Marcus, do you honestly think it makes a difference what was done?"

"Listen to me, John," Becker said, putting his arm around his brother's shoulder. "It was necessary. Things will be different now."

"My god, Marcus, you think after what happened it changes anything?"

"It's what we joined for, John."

"No," said Kirns, with a finger held up to his

brother. "Not what I joined for. I needed work when I came out the army and The Family gave me some. I never joined up for this kind of shit. There were some things I could go along with. Jesus, I even thought some things I did for them were justified. It's getting out of hand now, Marcus. We didn't join The Family to kill people. It was one woman. A woman like everyone else that had choices. I fought a war for those kinds of choices. Murren's out of control, Marcus, and you're just getting swept along with his obsessive crusade."

"John," began Becker, "look at me." Kirns looked up and Becker took his brother by the shoulders. "Truth is, I'm scared. I can't be as strong as you. I'm in too deep now. John, if I don't sort this I'm finished, The Family's finished. I know this reporter, John. He'll go after this all the way. Please help me?"

Kirns nodded, knowing the gravity of the situation his beloved brother was in. One didn't fuck things up in The Family. If one had a task, one saw it through. Any mess, it had to be cleaned up. If one didn't, one became a liability. Liabilities, like Sam Parker, were quickly eradicated. Kirns would never let anything happen to his brother, therefore, whether he liked it or not, this was one mission that he was unable to refuse.

Kirns rubbed his temples and let out a defeated sigh. "Tell the about this reporter?"

Becker was relieved. His brother was back on side. "His name is Jeramiah Stone."

"I've heard of him," said Kirns. "Isn't he the guy who has that column where he digs the dirt on the famous?"

"Yeah, that's him. He's good, that's why I'm concerned. This is one story Stone would like to get his teeth into. The more time we leave him to snoop, the more dangerous he becomes. We can't allow that to happen, John."

"What do you want me to do?"

Becker paused a moment. He never imagined that he would ask his brother what he was about to.

"I want you to kill him."

Kirns took a slow, deep breath. He knew it was coming. This was the only choice his brother had, but he felt saddened nevertheless. The killing was not a problem. Of course he didn't know Stone or have anything personally against him; he had killed many whom he had known less about. What saddened Kirns to the core was that his beloved brother had to ask such a terrible thing.

"We don't want Stone spooked," Becker went on, staring at the floor, ashamed to look at his brother in the eyes. "And we don't want him touched yet. We want to find out who's trying to reach out to him. Stone has a meeting with this photographer tonight." Becker paused a moment. "I want you to follow Stone. Find out where he goes and who he meets with. He's got to get negatives if he's going to get anywhere with this and he'll know that. We can't stop him playing until all of his toys are taken away. You understand?"

Kirns nodded. "Does The Family know you're asking me to do this, Marcus? I mean they have many others they could use. Have they sanctioned this?"

Becker rubbed his eyes. He was tired and his head

ached. "I've told Murren that it has to be you. He's okay with it. Besides, who else is there, John? You think I want to use those two psychopaths Murren likes so much? I want the best. That's you, John."

Kirns might have been flattered but not eluded. His brother had taken a risk in asking him to take the job on. He was ill, that's why The Family hadn't used him for what they considered the important jobs. What had happened to him in the Gulf was not a secret to any of the members and they all would be apprehensive to say the least.

"What else do I need to know?"

"Stone is going to Spain Monday morning, so he hasn't got any time to do any real damage," began Becker. "He's going to interview the artist Abraham Conty. I want you to get as much for me as you can before he goes. I know you haven't much time, but get what you can, John. We have to know who's trying to reach out to Stone." Becker paused for a moment. "Also, the job has to be done in Spain. That way it will be off British soil and therefore a Spanish problem. Make it look like an accident."

Kirns was thoughtful. "This doesn't give me much time, Marcus. There are things I need to plan. I need to gather intelligence."

Becker shook his head. "There is no time, John."

"How long is he in Spain for?"

"No timescale." Becker took a moment to look over his brother. "You know what I'm asking of you, John. You know what you have to do?"

"I understand." Kirns saw the strain on his

brother's face. "You didn't know this was going to happen," he reassured him.

Becker gave a weak nod in response then got up from the sofa. "You have all the resources of The Family at your disposal. I will have money deposited in your account; it will cover whatever you need and more. I will send a courier with your ticket for Spain. You will be on the same flight as Stone. Now, Murren's put some other operatives out to assist you. They won't get in your way; it's their job to see Stone's trail is tidied. You know who he'll probably use, so just keep out of their way."

Kirns nodded. Becker reached into his briefcase and handed his brother a small envelope.

"What's this?" asked Kirns.

Becker watched his brother take out more photographs from inside the envelope. "That's him, that's Stone," he said, watching Kirns sift through the many snapshots. "His address is on the back of the first photograph."

Kirns stared intently at a picture of Stone. The man that was causing his brother's misery would die for it.

As he studied his face something occurred to him. "Why didn't Stone come to you about this, Marcus? Why not the police?"

"He's not sure that he can trust the police," replied Becker. "He believes there's a conspiracy theory or government cover-up, so he won't go to authorities. As for me, he won't give this story up to anyone in the business, including his editor. He'll want all the glory of uncovering this himself. That's the kind of guy he is. You see, John, he doesn't give a shit about Diana or anything else. He just wants his name on the front pages again." Becker smiled. "I'm sorry that I ask this of you. Forgive me."

Kirns shook his head. "You're my brother. There's nothing to forgive."

Becker embraced his brother then stood back as a father might when suddenly realising how much his son had grown. "Now, John. Get everything from Stone. His luggage, any files, especially his laptop; anything that may need to be checked. You know the rules? I can't have any contact with you until this is over. You must never try and get hold of me until the job is finished.

Kirns nodded. He knew.

"Your contact with The Family will be through an operative on this number." Becker reached into his pocket and retrieved a folded piece of paper, handing it to his brother. "Destroy it once you have remembered it. The operative will get you anything you need. As always, any information you have for me must go through him. As soon as you get something, John, you get it to me. I'm meeting with the members tonight, so I'll need your report by then to give to Murren.

Kirns nodded. "I understand."

"Pull this off and you're in for a big pay-out, John, you know that?"

Kirns knew as well as his brother this was never about the money. If he didn't pull it off, then they were both dead. "Marcus, when this is all over, I'm out."

Becker nodded. "I understand, John."

Becker gave his brother a lingering look before heading for the door. "Are you sure you're well enough for this, John?"

Kirns took a deep breath. "Trust me, Marcus. I won't let you down."

"The thought never crossed my mind," Becker replied. He stood straight, playfully saluted his brother, and left.

As his driver sped him away from the apartment block, Marcus Becker had a dreadful sense of foreboding and, for a brief and horrible moment, wondered if that was the last time he was ever going to see his brother.

*

Rachel Martin stepped out of the shower and stood in front of the mirror. As usual she was disappointed with what she saw. On the outside, even by her standards, she was attractive, with long dark hair and a good figure for a woman in her early thirties. Unfortunately, Rachel could see right through her managed looks and fake-tanned skin, to the real Rachel Martin beneath.

She was fucking a man twice her age for nothing short of money just to make sure outside appearances were kept up. Becker loved her and she played on it. She was a woman alone who wondered if she would ever find a man that she could love and not use. Stone had come close, but he still loved another. With his flagging career, he wasn't the man to stick by anyway. Becker was by no means her future but he was her way out and so the justification for staying with him. Their relationship was secret of course. No one at The Informer knew of their relationship, not even Stone. Becker wasn't married so it wasn't an affair, but both felt it professional to keep things under wraps. Rachel was happy with that as it fitted well with her plans. By the time they *were* ready to tell the world, she would be long gone.

Not long now though. She knew Becker would retire soon a very wealthy man and finally she would have the money to start her new life. Becker had promised her financial security if she stayed with him. That was the deal. So she would be patient until then. She would let him have her for a little longer, then go, run from the sorry charade she was living and reinvent herself elsewhere. Then, a life where she would again be in control, where she would be strong.

She wouldn't end up like her mother; a woman married to a monster whose sole reason for staying with him was fear of being left alone and broke. Andrew Martin was a wealthy and powerful man who owned his own engineering firm. The Martins were comfortable and were the epitome of a happy, successful family whose head worked hard for their future. Behind the doors of that model home was a very different story. Anna Martin was once a beautiful woman, in love from the start with her husband. Rachel's arrival was the perfect addition and the young family's happiness was complete. But as Rachel grew into a little girl, the domestic bliss of the Martins had turned into a nightmare.

Rachel couldn't ever remember her mother talking about what her father did all the time she was alive. Sure, she would come up soon after her husband was finished and hold her little girl, but, as if incapable of accepting the truth, she never uttered a word against her husband. Her mother would cry; Rachel had heard that often enough. She had listened to her mother weep as her husband quietly walked the stairs to say goodnight after their meal together. Rachel would wait for him. She would curl up tightly so in some way he couldn't find her. He did. He always found her. And when he left, it was her mother, her weak and pathetic mother that would come in and comfort her.

Not until Rachel was fourteen had mother decided to act in some way. Rachel had come home from school to find her lying dead on the kitchen floor in a pool of blood after slashing both her wrists.

Rachel didn't see much of her father after that. Andrew Martin's business hit bad times and slowly he lost everything. He rarely stayed at the house as he had started seeing another woman, so Rachel was spared his nightly visits. Only once did he come into her room after the death of her mother. Rachel made sure it was the very last time.

When she had become mentally strong enough and the hatred was so profound, she'd ended it for good. As soon as her father finished with her, she crept out after him. He'd just made it to the top of the stairs. She'd backed up against the far wall of the landing, and then ran. She ran as fast as she could towards the monster that has caused her and her mother so much pain for all those years. She hadn't realised she could be so strong. She hadn't understood what she could achieve. She ran so fast, hit her father so hard, that his feet didn't touch the ground until he hit the landing where the stairs turned the corner. He hit his head on the newel post and was killed instantly. After the accident, Rachel, now parentless, was taken into care for the last two years of her childhood; the world oblivious then and now to what her father had done to her.

Rachel turned away from the mirror. She mustn't cry, not any more. As she went back into the bedroom to change, she noticed Becker's note. It was no surprise that Becker might have legal problems concerning the Shillingway story, she had wondered herself if Stone was pushing things a little too far. However, there was irritation that Becker had taken the photographs. He had promised her not to get involved until Stone asked for help, which was surely only a matter of time. Not that she thought it would come to that. A night's sleep brought her back to reality. A conspiracy theory concerning the death of the Princess of Wales seemed a little too outrageous in the cold light of the morning. Anyway, she was no better. She had promised Stone her silence but she had lied. Rachel just hoped Stone wouldn't come calling for them and find out what she had done.

Having just settled down to read the Sunday's edition of The Informer, the intercom buzzer sounded.

"Who is it?" she asked.

"It's me," came the sound of Becker's voice.

Rachel was hoping for a lazy Sunday on her own and reluctantly went to the door, letting Becker in. He looked terrible. His eyes were swollen from lack of sleep and strain was clearly visible.

"You look dreadful," remarked Rachel.

Becker didn't say anything. Instead he went straight through to the drinks cabinet and poured himself a large glass of whisky.

"You're starting a bit early, aren't you? It's eleven o'clock in the morning."

Becker downed the glass and poured himself another. "Yeah, well not to me."

"Obviously," replied Rachel, sarcastically. "How did it go?"

"How did what go?" replied Becker, his mind on something else.

Rachel frowned. "The meeting at the office? The reason you had to rush off this morning. Problems with the Shillingway story." Rachel held up the newspaper and waved it around. Shillingway was front-page news.

"Yeah, sorry," replied Becker. "Yeah, went okay. I thought we may have to drop it, but as you can see," he remarked, nodding at the paper.

"Why did you take the photographs?" asked Rachel.

"I told you," replied Becker, refilling his glass. "I'm having them verified."

"I told you not to take them."

"I'm only trying to help."

"Well, if you're trying to do that, let Stone come to you. I told you he doesn't want anyone getting involved until he's ready."

"Why the fuck are you looking out for him?" Becker snapped. "I'm the fuckin' editor! If I think I should get involved, then I will!"

Rachel glared at him. "I'm just saying that if he's onto something, it would be silly to jeopardise—"

"Onto something!" Becker shouted. "He's mad if he thinks this is for real. No one killed her. She had a fuckin' car crash. Stone's so desperate for the big one that he'll believe anything. Everyone knows he's past his best. He's still fucked over his wife. Rachel, you should thank me. I've given him Conty – the best story of his career, but still it's not enough for the great Jeramiah Stone. Or you, for that matter."

"What the fuck is wrong with you, Marcus?" Rachel asked, shaking her head. "Conty asked for Stone, Marcus, so don't you play Father Christmas with me. And you can forget canvassing support for your jealousy over Stone."

"Fuck you!" Becker snapped.

"No, fuck you!" shouted Rachel. She threw down the paper at Becker's feet and stormed out.

Becker immediately followed her.

"Look, I'm sorry," he said, grabbing her by the arm.

Rachel pulled away. "What the fuck is wrong with you, Marcus? Yes, I fucked him, is that what you want to hear?"

"It's not that," replied Becker. "It's not that easy not to get involved in things that my reporters do, but I'm the one that's ultimately responsible for who goes after what."

Rachel shook her head. "You've let him have a free reign before, Marcus. This is personal. I told you I don't feel anything for him anymore. Why can't you believe that?"

"I do. I told you I wouldn't do anything until he's ready to come to me. I'm just trying to stay close to this one."

"So there might be something in it?"

Becker sighed. "I don't think so."

Rachel studied Becker for a moment. She couldn't remember ever seeing him look so bad. "Then what the hell is going on, Marcus?"

Becker frowned. "I don't know what you mean?"

Rachel stared at Becker, trying to read something in his face. "You can stop a story over the telephone," she began, counting down with her fingers. "You take the photographs after promising that you wouldn't. You turn up at my flat and start drinking at eleven in the morning looking like shit, and you put it down to the strain of the fuckin' legalities with the Shillingway story. What is going on? You've had lawyers at your heels before."

"I don't understand," replied Becker. Rachel was smart and with the added burden of being exhausted he seriously wondered if Rachel was onto something.

"All right, Marcus, I'll spell it out. You think Stone just might be onto something and you want this story for yourself."

Becker stared at Rachel in disbelief. For a moment, he had seriously imagined that she could have been onto him and couldn't help but smile "Okay, okay, I thought about it," he said, holding up his hands.

"Jesus, Marcus, it never ends does it? This shitty business just gets shittier."

Becker took Rachel by the arms. "If this is all true, do you realise how much money a story like that would be worth?"

Rachel shook her head. "I want out of all this, Marcus. I'm not cut out to live this way. I want out, Marcus. I want us to get as far away from this stinking paper as we can."

Becker pulled Rachel to him. "I know, baby. It won't be long now, I promise."

Rachel backed away. "Promise me, Marcus that you'll keep out of this. I don't care about the money. You don't need it, you said so yourself. Please, Marcus. Just leave all this shit to Stone. Don't get involved in a war over this."

Becker held her tightly. "Okay, baby, I promise. We'll leave it to Stone," he said, admiring Rachel's reflection in the mirror behind them.

FIVE

A female officer and male detective got out of the car and made their way up the steps. The officer was wearing a black uniform with matching skirt, her hair tied back on her head with a black band. Around her slim waist was a utility belt, armed with gadgets that would give her the edge in case an arrest turned ugly. The detective was dressed in a dark suit, white shirt, and black tie. His determined demure indicated that, in the event of anything turning ugly, he had no need for any gadgets.

Having verified with the exchange company, they knew full well Stone had telephoned the resident. Now they needed to eliminate the occupant from their enquiries.

The officer pressed the intercom.

"Can I help you?" came the reply.

The officer looked up at the security camera. "Is this Mister Robert Sumpter?"

"Yes."

"I'm sorry to disturb you, sir. I wonder if we may have a word with you?"

"Of course."

The security door gave a gentle click and both made their way down the hall. Robert Sumpter waited for them at his door.

"What's all this about? Is there something wrong?"

"Would it be all right if we came inside, Mister Sumpter? We have some very important questions to ask you concerning a Jeramiah Stone."

Sumpter became concerned. "Yes. Yes, of course."

He showed the police through to the living room and cleared a space for them on the sofa. The officer sat down next to the detective. Both scanned the room, glancing at each other as they acknowledged the mess.

Sumpter stared at the woman. There was something familiar about her. "What's this is all about?" he asked. "Is Jeramiah in trouble?"

"What is it you do for a living, Mister Sumpter?" asked the detective.

Sumpter stared at the man. He didn't look like a policeman. He was dressed in an expensive-looking suit. His slick hair and handsome, youthful face didn't match the weary, brow-beaten features Sumpter associated with detectives. "I'm a photographer. Freelance."

"Mister Stone came to see you early this morning, is that correct?" asked the woman.

Sumpter nodded.

"Can I ask what he wanted to see you about, sir?"

"Err, yeah. I was in Paris the night the Princess of Wales was killed. He wanted to ask me what happened that night. He's a journalist, you see. He said that he wanted to know more of the facts. That's all."

"Did he ask you any details concerning the accident?"

"Yeah, some. Look, sorry, I'm confused. What's this is all about?"

"Did he talk to you about a possible conspiracy concerning the princess's death?" asked the detective.

Sumpter looked shocked. "Listen, I've told the Paris authorities everything I know about that night. It was nothing to do with us Paps. We didn't even go after the car!"

"Mister Sumpter," began the woman. "We aren't here to accuse you of anything. We just need to know what Mister Stone had to say to you."

"Did Mister Stone show you any photographs or talk to you about any at all?" asked the detective.

"No," replied Sumpter. "He just wanted to get an idea of what happened that night. I guess he may be doing a story from our side, you know, give an account of the night from the photographer's point of view."

"So he didn't talk to you about any sort of cover-up?" asked the detective.

Sumpter suddenly sat forward. "Jesus, is that what this is all about? You think she was murdered?"

The woman raised her hands up. "We can't say, Mister Sumpter. As you can appreciate, this is a very sensitive matter. Although I can tell you that we are following up possible intelligence information concerning her death. We just need to find out a few things concerning, Mister Stone."

Sumpter just nodded.

"Has he mentioned to you that he has received some photographs that could prove that the princess was murdered?" asked the policewoman.

Sumpter frowned. "No."

"So he didn't tell you of a photographer trying to contact him with certain information pertaining to the night the princess died?"

Sumpter looked shocked. "No, no he didn't… Is that true?"

The officer and detective looked hard at each other, and then looked back at Sumpter.

"Look," said Sumpter, "is Jeramiah in any trouble? He's a close friend of mine."

"No, sir," the detective replied, a little impatiently. "Now if you would be good enough to answer the questions, Mister Sumpter."

Sumpter stared at the female officer. "Look, have we met before?"

"No, I don't think so," she replied.

"Mister Sumpter, can you please answer the questions," said the detective. "There is more we'd like to find out."

Sumpter was still staring at the woman, and then

suddenly noticed it. Her fingernails. They were painted with bright red nail varnish. "I do know you! You were there!"

The woman tried to look confused. "I don't know what you are talking about, sir," she replied.

"You were the woman driving that truck! You were the one that held us up!"

"Mister Sumpter," the detective broke in. "I have to inform you that you must help us with our enquiries and answer the questions."

Sumpter turned his attention to the detective. "I'll answer anything you like, just as soon as you both show me some identification," he said, abruptly.

The detective was taken aback for a moment. "Of course, sir, I'm sorry."

With that, the detective reached inside his jacket, pulling out a 9mm, semi-automatic pistol with an attached silencer. He shot Bobby Sumpter twice in the chest.

"What the hell was that about?" asked Nathan as he put his gun away. "What was he talking about?"

Carla stared down at Sumpter's body. "He was there," she replied. "He was one of the photographers in Paris. He must have recognised me."

"No shit?" Nathan remarked, sarcastically.

"You think he knew anything about who's trying to get to Stone?" asked Carla.

"I don't think he had a clue," replied Nathan. "Best we search this shit-hole then get the hell out," he went on as he took off his jacket and loosened his tie.

*

Kirns tailed Stone for the whole afternoon. Time was 6 p.m. Two hours until Stone would meet with his informant. Kirns hadn't reported in yet as there was nothing much to tell. Stone had spent time at a graveside. Who the deceased Stone had visited was not known; however, Stone had spent an hour by the grave and seemed sorrowful when he had left so Kirns deduced it was obviously someone he'd been close to.

Kirns had then followed him to the Oriel Cafe in Chelsea where he had brunch, then waited while he had a drink in a wine bar. Kirns had now followed him to his home in the expensive side of Camden. Kirns pulled up just as Stone got out of the taxi. He watched as Stone went into his apartment. Now he would have to wait.

As Kirns slumped back in his seat, he saw the gas van roll up the street and stop outside the apartment block. He watched nonchalantly at first, and then sat up when he saw the two operatives he knew get out of the van.

Nathan and Carla were both dressed in overalls and carried large black holdalls. Kirns had an idea what they were up to and watched as they made their way up to Stone's apartment block.

Stone answered the intercom. "Hello?"

"Yes, hello, sir," said Nathan. "We have reason to believe there is a gas leak at this address, is that right?"

Stone didn't really need this. "No, no leaks here. I didn't call anyone."

"Oh, that's strange," replied Nathan. "Well, we definitely had this address. I could check quickly if you'd like? Won't take a few seconds. Could be dangerous. Better to be safe than sorry."

There was a brief silence, and then Stone answered. "Yeah, okay. But can you be quick?"

"Of course, no problem." Both operatives smiled at each other when they heard the door click open.

Stone waited for them as they turned the corner of the hallway. He was surprised to see that one of them was a woman; a stunning one at that.

"Really sorry about this," said Carla. "This happens all the time, but it's best to be safe."

"No problem," replied Stone, and showed both of them in.

Immediately the man searched his bag for the gas detecting equipment.

"Nice apartment," Carla commented. "You been here long?"

"Three years," replied Stone.

Nathan came from the kitchen. "I'll just do a sweep in the front room to make sure, if that's okay?"

"Yeah, fine," replied Stone.

"I love this part of the city," said Carla. "Feels so... *European*."

Stone beamed. "I like it," he replied. He noticed that the woman was wearing bright red nail varnish. Obviously she wasn't the one who got her hands dirty.

"Look," began Carla. "I've drunk a little too much coffee today. Could I use your bathroom?"

Stone blushed. "Err, yeah. End of the hall, first on the right."

As Carla made her way to the end of the hall, Nathan came out of the front room. "Doesn't seem to be a problem in there. I reckon it's a false alarm."

"That's good. I did tell you," replied Stone.

"We'll leave you to it," said Nathan. "Sorry to have bothered you."

Carla returned from the toilet. "'Thanks ever so much," she said, provocatively.

"We're done here," said Nathan to her. "I hate bothering people. Head office needs to get their act together."

"It's okay. Really," said Stone.

"Well we'll be off then," said Nathan.

Stone showed them both out. Carla made sure she left with a lingering look at Stone.

Pleased with what had been done, Nathan and Carla headed down the street for the van. Opening the back doors, both were startled to find Kirns sitting in the chair in the back.

"What the fuck?" Carla jumped.

"Find any leaks?" asked Kirns.

"What the fuck are you doing in here?" asked Nathan.

Both got in the van and closed the door. Carla sat in front of the surveillance rig and put the headphones on.

"You know what I'm doing here," replied Kirns. "You must remember to lock the van behind you."

Carla held up her hand for the others to be quiet. All were silent for a moment as she listened. "We're receiving," she said to her husband.

"So what's going on?" asked Kirns.

"Put a couple of listeners down," replied Carla.

"One in the bog, the other in the kitchen," said Nathan.

"If he talks to anyone, we're going to know about it," said Carla. "He's already leaving a nasty trail behind him."

"What do you mean?" asked Kirns.

"Stone's started snooping," said Nathan. "We had to pay a visit to a photographer friend of his. Seems Stone's been making enquiries about the night Diana was killed." Nathan winked. "Still, it's been sorted."

Kirns knew exactly what 'sorted' meant.

"I didn't think you'd get involved in all this," Carla remarked. "Didn't think you liked the important jobs."

"Well, I am involved, so don't get in the way."

"Hey pal, we won't," replied Nathan. "We're on the same team, remember?"

"Is that what you told Parker?" asked Kirns.

Nathan feigned a smile. "Oh, you do know a lot, don't you? But then I guess you would, given you have a brother who's a senior member."

Nathan made his point. Letting him know they

knew Marcus's brother was a senior member meant they were closer to Murren than he thought. Senior members were not something operatives usually knew anything about.

"Anyway, Parker was doing a runner," Nathan went on. "We only follow orders, just like the rest of them."

Kirns sneered at him. "And as long as you keep getting paid, you're happy to follow any of them, right?"

"We all do what we believe," replied Nathan.

"And what the fuck could you possibly believe in?"

"The cause."

"Arrh, the cause," mocked Kirns.

Nathan shrugged. "So, you decided to get in on the action after all?"

"Just cleaning up after the Paris fuck-up."

"That was no fuck-up," replied Nathan, proudly. "It was perfect, if I do say so myself."

"Then why are we here?"

Nathan decided to choose his words carefully. "Well, let's just say whoever was in charge of the Paris logistics made a few mistakes."

Kirns stated coldly at Nathan. "You're proud of Paris, aren't you?"

"I did what I had to do."

"Killing innocent people?"

Nathan ran his tongue across the front of his teeth. "We don't pick and choose. I'm told what to do, just like you. Besides, she had it coming."

Kirns shook his head. "You're sick."

"No," said Nathan. "This country is sick. I'm just part of the cure."

"And now you think it's better?"

Nathan remained unruffled. "You believe the same as I do. That's what we all joined up for. Maybe some believe more than others. I'm at the sharp end of things. I'm changing things."

Kirns was feeling claustrophobic all of a sudden. "All you've done is made it worse."

Nathan threw Kirns a cold stare. "Maybe you should think about what side you're on."

Kirns got up from his seat. "You threatening me?"

Nathan held his hand up. "Easy, big fella. We're just here to see who else this fucker is talking to, and then we're done. It's your show from now, Mister SAS Man."

"Wish I was in on it," said Carla, purposely breaking the tension between them. "Good looker that Stone. Wanna trade?" she asked, winking at Kirns.

Kirns had enough and let himself out of the van before he did something he wouldn't regret.

"Just stay out of my fuckin' way," he said evenly, and slammed the back doors.

SIX

7 p.m. Stone emerged from his flat to the awaiting taxi that would take him to Berrick Street, in the East End. Stone was nervous, looking up and down the street.

As the taxi pulled away, Kirns followed. He looked in his rear-view mirror, pleased to see that Nathan and Carla stay put in the parked surveillance van.

They reached the East End fifteen minutes before the scheduled meeting. Berrick Street was situated adjacent to the canal, mainly comprised of old warehouses, once servicing the barges which took heavy supplies out of London. Tourists, who rented narrow-boats for holidays, were the only ones that now used the waterway; the warehouses now derelict reminders of what the canal was originally designed for.

A handful of the large storage sheds on the opposite side of the canal had been converted into flats. Stone assumed number 27 would be one of those, until he came to the end of the footpath and discovered a warehouse with the number 27 painted in blue on the gable. A sign on the double doors proclaimed the building as unsafe and that no one was to enter.

Stone stopped outside, checking the address. The evening was still light, but the sun would soon be gone. He started to get a little nervous at being in such a quiet and seemingly deserted area on his own. Stone looked round for a moment, and then retraced his steps to the end of the footpath to see if he had made a mistake. He hadn't. This was it, 27 Berrick Street.

To the side of the large barricaded doors there was smaller entrance. Stone tried the lock. He thought it was secured at first but as he pulled the handle, the door gave. A musty smell came from within.

"Hello, anybody here?" he called, putting his hand to his face in attempt to stop the stench.

There was no reply

"Hello!"

Still none.

Stone stepped back from the door. He looked down the stretch of the canal but couldn't see anyone. On the other side stretched a row of Victorian terraced houses separated by a low fence. Still he could see no one.

Stone turned again to the door and peered inside. Nothing could be seen in the gloom. Taking one step inside, he shouted out again but still there was no response.

Stone wondered what to do. He looked at his watch, now 8.15. His adrenaline was running and he started to feel rather apprehensive about the inside of the building. Against his better judgment, he took a deep breath and went in. As he did so, he heard something. He stopped, listening into the darkness within.

"Who's there?" he shouted.

At first there was nothing. Then he heard some rustling.

His heart started to race. "Who the fuck is there?"

"Leave me alone," came the sudden reply.

Stone jumped at the sudden sound of the voice. He stopped forward and blinked into the darkness. As he did, a small light sprang to life.

Stone squinted to where the light was coming from. As he stepped closer, he could just make out the silhouette of the man's face. A tramp was curled up on a pile of old blankets and newspapers. He wore a thick woolly hat. His face was caked with dirt, accentuating two white, startled eyes that stared back at him.

Stone backed away as he smelt the heady aroma of alcohol.

"Leave me alone," the man said again.

"How long have you been here?" asked Stone, daring to kneel beside him.

"Leave me alone," slurred the tramp. "Go away!"

Stone coughed as he braved the smell. "Has anyone else been here this evening?"

"Leave me alone," the tramp moaned and the small flame of his lighter went out.

Stone emerged from the warehouse and into the welcome evening light. He took the piece of paper he had written the address on and looked at it again. Something was wrong.

Then, the realisation of the whole thing dawned on him – a set-up. There was never going to be anyone to meet him. Looking over at the houses the other side of the canal, Stone imagined someone, somewhere, laughing at him. Defiantly, he showed the houses the finger.

Deflated, Stone sat down a bench by the canal side and lit a cigarette. He'd been duped. The photographs were fake, the meeting a sham. Stone felt stupid and threw the cigarette angrily into the water. Then he got up and headed for the main road to get a taxi.

Kirns heard him cursing as he walked past. When Stone was out of sight, he emerged from the shadows and headed for the warehouse.

*

Nathan sat back in his seat and watched his wife snort up her line of cocaine. Carla dabbed the residue up with her finger and ran it along her gums. She turned to her husband and knelt in front of him. Nathan smiled and reclined in his seat. Carla had just started to unfasten his belt when Nathan bolted upright, tearing the headphones off.

"Jesus, Nathan. What's the matter?" she asked, orientating herself.

"He slammed the fuckin' door," replied Nathan. "Jesus, scared the hell out of me. Did you turn the sound up?"

"Fuck, Nathan, you're lucky I didn't have you in my mouth." Carla smiled.

"So he's back then." Carla slipped on the headphones. "And he sounds pissed," she said, listening to more doors being slammed.

Nathan lit a cigarette then put his phones back on. Both of them listened intently.

Jeramiah Stone stormed into the front room, poured himself a large whisky, and downed it. He poured himself another and went and sat at his desk. A picture of Milly on the mantle watched him. There was never a time when he needed her more.

He pulled the note from his pocket and read it again, wondering, or hoping, that he had got it wrong. He knew he hadn't. The whole night had been a waste of time. It was then that the intercom buzzer sounded.

Stone got up and ambled over to the door. "Yeah, who is it?"

"It's Rachel."

After a moment's contemplation, Stone pressed the buzzer.

Rachel came in to find him slumped in the chair. "I'll let myself in then," she remarked sarcastically. "Well?"

"Well what?" replied Stone.

"You know what... How did it go?"

"Err, let me see. Well, let's just start by saying someone had a good laugh at my expense this evening."

"What happened?" Rachel sat beside him.

Stone shook his head. "Nothing fuckin' happened," he growled, and downed his drink. "Nothing at all!"

"What happened, Stoney?" asked Rachel again and watched Stone refill his glass.

"Absolutely nothing happened," replied Stone, and took another long drink.

"Hey, why don't you slow down a bit, Jeramiah? What the hell is going on?"

"One friggin' chance," said Stone, holding up his finger. "Just once, I wanted a story. A real fuckin' story!"

Rachel took Stone by the hand. "Why don't you slow down and tell me about it?"

Stone ran his hand through his hair. "OK, you want to know? There was no one, Rachel. I went to Berrick Street. I don't know why they call it a street. It's an old walkway by the canal, full of warehouses. No one was there. Oh, no. Yeah, of course! There was someone there. Guess who was there to meet me?"

"Who?" asked Rachel, patiently.

"A tramp! I met a tramp that told me to fuck off because he was trying to sleep. I was set up. Someone played me good and proper."

"Why would someone try and set you up? I mean what's the point?"

"Could be anyone. We both know I've pissed enough people off to want them to get me back in some way."

"But the photographs looked so real?"

"Yeah, but you were right. A bit of digital make-over and someone has good old Stony running with a story that could make him look a fool and ruin his career. I should've seen it coming."

Rachel felt sorry for Stone. At that very moment she wanted to hold him. She knew more than anyone, how important this was to him. "Maybe they couldn't get there? Maybe they were held up for some reason?"

Stone frowned at her. "If those photographs were real, don't you think whoever was meant to meet me might have made sure they were there given the seriousness of it all? It's a set-up and you know it, Rachel, so don't bother telling me otherwise. Someone wanted me to run with this so I would look an idiot."

"We said that it might be a hoax, Stoney."

Stone laughed to himself. "Jesus, the last twenty-four hours I've been seeing ghosts. I've wondered if people were following me. Actually wondering whether I might be in danger because I was onto the conspiracy theory of the century." He laughed out loud. "I must be the most stupid fucker that ever walked the earth." He looked at Rachel. "I thought it was real, Rach. I thought for the first time in a long time that I could get back with this one."

"And you still can," Rachel urged. "Okay, so no one was there, and yes, maybe someone is having a laugh about all this. But you've still got a story."

"Oh, yeah?" replied Stone. "How's that?"

"You've been given possibly the greatest scoop you've ever had. Tomorrow you go and interview Abraham Conty, for God's sake. Most journalists would die for that interview."

Stone stared blankly at her. "Conty? Abraham Conty? You know what Becker wants me to do with that? He wants me to find some dirt on the guy so he can be just another obituary in my column. That's the career I have now. I spend my life dishing the shit about people."

"Then don't do it for God's sake. Go there and bring back a great piece. A piece that you can feel proud about again. One that just might make you stop feeling sorry for yourself."

Stone glared at her.

"Don't you dare look at me like that, Jeramiah." Rachel narrowed her eyes. "You can carry on like this if you want, making sure the world remembers you lost something. And believe me, I know. I know just how cold you make the world around you. Making everything and everyone fuckin' *accountable*."

Stone's eyes widened in anger. "You don't know what the hell you're talking about!"

"Don't I? Well I'm here to tell you that life's a bitch, Stoney. You think you're the only one that ever lost anything? Count yourself lucky."

Stone was dumbstruck. He laughed. "*Lucky?*"

"I'm sick of your gloom," Rachel went on. "Becker feeds you the leads and I write your bloody column most of the time. And what do you do? You sulk around waiting for a bit of good luck after all the self-pity you throw on yourself. If things go well you say, 'Well, it's about time they did, I deserve it.' If it goes wrong then you say, 'Well I told you so, life's shit.' Listen, Stoney, I know how important this was to you, but it's one story. And one story, any story, won't bring her back!"

Stone mouth nearly fell open. He just stared in disbelief. "Is that what you think this is about?"

"I think maybe it's about you wanting this story to be true. You wanted to believe Diana was murdered so you can be reassured that the world is as *bad* as you believe."

Stone was silent.

Rachel closed her eyes, regretting everything she had just said. "What's happened to you, Stoney? You've had knocks before. It's up to you how you write, not anyone else. You chose The Informer because it suited you, suited your frame of mind. You can't expect the world to change just when you think you're ready to."

Stone didn't say anything.

"Listen, Jeramiah," Rachel continued. "You don't have to write how Becker wants you to. Write how you want. How you always *used* to. You do remember, don't you?"

Stone looked at Rachel and smiled. "Yeah, I remember. You're right, of course. I'm sorry. Just been a bad day."

Rachel took Stone's hand. "No, it's me that should be sorry. I shouldn't have spoken to you like that."

"All I wanted to do, just for a change was, I don't

know, do some good. Chase the bad guys. Just make some good from all the shit."

Rachel grinned. "Well if you want to do that you'll have to get yourself a mask and a cape. I can't really see you in a lycra suit though, Stoney."

Both of them laughed. A simple silence rested between them. "What about you, Rach? You all right?"

"How do you mean?"

"You know, how are you? I haven't really spoken to you for a while. I mean properly."

Rachel winked. "You know me, Stoney."

"Do I?"

"Well, you know what I'm like between the sheets. I'm not sure you ever wanted to know about anything else?"

Stone let out a deep breath. "I'm sorry, Rachel," he said, softly. "You know, about us."

"Now listen, Stoney, just because I've given you a lecture, don't you go getting soft on me. I'm fine. It just didn't work out. I don't blame you for anything. I've got my own demons, as well you know."

"I know," Stone replied.

"So," said Rachel, tempering the moment between them. "What do you want me to do with the photographs?"

"File them. You know, the same place where we file the memos."

Rachel laughed. "I'll keep them, just in case. What you going to do now?"

"I guess I'll pack. But before that, you want a drink? Because I could bloody use another one."

Rachel slapped her hands by her sides. "Thought you'd never ask."

"Whisky?" asked Stone, moving to the kitchen.

"No ice."

Stone came back into the room and handed Rachel a healthy glass of Irish.

Rachel took a sip. "So, you ready for tomorrow, or is that a silly question?"

"It is and I'm not. Been a bit preoccupied."

"You mean no questions or anything prepared? No agenda?"

"None of the above. I've got a feeling Conty will have an agenda of his own though. If not, I'll wing it. Two grown-ups talking, how hard can that be?"

"I guess so. You know anything about him, Stoney?"

"I read some of Milly's stuff," Stone answered, gesturing to her study.

Rachel glanced at the room. She knew the study. She didn't know whether she was allowed to know, but did. Rachel recalled the night she had stayed at Stone's and woke the next morning before he had. On the way to get some juice, she noticed the closed door. The only room in Stone's flat she hadn't been in. Curiosity had got the better of her. Stepping into the room, something told her it had been Milly's. Walking around the room had confirmed her suspicions. The room was littered with the evidence of Milly's life. Sketches she had done, a pink, fluffy pencil holder, a large bear on the seat by her desk, Post-it notes on the side of the lifeless computer screen, pictures of friends, framed certificates, achievements and awards lining the wall above the desk and the many articles she had written pinned to a notice board.

Strangely, for all the evidence of another woman in that room, Rachel never felt intimidated or threatened. There was no ghost in that room, no presence to be afraid of. There was only sadness and Rachel knew the room which had been left untouched since Milly's death said more about Stone than the woman whose room it had been. That morning had been a turning point in their relationship. As the door was closed behind her, Rachel knew that she and Stone could never be.

"I went to the Tate to see his work," Stone continued.

The sound of Stone's voice yanked Rachel back to the present. "Oh, yeah? What did you think?"

"I thought it was outstanding," he replied, recalling his tour of the gallery.

"That good?"

"That good. I'm no art critic, but these were something special. You know anything about him, Rach?"

Rachel shrugged. "Not really. Like I said, you're going to be the envy of the world. I mean everyone wants to get a story from Conty. He and his wife are like this, *mystery couple*. She's beautiful. All the magazines have been after an exclusive from her.

Jennifer, that's it. Jennifer is his wife's name."

"Yeah, I know," replied Stone. "Given all that, don't you think it's strange? I mean, why me?"

"You'll find out soon enough." Rachel looked at her watch. "I better leave you to it, unless you want me to help you? I could stick around for a while if you want."

Stone contemplated the idea for a moment. "It's late, Rach," he replied.

Rachel smiled, a little embarrassed by the rejection. "Okay." She put on her coat.

Stone showed her to the door.

Rachel put her hand to Stone's face. "Listen, Stoney. You come back with a good one from Spain. Like I said, it's not Becker writing this up."

Stone looked her over. "I will," he said. "Thanks Rach. I mean, for everything."

"Get some rest," she said, and gave him a kiss on the cheek.

Stone, with some reluctance, shut the door.

*

Becker's evening was looking up. The news from his brother was good and he felt more at ease about passing that information onto Murren. Relaxed, he sat in the back of the car, enjoying the journey.

The Family's half-yearly dinner was the only occasion the members would all be present. They hadn't convened since the Paris job and, given the public mood; it was also the perfect occasion to assess their actions.

The car pulled up outside Murren's house. Two security guards flanked the main gates and one of them came to the driver's window. Becker noticed the guard's pistol tucked inside his sports jacket. The driver lowered his window. The guard looked inside and smiled politely when he saw Becker. He signalled to his colleague to open the gates.

As they started the drive up to the house, Becker could see other security guards patrolling the grounds. He wondered if this show of force was necessary, but then Murren did like to send a clear message to his guests of just how powerful the organisation was and, more importantly, that the organisation they were part of was heavily protected.

All The Family's security personnel were permanent members of the organisation, made up of ex-service men and retired police officers Murren had pensioned. They were never told of The Family's business and often never knew the identities of the men they protected, but their loyalty was unquestionable. Loyalty always had a price and they were all paid extremely well for it.

Becker saw the collection of limousines parked outside the mansion as he drove up. He smiled to himself; it was serious company. As soon as his car came to a stop, a member of security had the door open. Becker was then escorted into Edward Murren's residence, *The Family Home*.

Michael, as usual, was the first to greet him as he came up the steps. A formality that Becker enjoyed. He felt special – important.

"Good evening, Marcus," said Michael, and the

two men shook hands.

"Am I the last?" asked Becker.

"They're waiting in the study," replied Michael, and took Becker's coat. "Edward will join you all presently."

As Becker made his way to the sitting room, he noticed a side room with the door ajar. As he walked past he could see Murren with his back to him talking with someone. As he looked closer, he saw that Murren was in discussion with his pets. Nathan, on seeing Becker, smiled at him. Becker politely smiled back and walked on. His cheerful mood evaporated, replaced with a tinge of anxiety.

Becker walked up to the door of the study. Before going in, he inspected his attire. Standing up straight, he took a deep breath, and then opened the door.

Some of the most powerful men in the country stood chatting, all dressed in fine dinner suits. Captain Andrew Haines, retired naval commander, was in discussion with George Aron, publisher. Major Robin Rothmead, retired British forces, Queens Regiment, was busy pouring another brandy for Ian Bailey, Commander in the Metropolitan Police. Simon Losely of Losely Merchant Bank smoked with Jeremy Luflin, chief immigration officer at the Home Office and Lewis Wright-Smith, of the large city firm of solicitors bearing the same name, was busy filling a handsome pipe. The only member not present was Mitchell Seymour – financier, whose absence was tolerated because his mother was dying. All seemed relaxed, the mood of the room jovial, with ripples of laughter filling the room as the men exchanged amusing anecdotes with one another. The only one who seemed apprehensive was Becker.

As soon as he entered the room, his mood was lifted as the others enthusiastically welcomed him. The combined wealth and influence of the group made it a serious gathering of men and Becker was always in awe of the company. Becker was, in fact, the most recent recruit. Their illustrious leader had enrolled them all over a period of ten years, with Becker having joined just two years ago. Each had a role in The Family. Apart from their common dedication to the overall cause, each was expected to exact their particular influence as well. There was safety in their numbers, with the organisation being almost impenetrable from outside forces who might wish to bring them down. Murren had named their association, a family, one that each and every one of them was deeply proud to belong to.

The head of this illustrious group of men came into the room and greeted them like a father might to returning siblings. Becker was pleased to see that Nathan wasn't with him.

"Gentlemen, I'm so sorry to have kept you all waiting," announced Murren. He greeted them all personally. "Now that we're all here, shall we go through?" he said.

The members followed their leader through to an adjacent room. A large oval, mahogany table centred the room. There was a chair for each member. A taller chair with a high back at the head of the table was where Murren sat. Adorning the back wall, behind Murren's throne, was a large Union Jack with portraits of the Queen and her husband, the Duke of

Edinburgh. As soon as everyone was seated, staff hurried in with the evening meal. When the first course of salmon roulade and caviar had been set, Murren said Grace, toasted the Queen, and the meal began.

The Paris job was not spoken of. Policy was not to talk about any actions taken by the organisation. The events in Paris were no secret, but unless there were complications and it was necessary to inform the other members, the details of the job were never discussed. It was a system that worked extremely well. The less one knew, the less one worried. Also, in the unlikely event of a member being questioned by the authorities about any particular operation, they couldn't incriminate anyone else. If one didn't know anything, one couldn't inadvertently say anything. Given this, it was not necessary for Murren or Becker to inform the rest of the members about the recent events concerning Stone. Murren made it his duty to maintain morale in the organisation and the recent setbacks might just spook some of the members, especially as not all had been in favour of the actions taken in Paris.

The meal was, as usual, dominated by discussion of the organisation's business interests at home and abroad. The Family had a good year and was a good deal richer for it.

The Family's business was not just asset management, but also criminal activities. Blackmail was a big part as well as theft and money laundering. The organisation operated on a 'need to know' basis. All activities, and the details of them, were only discussed with the members that were directly involved in those activities. This was done in the way of one-on-one meetings, usually at Murren's home. Whether one were involved in a particular project or not, every member got a share of the results. It was fair, as by being a member one could rest assured that they would eventually be asked to contribute to the cause one way or another.

The only other senior member involved in the Paris job, other than Becker, had been Ian Bailey, Commander in the Metropolitan Police. He had been an essential role in passing on security details concerning the princess's movements. His involvement, like the rest of them, was ongoing and, following tonight, would be called on again. Nathan and Carla had left a messy trail since their deployment and Bailey would be asked to help clear that mess up. By tomorrow morning, the police would be investigating the brutal robbery and murder of a Robert Sumpter who had been shot at his home. The killing would be put down to drugs, as Bailey would make sure cocaine was found.

Samuel Parker hadn't been reported missing yet since his body, which had been dumped in a Surrey river, had not yet been discovered. The body would be found eventually, either by a rambler or maybe a fisherman. However it was discovered, Commander Bailey would make sure Parker's death would be put down to a vicious mugging. Guns were often used in and around London these days and so the fact that Parker had been shot before being thrown in the river would not cause any undue suspicion.

Bailey was part of the front line of the organisation but others would have their roles behind the scenes.

Lewis Wright-Smith, for instance, would handle all of The Family's legal considerations. Obviously this would mean representing the organisation and its member's interests in every way.

Others in The Family would have financial obligations, such as funding certain causes, asset management, blackmail, and financial corruption.

Becker's role was to handle the media side of things, making sure The Informer gave the right representation to the cause and to inflict maximum damage on the enemy where it could. The responsibilities, although rewarding, were also demanding. As much as Becker had the money and the will to retire, Murren would first have to replace Becker with a suitable recruit; one who would maintain The Family's strict media ethos.

After the meal, the members adjourned to the sitting room for brandy and cigars. As the members filed out, Murren motioned for Becker to stay behind. When the last of them had left, Murren shut the door.

Becker's heart raced.

"You know a man called Robert Sumpter?" asked Murren.

Becker thought for a moment. "Yeah, he's done some work for The Informer. He's a freelance photographer. Why?"

"I thought it prudent to monitor the phone calls that Stone was making," began Murren. "Lucky we did. One of the numbers he dialled was traced to a photographer friend. This photographer was, in fact, in Paris at the night of the job. Stone went to see him."

"Go on," said Becker.

"After Stone went to see him, I sent Nathan and Carla to pay him a visit. Turned out that Sumpter recognised Carla almost immediately."

Becker frowned. "*Recognised* her?"

Murren nodded. "Apparently he was one of the photographers in Paris. He was among the group of photographers that Carla held up."

Becker's eyes widened. "Is this who's trying to reach out to Stone? You think Sumpter took the photographs?"

"Well, this is what I thought initially. However, it's not the case. He was questioned and didn't seem to have a clue that someone was trying to reach out to Stone, let alone who it was. He also had no idea that Stone was sent some photographs. Stone merely went to see him to find out what happened that night, nothing more."

Murren poured himself a brandy.

"So Marcus, that brings us to Stone's meeting. How did it go?"

"It's very strange," replied Becker. "Berrick Street is in the East End. It's not a residential road. It's an old footpath that runs past a set of warehouses lining the canal. The address Stone was given was actually one of those warehouses. The strange thing is, Edward, no one was there to meet him."

Becker paused to wait for Murren's reaction but he said nothing. "He waited there for some time, Edward, but no one turned up at all."

"Yes, I know," replied Murren.

"You know?"

Murren smiled. "I also took the opportunity of having Stone's apartment bugged. It proved to be a fruitful exercise. Apart from knowing that Stone went to see Sumpter, there is other information that I was able to ascertain."

"I don't understand?"

Murren's accusing gaze made Becker feel uncomfortable. "Stone never came to you with those photographs, did he, Marcus?"

Becker felt his stomach turn. He knew Stone must have contacted Rachel. "No," he replied, softly. "She went to see him didn't she?"

Murren nodded. "I know what happened at the meeting because Stone told her," Murren went on. "She went to Stone to see how the meeting went."

Becker was angered that Rachel had been to see Stone. "I'm sorry I didn't tell you, Edward."

"Maybe you should tell me the truth *now*, Marcus," replied Murren. "Tell me about this woman."

"Her name is Rachel Martin," began Becker, unable to look directly at his boss. "She's Stone's assistant on his column. I guess Stone went to her with the photographs because he trusted her. You see, they used to be lovers." Becker looked up at Murren. "I was trying to protect her, Edward. I'm in love with her. I thought I could take care of this without her getting involved. I didn't want to deceive you on purpose, I swear it. I just didn't want any harm coming to her."

Murren stared at Becker. "It seems because no one

was there to meet Stone, they're both under the impression that this is all a hoax. I daresay she will not be a problem to us."

Becker ran his tongue across his top lip, tasting the salty deposits of sweat. "Thank you, Edward."

Murren's smile went as quickly as it had arrived. "But I want an eye kept on her. You know what I mean?"

Becker nodded. "She won't be a problem, Edward. I promise you."

"It's imperative that you inform me of *everything*, Marcus. This is not like you. Remember this is a family, Marcus. It is not a club where we work alone."

Becker rubbed the back of his neck. "I just panicked, Edward. I thought I could take care of it. It won't happen again."

Murren cleared his throat. "I'm glad to hear it."

"What do we do now?" asked Becker.

"We stick to the plan," said Murren, downing his brandy. "Stone goes to Spain tomorrow and your brother goes after him. As Stone isn't coming back, he won't be a problem to us anymore."

"Why do you think no one met with him?"

"That I don't know, Marcus. But we won't stop trying to find out. I'll have enquiries made, see what turns up."

"Is there anything you want me to do?" asked Becker.

Murren put a hand on Becker's shoulder. "You've done enough for now. Looks like everything is under control. Now if you don't mind me saying, Marcus, you look like shit. It doesn't look like you've had much sleep. Why don't you get off home? Probably going to be a late one here. The others won't mind."

Becker nodded. "I will," he replied.

"How's your brother? Is everything set?"

Becker nodded. "He knows what to do."

"Excellent," replied Murren.

Becker said his goodbyes to the other members then Murren showed him to the door. Murren opened the door just as Nathan started to descend the stairs with his wife. Becker looked up. Nathan gave him a wink.

"Goodnight, Marcus. Get some rest. I'll call you in the morning." Becker shook Murren's hand, and then got into his car.

Not until Becker was out of the main gates of Murren's estate did it dawn on him. The arrogant look on Nathan's face that told him everything, and he knew exactly what that wink had meant.

Becker started to shake. After two years with the organisation, Becker knew exactly what action would be taken. Get rid of all your liabilities at once. Rachel would have to be killed. It was stupid of him to think that Murren would let her stay alive knowing what she did. As for himself, well, he had made too many mistakes. First, he had messed the Paris job up. A photographer had gotten through the net and taken pictures with potentially horrendous consequences. He could have been forgiven that mistake, but not his second. He had lied to the head of The Family, and that was unforgivable. Trust was broken. His membership was effectively over. The appropriate orders would be sent to the network of operatives active in the capital and he would be taken out.

On the way back to his house, Becker asked his driver to drop him near a taxi rank. As soon as his driver had driven out of sight, Becker hailed a cab.

"Where to?" asked the driver.

Becker sat a moment and thought. He didn't know where to go. The realisation of what had happened was still sinking in. He could be dead by morning, maybe sooner.

"Hang on a minute," he said to the driver, and tried to organise his thoughts.

Where could he go? They would be waiting for him everywhere. He couldn't go home, not even back to work. The police? Impossible.

Becker opened the window for some fresh air.

They would come for him for sure – an accident, a suicide. He would be an obituary in his own newspaper. They would come for him, and then get Rachel.

No, they would go for her first.

Yes, of course! They would get Rachel first.

Becker gave the driver Rachel's address. As the taxi pulled away, Becker dialled Rachel's number, praying it wasn't already too late.

SEVEN

Rachel Martin sat at her kitchen table with her passport and her overnight bag packed. She looked at the clock, it was 3 a.m. Becker had phoned half an hour ago and she was spooked. He sounded scared. That wasn't like Becker. Why wouldn't he tell her why she had to pack a bag and get ready to leave as soon as he arrived? He'd always promised her they would run off together, but surely not like this?

Rachel got up and poured herself a glass of water. She had been here before. The same overwhelming sense of dread that she'd known as a child. Something was terribly wrong.

The door-bell suddenly startled Rachel. Quickly she hurried to the door and opened it to find Becker standing on the step dressed in a dinner jacket. Behind him on the street was a taxi with its engine running.

"We have to get out of here right now," he said, as calmly as he could.

"What the fuck is going on, Marcus?"

"Please, baby, you have to believe me. We have to get out of here. I'll tell you more later. Just fuckin' trust me on this one, Rachel."

There were thousands of questions, but Rachel knew they would have to wait. By the look on Becker's face, whatever trouble he was in, he was scared by it. "Okay," she agreed.

"Quickly, baby," said Becker, and picked up her bag.

As soon as they were both inside the taxi, Becker asked the driver to leave. The taxi sped off and Becker sank back in the seat. He unbuttoned his shirt and let a long sigh of relief.

Rachel stared at him. "What the fuck is going on, Marcus?" she demanded.

Becker sprang up and started to wave his hands in manner to calm her. "Not here." He motioned to the driver. "We have to get somewhere first," he whispered. "We need to get somewhere safe."

"Safe?" hissed Rachel. "Why do we need to get somewhere safe, Marcus?"

"Look," whispered Becker, glancing behind them to see if they were being followed. "You deserve an explanation and I'll give you one; just not here. Trust me, Rachel."

"Well can you tell me where we're going?"

"Away. First we're checking into a hotel. I'll tell you everything when we get there. Just trust me, baby, please."

Rachel, reluctantly kept quiet. She watched Becker wipe the sweat from his forehead and loosen his tie.

His actions terrified her.

Becker gave the driver instructions to go to a small hotel he knew just outside Heathrow; one he'd used before his association with The Family. It would be safe for the night and would give him time to think of a more suitable refuge for them both. Becker knew he had to be smart, to put his fear on hold for now. Fear had no place if he were to get Rachel and himself out of this mess alive.

An hour later and two miles north of the airport, Becker asked the driver to set them down about two hundred yards from the hotel. He paid the driver a large amount of money for his night's work and a little extra to keep quiet about ever picking them up. They waited until the driver was out of sight then made their way to the hotel.

They remained quiet as they kept to the shadows, hurrying along the road like refugees fleeing a war zone. Once there, Becker hurried Rachel into the lobby.

The hotel was a large, converted Victorian house. The reception was tiny, built under the stairs. To the left was a small restaurant, to the right a dingy bar. Becker went to the desk and rang the bell. An old lady bustled out of a small office behind the reception and smiled at the late arrivals.

"Can I help you?" she asked, politely. She was obviously used to people turning up at odd hours and showed no surprise.

"We need a room for just one night." Becker dabbed the sweat from his face with his sleeve.

"Just landed?" asked the lady.

"Yes, we have," replied Becker.

"I don't know why they have to come in so late. You'd think they could do all their flying during the day, instead of poor folks like you coming in at this hour. Do you know, we had a couple arrive, oh, it must have been Thursday last. They came in at five past four in the morning after being delayed for nine hours. No compensation – nothing. You would have thought that with all the money these airlines make they would have at least paid to put them up for the night. But nothing. Only a young couple as well. They were on their honeymoon, bless them. Imagine that? On your honeymoon?"

Becker smiled patiently. "Do you have a room?"

The old lady chuckled. "I'm sorry. You folks probably want to get to sleep, and there I am, rabbiting on."

Rachel was not so patient. "Yes, we *would* like to get some sleep. So have you got a room or not?"

The old lady looked flustered. She pursed her lips then looked down at the register. "Yes, we have one double. It's forty-five pounds a night. That doesn't include your breakfast."

Becker counted out the cash. "That's very kind. We shan't need breakfast. We have an early connection in the morning."

The old lady gave Rachel a distasteful look and got their key from the wall behind her. "Number twelve. Top of the stairs and turn right," she said.

Becker took the keys and hurried them both up the stairs.

"You've got to take it easy," said Becker, the moment they were in the room.

"Fuck you, Becker," snapped Rachel. "Now tell me what the shit is going on, or I'll do worse than that."

Becker threw the bag on the bed and sat. He buried his head in his hands then looked up at Rachel, who had her arms folded, waiting for an explanation. "We're in trouble. *Big* trouble."

"What trouble, Marcus?"

Becker lit a cigarette. "You'd better sit down," he said quietly, his gaze on the floor.

"I don't want to sit down," Rachel shouted at him. "Now, what is going on? Who are we running from?"

Becker went to the window. He looked out onto the street, which seemed deserted. Street lamps illuminated most of the road but there were still the persistent shadows. He watched a car drive up, pass the hotel, and go further up the road. He waited it until its taillights had disappeared into the night. He then turned to look at Rachel.

How could he tell her? How could he tell her what he had become involved in? How could he tell her about The Family? She wouldn't understand and would never forgive him for what he had done... He would lie! That was the only way that he could get her on his side and keep them both safe. If she knew, it would destroy her. God, if she ever knew.

"Why the fuck are we running Becker?" Rachel repeated.

"I had a threat."

"What sort of threat?" asked Rachel, nervously.

"A letter was sent to my flat. It said that they know about the photographs sent to Stone and that they want them. They threatened to kill me if I didn't hand them over."

Rachel let the information sink in. "So why aren't we going to the police?"

"Police! And tell them *what?*"

"Tell them that you're being threatened. We'll get some protection."

Becker shook his head. "They said if I go to the police they would kill me."

"So that's why we're stealing out of London in the early hours of the morning, because you got threatened?" Rachel shouted. "I've spoken to Stone. He didn't meet anyone last night. He said it was all a joke, some kind of prank."

"The photographs *are* real, Rachel," replied Becker, with the only piece of truth that he was prepared to give her. "I had them verified."

"So why wasn't there anyone there to meet Jeramiah?"

Becker shrugged as he really didn't know. "I don't know. All I do know is I'm being threatened by someone who wants those photographs back."

"Well give them back, for God's sake!"

"I can't, I have obligations to bring this out."

"*Obligations?*" Rachel asked, incredulously.

Becker rubbed his eyes. He was so tired. "Of course I do. If she's been murdered, I have an obligation to disclose it."

"Yes, to the police."

Becker sighed.

"And where do I fit into all this, Marcus? What the fuck am I doing here in this disgusting hotel room?"

"You said that you would come with me," replied Becker, angrily.

"I will!" Rachel boomed. "But not like this for God's sake."

Becker glared at her while putting his finger to his lips. When he thought Rachel would be quiet, he went back to the window, pulling a little of the curtain back. The headlights of another car drew up the road, stopping at a boarding house opposite. Becker froze. Was it them?

A woman emerged from the car, then a man. Both had luggage with them. The street lamp on Becker's side shone on the elderly couple. They didn't look like anyone he knew from The Family, but that made no difference. Becker was petrified.

"Why are you so scared?" asked Rachel, who was watching him at the window.

"I told you, I've received threats."

"And you don't know who from?"

"The letter was anonymous."

Rachel frowned. "Is Stone in trouble then, Marcus?"

"I don't know." Becker ears were trained to the road.

Becker was angry that Rachel always thought of Stone. He didn't give a shit about Stone. The only concern he had at that moment was to get him and Rachel out of the country. He had money and would get them as far away as possible. He had documents on The Family and might be able to use them. Maybe they would leave them alone if they knew he could ruin them all. Long shot, but it was all he had.

"You're not telling me everything, are you, Marcus?" asked Rachel, suddenly. "You'd better start giving me some answers or I'm out of here, you understand?"

Becker bowed his head for a moment then looked up to see Rachel waiting with her hands on her hips. "Don't you get it? She was murdered. The people that killed her want those photographs back. The photographs are very real, Rachel."

Rachel sat on the bed. "Shit," she said, rubbing her eyes. "You can't be serious?"

Becker nodded. "I'm afraid I am. I got you out because in the letter they said that if I didn't return the photographs or go to the police then I, and everyone I loved, would be killed."

Rachel was silent for a moment. Things were beginning to make sense now. Stone had been right about his hunch all along. But something didn't add up. "How the hell did these people, whoever they are, know you had the photographs?"

The question caught Becker off guard for a moment. "What?"

"You heard me. How the hell did they know?"

Becker shrugged. He was tired and this was all unrehearsed. "I don't know, baby."

"What the hell are we going to do now, Marcus? Stone could be in real trouble as well."

There it was again. Always thinking about Stone. "Yeah, well, I can't do anything about that right now, can I? Listen," he went on, lowering his voice, "we'll keep low. Give us time to think what to do. I'll make some calls to the airport, get us a flight somewhere. This time tomorrow we can be somewhere safe. If she *was* murdered, I need to work out what to do next. Okay, sweetie?"

Rachel winced. She could just about take the endearment before, but not now. Her immediate thoughts were to run as far away from Becker as she could. Just as they had time and time before, a man was messing up her sorry life.

Becker went to the window again and peered outside. Rachel moved to the bathroom to freshen up.

She looked at her reflection in the mirror. The face she looked back at was haggard and tired. *This is not how it was supposed to be*, she thought to herself.

Just as she was about to put her hair up, Rachel heard a strange noise – a dull thud. She opened the door to see Becker sprawled across the bed. At first nothing seemed out of the ordinary, and then as she came closer, she saw blood coming from his head.

She rushed to Becker's side and looked up at the window. A single hole was in the pane of glass. A sickening realisation of what had just happened smothered her. With some effort, she rolled Becker onto his back and saw he had been shot.

Rachel gasped. She started to whimper and shook

Becker to get some response. Becker's glassy eyes rolled in their sockets and blood streamed from his nose. Rachel looked at his wound. Bone jutted from the side of his head and she could see the dark hole where the bullet had shattered its way out

Rachel retched.

She clung to him while crouching down by the side of the bed. *This can't be happening! Not to me!*

Trying to control herself, she looked for the phone. Tears streamed down her face, stinging her eyes. She picked up the phone. It was dead.

Getting hold of Becker's face, she shouted at him to get up but it was a hopeless request. Becker's eyes rolled around as if he was trying to focus on her. He opened his mouth and blood sprayed over Rachel's face as he suddenly exhaled. Rachel shrieked and started to choke.

"I lied," Becker gurgled.

Rachel looked up, her vision blurred. Did she hear something? Did Becker say something?

She bent down, putting her ear closer to his mouth.

"I lied," repeated Becker, his voice stronger now that his airways were momentarily cleared of blood. "Get out," he moaned. "Run." Becker's breathing became laboured. "One-Nine-Two-Seven," he managed to say. The last of his breath left him with a dying wheeze.

Rachel stared at him. His lifeless eyes looked back at her. She fell back on the floor and started to creep away from him.

Fear gripped her and Rachel was unable to act or control her own body. She tried to get to her feet while leaning against the cupboard door. As she came level with the window, there was another dull thud against the window.

Rachel fell to the floor just as the bullet hit the side of the doorframe, exploding tiny splinters of wood across the room. She started to whimper, bundling herself up in a ball.

She lay there for what seemed like hours, but was really only seconds. Something was summoned within her. She was not consciously aware of it but, nevertheless, was controlled by it. Something deep inside her wanted to survive, wanted to live. She reached for the door handle and opened it, scrambling on her hands and knees into the hallway.

To the right were the stairs to the reception, to the left, a fire exit. Without even thinking, something inside her had elected for her to go left. She got up and sprinted to the exit. Crashing into the bar, the fire door flung open, out onto a metal stairway leading down to the garden of the hotel.

With the fire alarm ringing behind her, Rachel ran down the stairs and out onto the lawn without even looking back to see who might be behind her. Reaching the back of the garden, she came to a low fence which ran out onto the adjacent street. She threw herself over this, tearing her skirt and shredding her tights in the process. Once in the street, she ran for her life.

EIGHT

After checking in, Stone made his way to the first-class departure lounge. The flight had been delayed, which didn't bother him. He didn't like flying and the delay meant an extra hour on terra firma.

He went to the buffet bar, got a drink, then sat and watched the steady stream of first-class passengers coming through the glass doors of the departure lounge. One man that came through caught Stone's eye. He was well built, tall, about six foot four with closely cropped, greying hair. Apart from the man's appearance, the purposeful stride and posture captured Stone's attention. This man seemed to be walking much faster than anyone else.

Stone watched him go to the bar and take a beer from the cooler. As if he knew Stone was watching, the man turned and looked directly at him. Stone quickly looked away. When he glanced up again, the man was coming towards him. Stone nodded politely as the man walked past him. The gesture was not reciprocated. Without a further thought, Stone then turned his attention to Monday's edition of The Informer.

Stone hoped there might be something concerning his article on Shillingway the day before, but it seemed the politician had not started his denials of the accusation or even commented to the press. No doubt there would be something on the news that evening, but Stone didn't really care. His job was done. Becker would handle any subsequent stories on Shillingway.

He had to admit that given the last twenty-four hours things could be a lot worse. Soon he would be interviewing the most famous man in the world, all in a sunnier climate that just might lift his mood.

The call came through for first-class passengers to start boarding. Stone made his way to the plane. As they approached the tunnel leading to the cabin, Stone started to get pre-take off nerves.

A flight attendant showed everyone to their seats and Stone was glad to have been allocated a seat near the cockpit. Being near the pilot in the case of an emergency made Stone a little less nervous at first. However, overhearing another passenger informing his wife that the safest part of the plane was at the back obliterated any reassurance.

Once seated and belted he then started browsing the in-flight menu. The big man he had noticed in the departure lounge came and sat in the row opposite him. Stone stared again. The man's face reminded Stone of his father, with solid and weathered features. As Stone looked him over, he noticed a tattoo on the man's arm; a snake coiling itself around a dagger. Something was written around the fading tattoo, but Stone couldn't make it out. The man suddenly turned and looked straight at him again. Stone nodded. This time the man did smile back.

After the usual safety checks were made and the passengers informed of how to survive if anything went wrong, the cabin staff took their seats for take-off. Stone closed his eyes and gripped the side of his seat as the plane started its charge for the sky. He remained in this position until the flight crew was allowed to unbuckle and the plane showed every indication of staying airborne. Only then, did Stone open his eyes, immediately noticing the man in some discomfort.

Kirns leant forward, clutching his head. The stewardess went to him as soon as she unbuckled her seat.

"Are you all right, sir?" she asked.

Kirns held his hand up. "Yes, I'll be fine. I need to go to the bathroom."

He got out of his seat and went to the toilets. The stewardess was about to tell him that the seat belt sign was still on, but decided to keep quiet.

As soon as Kirns was in the cubicle, he collapsed on the seat. The pain was the most intense he had ever endured and he did all he could from screaming out. He quickly filled the small basin with water then plunged his face into it. Only a second of relief. The pain engulfed the whole of his skull and throbbed with ferocious malice. As Kirns pulled his head up from the sink the world around him started to lose its substance and everything started to melt into darkness.

The next thing that Kirns heard was a distant thumping. His eyes started to open slowly, the light stinging his eyes. The noise grew nearer, louder. At first, he was confused as to where he was. After orientating himself, he realised he was still in the toilet of the plane and the noise was someone hammering on the door.

Kirns looked at himself briefly in the mirror then went out. The stewardess and the first officer were waiting with concerned expressions on their faces.

"Sir, are you all right?" asked the stewardess.

Kirns was still unsteady on his feet and the stewardess helped stand him straight.

"Yes, I'm sorry. I guess I must have passed out. Have I been in there long?"

"About half an hour," replied the stewardess. "The gentleman opposite you alerted us."

Kirns looked to where the stewardess was pointing and saw Stone looking at him from his seat. Kirns nodded at him.

"I'll be fine, really."

The stewardess helped Kirns back to his seat and gave him some water. He tilted his seat back and closed his eyes. As always the pain was so intense that he could never remember it. But what he could remember was the fact that he had taken his medicine just before he boarded the plane. That fact either meant that the pills weren't working or they no longer had the capability to stop the attacks. For the first time in his life, Kirns was scared.

To Stone's relief, the flight was untroubled by turbulence and landed safely three hours later at Malaga airport. The arrivals hall was packed. Stone, and the other first-class passengers, were the first to emerge from the customs lounge. Expectant faces of people waiting lit up when they started to filter through.

Stone was jostled by a group of young Spanish people who screamed out their joyful recognition of a relative who received them with unrestrained passion. Dodging the ecstatic mob, he looked up to see his name written on a plaque being waved above the heads of the waiting entourage. Unable to see who was attached, he headed for the sign with renewed determination. The last few passengers got out of the way and Stone was confronted with his name bearer.

The man was very black and very big. He had a beaming round face, almost out of place perched on the rest of his mighty frame. He had a white shirt, which was masterfully pressed, and a pair of blue shorts hung down to the top of his thick knees.

Stone looked up at him and the man smiled. "Mister Stone?" he enquired, in a baritone voice.

Stone nodded. "Yes."

"My name is Deklin." He then engulfed Stone's hand with his own and shook it vigorously.

"Pleased to meet you, Deklin. Are you here to take me to Mister Conty?"

Deklin nodded and gave Stone a truly magnificent smile. "I am indeed. Come along with me, please, Mister Stone."

Deklin picked Stone's case off the trolley with such ease he might have been picking up an empty cardboard box. "Abraham is very much looking forward to meeting you." He grinned.

Stone grinned. Deklin's happiness was infectious. "Lead the way."

Deklin was clearly in a hurry and marched on. "Follow me, Mister Stone," he said, making sure that Stone was keeping up with him.

"You can call me Jeramiah," said Stone, following the giant out of the airport.

"Be happy to, Jeramiah," replied Deklin.

As soon as they stepped out of the air-conditioned arrivals hall, the heat washed over Stone, making it uncomfortably apparent that he was overdressed for the weather. Their mode of transport was a gleaming, white Rolls Royce Silver Shadow, which Deklin mentioned, to Stone's delight, was air-conditioned.

Deklin loaded the luggage in the boot and then opened the passenger door for Stone, who enjoyed the celebrity treatment. Deklin got in next to him, checked that Stone had everything, and then sped away at high speed from the airport.

"Did you have a nice flight, Jeramiah?" he asked, pulling onto the main drag.

"Yes, very nice. I must thank Mister Conty. I've never flown first class before. Have you?"

"Many times. Abraham has his own plane."

"You go away with Mister Conty a lot?"

Deklin was beaming. "Oh, yes. I always travel with

Abraham."

"Are you his bodyguard or chauffeur?" asked Stone, trying to pretend that Deklin wasn't driving as fast as he was.

Deklin chuckled. "You could say that I do a bit of everything. Abraham doesn't like to drive and he doesn't feel the need for a bodyguard."

Stone contemplated his next question, but the speed they were going made it difficult for him to concentrate on anything but the road. The Rolls raced past slower cars, Deklin overtaking anything that was in his way.

"Where are you from, Deklin?"

"Africa," replied Deklin with the almost permanent grin. "Mozambique originally. I came to Spain six years ago to find work. That's when I met Abraham."

"And you've worked for Mister Conty ever since?"

"Four years," replied Deklin happily. "Four good years."

"What's he like to work for?" asked Stone, pressing his feet further into the footwell as they overtook two cars at once.

"A fine man."

"Does he have a lot of visitors?"

Deklin beamed. "Many. However, you are the first journalist that has ever been to see him. Abraham doesn't like to talk to the media."

"Why not?" asked Stone, daring to take his eyes from the road to see Deklin's reaction.

"Abraham's a stickler for detail. I guess he's just not happy leaving the details to anyone else, if you get my meaning? You must be different from the rest."

Stone added the fact that Conty was a stickler for detail to his mental notes. "Is that what Mister Conty thinks, that I'm different?"

Deklin grinned. "I guess that's it, Jeramiah."

"So why does he want to be interviewed all of a sudden?"

Deklin turned to Stone and grinned. "I'm sure Abraham has his reasons."

"You sound fond of him." Stone gasped, as Deklin suddenly swung out and overtook a lorry full of oranges.

"You'll like him too. I'm sure of that."

"Do you like his work?"

"Oh yes," Deklin beamed.

Stone directed one of the air-conditioning vents so that it blew over his face. "Mind if I smoke?"

Deklin smiled. "Be my guest," he replied, and pulled out the walnut-fronted ashtray.

Stone lit a cigarette and took a deep drag. He peered in the side mirror and watched the other cars on the road disappear at speed behind them.

After an hour's ride, Deklin turned from the main highway onto a narrow road which snaked down up to a small pueblo nestled on the seafront. "What do you think?" he asked, as they travelled down. "Pretty isn't it?"

Stone nodded. The pueblo was nestled in a small bay on the undulating coastline. Expensive boats were moored alongside small fishing boats at the marina. Cafes had seating up to the harbour's edge shaded by bright-coloured parasols. Built into the cliff face were multicoloured villas and apartments with orange-tiled roofs. Deklin was right, it was very pretty.

As soon as the Rolls came to a stop by the harbour, a man was already opening the boot and retrieving the luggage. He then loaded it onto an awaiting Sun Seeker motor cruiser. The name on the side of the boat was *Jennifer*, obviously named after - Conty's wife, the first indication to Stone that he was nearing the acquaintance of the great man.

Deklin, with usual politeness, assisted Stone onto the boat.

"Sorry we're in a rush, Jeramiah," said Deklin, helping him aboard, "but we have to make high tide."

Stone sat himself next to Deklin in the cabin.

Deklin started the engines. "I'm afraid it's going to be a bit choppy," he advised.

He inched the boat away from its mooring. As soon as he was clear of the harbour, Deklin opened the throttle. The boat lurched in the air and raced away at high speed.

"How long does it take?" asked Stone, looking at the small landmass in the distance.

"About an hour in this crosswind," replied Deklin. "We would normally have used a chopper, but it's on the mainland fetching supplies."

"I don't suppose Mister Conty likes to come to the mainland himself?"

Deklin smiled. "Just easier, that's all. Besides, most guests like to arrive this way. Don't you think it's a lot more fun?"

Stone rocked around on his seat, his stomach bearing the brunt of the motion. "Oh, a lot more," he replied, uncomfortably.

Deklin pointed to a picnic hamper in the back of the boat. "There's some food in the back for you if you get hungry. And I believe some champagne."

Stone didn't feel like eating and instead turned his attention to the island in the distance. Conty Island.

*

Edward Murren stared at them across the table. "What went wrong?" he asked again.

"We lost her, sir," repeated Nathan.

"Well that's obvious!"

"I just couldn't get a clear shot."

"I can't believe you let her get away."

Both Carla and Nathan were silent.

"Well, she hasn't been to the police or we'd know," Murren went on. "That means Becker may not have told her anything about us. She'll be confused, which means she'll make a mistake soon enough. Won't take her long to realise she has no one to turn to, that she's in way over her head. Won't be long before she slips up."

"She might have told someone if she does know,

sir," said Carla.

"She might have," Murren agreed. "But I can't see that it matters. What could she do? From what she's been able to piece together, she probably realises she can't trust anyone. Besides, she has no proof of anything."

"She might have contacted Stone," said Nathan.

"It doesn't matter if she has. Stone won't be able to help her and he won't be around much longer anyway."

"Any news from Kirns?" asked Nathan.

"Operatives at the airport reported he got on the plane. He'll do what he's been sent to. We won't hear from him until the job's done."

"We could send backup to Spain," suggested Carla. "Just in case something does go wrong."

Murren shook his head. "No need to send the cavalry in just yet. Kirns can handle it. Nothing will stop him executing his orders. Not now."

"What happens when he finds out his brother's dead?" asked Nathan. "You know how close they were. He won't like it."

Murren lit a cigar. "He won't suspect us, I can assure you."

"She'll probably go to the police, sir," said Nathan.

"Doesn't matter if she does. But I've got a feeling she won't."

Nathan and Carla both looked at each other quizzically.

"Don't worry. I have a plan."

Carla and Nathan smiled.

"I don't know what you're smiling at. I want this bitch found. The more she's running around the more dangerous she can be. You to go where she might. Go to her home, maybe Becker's flat, anywhere, just find her. The next thing I want to hear from you two is that you've found her."

Nathan and Carla left Murren's mansion like a couple of scolded school children that had just been in with the headmaster.

*

Kirns paid a taxi driver to follow the Rolls from the airport, which the driver did with difficulty because of the speed it was travelling. However, the amount of money Kirns had paid the driver meant that he would have run after the car on foot if that's what Kirns asked him to do.

They followed the Rolls until it took a turn-off to one of the fishing pueblos about half an hour's journey out of Marbella. Kirns asked the driver to stop on a high point overlooking it.

Kirns got out of the car and watched the motor cruiser head out to sea through binoculars. Looking ahead of them, Kirns spied an island about twenty kilometres away. Scanning back to the shore, he watched a man get into the Rolls and drive it off. Kirns focused on the car until it was out of sight, and then went back to the taxi.

"Where are they going?" he asked the driver.

The taxi driver looked puzzled, so he asked him to

get out of the car. Kirns handed the driver his binoculars and pointed out to sea. The driver saw the boat speeding away, and then handed the glasses back to Kirns.

"I don't know, señor," he replied, in a heavy Andalusian accent. "Maybe they go to Conty Island."

"Do you know how I can get there?"

"No one go there, señor. It is a very private place. Some say it guarded."

Kirns turned and gazed defiantly at the distant piece of land. He had two choices – wait for Stone to return from the island, or go to the island. Waiting for Stone could be risky. If there was a landing pad on the island for a helicopter, Stone could be airlifted straight to the airport on his return. Given this, Kirns only really had one choice. He would have to go the island. As he didn't know how long Stone was going to be there, it was going to have to be soon.

Kirns rested himself against the bonnet of the taxi and thought. If he had time, he would have gone to the island that evening. However, there was one thing he needed before setting out. The question was how to get it? Ordinarily, anything that he needed for a job would have been obtained through connections with The Family, but Kirns liked to do things his own way.

"Where is the nearest town to here?" he asked the taxi driver.

"Marbella, Señor."

"Can you take me to a hotel there? Near the town centre."

"Si, señor," The driver opened the door for his high-paying fare.

Kirns got in, popped two pills and closed his eyes. He couldn't afford to have another attack.

NINE

Rachel was woken mid-morning by the sound of a magpie screeching for a mate in the tree above where she lay. It had been the place she had come to rest the night before. Better to stay still than to run through the streets where she may be caught. Awake most of the night, Rachel had only managed to grab a few hours of much needed sleep. She lifted her head and looked around. There was a shed in front of her and by it, tall rows of runner beans. If this was heaven, God was a keen gardener.

Disorientated, she got to her knees, which stung. She looked down and saw that they were all grazed. She was a mess, tights shredded, skirt torn and covered with blood. She winced and got to her feet. Looking around gave her the clues she needed to remind her of what had happened after fleeing from the hotel. She had ran into an allotment not far from the hotel and collapsed, exhausted. They hadn't found her. She was still alive.

It was early and she was cold. She searched her pockets and found a small vanity mirror. She looked at her reflection. Her face was covered in blood. The shock made her nauseous again and she nearly began to cry. Taking deep breaths, she tried to regain composure.

She needed to change and move. They would be looking for her, whoever they were. She got up, went to the shed. After rubbing away the moss from the window, she peered in. Inside were tools and a bench covered in plastic pots. She tried the door and was relieved to find the shed was open. Quickly, Rachel stole her way inside and shut the door.

A pair of overalls hung next to a large donkey jacket. It was all she had, and a lot better than what she was wearing, so she put the clothes on. The overalls stank, but she was warm. The donkey jacket was far too big, but it gave her a little comfort, just as coats always had since she was a child. Under a table, was a pair of large worker's boots. They were about four sizes too big, but more comfortable than high heels. After putting them on, she sat down out of the view of the window to collect her thoughts.

Realising her bag was still in the killing room at the hotel, she checked her clothes she had discarded to see what she had with her. All she found to her name was loose change, a handkerchief, a lipstick, and a key ring with three small keys on it. One was for her front door, the other Becker's, and the third for her desk at work. She wanted to cry. In her bag in the hotel was the rest of her life.

Rachel was troubled by what Becker had said, the memory of him dying as vivid as the moment it had happened. He said that he'd lied, and then had given her the numbers. What were the numbers? What had he lied about? The questions were many, but one thing was for sure, whoever killed Becker, wanted her dead too.

After a root around the shed, all she found was a sack full of half-rotten apples. Rachel forced herself to eat, if it were only to take away the taste of the night before.

She carried on trying to piece things together. They had used a silencer that was professional. In addition, they did it without any regard to who would find out. Shooting through the window of a hotel? None of it made sense.

There was more to it than Becker had told her, but she couldn't work it out. The numbers meant something, but what?

Rachel's mind was too crowded so instead she stuffed her clothes into the sack of apples, and then did her best to get the blood off her face with a rag and plenty of spit. She found an old cap, wrapped her hair in a bun, and put it on. Unwittingly, it was the best disguise she could have made. First things first; she had to phone the police. She had to get safe.

After preparing to venture out into the hostile world awaiting her, Rachel carefully opened the door and peered out. The allotment seemed deserted. Against her better judgment, it was time to get going. The first thing she had to do was get to a phone.

They would be close. They knew she was on foot, which meant they knew she couldn't have gone far. She ran over to a small orchard and kept in the security of the trees. Anyone who saw her from a distance, she hoped, would think there was an early riser tending their patch of the allotments.

As she came to the last row of trees, she noticed a lorry full up with bottles of gas in the road adjacent. Rachel stopped, planning her next move. The truck was parked outside a house with the lights on. She made a guess that whoever drove the lorry was getting up for work. Her next move was the best thing she could think to do and an easy way out.

Creeping to the edge of the fence dividing the allotment from the road, she looked up and down the street. When the coast was clear, she sprinted as best she could with the large boots across the road. As soon as she reached the truck she ducked down by its back wheels. After checking around again to see if she had drawn attention, she stepped onto the top of the back wheels, then up the tailgate and into the back. Squeezing herself in between the tall bottles, she lay there getting her breath. She wasn't going to move an inch until as far away from the vicinity as she thought safe.

As she lay there, something odd struck her. She hadn't heard sirens through the night, or that morning. There had been a shooting and she hadn't heard a sound. No dogs, helicopters – nothing?

Rachel didn't have to wait too long for her ride. There was a slamming of a door and then someone stepped up into the cab. The engine started and the lorry began to move off. She then sat up and watched the road they were leaving. The truck turned onto the street where the hotel was. Rachel tried to make herself smaller as they passed it.

Nothing. Not a police car in sight.

The start of the day had been on Rachel's side. The lorry drove into the outskirts of London and stopped outside a café. The driver locked up and went inside. Rachel decided it was time to get off before he started his deliveries and she got caught. She clambered over the side of the lorry and into the main road. Some drivers who went passed tooted angrily at her. From there, Rachel ran up the street towards a phone box. Shops were beginning to open and as she ran past a parade of retailers, something caught her eye.

She halted for a moment, as her brain registered what she had seen, then backed up.

What she noticed was a shop selling televisions. About twenty different types of sets lined the front of the shop, all showing the morning news. As Rachel stepped up to the glass she saw a newsreader speaking, although she couldn't hear what he was saying. The photograph behind the newsreader is what froze her to the spot – Becker.

Rachel quickly hurried into the shop and stood in front of one of the televisions. The news coverage flashed to a press conference. There was policeman at a desk talking to a group of the media. The name on the desk in front of him was Commander Ian Bailey of the Metropolitan Police.

Rachel watched as Bailey told the press that Marcus Becker, editor-in-chief of The Informer, had been found dead at the Abercaveny Hotel in the early hours of this morning. He had been shot in the head.

Rachel sighed with relief. At least the police were

onto it. Now she could go to them. Tell them that the people that did it had also murdered the Princess of Wales. She was safe.

Bailey then went on to give the press more information. The police were now looking for a Rachel Martin who had checked into the hotel with Mr Becker. Her bag had been found which led to the identity of his companion and Miss Martin is believed to be responsible for Becker's murder. The landlady of the hotel has been extremely helpful with the police enquiries, saying that she had heard the couple arguing in their room. Miss Martin is said to have fled the vicinity after murdering Marcus Becker. A manhunt was now in progress and the police had every confidence she would be caught. All members of the public were told not to approach her.

When the image of her came up on the screen, Rachel staggered back. She felt sick and wanted to cry. What she was witnessing was almost unbelievable.

"Hey, you!" shouted a voice, suddenly.

Rachel jumped when she heard it. She turned to see a salesman coming towards her.

"Get out of here! What the hell did you think you are doing? Go find somewhere else to keep warm!"

Rachel realised of course how she was dressed. The salesman thought she was a vagrant who had come in from the cold morning to get warm. He grabbed her by the arm and manhandled her out of the shop and into the street, slamming the door behind her. Rachel turned and stared at the image of her, which was still on the television screen.

She leaned against the wall by the shop, slid to the floor and buried her head in her hands, trying to get her brain around what was happening. *All of those people*, she thought, *but no one to turn to.*

Rachel was now a fugitive and so had to be careful of her next move. There was no going to her flat, in fact, nowhere where she would normally go. They would be waiting for sure.

Her disguise was the best thing she had going for her. The police weren't looking for a tramp. This might give her time. Time to find out what the hell was happening.

Things were as bad as they could be. She had no one to turn to and was on her own. Rachel wanted to cry; to curl up in ball just as she had as a child, wanting the world and everything bad in it to leave her alone and go away. But it couldn't be like that now. She had to be strong. If there was any chance of getting through this nightmare, she had to be strong. Just like she had before.

The only way out was to try and piece together what was going on and who the killers were. The answer had to be in Becker's last words. "I lied," is what he had said.

What the hell had Becker lied about?

The photographs were real, that's what he'd told her, so the people that had Diana assassinated must be the same that were after her now. And obviously, whoever they were must have a position of influence in the police. Who the hell had that much power? Then there were the numbers that Becker had told her just before he died.

What were the damn numbers? *One-Nine-Two-Seven*. What did they mean? As she thought hard, it came to her. It must be a safe. The numbers must be the combination to some sort of safe. But whose and where?

Rachel stood. The only attention she attracted was the odd sneer by people seeming to pick up their pace as they passed her. Feeling a little safer under her disguise, she headed for the city centre. She would go to Becker's flat. There she would find the answers. There had to be some evidence there that would free her from these terrible accusations.

As she walked on, she came to a phone box and went in. She had to contact Stone and warn him. He'd seen the photographs too and they would be after him for sure. For now, Stone was safe in Spain, but Rachel knew that they would be waiting for him on his return.

"The mobile you are calling is currently switched off," came the recorded message from Stone's mobile service.

Rachel slammed the receiver down. "Damn it, Stoney!"

She pondered the photographs Stone had showed her. She knew they were real, which meant whoever sent them to Stone in the first place was real too. But why didn't they meet him? And who the hell were *they* anyway?

The questions, for the moment, would have to remain unanswered. Rachel was on her own, just as she'd always been. Taking a deep breath, she took control of herself and went outside the phone box.

The boots were already hurting so after a root in a bin she found an old newspaper and took a moment to stuff several of its pages into the toes. A little more comfortable, she started walking. Becker's flat was fifteen miles away. Her day was going to get worse.

*

Stone couldn't remember the last time he was so pleased to see land. Deklin dropped the throttle of the motor cruiser and it idled towards the small wooden jetty. A young man dressed in a pair of blue shorts and matching shirt waited for them next to a Jeep.

The young Spaniard who came to greet them helped Stone out of the boat. Stone noticed a revolver attached to the side of his belt. Although Conty didn't see the need for a bodyguard, he nonetheless felt his island needed security.

While waiting for Deklin to moor the boat, Stone looked around the home of the most famous twentieth-century artist. The immediate vicinity was densely populated by palms and rambling undergrowth with no obvious road or exit from the beach once they had changed vehicles. In the distance, dense pine forests crowned a small range of hills. Conty certainly wasn't joking when he said he liked his privacy. Other than the two men around him, the only other signs of habitation were the birds, who, apart from loud screeches, gave no visual indication of their presence either. The golden sands stretched as far as he could see – not a bather or sun worshipper in sight. Stone looked at the mainland, now a thin line of white buildings on the horizon, and felt a twinge of anxiety at being so far from what he knew.

Deklin, smiling as usual, came ashore carrying Stone's luggage. He and the guard talked for a brief moment, then the guard shook Deklin's hand, nodded politely at Stone, and left to continue his lazy patrol of the coastline.

Stone didn't have to lift a finger. His bags were put in the back of the Jeep and when Deklin was sure Stone was comfortable, they headed off, following a single track away from the beach.

"How long now?" Stone asked.

"About an hour," Deklin replied. "Not a very big island," he said, grinning at his passenger. "We have to travel overland because there are too many reefs around the estate for us to take the boat in. I hope you don't mind?"

Stone lit a cigarette. "I see when Mister Conty wants privacy he means it."

Deklin laughed. "I guess you could say that."

"Does Mister Conty have much security?"

"I can't tell you much about that for obvious reasons, Jeramiah. We have enough to watch for unwelcome arrivals. The Coast Guard helps us by keeping an eye out for the determined fan."

"The Spanish government must regard Mister Conty quite highly."

Deklin smiled and turned briefly to look at Stone. "We have a few problems in Spain. You know of ETA, the Basque separatists?"

Stone nodded.

"Well the government fears Abraham could be a

target for kidnapping."

"I see," replied Stone. "Yes, of course."

"Abraham doesn't like it," Deklin went on, "but the government insists on providing a small amount of security."

"Why Spain? I mean why did Conty decide to live here?"

"You'll have to ask Abraham." Deklin beamed.

"What can you tell me about Jennifer Conty?"

"You'll meet her and Abraham soon enough."

The road they were travelling on was, to Stone's satisfaction, not at all bad. Although obscured from the beach, the dusty path was well maintained for the limited amount of vehicles that used it and the journey was not too uncomfortable, although Stone was not letting go of the roll-bar just yet. After around thirty minutes, he noticed the jungle vegetation thin to an open, rockier expanse of land. On further through arid countryside, they topped a hill and Deklin brought the Jeep to a stop. Below was a stretch of beach with an estate settled around like an oasis of habitation.

"There it is," said Deklin, pointing to Conty's estate.

Stone was taken aback. The trip had been worth it. Built on a sandy shoreline were a group of large, white-painted villas with red terracotta roofs. The region was mountainous with dense vegetation all around it. Conty's estate was the epitome of solitude.

"Wow," Stone remarked.

"Beautiful, isn't it?" asked Deklin. "Maybe now you know why he chose Spain."

"Does he have many guests? Any famous ones?" asked Stone, curious of the company Conty kept.

"Some," replied Deklin.

"It's a pity I'm here on business," said Stone, feeling the sun on his face as he admired the view below.

Deklin laughed. "I think maybe you'll get a chance to relax here, Jeramiah. Most do."

Stone took in a deep breath. "Well, let's get down there, shall we?"

"Of course," replied Deklin. "Hold on tight."

By the time they made their way down the steep road to the Conty estate, evening was approaching. Whilst Deklin unloaded the Jeep, Stone got out to look around. The first thing he did was walk down to the water's edge. The sun gently dropped to the horizon, casting brilliant orange light and the last of its afternoon warmth around Conty's retreat. A large villa surrounded by lawns was further up the beach with smaller apartments dotted around the estate. Palms swayed above its roof, shading balconies filled with sun lounges that stretched the whole of the building. Stone saw who he presumed to be a maid coming out one of the villas with a basket of laundry.

Taking his shoes off, Stone waded in the warm Mediterranean water. He noticed stables under the shelter of the surrounding woodland and a pool, which a staff member was cleaning with a pool net. He lit a cigarette just as a woman came out of the main villa and started towards him along the lawn.

Stone put his shoes back on and threw his cigarette in the water. At the same time he realised he felt a little nervous. Deklin waved and headed up to meet the woman.

Stone smiled and turned to the woman as she approached. He recognised her instantly, though photographs did not do her justice. She was strikingly beautiful, dressed in a light blue cotton dress that hugged her slight figure and highlighted her even tan. She had long auburn hair tied at the back with a matching ribbon.

"Mister Stone, you're very welcome," she said, holding out her hand. "I'm Jennifer Conty."

His hostess's rich hazel eyes were as welcoming as was her infectious smile. Stone knew he stared and wondered if he were even blushing. He couldn't help it. Jennifer Conty was one of the most beautiful women he had ever seen.

"Nice to meet you Missus Conty," he said, and shook her hand.

"Do call me Jennifer. I hope Deklin has been looking after you?" she asked, smiling over to him.

Deklin winked at Stone. "Yes, very well indeed. Thank you."

"I hope the journey hasn't been too bad. The chopper's on the mainland getting supplies and a service."

"Oh, that's all right," replied Stone, aware that he was trying exceptionally hard to be polite. "It's been quite an adventure. It really is beautiful here." He felt his face reddening. "I think I've caught the sun already."

Jennifer smiled. "I think you probably have," she agreed. "Abraham's on the other side of the island at present. He should be back tonight. If not, tomorrow morning. He said to tell you he's sorry, but he has some pressing matters to attend to. I hope you don't mind."

"Not at all, I'm in no hurry," replied Stone honestly, and he realised he was staring again.

"Good," said Jennifer. "I'll show you to your apartment."

"Thank you."

"Are you hungry?"

"A little."

"Well, why don't you get yourself settled in? I've prepared a meal for us this evening. I hope you don't mind me for company?"

"Not at all. That's very kind."

"Dek, would you put Mister Stone's—"

"Do call me Jeramiah," Stone interrupted.

Jennifer smiled. "Dek, do you want to put Jeramiah's things in the guest villa?"

"You bet," replied Deklin. "I'll see you around, Jeramiah." He then headed off with Stone's cases.

"Come, I'll show where you'll be staying," Jennifer ushered. "We haven't had a visitor for a while now," said Jennifer, as they walked. "Have you been to Spain before, Jeramiah?"

"Only when I was younger."

"You'll love it here," Jennifer assured him. "Different than the hustle and bustle of London I imagine."

"It is," replied Stone. "I feel as though I've just arrived on holiday."

Jennifer smiled at him. "Good. I'm sure you'll find some time to relax. There's plenty for you to do."

Stone followed Jennifer up the lawn towards one of the small villas. He couldn't help wondering about her. She was certainly much younger than Conty and, although he had met plenty of celebrity wives that tolerated a lot of things for money, she seemed to be very different from any of them. There was a refreshing simplicity about her, a woman clearly not overwhelmed with the wealth and status. Stone would have felt totally at ease in her company had it not been for her beauty. She was sure and self-confident without being threatening, and seemed undaunted at having a journalist as her guest. *If this is all true*, thought Stone, *then Jennifer Conty is a rare breed. If not, her demure is very well rehearsed.*

He followed her into the apartment where he would be staying. Air conditioning had been put on beforehand. The furniture was sparse, but expensive. In the middle of the room was an oval glass table with white leather sofas around it. Along one wall was a variety of reading material. On the walls there hung a few paintings. Stone noticed one of them was a painting of the beach. Another was of Jennifer sitting by the pool. Stone thought it ironic that these private paintings worth millions should hang so unassumingly on the walls of a guest room and not in a major art gallery.

"I think you'll be comfortable here," said Jennifer, opening the patio doors out onto the sun terrace where the pool was situated. She turned to Stone for his reaction.

As the light washed over Jennifer's dress, Stone could just make out the outline of her slim figure underneath. "It's beautiful," he replied.

Jennifer smiled. "Your bedroom's upstairs. There's a phone on the wall, there," she said, pointing. "I'm sure you'll want to keep in touch with your office so there's a separate line to use if you want to go online." She pointed to another phone socket. "That way we can keep the main line free. If you need anything, just phone Maria. She's our maid. You can get hold of her by pressing zero on the phone. I'll let you settle in then come and get you for dinner in say, an hour?"

"Sounds good," Stone replied.

Jennifer gave one last look around the room. "Great, I'll see you then. By then I should know what Abraham is up to. Oh, by the way, don't forget to put your watch forward an hour."

Stone shook his head. "I won't."

"Well, I'll leave you to find your feet."

"Thank you." Stone showed her to the door then watched as Jennifer crossed the lawn.

After putting his watch forward, Stone then took his things upstairs. A bowl of fruit had been set on the table next to his bed. In the corner of the room there was a music system and a shelf of CDs. There were more paintings in the room he assumed to be by Conty. Some were obvious scenes from the island or other parts of Spain, probably all worth a small fortune. Stone chuckled to himself. He thought of how pictures in hotels were so firmly fixed to the wall that they would defy the most cunning criminal mind to try and steal them. Conty's masterpieces, however, could simply be lifted off the wall and stuffed into his suitcase like the odd bath towel. Strangely, though, the paintings had a mystical quality, ancient works of art adorning the walls of something far more sacred than a hotel bedroom; art that was hard to bring oneself to touch, let alone steal.

After unpacking his things, Stone switched on his laptop and went online to see if he had any e-mails. He didn't. He thought Becker might have at least enquired about his trip. He unpacked his mobile phone but decided to leave it switched off. For the time being, Stone was rather pleased to be cut off from The Informer, the rest of the world, and everyone associated with it.

The evening was comfortably warm, so Stone decided to have a swim. After a few lengths he went to the bar, poured himself a drink, and sat outside on his balcony watching the last of the sun melt away over the horizon. The ocean had mellowed since the journey earlier and water lethargically lapped the edge of the beach. Tree frogs started their hypnotic evening chorus. The air was clean, with the faint smell of the pines sheltering the balcony peppering the ever so light sea breeze. Stone sank into the chair. He was on one of the most famous locations in the world to get an interview that would be the envy of his profession. Things were surely looking up.

*

Kirns watched the Jeep for over an hour but patience was one of the things he had mastered while in the army. However, it seemed the waiting game was now over. Kirns was relieved to see one of the officers heading off into the throng of the town.

The Guardia Civil Jeep was parked in the middle of a busy square in the centre of Marbella. This part of town was a popular place for locals and tourists alike. A handsome sixteenth-century church dominated the square, surrounded by bars and restaurants and a handful of boutiques. Given the mass of people, the Guardia Civil stationed themselves in the centre of town, mainly as a presence to deter pickpockets and petty thieves preying on the unsuspecting holidaymakers.

Kirns watched the second officer walk a fair distance down the street while the first remained in the Jeep. Time wise, it was a small window but plenty for what Kirns had planned. When the second officer was well out of sight, he made his move.

Walking to the side of the Jeep, Kirns got in character. He went up to the window and rapped frantically on the glass. The officer inside was startled and his cigarette popped out of his mouth.

The officer stepped out of the Jeep.

"Si?" he asked, with a frown.

"Quick, quick, you must help me," Kirns ranted. "Please!"

Kirns started to walk off, waving for the officer to

follow him.

He could see the officer was reluctant to leave the Jeep at first, so ran back, grabbing him by the arm and urging him to follow.

Kirns led him away, keeping in character by babbling on about being robbed. Kirns knew exactly where he was leading the officer, of course. Everything had been planned in advance. He picked up the pace, inclining the officer to do the same.

They left the square and started down a narrow street. Kirns knew at the end there would be a deserted alley behind a restaurant, where rubbish was dumped; a place where it would just be the two of them.

Kirns ran into the alley with the officer following. Kirns suddenly stopped by two large rubbish bins. Lights from the restaurant kitchen illuminated the alley.

As the officer came to a stop, he looked around, then at Kirns with a confused expression. He began to ask why Kirns had brought him there, but didn't get a chance to finish. Kirns punched him square in the face. The officer fell straight to the ground but was not out. Disorientated, he tried to get up but fell back on his haunches. Kirns was ready with his next move. With a ferocious roundhouse kick, he brought his boot across the side of the officer's jaw, this time knocking him out.

Kirns retrieved the semi-automatic pistol from the officer's holster. He checked the clip, which was full – mission accomplished.

He tucked the pistol in the back of his jeans then left the alley. As he made his way back to the square, he saw the second officer had returned to the Jeep. He was looking around for his partner, scanning the throngs of tourists that packed the square for a familiar uniform. Kirns smiled as he walked past him. Time to get something to eat. Everything was going to plan.

TEN

Rachel lay down against a tree in the small park opposite Becker's flat. Her feet were in a bad way. Ironically, the pain was an almost welcome distraction from the danger.

Unintentionally, her disguise had been brilliant. No one had paid her any attention during the fifteen-mile journey to Becker's flat and didn't take long for Rachel to realise the effect her clothing was having. True to her character, she even on occasion took to inspecting the odd dustbin. She was just another poor and ignored unfortunate, sleeping rough under a tree in the park. No one cared. No one bothered her. She was, to everyone who noticed her, of no consequence.

The time she spent walking to Becker's enabled her to collect her thoughts. Whatever Becker was into, the answers had to be at his flat. The numbers he had gurgled before he died had to have something to do with that flat also.

One-Nine-Two-Seven.

They sounded like a safe combination.

Rachel had seen very little police presence and surmised that they were still hunting for her in the vicinity of the hotel where Becker had been killed. She had also worked out that whoever killed Diana was definitely connected to the police in some way. Rachel had been set up. Becker's killers and the police had to be the same. This was almost too unbelievable to be true. If the pain in her feet hadn't confirmed her of reality, she might have actually been convinced this was just a dreadful nightmare she was in.

The coat wrapped tightly around her and cap pulled down far enough to shade her face from view and recognition, Rachel wandered closer to the road, scanning the front of the flats. The place looked deserted from the outside. She watched everyone entering or leaving the flats, including all passers-by. Everyone looked suspicious but no one seemed like a killer. If there were police in the vicinity, she hadn't noticed them.

She sat and waited, deciding when to risk going in. She could wait until the cover of darkness but that gave her killers the same advantage. At the same time, the sight of a tramp walking into expensive flats in sight of all the other residents might bring more attention than she needed. If someone phoned the police, it was all over. Despite the desire to change and clean up, Rachel decided to wait for nightfall.

*

A knocking woke Stone out of a light sleep. He got up and pulled on a pair of jeans then went to the door downstairs. Jennifer Conty stood in the doorway wearing a long white dress. The moon behind her illuminated the outline of her concealed nudity. Stone wondered if he were still dreaming.

"Sorry. Did I wake you?" she asked.

Stone tried his best to flatten his hair. "I must have been more tired than I thought," he replied, feeling a little inadequate in her presence. "I'm really sorry."

Jennifer smiled at him. "No need to apologise. It you're too tired then I can have some food sent to you instead."

As Jennifer came into the light of his room, Stone noticed broken capillaries in the whites of her eyes. Jennifer had been crying.

"No, no," replied Stone. "It will only take me a few minutes to get ready. Will you wait?"

Jennifer nodded, stepping inside. Stone ran upstairs and got a shirt. He came down to find Jennifer putting together a drink at the bar.

"Is your husband back?" he asked.

Jennifer turned to face him. "No, I'm afraid Abraham's a bit tied up. He sends his apologies. I hope you don't mind?"

Stone shook his head and smiled, although he had to wonder whether Jennifer minded.

"What does Abraham do over the other side of the island?" he asked, buttoning his shirt.

Jennifer handed Stone a drink. "Paints," she replied. "He often spends days away over there."

"Over there?"

"In the north, at his studio."

"I see. Do you mind him going off?" asked Stone, then realised the question may have been a little too forward.

"No. I knew who I married. I guess you can say it goes with the territory." She put her hands together. "Hungry? We can talk more over dinner."

"Starving actually," Stone replied.

"Good," she said, moving towards the door. "Follow me."

Stone walked with Jennifer along the beach to the large, brightly lit villa. They passed through a large entrance hall, then into the main living room. The place was homely and not anything like Stone had imagined. Bean bags littered the room, with books strewn over a large oak coffee table. Paintings adorned most of the walls. Stone immediately noticed a portrait of Deklin. Others were scenes presumably from areas around the island. Large ornate candles burned sleepily, illuminating the room with flickering light. Incense filled the villa with an exotic aroma.

"This is nice," Stone remarked, looking around the room.

"We like it comfy," Jennifer replied. "Through here." She led the way out to the veranda.

They both stepped onto a large balcony overlooking the sea. Hanging lanterns illuminating a grape-covered pergola. Under it was a table adorned with fruit, cheese, and a couple of bottles of wine. Two places were set.

Stone followed Jennifer through to the kitchen so

they could talk while she prepared supper. Stone thought it a good opportunity to find more out about the Contys.

"Where are you from originally?"

"Murcia," replied Jennifer, "although I seldom go back home. Both my parents are dead. I have no other family."

"You speak English perfectly."

Jennifer was flattered. "I spent a lot of my time in America and in England studying."

"Where did you meet your husband?"

"We met at a gallery in Barcelona. I was visiting the gallery at the same time Abraham was opening a small exhibition of his work there. The rest, as they say, is history."

"How long have your been married?"

"Two years," replied Jennifer, with obvious affection. "I know what you must be thinking. Why would a young woman like me marry a man thirty years my senior?" She winked at Stone. "A very wealthy man at that."

"I wasn't thinking that," Stone lied. "But seeing as we are on the subject, do you mind what people might think?"

Jennifer shrugged. "No," she replied, pouring Stone a glass of wine. "He's a remarkable man, Jeramiah. You'll like him." She then eyed Stone, at the same time sipping her wine. "Am I being interviewed?"

"No," lied Stone again. There was a pause but he couldn't help himself. "Why an island in Spain? I mean you could live anywhere, I assume?"

Jennifer put her glass down. "Abraham adores Spain. He loves the people, the Spanish culture. The island has more to do with the Spanish government than Abraham. He wanted to settle in Spain and the Spanish government offered him this island. They thought it best to give Abraham the privacy he needs, more importantly, the security. The Spanish and its royal family are very fond of Abraham."

"Is that something you both worry about?" asked Stone. "Security."

"Not really, but you have to be careful. Abraham keeps all of his work here so you can understand he could be a potential target for thieves. The Spanish government offers a small amount of security. The Coast Guard looks out for us by keeping the odd nosy tourist away. But there are also justified reasons why security is needed. The government is concerned about a possible threat to Abraham's life."

"To his life?"

Jennifer nodded. "We have problems with ETA in Spain. The authorities feel that Basque separatists could pose a threat. Kidnapping is something they worry about. We've had some threats in the past."

"Yeah, Deklin told me about that? What's the story with him by the way?"

Jennifer smiled to herself. "Deklin's been working for Abraham since they met." She ran her finger around the lip of her glass, thoughtfully. "Deklin was employed as a labourer on a building site on the mainland. It happened to be the same site where Abraham was looking to purchase some property.

The company employing Deklin was using him and the other illegal immigrants as cheap labour. Apparently, Deklin's conditions were appalling. They gave him a tiny hut to live in onsite and paid him barely enough money for even his food. Well, just across the water was a very wealthy artist living on an island. Deklin was desperate to change his life and saw that Abraham, one way or another, could change it." She shook her head and laughed. "Well, the story goes that Dek stole a fishing boat and sailed to the island one night with the intention of stealing a painting."

"You're joking," Stone gasped. "And now Deklin *works* for him?"

Jennifer giggled. "That's typical of Abraham. He caught Deklin as he was actually lifting a picture off the wall in the living room. Abraham surprised the hell out of him. Deklin was so shocked that he nearly dropped the painting. Abraham asked Deklin if he could wrap it for him and give him a lift back to the mainland.

"Well Deklin didn't know what to say. He didn't speak much English and his Spanish wasn't much better either. Abraham needed someone to help around the place so instead of reporting him to the police, he offered Deklin a job. Deklin couldn't quite believe it. Abraham sent him to school, helped him get residency. They've been friends even since. Don't tell Dek I told you. He gets very embarrassed about it."

"Sounds like your husband is more forgiving than I would have been."

Jennifer nodded her agreement. "He seems to see

the good in people. Deklin would do anything for Abraham. We are both very fond of him."

Jennifer took the sardines out from under the grill and transferred them to a large plate. She then served an assortment of tapas. "Follow me," she said, heading to the table. "I hope you've got an appetite. I've probably made way too much."

Stone took some of the dishes and followed Jennifer to the veranda. The warm evening was accompanied by a nearly full moon, which illuminated the cove. Stone didn't know whether it was the company or location that relaxed him, but he was glad of it. If it were all a ploy by the Contys to woo him with a charming location and indulgent hospitality, he was falling for it.

Jennifer put two sardines on Stone's plate then passed him the salad and bread. Stone had to stop himself from laughing out loud. He was having dinner with the beautiful wife of one of the most famous artists in the world, by the ocean on the most exclusive island on the planet. To say it was surreal would have been an understatement.

"What are you smiling at?" asked Jennifer, as she poured the wine.

"Oh, I was just thinking that I wish all my assignments could be like this."

"Well here's to new ways of doing things," toasted Jennifer.

Both looked at each other and they clinked glasses.

"How many people are actually on the island?" asked Stone.

Abraham, me, Dek, and Maria. There is staff that we have over from the mainland to look after the grounds and the horses, but they are taxied here by boat every morning. We travel a lot and Deklin runs the place while we're away. Maria does all the cooking, when she hasn't got a night off like tonight," she said with a smile. "I hope I've done okay?"

"Delicious," replied Stone, unable to take his eyes of his hostess. This world seemed to suit her. He wondered if she would look the same on a rainy day in London. Whether she would stand out and catch his eye in a windswept street. "So, what's it like living in paradise?"

"It has its ups and downs."

"Do you get to leave the island much?"

Jennifer took a sip of wine but maintained eye contact. "We're not as reclusive as people say we are. Abraham has more autonomy than you might think. We often go to the mainland. I handle Abraham's business affairs so I travel often. You'd be surprised. Very few recognise him, so we're able to move about quite freely."

"But you do go to some lengths in keeping your privacy," Stone remarked. "There's very little known about you and your husband."

"You make it sound as though it's a crime."

"Not a crime, but certainly unusual. Is there a reason for it?"

"Does there have to be one?"

Stone was finding it difficult to be the journalist. He could smell Jennifer's perfume and at that moment it was the most delicious fragrance he had ever smelt. "I guess the public would like to know."

Jennifer pondered the question. "Public or the press?"

Stone considered the remark. "Both, I guess."

"Does the world know about you?"

"No, but then I'm not one of the most famous artists in the world."

"Being good at something doesn't mean you become the property of the press, does it?"

Stone shook his head. "I guess not. But, it does mean you are in a position of influence."

Jennifer poured them both some more wine. "Surely your job means you have far more influence than my husband does?"

"Maybe. Why has he never spoken to the press before?"

"You'd have to ask Abraham about that."

"Why now?"

"Why now, what?"

"Why is your husband suddenly giving an interview?"

Jennifer studied Stone over the top of her wine glass. "We told you, to coincide with his exhibition at the Tate."

Stone wondered if Jennifer was lying. If she was, then she did it well. "Then why me?" he asked. "Why did your husband ask for me?"

"Why, has he made a mistake?"

Stone laughed. "I hope not. It's just that I don't know much about art."

"Abraham knows what you do. I'm sure he has his reasons. I've never known him do anything without thinking it through. Besides, Abraham doesn't much like the art critics. Maybe that's why. You'll see him tomorrow. You can ask him then."

"This is delicious," said Stone, changing the subject.

"Eat as much as you like," replied Jennifer. She then sat back and crossed her legs. She gave him a quizzical look. "How about you, Jeramiah?"

"Me?" puzzled Stone, as if others might be in the room.

Jennifer nodded her head slowly then smiled. "Yes, *you*. My turn to ask you a couple of things."

Stone started to feel a little uncomfortable.

"I've read your articles in The Informer. That's about all I know about Jeramiah Stone."

"Not much else to know."

"Married?" asked Jennifer, pointing to the ring on Stone's finger.

Stone shook his head. He hadn't expected to be reminded of Milly and immediately felt guilty over some of the thoughts he'd been having during the evening.

Jennifer noticed the reaction. "I'm sorry. I didn't mean to pry."

Stone took a deep breath. "My wife died two years ago."

"I'm so sorry, Jeramiah."

"Yeah, well," was all Stone could manage.

"I lost my parents suddenly in a car accident," replied Jennifer. "I like to think something good comes out of something tragic like that."

Stone finished his wine. "Maybe."

"You enjoy your work?" asked Jennifer, changing the subject.

"Sometimes."

"You good at what you do?" she coaxed, looking him straight in the eyes.

God she is so beautiful, Stone thought to himself. He could feel himself starting to get quite flushed under her gaze. "I've been known to be," he replied. "Things haven't been going that well since..." He paused. "Well, they haven't been going that well, although your husband might have helped by giving this interview. I'll be the envy of Fleet Street."

Jennifer winked at him. "Maybe everything happens for a reason. Anyway, enjoy your stay here. Think of it as a vacation. Abraham won't bite and he'll probably want to have some fun while you're here. That will be the deal. Don't tell him I told you, but I understand he wants to take you out on the boat. There are some fantastic lagoons around the island."

"I look forward to it."

There was silence between then for a moment as they ate, then Jennifer stood up.

"You fancy a walk along the beach?" she asked. "That's if you're not too tired. It's a beautiful night."

Stone looked up. "Why not?"

As they stepped onto the sand, Jennifer put her arm through Stone's as they walked. "Look," she said, nodding to the sky.

Stone looked up. "Wow!" The universe was a mass of bright stars.

"I love the sky at night here. It's so beautiful. You don't get that in England."

They walked on to where a small boat lay upturned near the water's edge.

"I have to go to the mainland tomorrow," Jennifer began. "There's a festival in the town. You know it actually; it's where you got the boat."

"Oh yes the pueblo. Very quaint."

"Every year we sponsor the celebrations. The town has been so good to us. They look out for us. We love doing it. One year, we had the festival here on the island. Abraham ferried the whole town here. All the families came. The children were so made up."

Jennifer sounded excited but Stone was again aware of a sadness that he had noted during supper. If he had to guess it was because she was lonely.

"Do you have any children?" he asked.

"No," replied Jennifer, softly. "I found out some time ago that I can't have children."

"I'm sorry."

Jennifer feigned a smile. "Some things are just not meant to be."

"Are you going to stay for the festival tomorrow

evening then?"

"Not this year," replied Jennifer, sadly. "By the way, is there anything you'd like me to get for you while I'm there? Anything you need?"

"I can't think of anything," said Stone. Again he noticed something bothered his hostess. He wondered then if the Conty marriage was as tight as Jennifer made out.

"Is everything all right?" he asked, boldly.

"Yes, of course," Jennifer said quickly, without looking at Stone directly. "Why wouldn't it be?"

Stone regretted asking the question. "I'm sorry, I just wondered."

"You must be tired," said Jennifer.

Stone was disappointed that the evening was obviously coming to a close. "A little. I'll walk you back," he said.

They arrived back at the estate. "Thanks for a really nice evening," said Stone.

"You're welcome," said Jennifer. "It seems we have a few things in common, Jeramiah."

Stone looked puzzled. "We do?"

Jennifer nodded, but didn't explain herself.

"Well, I won't see you until tomorrow evening for dinner. That means you'll have the whole day with Abraham. You'll have fun if nothing else."

Stone wanted a few more hours of Jennifer's company. The night was over far too quick. "Have a nice day on the mainland."

Jennifer glanced back at her villa. "Well, goodnight, Jeramiah."

"Goodnight," said Stone, and reluctantly watched her make her way back inside.

Once inside himself, Stone lay on his bed staring up at the fan. He thought about Jennifer.

She was a distraction he hadn't counted on.

ELEVEN

Rachel was cold and pulled the old coat tightly around her. She wondered how anyone could survive on the streets. She had watched Becker's apartment for hours; a horseshoe of expensive homes surrounded a miniature park in a cobbled courtyard. She lay under a large oak tree, camouflaging her from the hostile world waiting for her just a few feet away.

Rachel had always found it somewhat mysterious that Becker could afford to live where he did. This exclusive area of Kensington meant that one had to be rich to dwell here and it seemed remarkable that an editor, although well paid, would have been able to afford such an expensive address. Rachel knew Becker had money. He had told her that he'd recently inherited money from an aunt, but it would have to be some inheritance; one that she would never now be able to share in.

In all the time Rachel had watched and waited, there had only been two people who had entered the building. One was an old lady who struggled with her bags up the steps to the flats – too old and frail to be a killer. The other was a young woman. She had arrived by taxi. She paid the driver and ran straight into the apartments. A woman just coming home from work, that was all; or so Rachel hoped. Still there was no sign of any police.

This was it, now or never. Rachel stood up, and then pretended to wander aimlessly out of the park and into the open. She also pretended to have a limp and hobbled out into the street, looking up each end to check for anything suspicious. The road seemed deserted so she crossed just a few yards from the apartment entrance and sat against the black iron railings which ran in front of them. After a deep breath and one more look up each end of the street, she got up and walked purposefully towards the steps leading to Becker's front door.

She wondered if she could go through with it. Her mind told her to walk on, to walk past and forget she was ever involved. *No!* She thought to herself, *I can't run. I always run.*

Rachel turned and walked straight up the steps. She retrieved Becker's key and put it in the lock, turned it, then pushed the door open and quickly stole inside. She'd done it.

Rachel elected to take the stairs. Becker's apartment was on the first floor. She hurried up the stairs and stopped abruptly on the first floor landing. She leaned against the wall, holding her breath, and then peeked out so she could see down the corridor. To her relief, it was empty.

She then hurried to Becker's apartment. Once outside she pressed her ear to the door. Apart from the thump of her heart she could hear nothing. Slowly she raised the key to the lock, her hand shaking. Very gently, as though the lock were a bomb, she pushed the key and turned it. The door opened with a gentle click.

She went in.

The room was dark. She closed the door behind her and stood in silence. She could see nothing in the gloom and felt for the light switch. With her finger on the switch, she paused for a moment.

Death will have me now, if it were going to at all, she thought. As soon as the light went on they would murder her. She would come face to face with Becker's killers probably for only a few seconds, and then they would do the same to her as they had done to him. At that point, she knew she couldn't face it, could not look at them. If she were to die, it would be this way, with her eyes closed.

With that, she flicked the switch.

Nothing happened.

Rachel opened her eyes. In front of her was the living room. There was a sofa, with two easy tables either side. To the right was the kitchen. To the left was the bedroom. In the corner of the room was Becker's desk. She scanned the rest of the room hoping to find some clues.

Rachel hurried into the kitchen. She opened the fridge door to find it quite well stocked. The sight of the food made her stomach growl. She got some slices of ham and stuffed them into her mouth. She then went to the bathroom to wash. The warm water and soap was a much needed tonic. Rachel had to fight the urge to run a hot bath but there was no time for such indulgences. She towelled her face, and then proceeded to check the rest of the flat.

In the bedroom she hunted around for what she hoped would give her some answers. She opened one of the bedside draws. There was a book, cigarettes, and lighter. Rachel picked the book up and shook it upside down as though some shattering clue would fall onto the carpet. Nothing.

She then checked the en-suite bathroom. Nothing to help her piece together what was going on and why Becker had been killed. She went back to the living room and sat on the edge of the sofa collecting her thoughts. If there were a safe, where would it be? Or maybe it wasn't a safe. If not, what did the numbers mean? For God's sake, what did they mean?

She got up and searched the flat again, this time more thoroughly but was only brought back to the same place – on the edge of the sofa staring at Becker's desk. There was no safe. She'd wasted her time. Whatever Becker wanted her to know, the answer was not in his flat. She had spent all night under a tree, waiting and hiding, cold and hungry, only to draw the shortest straw of her sorry life. What did he mean? What were the numbers?

One-Nine-Two-Seven.

Rachel couldn't think any more, so she got up and went to the fridge. She gathered as much food as she could stuff into her pockets and got ready to leave. She went to the door and scanned the room one more time; as if by some miracle the answers to all her questions would pop up from behind the sofa and declare themselves.

There was no miracle. Nothing popped up. Time to get the hell out and she was glad of it.

Rachel had made her mind up what to do next by the time she had made her way out to the road. She strode purposefully away from the flat, towards the nearest bus stop. She only had to wait a few minutes before the right one turned up that would drop her where she lived.

The journey took an hour. She got off the bus and started to make her way to her flat. She kept her head down but her gaze fixed on her home. The street seemed quiet enough, with nothing suspicious as a car full of killers waiting for her to return home after the most frightening night of her life. There was no sign of any police either. She guessed they wouldn't be waiting for her on the account that it would be the first place they'd look. She needed a change of clothes and money if she was to get somewhere permanently safe.

She quickly ran up the steps to her front door and put her ear to it. All seemed to be quiet. Another deep breath, then she put her key in the lock and opened it.

Once inside, Rachel flicked the light switch.

"You can come out now," she shouted.

No murderers replied.

Rachel let out a deep breath then shut the door behind her. She had to be quick, get some money and a change of clothes then get out.

After a quick shower Rachel moved to the

bedroom and changed into a pair of jeans and a jumper. Changing her shoes was not easy given the way her feet were blistered but it felt good to finally get out of the workman's boots. She cleaned her teeth then gathered up what a fugitive might need for a life on the run. She got a chequebook, her driving license, some cash and a credit card. She then packed a holdall of clothes and toiletries. Time to get out. She started to head for the door, but caught a reflection in the living room mirror.

She turned. Becker had left his laptop on the table.

One-Nine-Two-Seven.

Surely not?

She stared. Her heart begged for her to leave, but her mind said otherwise. She went to the desk and sat. Slowly she lifted the screen and turned on the computer. The machine hummed and whined until eventually a welcome note flashed up to Becker telling him he was the most important man in the world.

Rachel moved the mouse along the range of Windows icons and placed the arrow onto the start button. She clicked it and brought up a sub menu. One of them was marked Files. She clicked the icon and a list of sub files popped up in that location.

Rachel sighed as she saw how many there were. She looked for ones that seemed unusual and clicked on one marked Favourites. Thumbnails of naked women. Rachel fought the tears and exited the screen. She was back to the main menu with a hundred file names in front her.

The task was daunting. Rachel flicked through various files, most work related, saved memos, articles and accounts. She was getting nowhere and threw the mouse against the machine and sat back. Another blank. She stared at the screen then rubbed her tired eyes. When she looked back at the screen, she noticed a file name that intrigued her. The Family. Becker didn't have a family?

Rachel clicked the file name. The screen flashed away then brought up another command prompt.

"Confidential. Please type in password."

Rachel eyes widened. There were four spaces. She knew four numbers.

With renewed urgency, she typed in the appropriate numbers in the space provided. *One-Nine-Two-Seven*. Holding her breath, she pressed the return button.

At first, Rachel thought it was just another file relating to work, but as she read, it became apparent this file was what Becker wanted her to see.

As she sat reading, the reality of her situation was more shocking than she could ever have imagined. The more she read the more she knew she was dead.

Rachel read the last few inputs from Becker before his death. It was just too much. She stopped reading and started to sob.

When Rachel had no more tears to shed, she looked up at the screen. The evidence was still there, she was not dreaming. Now it was clear why they wanted her dead. Stone had been right all along. The police *were* involved. The file gave detailed evidence of their part in it, and now she knew just who Commander Ian Bailey really was. And to top it all, the owner of the paper she had worked for the last five years was the king-pin.

Rachel had to decide what to do. The file could send them all down and prove her innocence. If she could just somehow get the evidence to the authorities – to someone that wasn't part of this organisation – she would be safe.

She hunted in the drawer to look for a disk to transfer the file but couldn't find one. No matter, she would just take the laptop instead. As she went to close it down, Rachel realised she was making a mistake. If they found her or she was arrested they would confiscate the computer. They would find the file and destroy it. Where would she be then? She would have nothing. No, she couldn't take it. She had to get it to someone, get the file in safe hands. Then it struck her. She could send it to Stone. That way he would know what trouble he was in and maybe, just maybe, he could get help.

Time, like everything else, was not on Rachel's side. She quickly dialled Stone's mobile number. She waited, and then winced as she was told again that his mobile was switched off.

What now? Think!

She looked back at the screen. Rachel had an idea.

Quickly she went online, and then scanned the e-mail addresses Becker had on file. Stone's name came up and she selected it. She would send the file to him. Stone would know what to do. She typed a short note for him then attached the file to the e-mail. She stared at the screen one more time then hit the send icon.

Rachel prayed Stone would get it. As soon as the

server told her the e-mail had been sent, Rachel erased the file. She couldn't risk them finding it. As soon as that was done, she packed away the laptop and put it under the table. Checking she had everything she needed, Rachel made for the door. She had already spent far too much time in the house. It was time to get the hell out.

As she went to open the door, it was flung open, knocking her to the floor. Momentarily disorientated, she tried to get but someone was already on top of her and pinned her down. Her attacker rolled her onto her back and she stared up at the man holding her.

Standing behind him was the woman she'd seen going into Becker's apartment block earlier. Rachel moaned at her own stupidity and the woman grinned down at her. She tried to free herself again, thrashing around on the floor. She screamed and the man hit her hard across the side of her jaw. The room blurred and the woman's face became horribly distorted. Then there was darkness.

TWELVE

Kirns checked out of his Marbella hotel early. A taxi took him to the pueblo where Stone left for Conty's island the day before. On the way, he noticed a heavy police presence along the main road. They had only gone a couple of miles when the taxi was hailed into a police checkpoint along the highway. Kirns hoped he wouldn't have to use the gun tucked in the back of his jeans.

As soon as the taxi came to a stop, an officer of the Guardia Civil asked the driver to step out. The police now knew that the perpetrator that had attacked an officer the night before and stolen his weapon was foreign. The driver was asked if he had been working the night before and seen anything suspicious.

Kirns retrieved the pistol from his jeans and held it by his side. He watched as the driver gestured to the car. The officer looked past him, seemingly looking at his passenger. Kirns remained calm.

The officer turned his attention back to the driver. They talked for a few minutes more, and then he came walking back to the car.

"What's going on?" asked Kirns, as they drove off past the checkpoint.

"A policeman was attacked last night in Marbella. They stop all taxis from here, all the way to Gibraltar. Crazy people!" he stirred his finger against his temple as he spoke.

Kirns relaxed back in his seat and tucked the gun into his jeans. He was clear.

A few miles later, he was dropped off at the pueblo. He reached the small village in the middle of the morning fish auction. Locals haggled furiously and it was obvious that he was not going to get anywhere during the commotion. He headed into the main strip, looking for ways to pass the time.

Restaurateurs set up the tables and displayed large boards with photographs of their meals, while souvenir shop owners put out revolving postcard stands in the walkways. The aroma of roasted almonds filled the streets, sold by a young boy turning the almonds over a hot skillet. Kirns purchased a small carton of them and continued walking.

He noticed a small shop with a sign announcing 'Daily boating trips.' Kirns headed for it.

"Can I help you, señor?" asked the Spanish gentlemen behind the desk.

Kirns cleared his throat. "Yes. I was hoping to get out on a boat. I'm a photographer and would like to take some pictures of the coast."

"Arrh, Si, señor. We have plenty of boats here."

"Good, I'd like to hire one for the day."

The Spanish man shook his head and tutted. "Not today, señor. There is no boats going out today. Sorry."

This was not good. Kirns had plans and didn't like them being changed. "I really would like to go out today," he pressed.

The Spanish man smiled. "I'm sorry, señor, all the boats are back now. Tomorrow will be good. You book for tomorrow?"

"Maybe I could ask one of the fishermen?" replied Kirns.

"Señor today is the festival. No boats go out today. Holidays now. Tomorrow, I take you myself. No problem."

Kirns left the shop and walked towards the small harbour. He scanned the many boats, deciding how best to get to the island. He knew he would have to steal a boat.

Getting out his binoculars, he then looked out towards the island. As he scanned its coastline, he saw a boat heading in the direction of the pueblo, the same boat that had taken Stone across the day before. Kirns wouldn't have to steal a boat after all. His transport was on its way.

*

Stone was up early, already washed and dressed in preparation to meet Conty. He contemplated checking his e-mails but decided against it. The Informer seemed a million miles away.

He made his way downstairs, just as there was a knock at the door. He looked at his watch, which said 8 a.m. He was a little nervous as he went to the door. This was it. Finally he was going to meet the great man. He took a deep breath then opened the door.

Light streamed in and, for a moment, Stone couldn't see a thing. As his eyes adjusted, he saw that in fact it wasn't Conty at all. A large woman with a pretty face was holding a tray out in front of her.

"Buenos dias, Señor Stone," she greeted him.

Stone nodded politely and moved out of the way. The woman walked in and placed the tray on the living room table.

"You must be Maria?" asked Stone.

"Si, Maria," replied the maid cheerfully, and then let herself out again.

Stone lifted the silver cover and found a full English breakfast had been prepared for him.

He took his meal out to the veranda, squinting as his eyes became accustomed to the morning sun. An old man, wearing far too many clothes for the time of year, was cleaning his pool. The morning seemed perfect. The sun was already high and the cloudless sky indicated today would be a hot one.

After finishing his breakfast, Stone decided to look for his host. If Conty wasn't going to come to him, then he would go to Conty. As he opened the door the sun streamed into his apartment. Stone, cursing the fact he had forgotten his sunglasses, shaded his eyes with his hand then stepped out onto the soft sand. At first, Stone could see nothing, not even the sea only yards from him. Through the slits in his fingers, he saw a shimmering figure emerge from the light.

The man came up the beach. He was dressed in a loose cotton shirt, white slacks, and was barefoot. As the man came closer, Stone could see him more clearly. His hair was almost white, closely cropped. He was tall, with lean build.

The man reached Stone. He was incredibly attractive with a warm complexion, tanned and weathered by the sun. Although lines creased the sides of his eyes and around his forehead, there was something extraordinarily youthful about him. The most striking feature was the man's eyes. The bluest Stone had ever seen. They shone brightly, and were so unique that they wouldn't have been out of place on an oriental cat. Stone knew who he was without being told.

"Jeramiah Stone," said Conty in a soft, well-spoken voice, and held out his hand. "I'm, Abraham."

Stone flushed with awe. Conty's presence was quite electrifying. "Pleasure to meet you, sir."

"Well, there's a thing," Conty said with a warm grin. "I've never considered myself a *sir* before. Please call me Abraham. There are no need formalities here."

Stone nodded rather embarrassed. "It's a pleasure, Abraham. Jeramiah Stone."

Conty took a moment to look his guest over. "I'm so sorry you've been kept waiting. I hope you'll accept my apologies, Jeramiah. May I call you Jeramiah?"

"Of course," replied Stone. "No formalities here

either. Apologies are unnecessary. I understand it can't always be easy to leave your work."

"Yes, my work," remarked Conty, distantly. "Well, thank you for your understanding. I'm sure Jennifer has been looking after you. Have you settled in okay? I hope you are comfortable?"

"Yes, thank you. Everything's fine."

"Good."

"I don't know how you want to do this," began Stone. "Would you like to get started right away? I'm sure your time is limited."

Conty ran a hand over the top of his head. "Ah yes, the interview. I thought it might be nice for us to get to know each other first, Jeramiah. What do you think?"

Stone nodded. "Sounds a good idea."

Conty studied Stone again. "Excellent," he said, clapping his large hands together. "You like fishing, Jeramiah?"

"I've never been fishing."

Maria emerged from the Conty villa and walked towards them unsteadily, struggling with a large cooler box. Conty quickly went to her side, taking it from her. "Gracias, Maria." He kissed the maid playfully on the cheek. "I've got a picnic for us," he said, tapping the cooler box. "Although we'll have to catch our main course. It's just you and me, Jeramiah. Deklin and Jennifer have gone to the mainland. Come," he ushered.

Conty led them along the beach to a small jetty. In the shallows was a powerful ski boat, an awning shading the white leather loungers behind the wheel. Conty boarded first and then helped Stone aboard. Conty powered the boat up, then took them out.

"So, Jeramiah, you like it here?"

Stone leant back in the lounges, his arms resting each side of the soft leather. "Yes, thank you. I must say it's one of the most relaxing assignments I think I've ever had."

"Good," said Conty. "There's a nice spot just around this headland. He pointed ahead. "It's a small cove where the fish gather in the shallows. I reckon we're going to be lucky today!"

They followed the picturesque coastline of the island. Conty pointed out various places of interest, whilst giving Stone a brief history of the island. Stone was told that, originally, the Moors used the island as a fortification to the mainland. Right up until Conty bought the island, it was used by the Spanish Army for training manoeuvres. The Spanish government gave it outstanding natural beauty status.

After half an hour, Conty brought the boat to a stop in a small cove with a tiny white-sand beach. Cliffs rose to the ridge of a pine forest, giving them total seclusion.

Conty dropped anchor. He then opened the cooler box and handed Stone a beer. "Not too early, I hope?" Conty sat on one of the lounges. "Pretty, don't you think, Jeramiah?" he asked, gesturing to the beach.

"I think it's beautiful," remarked Stone, admiring the scenery. "I recognise the cove. Isn't there a picture of this beach in my apartment?"

"That's right," said Conty. "You're very observant."

Stone scanned the bay. The water was like a mill pond. Insects could be heard all around, their chirping coming from secret destinations within the clifftop flora. The air was fresh, with the heady smell of the ocean. "You must be very happy here?"

Conty's eyes sparkled as if a master jeweller had set them in his sockets. "I am. It can be a little too quiet at times I suppose, but I don't mind that. I like my solitude. However, Jennifer gets lonely at times." Conty was thoughtful. "She's very tolerant. My work takes up a lot of my time lately. And I'm afraid I'll have to ask you to put up with that as well. I hope you won't think me rude, Jeramiah, but I have to leave you this afternoon. I have a great deal of work to finish at my studio. Jennifer will be back by then. She will take care of you. I'm so sorry about all of this, but I did explain to Mister Becker in my letter that I may keep you for at least a couple of days to do this interview."

"It's fine," said Stone, honestly. "I don't mind being away from the office for a few days anyway." What Stone omitted to tell his host was that he didn't mind spending another evening with his host's wife either.

Conty clapped his hands together. "Good. That makes me feel a lot better. If there's anything you need, Deklin will take care of it. He takes care of most things around here."

"Quite a character," said Stone.

"Indeed," Conty agreed.

Stone considered his next question. "What are you working on, by the way?"

Conty seemed momentarily thrown by the question and looked at Stone as if he hadn't heard him correctly. "Oh, err, a painting," he replied. "Trouble is, once I get my teeth into something, you know?"

Conty then got up and went to the front of the boat, returning with two fishing rods. He handed one to Stone.

"I hope you're not hungry," said Stone, taking the rod. "I'm not sure I even know how to use one of these."

"Easy, Jeramiah. When you feel something pulling on this bit," Conty pointed to the hook, "then you wind this bit in." Conty worked the reel.

Conty showed Stone how to bait his hook with a small sprat, then how to cast. He rested both rods in mounts on the side of the boat.

"Easy as that," said Conty, sitting back down. "Now we wait. That's fishing."

"Do you have many unwelcome visitors here?" asked Stone, noticing a boat out to sea.

Conty followed Stone's gaze. "No, not many. People tend to leave us alone. That's the Coast Guard. They keep an eye on the place for us."

"Can I ask why you live here? I mean, people would want to know why you're so isolated." Stone realised he had no pen or paper to document this time with Conty but had a feeling he wouldn't forget.

"It's not as remote as you may think," Conty replied. "We have many friends that come over and we go to the mainland fairly often. But to answer your question, I like it here. I like the sense of space. It's extremely important for my work."

"Are you aware of the reputation you have because of it?" asked Stone.

"And what reputation is that?"

"That you're a recluse."

Conty leant closer to Stone. "What do you think, Jeramiah?"

"I hadn't given it much thought. The invitation to come here was quite a shock. I did some research on your background and the information was well, let's say limited."

"And what did you manage to find out about me?" Conty asked, narrowing his eyes mockingly.

Although Conty was teasing, Stone felt awkward under his gaze.

"Not much. You're probably the most famous living artist, whose importance in the art world is unrivalled, your work internationally acclaimed. You're wealthy." Stone gestured to the boat they were sitting in. "You donate to various charities, specifically to children's charities." Stone thought hard. "You were born in Norwich." Stone spoke a little softer. "You lost your first wife, Louise, in eighty-eight and are now married of course to Jennifer, who told me that you met when you opened a gallery in Barcelona. You have no children. That's about it. In fact, that's about as much as any of the media know about you. You are, as they say, a mystery."

"It would seem I am," Conty mused. "Therefore, you seem to be in a rather enviable position."

Stone took a swig of his beer. *Time to get to the point*, he thought. "Yes, it does. Which brings me to the obvious question."

Conty folded his arms. "Why you?"

"Precisely," replied Stone. "This is the first time you give an interview and you want me? Of course I'm flattered, but you could have any of the television networks here. Art critics would have given their right arm to have this opportunity. So yes, why me? Or more importantly, why would you want to give an interview to The Informer? It doesn't strike me as your kind of reading material."

Conty was thoughtful for a moment. "Why would you think I wouldn't have asked for you, Jeramiah? You're a good writer, are you not?"

Stone cocked his head. "I'm a journalist for a daily newspaper. Not the sort of paper you expect to find an interview with Abraham Conty in it. As for me, well, let's just say I'm not the sort of journalist celebrities usually like to be associated with." Stone raised his eyebrows. "Unless of course, you don't know what I do, which I very much doubt."

"Okay, it's my turn," Conty began. "You are thirty-eight years of age. You career started in your hometown of Croydon, Surrey, for the Croydon Echo where you began as a junior journalist, after studying journalism at Goldsmith College, London. You did well there and, after four years, were offered a junior placement with The Global on Fleet Street. There, you started to build a reputation as an enthusiastic reporter with an appetite for the truth. You worked exceptionally hard until you were promoted to the position of overseas correspondent, which I believe, was a boyhood ambition."

Stone folded his arms and sat back. "Very good."

"Out of all that one thing puzzles me, Jeramiah."

Stone was uncomfortable and sat upright. "Which is?"

"Why you suddenly gave it all up? I mean, there you are at the top of your game, a move into television the next step forward surely, and you give up. Eighteen months later you return to journalism, only this time to work for The Informer writing a column called 'Blood from a Stone'. Quite a different writing style from what I've read of yours in the past, Jeramiah."

Stone could feel the back of his neck burning and pulled the collar of his polo shirt up. "I needed a break."

"Why The Informer?"

"It has a massive readership. I thought it would be good for my career."

"But not so good for the careers of the people you write about?"

"The people that I write about deserve all they get."

"Is that so?"

Stone looked out to sea, avoiding Conty's gaze. "The public has the right to know."

"Do they?"

Stone turned back to look at Conty. "I can see you don't agree."

"It's not that. I just don't understand why a man with your career would go the way you have."

"Which way is that?" asked Stone, containing his anger. The tables had been turned and he didn't like it.

"Well, the world you reported on when working at The Global would make any man cynical. You must have seen some pretty terrible things while you were their overseas correspondent. However, I never detected any cynicism in any of your reports, just the facts. The honest account. No judgments. No moral high ground."

Stone's eyes narrowed.

"And now," Conty went on, gauging Stone's reaction. "Well now, you wreck the careers and lives of people who are, in your view, morally challenged. All in the pursuit of your career."

Stone stared hard at Conty, barely able to contain his frustration at being pushed into a conversation he never expected to have. "I lost my wife, if you must know."

Conty looked saddened.

Stone took a deep breath. "She was killed by a motorist."

"I see." Conty bowed his head. "I'm sorry."

Stone sighed. "I couldn't work properly after that. The Global let me go. Eighteen months later, The Informer took me on."

Conty didn't say anything. He just stared at Stone.

"So, given what you know about my career, I still can't see how you came to the conclusion that you wanted me to do this interview."

Conty shrugged. "Like I said, I think you're a good writer."

Stone threw his host a sour look. He knew he was lying. If Conty liked to play games then Stone was happy to play too. "Why now, Abraham? Why, after all this time, do you suddenly want to give an interview?"

Conty stood up and went to the side of the boat, checked the fishing lines, then sat down. He stared straight at Stone. His eyes seemed to brighten and shine unnaturally under the fierce blaze of the sun.

"Because I'm dying, Jeramiah."

Stone eyes widened at the bombshell. Stone could never have considered this. At first, he didn't know what to say.

"What's wrong?" Stone asked, after some time. "I mean..."

"Let's just say it's my heart," smiled Conty.

"I don't what to say. I mean... How long?"

"Not long now, Jeramiah."

"I'm so sorry."

Conty shook his head. "Don't be."

Stone didn't know what else to say for a moment.

"Something good always comes out of something bad," Conty went on. "We are all here on a journey, Jeramiah. Mine is coming to an end."

"How do you figure any good will come out of your death?"

Conty beamed. "Well, for one thing, you're going to take back one hell of a story."

Stone didn't find the remark funny, though he had to admit Conty was right. Stone could imagine the headlines of how he would be the only man to ever interview the great Abraham Conty before he died. The story would be huge, he knew it. However, Stone felt strangely hollow at the thought.

"Can I ask you something, Jeramiah?"

"Yes of course. What is it?"

"Jennifer doesn't know. I'd appreciate it if you didn't say anything while you are here."

"Of course not," agreed Stone, solemnly. The admission shocked Stone. Again he was forced to ponder what relationship he had with Jennifer to hold back such information from her.

At that moment, the reel of one of the rods started to whine. Conty rushed to it.

"Lunch, Jeramiah!" He laughed. The reel whirred and Conty had to steady himself. Stone went to Conty's side, both men pulling on the rod.

"And maybe dinner as well!" boomed Conty.

For a brief moment, both men forgot what had been said, concentrating their efforts on what surely had to be a whale. Conty couldn't stop laughing and it was a wonder to Stone that he could be so happy about anything, let alone the prospect of catching a fish. Both of them heaved on the rod. The line suddenly snapped, propelling both men into the far side of the boat.

"Whatever that was," roared Conty, "I'm almost glad we didn't catch it."

Stone managed to get himself up then helped Conty to his feet. Both sat, out of breath but managing to laugh.

Conty reached into the cooler and fetched two beers. He slapped Stone on the back. "Better luck next time, Jeramiah."

"Are you sure you should be exerting yourself like this?" Stone asked.

Conty laughed. "Let's not spoil our fun, Jeramiah. My heart can take a little disappointment."

Stone gave a weak smile.

"I'm sorry; you must think I'm being flippant about all this."

"It's not my business how you handle things," Stone considered. "We all have our own ways of doing that, I suppose."

Conty let out a slow breath. "Yes, we do, don't we?" he agreed.

Both men stared at each other for a brief moment. For Stone it was as if time had momentarily stopped and he was given an endless amount of time to scrutinise his host. Conty's eyes shone brilliantly; a rich and deep blue, full of youth, making it almost impossible to believe Conty had anything wrong with him, let alone be dying.

"Now, let's not have all this sombreness," Conty said suddenly. "There's plenty more fish in the sea."

He then set about re-baiting the lines.

"So now I know why I'm here," said Stone. "To prepare your obituary."

Conty sat down. "Why not? You do a fine obituary. I read the one you gave about Diana. It was a lot nicer than some of the things The Informer wrote about her while she was alive. I'm sure she'd have found it rather flattering."

Stone frowned. "You knew her?"

Conty put his hands together and rested his chin on them. "Yes I did. She was a dear friend."

"When did you last see her?"

"A couple of weeks before she died. She was here for a break. She often came to the island."

"How did you meet her?"

"At a charity auction we both support. She was bright and very beautiful. I fell in love the moment I saw her. We became good friends. Jennifer was extremely fond of her too."

"It must have come as a shock," said Stone, thoughtfully.

Conty didn't reply at first. Instead he got up and moved to the front of the boat, bringing back two paper plates with him. Reaching into the cooler, he prepared the lunch Maria had packed.

Stone watched him. "Are you angry with the press?" he asked, tentatively.

Conty looked up from what he was doing. "You mean do I blame them for her death?"

Stone nodded. "I guess so, yes. That's what a lot of people think."

"To blame the press would mean, in some way, I hold them all accountable, including you, Jeramiah. Which I don't."

"But you think that she was being chased by paparazzi photographers who caused her car to crash?"

Conty stopped what he was doing and gave Stone his attention. "There could have been two things that killed Diana, Jeramiah," he began. "First, it was an accident that happened because she was running from something. That something could have been the press, yes."

"The second?"

"The second is that she was murdered."

Stone felt a familiar hollow feeling in the pit of his stomach as he absorbed Conty's statement. "I know a photographer that was in Paris the night the princess was killed. He said the paparazzi chasing her could never have caught up with her car that night."

"Is that so?" Conty remarked.

"The paparazzi were held up by a truck pulling out in front of them just as they left the hotel. The princess's car was already on its way before the photographers had a chance to reach her. People talk about a conspiracy theory. Some even say it concerns the Royal Family, but I don't believe that. I don't believe she was that much of a threat to the establishment. I believe it was just a freak accident."

"And if there was a conspiracy, how do you know it wasn't someone else?"

"Because it would have come out by now. You can't cover up a thing like that," said Stone.

"What did you think of Diana?" asked Conty.

"She was popular," Stone reflected. "Her funeral proved that. But what concerned me was the public's reaction to her death. I think it's sad she could have had that amount of impact on people. I found myself feeling embarrassed. I found people hypocritical. I think people hoped her death marked a new beginning. A unity we hadn't had since the war."

"And it didn't?" asked Conty.

Stone was suddenly saddened by his own findings. He bowed his head and stared at the patches of wet sand on the floor of the boat. "It may have for a while. But people just went back and did what they were doing before she died – nothing changed. Some still went home and brought up their children to be racist. Others still stole. Others were still intolerant. There is still war. People still get killed. If she changed anything, I don't see it."

Conty slowly shook his head. "Is that how the world really is, Jeramiah? Or just how you see it?"

Stone looked up. "I'm sorry if I've offended you," said Stone.

"You haven't."

"What do you think then?" asked Stone.

"Regardless of her private life, there are a number of things she could have done with her popularity and status," said Conty, thoughtfully. "She chose, in her own way, to do some good with it. Trouble is the press don't seem to like it when people do some good. Instead of celebrating her, the press abused her. Do you know what it's like for someone trying to do some good, but are hated for it?"

"The press have responsibilities," Stone replied.

"Yes. Yes, they do," Conty agreed.

Stone eyed Conty, sceptical of his concurrence. "Plus the fact, they give the people what they want. It was the public who had an appetite for knowing about Diana's private life, not us."

"What the public wants," Conty began. "The power of the media is unrivalled. The public will want whatever you give them. So what do you do? You give them gossip, tales of corruption, stories of fallen heroes – in fact, anything bad. You could tell them about what *good* people do. The achievements of their fellow human beings. If you, the press, had the interest of this public you seem to be so protective of, then you could change the world they live in, make it a better place. But the press are not really interested in what they give the public, only in selling papers."

"Some would say she used the media," replied Stone, defensively. "She used them when she needed them. She often courted the photographers. If you're in the public eye, then you must accept your life will be public. She was accountable, like everyone else."

Conty sat back and put his hands behind his head. "You're a bright man, Jeramiah, and a good one, I believe. I don't think you believe in the paper you work for any more than I do. It is not interested in its readers or whether they have the right to know about something. It's interested in sales. Therefore its interest is financial. Unless of course it has a hidden agenda. I'd take a guess that you're familiar with the latter, Jeramiah."

Stone eyed Conty suspiciously. "Your point?"

Conty sat forward. "My point is, grief can lead us from ourselves sometimes. It allows us to stop believing in goodness. It legitimatises our contempt of the world.

Stone eyes narrowed. He shifted uncomfortably. "I didn't really care for Diana, if you want the truth."

"I'm not talking about Diana. I'm talking about your wife."

Stone sat up suddenly, his cheeks flushing with anger. "What the hell has this got to do with my wife?"

"Everything," replied Conty. "I think you're man who can't understand why your wife was killed. I think you dislike the world, and the way it works, so you spend most of your time trying to prove yourself right about that world. That it is indeed, a bad place. A world in which you don't accept the likes of Diana because she breaks the spell. Because if the world was any other way, then how could you possibly begin to understand why Milly was taken from you?"

Stone wasn't prepared for Conty's remarks. Then something struck him. "How the hell did you know my wife was called Milly?" he asked, angrily.

"Like you said, Jeramiah, I do my research. And so now that's why you now write for a paper like the one you do. Because you're angry. And The Informer has made it legit."

Stone stood up. "I'm a journalist. Journalists work

for newspapers. That's what I do."

"You look for weaknesses. You look for the joins, the illusion. Anything to prove that good is all an act."

Stone pointed down at his accuser. "Listen, if you don't like what I do or the paper I work for, why did you ask me here? I don't destroy people, they do that themselves. People in positions of influence should be accountable, and if they're not, yes, I bring them down."

"How was your wife killed?" asked Conty, suddenly.

Conty's arrogance infuriated Stone and he was mortified that he should ask such a thing. "She was hit by a drunk driver."

"And who was responsible?"

Stone took a deep breath, his patience wearing thin. He was sweating now, and wiped his forehead with the back of his hand. "It was a government minister, if you must know. He was drunk after attending an all-night party. He was four times over the limit, but still drove his Bentley home. He hit my wife who was on her way from the doctors to tell me she was pregnant. He served two years' probation and was banned from driving for two fuckin' years! You happy now?"

There was silence.

Conty looked up. "You must know I don't mean to offend you, Jeramiah."

Stone was angrier than he could remember. He sat down. "What is all this? Why are you so interested in my life?"

"Because you're going to write about mine," replied

Conty. "And let's just say I have a vested interest in you. My obituary, remember? I have a responsibility to know the man that's going to write it."

Stone sighed. "Look, I'm not sure I am the right man for what you want. We haven't got off to the best of starts."

"You're the only man for the job," replied Conty, adamantly. "I trust you, Jeramiah. I want you to do this. I think we could be of use to each other, Jeramiah. All I ask is that you trust me. I mean you no harm and very sorry if I've offended you in any way."

Stone wondered what Conty was all about. Why Conty had made it his business to have researched Stone's background quite so thoroughly was unsettling to say the least. For some reason though, Stone did trust him.

"You haven't offended me," he replied, sitting down.

Conty put his hand on Stone's shoulder. "I'm glad, Jeramiah. I would never want that."

For a brief moment, silence hung between the two men.

"You know," Stone began, "one thing about Diana made me realise I would never like to be in that position. All that responsibility. The media. The constant attention. I don't blame you for keeping out of it all."

Conty briefly looked up at the sun. "I don't consider myself public property, Jeramiah."

"But what's it like? What's it like knowing you're one of the most famous people in the world? That every painting you sign will be worth a fortune?"

Conty shrugged. "It serves a purpose, that's all. I try to put most of my position to good use. None of the rest is important, I can assure you."

Stone held his arms up. "But how can you say that? It's changed your life, surely? The money allows you to have your freedom."

"It has. However, the money doesn't prevent things from happening. And when it does, the money certainly doesn't change it for you. As soon as you know that, the sooner you know none of it matters."

"You sound pretty sure."

"I am," Conty ensured. "I know because I'd trade it all if I *could* get it back."

"And what is it you'd buy back?" asked Stone.

Conty considered the question whilst looking out to sea. "More time."

Stone studied his host a moment. "Time for what?"

Conty turned from the sea and met Stone's gaze. The sun seemed to have filled his eyes with an intense reflection of the ocean. "Living," he said.

Stone looked at Conty's large hands, imagining the brushes they controlled to paint the magic they did. "Are you aware of your greatness?"

Conty looked up suddenly as if genuinely surprised by the question. "I'm aware of many things. *Greatness*, as you put it, is not something I contemplate."

Stone recalled his visit to the Tate gallery.

"There was another painting I viewed before coming here," he began. "It had no title. It's the one where you're sitting before your canvass, painting A Blind Eye. You have in angel sitting next to you, watching you as you paint."

Conty nodded.

"What does it mean?" asked Stone. "Do you feel that you have a gift, I don't know, from God or something? Are you a religious man?"

"Maybe I just believe in angels."

"What about A Blind Eye?" Stone went on, remembering the paintings he had seen. "What's that painting about?"

Conty looked directly at Stone, eyes gleaming. "What do you think it's about?"

"Well firstly, I thought it was amazing," Stone responded, recollecting the painting.

"But you would like to know why everyone in the painting ignores the man drowning, yes?"

Stone shrugged. "Doesn't everyone who sees it?"

"Why do you think they ignore him?" asked Conty.

"I don't know," considered Stone. "Maybe you're trying to say something about society, the way people don't care about each other anymore? Maybe the painting's a reflection of the way you feel about people, about life? Maybe that's why you live here on this island away from anyone, because of your own disappointment in people?"

"The painting is simply about what the name

suggests," Conty revealed. "A man has fallen in the water, right in front of everyone around him and no one does anything. They all turn a *blind eye*."

Stone was confused at squinted at Conty. "But why? Because they don't care?"

"They care," revealed Conty, "but not enough to help. They're scared."

Stone shrugged. "Of what?"

"Of change. Being responsible."

"I don't understand," Stone admitted.

"The painting is a metaphor," began Conty. "If any of those people were to save that man, it would change their lives in some way… Forever. Each and every one of them hopes someone else will take care of it. Rather like the way you said people saw Princess Diana. She took the responsibly for us, and the consequences with it.

"It would be such a simple act to save him. That's the power each and every one of us has but, all too often, we just do nothing. We are passive."

Stone wiped the beads of sweat from his forehead. "So you're disappointed in the human spirit?"

"I see the power I speak of used in disappointing ways," Conty explained. "I see people wielding it to cause pain, rarely to save. I am however, hopeful."

"Are you a religious man?" asked Stone again.

Conty seemed to study his guest. "Why do you ask me that?"

"You talk about angels, responsibilities, and the power we all possess. You seem to be a man of faith."

Conty contemplated the question. "We all have faith to begin with, do we not? You have it right from a child, given you rely on others so much when young. The trick is holding on to it… And you, Jeramiah? Do you have faith?"

Stone shook his head. "I might have once. Not now."

"Because something precious was taken from you?"

"Something like that."

"Which one are you?" asked Conty.

Stone frowned.

"Are you one of the people on the riverbank or are you the man drowning?"

Stone considered his reply. "Depends. What's the man's fate? Does he drown or does someone eventually save him?"

Conty was thoughtful for a moment. "The man's circumstances have been forced upon him, but he, like them, has two choices. Someone either saves him or lets him drown, that is out of his control. But he has another choice.

"Which is?" Stone asked.

"He can save *himself*."

Stone smiled. "But he can't swim?"

"He doesn't have to," replied Conty, looking out to sea. He then turned directly to look at Stone. "When you get a moment again, look closely at the picture. There are children paddling not far from where he is. So the water is not deep. He is in the shallows. He doesn't need to know how to swim to save himself."

Stone felt a little awkward under the pressure of Conty's piercing gaze.

"I have a print of A Blind Eye in the villa," Conty went on. "Maybe you should take another look at it; a good look. Paintings have a habit of revealing much more than at first sight."

With that, Conty handed Stone a plate of langoustines, olive bread, and a cold beer. Stone's stomach growled at the sight of the food. Conty looked at his watch. "I need to go back after lunch, Jeramiah."

"Is everything all right?" asked Stone, seeing Conty's anxiety.

"Everything's fine. There's something I need to attend to this afternoon."

After lunch, they headed back to the Conty estate.

"I'm so sorry to cut the day short, Jeramiah," Conty said again, as they walked up the beach.

"Would you like me to come with you?" asked Stone. "I'd very much like to see your studio."

"No," replied Conty, firmly. "I'm sorry, I didn't mean to sound blunt, it's just that no one is allowed at my studio. We'll pick this up later, Jeramiah. I have very much enjoyed our time together this morning. Jennifer and Deklin will be back soon. If there's anything you need at all until then, please ask Maria. Relax and enjoy your stay. We have much to talk about."

Stone nodded. "I will. Thank you."

Conty put his hand on Stone's shoulder then left him. Stone watched as he went to a Jeep and sped off, heading towards the other end of the island.

Stone was left confused. Slowly he made his way back to his villa. His short time with Abraham Conty had been one he would never forget. Conty was dying, and he was on the verge of the greatest story of his career. Ironically, that didn't please Stone. Conty had given him a rough time. However, he couldn't help liking him. Something wasn't right though. Conty seemed to be a troubled man.

Stone remained thoughtful as he went inside. There was something else. What was at the north of the island that kept stealing Conty away? Maybe it *was* his art, but given what Stone had learnt about Jennifer's apparent sadness, he guessed there was more to it. Whatever it was, one way or another, Stone was going to find out.

*

Kirns sat outside the bar sipping his coffee whilst watching the man and woman who had come in on the *Jennifer*. He was travelling light, with only a small rucksack containing the things he would need to finish the mission. Patiently, he waited for the couple to finish their lunch.

He had found a number of things out since they had arrived. Pretending to be just another tourist, he had followed the couple around the pueblo as they visited a number of shops and stores.

All the locals seemed know these two by the warm welcome they received. The beautiful woman was none other than Mrs Conty, wife of the famous artist while the other man was a mystery, though Kirns knew it wasn't her famous husband. Kirns remembered seeing Conty's image on the television and he didn't recall the great Abraham Conty being a large black man. Kirns surmised the man was either a friend or possibly security.

Kirns had followed them to the local town hall. From the conversations overheard between the couple and the locals, he was able to ascertain that Mrs Conty and her husband were treating the town to a festival that evening.

Now, Mrs Conty and her chaperone sat at a table opposite him, eating tapas of calamari, and chorizo sausage. From the snippets of dialogue he had overheard between them, it seemed that they would soon return to the island. Kirns was pleased he'd waited. He needed transport to get to the island and they had it.

As Kirns was about to get up, he saw the familiar cream and green Jeep of the Guardia Civil. The Jeep drove straight past him and stopped just past the bar he was sitting outside at. Peering over the top of his coffee cup, he watched two officers get out of the Jeep. They started talking with the barman who had come out to greet them. One of the officers showed the barman a police sketch of the man they were looking for. Kirns felt into his rucksack and put his hand around the pistol. The police said their goodbyes, and then walked towards him.

Kirns was ready with the gun. The hairs on the back of his neck stood on end and the adrenaline suddenly rushed through his body. It didn't want this, but was ready nevertheless.

The officers kept coming. Kirns readied himself. As they came towards his table, he started to ease the pistol out of the holdall. He was about to stand up and confront the inevitable, when he realised that they were not coming for him. Instead, they walked casually past his table and on into a small hotel next door to the bar.

Kirns waited patiently. If they were to question him, he would kill them both, steal their Jeep. Later, he would dump the Jeep near a busy town or city where it would be almost impossible for the authorities to find him. All was planned in his mind within minutes.

The officers eventually came out, walking past Kirns's table, and got back into the Jeep. One of the officers glanced at him, but paid him no mind. He watched the Jeep drive further up the main street and stop at the next bar. Only then, did Kirns release his grip on the pistol.

It was time to get going. Kirns finished his fourth espresso then got up and headed towards the marina at the end of the town. He wandered casually down the small wooden jetty, admiring as any tourist would, the myriad of boats, moored either side of the walkway. He came to the Sun Seeker. On the side of the boat was its name. *Jennifer*. Kirns smiled at his sudden deduction. He now knew Mrs Conty's Christian name.

Pretending to tie his shoelace, Kirns glanced back at the town centre. Mrs Conty and her chaperone were making their way towards the boat. With a glance to see if anyone in the marina was watching him, he stepped onto the stern of the Sun Seeker. He then stole below, down the few steps to the berth below. The master bedroom was right in front of him. A curtain divided a small recess that was used as a wardrobe. Quickly, he hid inside. Just in time; he heard the man and woman come aboard as he drew the curtain.

"It's a pity, Dek," he heard Mrs Conty say. "I know this isn't the time for celebration, but it would have been such fun to stay tonight."

"Sure would," replied the man she called Dek. The engine rumbled to life.

"I'm just going to change," she said.

Kirns stood perfectly still, feeling the engines roar up as the boat was taken out of the marina. He then heard the woman come below. Kirns pushed himself deeper into the wardrobe, peering through a gap in the curtain to see the woman enter the bedroom.

She was beautiful. Kirns stood perfectly still as she started to undress. First her shirt came off, then her bra. Kirns just stared in disbelief.

Then she took off her jeans. She had no knickers on. Kirns saw the small tattoo of a rose just below her navel. The woman put on her bikini and went back on deck.

The experience of watching the woman change had been pleasant but, as always, non-sexual. At that moment, Kirns wished more than anything to know what it felt like to be a real man again.

After an extremely uncomfortable journey, Kirns was relieved to hear the boat engines slow. As quietly as he could, he stepped out of the wardrobe and went to the window. They approached a beach, with a wooden jetty. As the boat came to a stop, he heard a number of voices above.

Kirns crept to the doors which led out on deck, opened them slightly and popped his head up to see the woman and the man talking to another man on the beach. Obviously, by the man's attire and pistol holstered to his belt, he was a security guard. Kirns had contemplated taking the woman hostage in order to save time and get directly to Stone, but that would only mean a confrontation with the security guard. For now, Kirns decided to take another option.

After a short wait, Kirns heard a vehicle start and then drive off. Creeping up on deck, he saw a second security guard talking with his colleague under a small wooden shelter, topped with palm leaves. Mrs Conty and the man he now knew as Dek were gone.

Kirns went back below. He surmised that the boat wouldn't be going anywhere until the morning, so decided to stay on board and rest until it was nightfall. Then he would find Stone.

Getting his medicine from his rucksack, he emptied the last four pills in the palm of his hand. Ordinarily he might have panicked at running out but it didn't matter now. He wouldn't need them anymore. After swallowing the pills, he laid himself on the bed and closed his eyes. It was time to get some rest before the final assault.

THIRTEEN

Rachel slowly opened her eyes, focusing on the world around her. The pain in her jaw reminded her it was still a very bad place. She ran her tongue around her mouth, feeling the lacerations on the inside of her cheek. The blow, combined with her exhaustion, meant she had slept for hours.

She sat upright in a chair, hands bound behind it. Her head thumped when she moved but she did her best to get orientated.

She was still in her flat. A woman was sat at her desk eating a sandwich. The man who'd struck her was sat on the sofa watching cartoons on television. Rachel wondered why she was still alive.

"What are you going to do with me?" she asked. She winced at the sudden sharp pain in her head.

The woman at the desk turned to face her. She grinned. "Sleeping beauty awakes."

"You must be pretty proud of yourselves,"

mocked Rachel, remembering horrors she'd read in Becker's file. "*Really* proud."

The man got up from the sofa and came towards her. Without warning, he slapped her hard across the face. "You're alive, bitch, be thankful for that."

"What are you waiting for?" Rachel cried out. "What do you want me for? Why don't you just kill me?"

Nathan sneered at her. "If it were up to me, I would," he said. "In time though."

He went back to watching Jerry kicking the shit out of Tom.

The muffled ringing of a mobile phone sounded. Carla retrieved it from inside her bag and answered it. "Yes?" she asked. "Yes, she's just woken up." She ended the call and looked at Nathan. "He's on his way."

Nathan glanced at Rachel. He reached into his jacket and produced a pistol. He checked it over, put it back in his jacket, and then got up. Rachel thought he was coming to her but instead he went and stood behind Carla. He reached forward and massaged her shoulders. Carla let out a sigh and rolled her head. Nathan then reached down and started to caress her breasts. He gazed at Rachel as he did so.

"You'll never get away with it," Rachel assured them.

Nathan stopped his actions, to Carla's disappointment. He kissed her on the top of the head.

"Did you hear me?" Rachel screamed. "It's over!"

There was a knock at the door. Nathan went and

opened it. Three men quickly filed in. The oldest of the three stepped forward. He took off his a scarf and removed his dark glasses.

Rachel recognised Murren immediately.

Carla got up and went to her husband's side.

"You searched Becker's?" asked Murren.

"Yeah," replied Nathan. "Nothing there, except for these," he said, passing Murren an envelope containing the photographs. "We turned the whole place over."

Murren grimaced at Rachel as he tore the envelope into little pieces.

"How's our guest?"

"She's just come around," said Carla. "And she's a bit crabby."

Murren knelt in front of Rachel. "If you're wondering why you're tied up, it's because we don't want you running off."

"Fuck you," Rachel snapped at him.

Murren shook his head. "Now, now. There's no need to be like that."

"Fuck you, Murren," she said again.

"Well, I suppose the fact that you're not surprised to see me indicates Becker told you everything about us?"

"Everything," Rachel spat. "You'll never get away with what you've done. You make me sick."

"Oh, my dear," began Murren, wiping a tiny bit of spittle from his face, "we *have* got away with it. You think it matters what Becker has told you? The fact is you have no proof, and even if you did, I'm afraid there's nothing you could do about it now."

On hearing this Rachel realised what Murren didn't know. The truth was that Becker hadn't told Rachel anything, but the file she read certainly had. She glanced briefly at the desk, noticing Becker's laptop still in its case underneath it. Psychologically, it was everything. She had proof, or at least, she hoped Stone had it. Rachel knew she probably wouldn't get out of this alive but that was OK. She had been close to death before, almost yearned for it after what her father had done to her. All she cared about was that the evil that was smiling in front of her could somehow he brought to justice.

She suddenly started to laugh. She had something over them, and, in a macabre way, she found it hysterical.

"How about our mutual friend, Mister Stone? You told him anything?" asked Murren, ignoring her show of defiance.

Rachel didn't answer. Instead she poked her tongue out which made her laugh again.

Murren shook his head. "I see. Well, it really doesn't matter if you have. Stone won't be around much longer, anyway."

"What do you mean?" snapped Rachel.

"Oh, do I have your attention? Didn't Marcus tell you? Well let me enlighten you, my child. One of our best men is in Spain with the sole purpose of exterminating your boyfriend. The fact that Stone hasn't made contact with the office, or indeed your good self, would probably indicate his mission has already been successful. I really am so very sorry."

Rachel bowed her head. The tiny piece of hope evaporated.

"Like I said, I'm truly sorry. But we can't have Stone running all over the place with information you might have given him, now can we?"

"How could you do it? Why did you kill Marcus?"

Murren tutted. "Marcus was becoming a little clumsy. And let me remind you, my dear, that we didn't kill Marcus. You did."

Rachel wanted to cry again. "Fine!" she spat. "Get the police. You can't have them all in your pockets. I'll tell them everything, you bastard!"

The room erupted with laughter. "You're naiveté is quite endearing, my dear," said Murren. "I have no intention handing you over to the police."

Rachel just stared at him.

"You see," Murren went on, "after you killed Marcus, you then turned the gun on yourself. The only things the police are going to find are you lying dead in your own apartment." He clapped his hands together. "Case closed, as they say."

Rachel glared at the man she now hated more than anything in the world. "You bastard!" she screamed at him.

"So, what next?" asked Nathan.

Murren stood up. "Keep her here for the moment."

"Why?" asked Carla. "Why don't we just get rid of her now?"

Murren ushered his operatives out of Rachel's earshot. "I'm going to let Kirns have the pleasure of executing his brother's killer."

Both Carla and Nathan looked like children that had just had their toys taken away.

Murren leant closer to them. "I have to give Kirns something on his return. I don't want him getting suspicions about what happened to his brother. If he thinks I have his brother's killer, it will keep him quiet. Then you two can have the pleasure of killing Kirns."

Nathan and Carla beamed at each other.

"Now, keep her here until I tell you otherwise," Murren went on. "And no games, understand?"

Nathan and Carla nodded obediently.

"Are you sure you searched Becker's flat thoroughly? I don't want anything popping up that could incriminate us. I don't trust that bastard."

"Nothing," replied Nathan, adamantly. "We searched it top to bottom."

"Very well. We're back on track."

"It's over," said Rachel, suddenly. "Stone will go straight to the police. You're finished. I told him everything!"

Murren walked back to Rachel and knelt in front of her again. "If he had, we would have heard by now." He put his hands together and pointed with both fingers. "I think your efforts have been in vain, my dear."

Murren went to the door. "Keep an eye on her,"

he said, looking at each of them in turn. He left the room, taking the other two operatives with him.

Nathan turned to Carla and took her in his arms. "We're going to be all right, baby," he whispered.

"Yeah, I know," Carla agreed. She then looked over her husband's shoulder towards Rachel. "Let's have some fun shall we?"

Nathan followed his wife's gaze. He knew what Carla had in mind and went hard. "Yeah, let's."

*

Stone sat in front of his laptop staring at what he had written about Conty. His initial meeting with the artist had been nothing like he'd expected and left him contemplating the experience.

Stone felt as though he'd been the one interviewed and that Conty knew much more about him than he did about Conty. It made sense for Conty to find out a little about the journalist conducting his one and only interview, but Conty seemed to know a lot more than expected. Why the artist seemed to be concerned with Stone's wellbeing was just one of the mysteries. Stone knew Becker would be expecting some dirt on Conty, but he already had far more than Becker would have hoped for. The most celebrated living artist was dying; it would be the story of the year.

Oddly enough, Stone got no satisfaction from this. Clearly the media were not on Conty's Christmas card list and it still puzzled Stone as to why he was invited at all. Somehow, Stone knew there was far more to Conty than met the eye.

He sat back and rubbed his eyes. He thought

about checking into the office but he didn't much feel like speaking to anyone connected with work. Being away made him feel better than he had for some time. In fact, he began to understand why Conty lived the way he did. Isolation was medicine and Stone was happy for the dose.

Looking out of the window, he noticed the sun beginning to set. He felt sleepy, so decided to go for a swim.

Stone was glad he did. The water was cool and refreshing and he let himself just float on his back, enjoying the last of the sun washing over his face. He looked up at the sky dreamily. With ears underwater, the world was shut out; the only sound was the humming of the pool filter and his amplified breathing. For a moment, he was transported. His thoughts turned to Milly. He wondered, after his conversation with Conty, whether there really were angels. As he looked up at the cloudless sky, he considered whether she might be looking down on him. Hoping she was, Stone smiled back up at her.

Floating in the pool, Stone let his legs drop to the bottom. Then he stood up and wiped water from his eyes. When he opened them again, Jennifer Conty stood on the edge of the pool looking down at him.

"Hello," she said.

Jennifer wore a black bikini and a white sarong. Long, dark hair shimmered in the afternoon sun, making the whole image incredibly provocative. She closed her eyes briefly as she gathered her hair back, and Stone looked her over. If angels really did exist, then it seemed that one had fallen out of the sky.

"Hello," said Stone, a little shyly.

Jennifer sat on the edge of the pool and dangled her legs in the water just in front of him. "So, how'd it go?" she asked.

"How did what go?"

"Your day out with Abraham?"

"It was fine," replied Stone, unconvincingly.

"Did Abraham give you hard time?"

Stone shrugged. "A little. I'm not sure who the interviewee was."

Jennifer laughed. "That's Abraham for you," she said. "Don't mind him, Jeramiah. He's fond of you."

Stone stared at Jennifer for a moment. She was more beautiful than he had remembered and he realised how glad he was to see her. It was then that Stone noticed the faint red lines around her eyes

"So you've seen him?"

Jennifer nodded. "I went to see him at the studio before I came here. Deklin's with him now."

"What's he doing?"

The question was obviously uncomfortable for Jennifer. "Painting," she replied.

"And what does Deklin do up there?"

"Helps him out. Mixes paints. Moves things around. General stuff."

Stone nodded, knowing she was lying.

"Are you hungry?" Jennifer asked, avoiding the subject further. "I hear you didn't catch any fish today."

Stone laughed. "You're right. We didn't."

Jennifer got to her feet. "In an hour, at my place?"

"Sound good," agreed Stone.

Jennifer gave Stone a lingering look then left. Stone watched her until she was out of sight. He mused over why she had been crying again. Was it Abraham? Was their marriage in trouble? His thoughts were wrong, he knew it, but he couldn't help it. He had feelings for a married woman and to make it worse, her husband was dying and she didn't even know it. Jennifer Conty was untouchable; a woman Stone had no business desiring.

After an extra cold shower and a change of clothes, Stone walked along the beach admiring the sunset as he made his way to the Contys' villa. Checking his attire, he knocked on the door.

Jennifer answered the door and it was clear that she had gone to the same amount of effort as Stone. She had on a long blue dress that hugged her slender figure. Her long, shiny hair fell over her bare shoulders.

"Good evening, you look beautiful," Stone blurted out, much to his own amazement.

Jennifer gave Stone a playful wink. "Don't look so bad yourself."

She showed Stone into the house. "Would you like a beer?"

"Beer would be good."

Jennifer handed Stone a cold one. "Make yourself at home. I won't be long." She went upstairs, leaving Stone alone.

He took the opportunity to look around the villa. He went into the sitting room then on through to the dining room. A large oak table centred the room and paintings covered most of the walls. Most of the works were landscapes from around the island. There was a handful of portraits, one of which was Conty himself. The others were of Jennifer and Deklin. Stone stepped up to Conty's self-portrait. The image was almost photographic; the detail of Conty's face was remarkable, as though Stone was literally staring at the real face of his host. The skin looked so lifelike, with the most incredible detail. The eyes had been reproduced perfectly, as striking as they were in life. Stone, feeling a little uncomfortable under the man's gaze, turned his attention elsewhere.

He wandered out of the dining room along a small hallway. At the end, he entered the library. Books covered the walls from floor to ceiling. The Contys were obviously well read, seemingly interested in just about every subject there was. Biographies sat alongside fiction, which nudged neatly up against volumes of science, geography, and architecture. At the far end of the wall was a painting he recognised immediately; the print that Conty had told him about. 'A Blind Eye' covered the whole of the south wall.

Stone's spine tingled as he approached the painting. He stood in front of the masterpiece, studying what he'd already seen in the Tate with more scrutiny.

The figure in the middle of the lake still drew his gaze. The man, only the top half of his body above the water, waved his arms, frantically trying to attract attention. Conty was right. There were children paddling nearby, suggesting the man was indeed in shallow water.

Stone felt cold as he studied the anguish on the man's face. The bank was littered with people, all seemingly ignoring the man's desperate struggle. As Stone considered the people on the bank, he felt there was something different about what he had remembered from before.

At first it was a muddle. A hundred different faces looking everywhere but at the drowning man. Stone flicked his gaze over them all. Something was different. Stone wasn't actually aware of what it was but nevertheless, something definitely was different than before. He stepped back, and, as if the picture came into proper focus, he saw it. Or rather, *him*.

On the bank, standing near to the priest, was the lone figure of man. Stone couldn't see the man's face as his back was turned to the viewer, but he was unmistakably different from anyone else. He was dissimilar because he was the only person to be actually facing the drowning man. More than that, the figure seemed to be looking straight at him. What it meant, Stone didn't know. He had certainly missed it the first time at the Tate. But then, he remembered Vincent, curator of the Conty exhibition, hadn't pointed him out either.

Turning away from the puzzle, Stone noticed a louvered door. He went to it and peered through the slats but couldn't see into the room within. Stone went for the handle and started to turn it.

"No, Jeramiah," Came the sharp command from behind him.

Stone whipped round to see Jennifer coming towards him, a concerned look on her face.

"I'm sorry," he said.

Jennifer's face softened. "It's Abraham's study. No one's allowed in there. I'm sorry if I sounded sharp, it's just that he's very private about some things."

"I'm sorry," said Stone. "I was just looking around. I didn't mean to..."

"It's okay," Jennifer reassured him. "You weren't to know. Dinner's nearly ready. Are you ready to eat?"

"Whenever you are," replied Stone.

Jennifer turned and ushered Stone away. "Follow me."

Stone followed Jennifer out of the room. He glanced back at the painting and then at the door he wasn't allowed through. Judging by Jennifer's reaction, something was in there Conty didn't want anyone to see. Which meant he had to find out.

Jennifer had laid a table outside by the pool. A pretty setting, with blue pool lights shimmering under the still water. Lanterns illuminated the table and candles flickered in what little breeze the evening had to offer.

Jennifer handed Stone another cold beer. Maria, the maid, came from the kitchen with a large plate of mussels. She nodded politely at Stone and set them on the table. The smell of fresh seafood filled the Mediterranean air.

"Gracias, Maria," thanked Jennifer, and ushered for Stone to sit down. "Tuck in," she said and passed him some bread. "They're fresh this morning."

"These are delicious," Stone said as he scooped out the fleshy middle of a large mussel.

"I picked them up from the mainland this morning. There was lots of fish caught for the festival."

"Of course," said Stone. "Would you have liked to have gone?"

Jennifer nodded. "You bet. We usually go every year."

"But not this year?"

Jennifer seemed saddened and shook her head. "No, not this year."

Stone decided not to ask. "What exactly is Abraham working on at his studio?"

Jennifer didn't look up. "I told you, a painting. It's taking up all his time at the moment."

Stone felt sorry for her. Whatever it was she was covering up, it was putting a great deal of strain on her. Stone had to wonder if the marriage was going sour. Second night on the island and once again Conty was not present at his wife's side. Stone was determined to find out why.

"I've got something to show you later," said Jennifer.

"Oh?" asked Stone. "What's that?"

Jennifer tapped her nose with a finger. "It's a surprise… Tell me about your day with Abraham."

Stone shrugged. "Short and sweet. As I said, Abraham seemed much more interested in me."

Jennifer put her hands together. "He was?"

"He knew quite a bit about me. He's certainly done his research."

"Do you mind?"

Stone watched Jennifer as she ate. *God, she is beautiful,* he thought. It wasn't easy for Stone, being in Jennifer's company. Guilt was always nagging at him. "No, I don't mind. I suppose for Abraham's first interview, he would have to check up."

Jennifer thought the remark funny. "*Check up?* Maybe he just likes you. Maybe he's just interested in you."

"He doesn't know me," said Stone.

"Abraham has a knack of knowing a lot more than you think he does," Jennifer revealed.

And there it was, that contented look. Stone was confused. This was not a woman who seemed to dislike her husband. In fact, on the contrary, every time she spoke of her husband, it was with obvious affection. If there were problems with the marriage, Jennifer Conty was a master at hiding it.

"Your husband seems to have me all worked out," Stone admitted.

"Maybe he has," agreed Jennifer. "You shouldn't be suspicious of him though. I told you, he's fond of you."

"Why?" asked Stone. "It's not that he knows me very well."

"He cares about people. About you."

Stone scratched his head. "I'm flattered, I think."

Jennifer took a sip of wine. "Maybe you've got something in common."

"Is that right?" said Stone. "I can't really see what I could have in common with your husband."

Jennifer waited a moment. "Grief," she concluded.

"I see," Stone remarked. He thought it an odd thing for Jennifer to say. He went along with it. "And what does your husband grieve?"

Jennifer stared at her plate. The strain was all too evident in her rich, hazel eyes.

"Abraham's ill, Jeramiah."

Stone was taken aback by the remark. Conty had made him promise not to say anything to Jennifer but it seemed she knew already. "How do you know?" he asked, doing his best to sound shocked.

Jennifer's eyes filled with tears. "I see it," she admitted. "He hasn't said anything, but I know. There's a... well, I just know, that's all."

Stone wanted to get up at that moment and go to her; to hold her.

Jennifer wiped her eyes. "He's tired, Jeramiah. He's tired of it all."

"Tired of what?"

"Of..." She paused. "Of the devotion."

"To his art?" asked Stone, desperate to understand.

Jennifer was thoughtful. "Yes, to his art."

Stone reached out, wondered if it had been the wrong thing to do. To his relief, Jennifer took his hand. They both gazed at each other knowingly.

"I'm glad you're here, Jeramiah. It's as if I've known you for ages."

"I don't know what to say, Jennifer. I'm sorry that you hurt."

Jennifer squeezed Stone's hand. "It's funny you know, but whatever happens, I just know things are going to be all right."

"Of course they will," Stone assured her.

"Come on. Let's not be gloomy," Jennifer decided. She took a deep breath and took up Stone's plate. "You had enough to eat?" She got to her feet.

"Plenty," said Stone. He was a little disappointed that the moment of intimacy was over.

"Good," said Jennifer, and clapped her hands together excitedly. "There's something I want to show you."

"What is it?" asked Stone, watching her go to the kitchen.

Jennifer returned with a cooler and some glasses. She handed them to him. "Wait and see."

"Where we going?"

"Follow me."

Jennifer led the way out through the house.

As soon as they were outside, Jennifer told Stone to get in the Jeep. She then drove up the road leading to the top of the island.

*

Kirns opened his eyes and sat up. He got up and

went to the window. Now dark, the beach was illuminated by a full moon. He could see the small security cabin on the beach and could hear the faint sound of voices coming from within.

Looking back to the bed, Kirns saw the empty bottle of pills. He remembered he had taken the last of them, which explained why he had slept for so long. Now, they were all gone, but it didn't matter. The mission was nearly over and he had no intention of coming back from it. Finally, he would have no need for any more medication.

He stretched last of the sleep out of his joints then put on the hold-all. He checked the pistol's magazine and tucked it in the waistband of his combats. Time to get going and bring matters to a close.

Making his way to the deck, Kirns scanned the moonlit beach. A faint flicker of light came from within the small security hut. From what he could determine by the voices coming from inside, he deduced there were just two security guards. Parked alongside the cabin was a four-by-four. Kirns figured he had two choices. One, steal the truck, which would get him to Stone quicker. That choice would probably mean someone getting hurt, making it risky. Besides, Kirns had no intention of taking out innocent parties.

The second choice would be to head off on foot and follow the road heading south, away from the beach. This option would be slower but he could move more easily without being detected. The island was small and Kirns figured he wouldn't be hiking for too long.

Decision made, Kirns stole over the side of the boat

and lowered himself quietly into the shallow water. He waded the last few feet to the beach, keeping in the shadows of the rocks. As he brought himself onto the shore, the door of the security cabin opened.

Kirns dove to the ground.

He lay still as the guard came out of the hut and switched on his flashlight. He aimed the beam at the boat, scanning the bridge. Kirns raised his gun and aimed it. The moon gave him enough light to see that the guard was a young man, seemingly just doing his rounds. He said something aloud in Spanish and another guard came out of the hut. Both lit a cigarette and chatted to one another.

Kirns lay motionless, going over his options. Confrontation was the last thing he wanted. He waited patiently until both men went back inside. He got up and made a dash for the trees lining the beach. He was about to run up the track leading away when he had an idea.

By morning, the security might find his footprints on the beach, so Kirns decided to slow up any possible pursuit. Keeping to the trees, he crept around the back of the hut and dropped down by the side of the truck. Taking a knife from his rucksack, he crawled under and began making a hole in the fuel tank by twisting the point of his knife through the outer metal shell. He caught a whiff of a BBQ and his stomach rumbled, reminding him he hadn't eaten.

Just as Kirns got out from under the truck, one of the guards came out of the cabin. If luck was with Kirns before, it left him now. What he feared most, it seemed, was going to happen. The guard walked towards the four-by-four.

Kirns scrambled back under the truck. He watched the guard's feet and feared the worst as the guard came towards him.

He froze. The guard's feet were a few inches from his face. The guard opened the door of the cab. Petrol dripped onto the ground. If the guard smelled it, he would surely look underneath. Kirns slowly inched his weapon out and put his finger on the trigger. The guard slammed the door but stood still for a moment. Kirns imagined he was sniffing the air, which carried the smell of the petrol. He aimed the gun at the guard's leg, ready to fire if he bent down to look under. A smoking match fell by Kirns's face and the guard moved off.

Almost immediately, Kirns rolled out from under the truck and stood up. He heard talking from the cabin. The guard was back inside. Kirns left through the trees and joined the track heading south.

Geographically, he didn't know the island, but the only road led away from the beach. He concluded that if he kept going it would eventually bring him to Conty's home and, more importantly, to Stone. He relaxed as he marched on but the feeling was short lived. All of a sudden, there was the sound of gunfire.

Kirns dived off the path and into the undergrowth. He lay there, eyes darting about to see where the shots had come from. Looking up, he saw bright, multi-coloured lights explode in the sky and rain down. The fireworks display on the mainland had begun.

Kirns sat up. With the sky bright with myriad colour, he took a moment to reflect.

Kirns had decided some time ago that here, on the island, he would end it all. There was no point in going back to England to kill himself. Besides, he didn't want Marcus to find him curled up in his flat with a bullet in his brain lying in a pool of blood. No, not like that. He would do it here, somewhere peaceful, in the tranquillity of the forest.

Kirns thought about contacting Marcus, tell him he wouldn't see him again, but he couldn't. Once on a mission, he wasn't allowed to contact a senior member of The Family. He just hoped, somehow, that Marcus would understand.

Kirns found it strange that he could be so calm about suicide. There was no feeling of dread or the contemplation of whether he could actually do it or not. He knew he could do it. To prove it to himself, he got the pistol and put the muzzle against his temple. Yes, he could do it. Kirns was never going to have a wife, never going to get his brother back, and he was dying anyway. No, it wasn't hard at all. In fact, Kirns realised he was actually looking forward to leaving the world that had been so cruel to him.

Resigned to his own demise, Kirns pondered his brother's future. He would rid Marcus of the Stone problem but that wouldn't be the end of his brother's worries. Marcus had been part of a terrible act, one that he would surely be punished for.

In the past, he'd tried talking Marcus out of his association with The Family, but, he was in too deep. Murren had given Marcus everything he thought incapable of having otherwise. Ever since they were young, Kirns remembered Marcus wanting so much more than their foster parents, children's homes, and assumed families could have given him. Both being abused as young boys by one of these sets of parents had tainted Marcus forever. Kirns was adopted by new family, the Army, but his brother was left alone. Kirns had always felt responsible for that.

Some would have been proud at having made something of themselves after what Marcus had been through, but it wasn't enough. Even though Marcus had achieved editor of the largest circulated newspaper in the country, he still wanted more. Marcus wanted status, wanted real money that he knew he could never earn. He wanted to be like Murren, and so Murren became his patron. He had bought his brother and now owned him. And what did Kirns do? Stood by and watched his brother get deeper and deeper.

Kirns stood up and swung the rucksack over his shoulder. As he marched on up the road, he felt a certain sense of shame at not having gotten his brother out long ago. But none of that mattered now. He was out of medication with his mission, and his life, almost over. Time to finish up what he came to do. Marcus, once again, would just have to take care of himself.

*

Jennifer took hold of Stone's hand and ran the rest of the way up to the very top of the hill. "Quickly," she said, "they've started."

Stone was almost dragged to the top just as another volley of rockets screamed towards the sky.

"This is the highest point on the island," Jennifer declared. "Not exactly Everest, but it'll do."

Both of them sat down on a small bench with a view out across the water to the mainland. Tiny house lights flickered in the distance, stretching along the coastline. The dull thud of the music could be heard, while colourful explosions were followed by sporadic bangs of the fireworks. The star-filled sky added an impressive backdrop.

"Isn't it beautiful?" Jennifer clapped.

"What is this place?" asked Stone, looking around at the broken walls.

"This is the old lookout post. It was a Moorish fort once upon a time. I always come here. My special place."

Stone looked Jennifer over as she watched the colours breaking out below the stars. As if feeling his gaze, she turned to him.

"Here," she said, reaching into the cooler and retrieving two glasses. "Will you do the honours?"

Stone took out the bottle of champagne. He popped the cork, and then filled both glasses.

"Your toast," she said, holding up her glass.

Stone thought a moment.

"To new friends," he said, tipping her glass.

"New friends," Jennifer agreed.

"It's nice to see you happy," said Stone, looking up at the sky.

"Don't I seem happy?"

"I noticed you've been crying a lot lately."

Jennifer bowed her head and didn't say anything.

"I'm sorry. I didn't mean to pry."

"It's okay. Things have been a little difficult for us all lately."

"Is everything all right? I mean, with you and Abraham?"

Jennifer was thoughtful. "As well as it can be at the moment." She turned to him. "There's something I didn't tell you."

"What is it?"

"Remember me telling you that I met Abraham at a gallery he was opening in Barcelona?"

"Yes."

"Well..." Jennifer paused for a moment. "Well, I was upset."

"Upset?"

Jennifer nodded. "There's more to it than that." She hesitated. "I'd always loved painting. Have ever since I was a little girl. I went to that gallery to spend some time. I didn't even know Abraham was opening the gallery. I just went there to see what beauty there was before..."

"Before what?"

"I was depressed, Jeramiah. I mean really depressed. I had just lost my parents. I had no money. I had been travelling on my own for some time and was just wandering aimlessly, not having a clue what to do or where to go. I was in a very bad place. I went to that gallery knowing it would be the last time I went anywhere."

"I don't understand," said Stone.

"I had the bottle of pills in my bag," Jennifer continued. "Sleeping pills and a bottle of whisky to take them with. I wanted one last look at something beautiful before I took them. Before I…"

Stone was silent. Without thinking, he took her hand.

"I remember sitting down opposite a watercolour. I can't even remember who it was by. I was in a dream, I guess. I hadn't even noticed Abraham and all the press come into the room. But he noticed me."

She gazed out to sea. "It was as if he knew, Jeramiah, as if he actually knew what I was going to do. He just broke away from everyone in that room and came straight up to me. I remember looking up at him. His eyes were so beautiful. At first I wondered if I was dreaming it, wondered if you see things differently when you're in that frame of mind. He just smiled at me and my insides went all warm."

Jennifer shrugged and let out a deep breath. "I can't explain it. Somehow, I knew that everything was going to be all right. He held out his hand to me and I took it. He pulled me up and asked me to walk with him. We just walked around the gallery looking at his work. The rest is history."

Stone squeezed her hand. "I'm glad."

Jennifer turned to him. "That's why I love him, Jeramiah."

Stone nodded. "Of course you do," he replied, sadly. Jennifer confirmed what he didn't really want to know. She clearly loved her husband and although he was happy for her, Stone couldn't help acknowledging his own disappointment. He knew then he wanted her more than ever.

"But as much as I know I love him," Jennifer went on, "I know that he's letting me go."

"I don't understand."

"I'm not sure I do. He's ill, as I've said. I think he knows it won't be long. I think he knows that after..."

"After what?"

Jennifer shook her head. "It doesn't matter."

Stone didn't push it, although he knew she was trying to tell him something. Instead, without even thinking, he leaned forward and kissed her. He regretted his actions immediately.

Jennifer put a hand to the side of his face. "Do that again."

Stone did and Jennifer responded. Under the finale of the fireworks, they embraced and kissed passionately. Stone felt the years of mourning, the years of hurt, melt away. For the first time in a long time, he felt something he hadn't since Milly had died.

They stopped kissing and Stone started to speak but Jennifer put her fingers to his lips "No, don't say anything," she whispered.

Stone gently wiped a tear from Jennifer's cheek. There was so much he wanted to say, so much he wanted to know.

"We'd better get back," she said.

Stone let out a slow breath. He wanted to say no but reluctantly agreed.

They didn't say much on the short journey back to

the villa. By the time they arrived at the beach, Stone was convinced that the kiss had been a huge mistake. His mind was on Abraham. He was dying and Stone had betrayed his trust. His wife was vulnerable and he had surely taken advantage of a situation. His elation of at the possibility of loving someone again was short lived. Guilt was setting in and Jennifer's silence made it more unbearable.

Stone walked with Jennifer back to the Contys' villa. Both of them stopped by the door.

"What now?" asked Stone.

Jennifer shook her head. "I don't know, Jeramiah."

After a moment of awkward silence Stone said, "I guess I'd better turn in."

Jennifer nodded.

Stone made his way back to his apartment. He knew he should have stopped her. There was so much that hadn't been said and he was furious with himself that he'd left it like this.

As soon he was inside, Stone poured himself a large whisky from the drinks trolley and sat down. He knew he'd committed a terrible crime. It had to be a crime; why else would he feel so guilty? If Jennifer had told him different, the kiss would have been OK. She hadn't. Stone knew that it had been a dreadful mistake. He had fucked up again, just as he always had.

Sitting at his desk, Stone mused over the situation. He picked up his mobile phone and for the first time since he had arrived, switched it on. Staff would still be working at the office this late and he contemplated phoning in. Staring at the screen, he knew he didn't really want to talk with anyone, so he put the phone to one side and took his drink upstairs.

After a shower, he got into bed. He wouldn't sleep, but then he didn't deserve to. The night would be spent trying to work out what he should do. Maybe he should leave. Yes, he should leave. Return to England without the interview and without a job. One kiss, one hopeless and thoughtless kiss, would change everything.

He lay back, looking up at the fan whining noisily above him, keeping him from slumber. Suddenly, he was aware someone was in the room. His heart began to race and looked up to see a shadowy figure in the gloom. Quickly, he flicked the light switch. Jennifer stood at the end of the bed.

Stone didn't know what to say.

Jennifer slowly came forward to the side of the bed.

Stone watched as she untied the front of her nightgown and let it slip to the floor. She stood for a moment, naked in front of him. She smiled awkwardly, waiting for reassurance.

Stone gave it to her. He held his hand out and she came to him.

FOURTEEN

Rachel was being moved. She knew this from snippets of conversation she overheard between Nathan and Carla. Rachel also knew she wouldn't be alive much longer. How could she be? They certainly hadn't treated her like someone they intended to keep alive.

The sickos now sleeping so innocently in the next room, had abused her. While Carla had kissed her neck, stroked her hair, and whispered disgusting things in her ear, Nathan raped her. Even now she could feel his hands on her, probing her body with his fingers and tongue. Then, when he was done with her, she had been made to watch while he and Carla had sex. She could still see their faces, contorted in ecstasy, leering at her. No, Rachel knew, she didn't have long to live.

And in a way, she didn't care about dying. This was the worst thing they could have done to her. She could have handled anything else – a painful torture that might scar emotionally or mark her frail body, but not this. Not again.

She had endured this kind of abuse before from her father. She remembered his hot breath just as she had felt Nathan's, remembered how he had touched her, caressed her with a savage intimacy.

And like before, she had closed her eyes and gone to that place again. The place she'd always gone when her father came to her. With her eyes shut tight, until the muscles in her eyelids ached, she had started to moan – and she had kept moaning, until that sound became almost hypnotic, until that sound transported her into a world of numbness. Only when they had left her and she opened her eyes, could she then feel again. Only then did she cry. Only then did she allow herself pity.

Now, she sat in the middle of her own bathroom; her prison. She had stopped sobbing and stared blankly at the bath in front of her. Through the small bathroom window was the faintest of lights. Soon it would be dawn and she would know her fate.

Where they were taking her, she didn't know. The conversations she was able to make out were limited, but she had definitely heard Nathan say they were to move her first thing in the morning. So, Rachel surmised, it was probably just a few hours to go before she was taken somewhere to be executed.

Escape seemed impossible. She knew her own bathroom well. The window in it was too small for her to crawl out. Besides, she would have to drop from the first floor which would surely mean breaking something and hamper her escape. But she couldn't just sit here; couldn't just wait for the next terrifying instalment of her tragic life. No, she would die trying.

She got to her feet then knelt in front of the door. Putting one eye to the keyhole, she peered through to the adjacent room across the hall. Their door was ajar. She could see them wrapped up in each other's arms on the bed. She could see Nathan's face and wondered how something so evil could look so peaceful in its slumber. How she wished for just an instant for no divide between them. No door to stop her. With her life in the balance, she would have traded what was left of it for that door to be open. And with the last of her life and might, she would grab the scissors from the medicine cabinet and stab them. Stab them both until they were dead.

As Rachel visualised that terrible act, it came to her. If she hadn't have been so hate-filled at that moment, hadn't have wanted to hurt them so badly, she wouldn't have thought of it at all. The very weapon she had used in her mind to butcher them could also save her life. The scissors!

Rachel got to her feet and opened the cabinet. A small pair of nail scissors gleamed at her from the gloom like a precious gem out of the pitch of a mineshaft.

Rachel stared at them. What was she to do now?

Kneeling by the door again, she looked at the sleeping devils. As she pulled away from the keyhole, she saw the three screws that attached the doorknob to the frame. They were small, but so were the scissors. Quietly, she inserted one blade of the scissors into the groove of the first screw.

Holding her breath, she turned it.

No good. The screw held fast.

Without trying again she went to the next screw. This one gave. She put her eye to the keyhole. Evil hadn't stirred.

After several turns the screw came away and fell to the carpet. She went to the next screw. Holding her breath again, she did the same.

The screw gave.

After another check at her captors, she unwound the screw and it too dropped to the floor. Rachel gave the doorknob a gentle tug, which was now loose.

One to go!

Rachel prayed. To who or what she didn't care. She just prayed, hoping someone listened. She put the blade into the groove of the final screw and turned it.

It didn't give.

She tried again.

The screw held fast.

Paint glued it tight.

Gently, Rachel scratched the paint away until she thought the screw was clear. As she put the blade in the groove, she heard movement.

Rachel peered through the keyhole.

She saw Nathan stirring. He let go of his wife and rolled onto his back, groaning.

Rachel knew the groan. She winced and prayed

again. If he got up now, she was dead.

She watched him. Nathan stayed where he was. She could see his breathing go shallow. He was still asleep.

Her heart was pounding. She inserted the blade into the groove of the last screw. With a delicate might, she gritted her teeth and forced the blade round.

Suddenly, it slipped from the groove and popped out, the blade cutting across her forefinger.

Blood erupted from the wound and she nearly yelled out.

Rachel clutched her finger tightly and started to cry. Putting her finger in her mouth, she sucked hard in defiance.

She wouldn't cry. She wouldn't!

Grabbing a tissue from the roll, she wrapped it around the wound.

Rachel then turned back to the task.

Again she put the blade into the groove, this time holding the blunt edge with her palm of her other hand. She then turned it sharply.

The sudden jolt loosened the screw from the paint and started to turn. After just a few rotations, it dropped to the floor.

She'd done it!

After a check on them both, Rachel then gently slid the doorknob from the centre pin, which came away, leaving the cylinder and lock visible. She then used the closed scissors to slot in the cylinder and turn it. With the same principle as the last screw, she gave it a quick yank. The lock gave suddenly, but far too loudly.

Rachel heard a noise from her captor's room. She closed her eyes tight. They must have heard her. She was dead.

After several seconds, Rachel opened her eyes. The door hadn't come crashing in. No voices were heard. She peered through the keyhole. Both were still asleep.

Rachel inserted the scissors into the lock chamber and turned. The door came open.

Slowly she crept towards them, avoiding creaking boards she knew well. She felt light as air. No one could hear her. She felt invisible.

She was near the entrance to her bedroom now. There they lay – the evil ones. She gripped the scissors, point protruding from her clenched fist. She knew exactly what she would do.

With a mind of an assassin – a mind of one that felt nothing but hatred – she would stab repeatedly at their faces, their necks and eyes; the places where the most amount of blood would be lost in the shortest time. Sure, they would kill her, but not before she knew they would die soon after. Not until she was sure both of them would bleed to death.

As she crossed the threshold into her bedroom, she raised the scissors above her head. She stopped briefly to compose herself before bringing the first of many blows raining down upon them. With just the smallest part of her being not consumed by hatred, she suddenly noticed it.

Lying on top of the bedside drawer was her own mobile phone. She knew why they had it. They had to see if Stone would contact her so they would know if he was alive or not.

Rachel stared at it as her hatred-filled mind processed what it meant. Everything, in that fraction of a moment, was brought home to her. The last hours had been all about them – the monsters lying in her bed. But it wasn't just about them. There was a far more dreadful nightmare than just her ordeal. This was about The Family and what they had done. This was about the princess. The murder of Becker... Stone.

Rachel lowered her arms. However much she wanted them dead, Rachel knew there was more she should do. She had sent Stone an e-mail that could bring this group of people crashing down. He might already be dead of course, but maybe, just maybe he was still alive. And it was that faint glimmer of hope that she had to go with. Rachel had to warn him, had to tell him that he must look at his e-mail. Tell him to get safe. If she could do this one thing, then she could accept the fate awaiting her. She could die knowing that The Family just might die with her.

The options went round and around in her head. Rachel didn't know what she should do first. The phone was a lifeline. She could contact the police. Or could she? Of course not. The Family had police working for them, so how could she be sure to trust them?

Rachel was sweating now. She had to decide what to do. She could run? Yes, of course, that was it! Get the phone and get out the flat.

Rachel stepped closer to the bed. If she was light and invisible before, she was now heavy and all too present. Her shadow was cast over their faces as she inched forward. Rachel was there now, right above them, the phone lying inches from her right hand.

Rachel looked up at the window. Light crept up the curtains. The room was becoming brighter. Now or never.

Rachel inched her hand towards the phone.

She wanted to take a large breath after the continuous shallow breathing but knew she had to hang on. Rachel put her hand around the phone and raised it from the table. Then she backed up the way she had come.

Each step was excruciatingly slow and painful. Only when she'd crossed the threshold was she able to take a deeper breath.

Slowly she turned and started for the stairs which would bring her into the hallway.

The first step of the stair creaked and she put her hand to her mouth and winced at her stupidity.

The beasts didn't stir.

Feeling a little more confident, Rachel descended the stairs as quickly as she dared. On the way down she looked at the mobile phone screen and pressed the first button on the speed dial memory. Stone's name lit up in a soft blue light like a beacon of hope.

Once downstairs, she stole to the front door and tried the handle. Her captors had locked it and taken the key.

Rachel put her hand to her mouth and started to

cry. She bit her finger to stop the moan of anguish leaving her lips.

She looked down at the phone. The name was still illuminated. Without a thought for the police, she hit the dial button and put the phone to her ear.

At first nothing happened. The call had to travel to Spain. Then, all of a sudden there was a ringing tone.

"Come on! Come on!" she whispered, as the call went on ringing.

She wanted more than anything to hear a voice. But, not just any voice, one she knew; one that reminded her of life on the other side of the hell she was in.

The call was put through to Stone's recorded voicemail.

Rachel winced. "Stoney," she whispered, urgently. "Go to your e-mail. Please, please read your e-mail. You're in danger. You must get away, get safe. Whatever you do, don't go to the police. You must get safe!"

Rachel ended the call. There was nothing more she could do. Now she had to think of herself. She had to get out or she was dead.

She hurried to the window and tried the handle. It was held fast. Someone had secured the window shut with screws. Quickly she hurried to kitchen back door – locked too, the key taken out and all the windows secured. Panicking, she ran back into the front room. She opened a bureau drawer where she knew there would be a screwdriver and rummaged around.

In that moment of urgency, all other senses left

her. She had never heard anything else, or noticed how loud she had become.

All of a sudden, she was spun on her heels. Nathan stood in front of her.

"You stupid bitch!" he hissed, and then hit her hard in the face.

Rachel buckled to the floor.

Dazed, she looked up and started to back away. Nathan came forward, levelling his pistol at her.

Rachel glared up at him. She had done all she could. Resigned to her inevitable fate, she simply closed her eyes and waited.

An odd thought crossed her mind at that moment. Movies had taught Rachel that she would die before hearing the shot. She took no comfort from the fact.

*

A ringing mobile phone woke Stone from a deep sleep. He reached for it and looked at the call he had just missed. Rachel's name was on the screen. A small icon told him that she had left a voice message. Stone moaned wearily then put it back on the night stand. He couldn't be bothered to talk to Rachel, not now. Besides it was six o'clock in the morning. *What the hell was she thinking?* he thought.

Stone rolled over to find Jennifer gone. She must have just left as her side of the bed was still warm. There was no note, no explanation.

Their lovemaking had been the most pleasurable and intimate thing he'd done with a woman since Milly. During the act, feelings of guilt came and went, but now none of these negative feelings remained. In fact, he felt the opposite. But it didn't matter. She was gone with so much left unsaid.

Abraham would be meeting him today to conduct the rest of the interview. Stone would have to do this knowing what he had done with a dying man's wife. The joyful morning was short lived. Elation turned into guilt.

Stone got up and took a long shower. His mind raced. Now, he didn't even know if he could face Conty. The night before had been perfect. Now, things were complicated. Stone wondered if he should leave the island.

After dressing, he thought of accessing his voicemail but didn't feel like talking to Rachel, or anyone else for that matter. He sat in front of his laptop with the intention of writing up the interview so far. He lit a cigarette and stared out the window for inspiration, when he saw Jennifer emerge from her villa with Deklin.

Stone moved to the window and watched as Jennifer went to the Jeep. She was visibly distressed and Deklin tried to comfort her. Stone watched Deklin hug her, then, Jennifer got into the Jeep and raced off, taking the road northwards to Abraham's studio. Deklin watched her leave then went back inside.

Stone stubbed out his cigarette and hurried outside. Something was wrong. Very wrong.

He hurried along the beach to the Contys' villa. He went up to the front door and knocked.

No answer.

Stone went to the side of the villa to see if anyone was by the pool. He saw another Jeep parked under a carport. He looked inside and spotted the ignition. For a moment he considered going after Jennifer. Instead, he went to the door at the side of the villa and found it open. Stone stepped inside into a laundry room. Another door led into the main house. He went in.

He stood in the main hallway. To the right he knew was the kitchen and living room. To the left, was the library.

Stone called out.

No answer.

He called again.

Still no answer.

Stone considered his next action. He knew he should go back to his villa and wait for Conty to arrive, but something told him that wasn't going to happen.

Turning left, Stone went into the library. On the far wall hung 'A Blind Eye'. He stood in front of the painting again. As usual, the drowning man image drew him in.

Stone scanned the painting, looking for the lone figure he'd witnessed the day before, the only figure that paid the drowning man any attention, but couldn't see him. Stone was sure he'd seen him. He scanned the hordes of people where the figure had been before. The crowds seemed to be larger this time, appearing to hide the character. Stone moved closer to the picture. He stared hard, looking for the man that he knew had seen, but nothing. The mystery man had vanished.

Stone stood back from the painting and shook his head. He had obviously imagined it all. The island was enchanted.

Stone was about to leave the room to find Deklin when he noticed the louvered door. He remembered Jennifer's reaction the day before when she'd caught him about to open it. Conty's mysterious study became a huge temptation.

Again Stone tried to see into the room through the slats in the door, but couldn't. He stood back, waiting for the best part of his brain to talk him out of it. However, after what happened last night it was clear the best part of his brain didn't seem to be functioning anymore. Stone grasped the handle of the door and turned it slowly. In a way, he would have liked the study to be locked so he wouldn't have a choice but to mind his own business. That would have been too easy. The door opened and Stone stepped inside.

The room was small. A leather-bound desk occupied along one of the walls, a tall leather chair in front of it. Another wall contained a shelf of books. By the side of the desk sat a safe. On top of it, a fresh bouquet of flowers.

Stone scanned the room. Another bookshelf was full of files. Stone stepped closer to them. Most were accounts with labels of the names of many charities Conty supported. On the desk was a laptop, a printer, and piles of various reading matter. On the right side of the desk were three drawers. Stone stared at them for a moment, and then did what he shouldn't have.

In the top drawer was a pile of papers, mostly accounts and letters. He rummaged through some of the letters. Most seemed to be from adoring fans or formal invitations to various overseas functions. The second drawer contained much the same thing. Stone then opened the bottom drawer.

At first, it seemed to house just another pile of papers. Stone moved the top letter. Underneath was a pile of newspaper cuttings. He got them out and laid them on the top of the desk. As he started to flip through them, he was shocked to find that they were all from his column, 'Blood from a Stone'. The most recent, concerning Shillingway. The next was an article he had done a month before about a government minister by the name of Michael Tanyard.

Tanyard had been a Labour backbencher named by Stone as having an affair with his secretary. That secretary was Andrew Marsh. Their homosexual affair had apparently been going on for two years unbeknown to Tanyard's wife. Tanyard resigned two days after Stone's article was printed.

The next was a month prior, concerning a wealthy financier by the name of Pannaup Patel. Stone's article exposed the chief executive's corruption. Subsequently, the police investigated him and the pharmaceutical company he was majority shareholder in. Patel was arrested following the accusations and the company's share options collapsed.

Stone read over the many articles he had done since joining The Informer. They made for gruesome reading. Carefully, he put the cuttings back in the drawer. Conty had indeed researched him well.

Stone turned from the desk. He should be leaving, but wondered if there was anything else to be found out about his elusive host. His gaze fell on the walls. Along one of them were photographs of Conty with other celebrities. In one, he stood on the beach with Mick Jagger. Another was Deklin, Conty, and David Bowie. Others were of Conty with artists that had obviously stayed on the island. Some Stone recognised; others, he didn't. Another of the photographs was Conty, Jennifer, and the Princess of Wales, standing by a pool. The princess wore a bikini and Stone instinctively knew it would be worth a fortune on the open market.

He scanned the other walls where many of the paintings hung. Stone looked at them one by one. Lots were of the princess in locations on the island. There was a portrait of Jennifer and of Deklin.

Stone looked at a few more and was about to leave when his eyes fell on a portrait, freezing him to the spot. Stone's eyes widened and his mouth went completely dry. His stomach sank and his whole body shook as if the room temperature suddenly dropped below zero.

At first he couldn't believe who he was looking at. He closed his eyes then opened them again. The image wasn't going to go away. Next to the portrait of Deklin was another he could never have expected to see. The features were painted perfectly; features he knew intimately. Long chestnut hair, green eyes. The warm and carefree smile. It was his wife, Milly.

Although seeing the portrait shocked Stone, he realised it was familiar to him. He'd seen it before. Then it came to him. Stone reached into his back pocket and retrieved his wallet. He then took out the small sketch from the book Milly kept in her study. Stone held it up. The picture was the same. In fact, identical. The words under the sketch now made sense. "August is fine." *Milly must have been here at some time in the month of August*, he thought. Stone stared hard at the picture, trying to remember a time when Milly had gone away. He couldn't.

Milly's gaze was almost haunting. Stone put his hand to his face, not knowing at that moment what he should do. Questions bombarded him. Conty had painted Milly but she had never told Stone she'd even met him. Maybe she hadn't. *Maybe Conty took it from a photograph?* Stone thought. *No, the beach was behind her.* She *had* been here. Impossible as it was, Milly must have been to the island. *But why hadn't she told him?*

The more Stone stared back at the picture of his wife, the angrier he grew. This was too much. The island was tainted in some way. Ever since he had arrived, strange things had been going on; secrets, lies and riddles, seemingly orchestrated by the very man that had invited him here. And now this – a picture of his wife. Stone clenched his fists. He had to see Conty.

Moving from the room, Stone ran out into the library, and then stopped abruptly. By the door stood Deklin.

"Jeramiah?" he said, a look of surprise on his face.

"Where is he?" asked Stone, angrily.

Deklin just stared for a moment. "What is it,

Jeramiah? What's wrong?"

"Where's Conty?"

"He's at the studio."

Stone walked toward the door but Deklin stopped him. "You can't go there, Jeramiah."

"Take your hands off me, Deklin," said Stone, patiently.

"You can't go there," repeated Deklin, taking his hand away. A bead of sweat lined his brow. He looked anxious, his hands trembling as they were held by his sides.

"Why?" blasted Stone. "I want to know why a picture of my wife is on his wall. Why didn't anyone tell me she was here?"

Deklin looked past Stone to the door of Conty's study, which was still ajar. He closed his eyes for a moment, understanding what Stone had seen. "You can't go to the studio," he said, holding his hands up, desperately trying to calm the situation. "I'll call him for you. I'll get him to come here."

"I'm going to him," said Stone. "No more fuckin' games!" Stone started to walk off.

Deklin clasped his hands together as if in prayer. "It's bigger than this, Jeramiah. There are things you have to..."

His voice trailed off. Stone had left the room.

Deklin ran after him and found Stone already in the Jeep. Deklin tried to open the door but Stone had locked it.

Stone glared at him and started the engine. Deklin

tried frantically to open the door, but it was hopeless. Stone reversed the truck, slammed into first, then raced off up the beach. Deklin could only watch as Stone sped away northwards towards the place no one was allowed to go.

After half an hour, Stone drove up a steep incline and over the top of a ridge. As he came over the top he saw the studio – a white building situated near to the edge of the cliff. He saw two Jeeps parked outside.

As he drove down the steep incline to the studio, Stone spotted the large area of tarmac with a red 'H' painted in the middle, indicating a helicopter pad. No one was outside. He drove up to the building and stopped, waiting for a moment. No angry welcoming committee came out to greet him. The place seemed eerily quiet.

Stone didn't know how he was going to play it. He shouted out but no one replied, no one came out. Looking around, there were no obvious signs of entry from where he stood and so he went round the side. Turning the corner, he came to a set of small steps leading up to a doorway. Stone ran up the steps and put his ear to the door. No sounds came from within and he tried the catch. The door creaked open. Stone slipped inside and closed it behind him.

He stood in a large room covered in sketches and unfinished paintings. In the centre of the room was a grand oak table strewn with brushes and paints. The paintings hung on the wall were mostly scenes of the island. There was an easel in the corner and to the side of it was a wheelchair – a stark reminder Abraham was indeed unwell.

As Stone looked around the room, voices drifted in. He crept over to the door and put his ear to it. Several people spoke, but Stone couldn't quite make out what they were saying. One of the voices was Jennifer's.

Stone looked over the old door and noticed a tiny gap in the frame. He put his eye to it and peered inside. He was looking into another large room, bright, with white-washed walls. Stone could see Jennifer, leaning over a hospital bed. Monitors and medical equipment took up most of the room on the opposite side of the bed.

Now Stone knew why she had been so upset, why Conty spent so much time at the studio. Abraham Conty wasn't coming here to paint. He was obviously coming here for treatment.

Stone watched as Jennifer turned to face him. For a moment, he thought she looked straight at him until she started to speak to someone. Stone couldn't make out what was being said.

Confused, he stepped away from the door. His mind raced. He put his eye back to the cracked frame and scanned the room.

Jennifer sat at the side of the bed. Stone tried to get a better look at Conty, but couldn't.

Stone stood up. He had to go in, had to know what this was all about. As he gripped the door handle, a presence behind him made itself known. Slowly he turned, and then froze.

Abraham Conty stood in the doorway.

With everything that should have been said, Stone,

for a moment, couldn't say anything.

"You journalists do have a tendency to live up to your reputations," said Conty. He didn't seem surprised to find Stone.

Stone, however, was dumfounded. "I thought you were sick."

Conty didn't say anything.

Stone decided to go on the offensive. "Why have you got a portrait of my wife?" he demanded. He then produced the small sketch of his wife that he had in his wallet. "Did you send this? What's it mean, August is fine?" Was it okay for Milly to come here in August? Is that what it means? What the hell is going on, Conty? Was my wife here or not?"

Conty nodded. "Yes, she was here."

"Why the hell didn't you tell me?"

"I couldn't."

Stone's patience wore thin. "I want some answers, Conty! What the hell is going on here?"

Conty sighed. "Very well," he began. "Yes, Milly did come here. But it was before you both met."

"Go on," said Stone.

"Milly wrote to me. She wrote to me a lot."

"About what?"

"She wanted to interview me. Of course I said no, but she was very persistent. I had read her articles and interviews through the magazine she worked for. I knew she was a respected art critic. She seemed genuine in her motives. The magazine she represented was a reputable one. After some time and after a great deal of correspondence, I granted her the interview. Like you, I invited her here."

"Why didn't she tell me? Why was the interview never published?"

Conty bowed his head.

"Why?" Stone asked again.

"Because while she was here she..."

"She what?"

Conty closed his eyes. "She found something out. Something I didn't want anyone to know about."

"What?" asked Stone, urgently. "I have a right to know."

Conty nodded. "Yes you do, Jeramiah." He gestured for Stone to go into the other room. Stone hesitated, but did as he was told.

The room he entered was not unlike a private room in a hospital with the familiar, sanitised smell of any conventional ward. Walls were brilliant white with just a few of Conty's pictures hanging up. Against the far wall were bookshelves and a desk with a computer on it. Below the window, which looked out to sea, was a hospital bed surrounded by sophisticated monitoring equipment, intermittently beeping.

Stone stopped when he saw Jennifer looking out of the only window in the room. She turned to him. Her face was red and her eyes bloodshot.

"Hello, Jeramiah," she said, softly.

Stone stood where he was. Conty walked past him to the bed. He put his hand on the head of someone, but Stone still couldn't make out who it was.

At that moment, a nurse entered the room from another door. She was shocked to see Stone at first, but then carried on to the bed. She looked down at whoever was in it. She checked the monitors and added the information to a clipboard at the end of the bed. The nurse then checked the patient, taking her time to arrange the blankets. She nodded at Conty, gave a distasteful look to Stone, and then left the room as silently as she had entered.

"What is this place?" asked Stone, looking first at Conty then at Jennifer for the answer. "What's going on here?"

Conty ushered for Stone to come forward. "This is my son," he said, looking down at the bedridden person.

Stone frowned in disbelief. "But you don't have a son," he said, dumbly, looking at Jennifer then back at Conty.

Slowly he walked towards the bed. Lying still, his eyes closed, was a young man with a bandage around his head. Tubes were coming from his nose and mouth, connected to a pump that hissed as it compressed every few seconds. One hand lay on the starch white covers with a drip connected to the inside of his wrist. The boy's age was hard to tell, as he was disfigured. His face was terribly scarred from burns.

Stone just stared. He then looked up at Conty for an explanation.

"His name is August," began Conty, putting his hand on the boy's forehead. "We named him after the month he was born."

He smiled fondly at his son then turned back at Stone. The youth seemed to ebb away from his eyes and at that moment seemed as though the weight of the world rested on his shoulders.

Stone was aware of the measure of pain Conty was feeling but he needed to know things. "So that's what it meant under the sketch. *August*, meaning your son?"

Conty took the sketch from Stone. His hand was trembling. "That's right," he replied. "Milly wrote to me asking how August was. I told her he was fine."

"What's this all about, Abraham?" asked Stone. "Why didn't Milly tell me she came here?"

Conty handed the piece of paper back to Stone. "Very well, Jeramiah. You deserve an explanation."

Jennifer came to Conty's side and put her hand on his arm.

"My son is dying, Jeramiah," began Conty. "He has a brain tumour. The doctors have tried to remove it, but they can't. He has been ill for some time and has just a few days left. It's the reason I've been spending so much time here."

Stone sat down on a stool. He didn't know what to say.

"His brain was damaged after an accident," Conty went on, looking over his son and stroking the blond curls visible from the bandage.

"September twelfth, nineteen eighty-eight. August was fifteen. My wife, Louise and I decided to take August on holiday to Spain to see the galleries of Madrid. That morning we left the hotel it was a beautiful day. The sun, high in the sky. *Too* high. The driver of the truck that hit us had been momentarily blinded by it as he came out from a tunnel. He hit us head-on." Conty paused for a brief moment. "My wife was killed instantly. I was thrown clear. The car turned over and caught fire as it hit the central reservation."

Conty looked out the window as if the image of the crash played out in front of him.

"August couldn't get out. He sustained eighty percent burns. It was a miracle he survived at all."

Stone stared at the floor as he listened. "Jesus. I'm so sorry," he muttered. "But why didn't you want anyone to know this? I mean, no one knows you have a son." Stone turned to Jennifer. "I don't understand."

Conty took a deep breath. He was about to speak when Jennifer stopped him. "You don't have to do this, Abraham," she said.

Abraham put his hand on the side of Jennifer's face. "Yes, I do, Jennifer," he said, solemnly. He turned to face Stone. "Things will be clearer when I tell you about Milly." He took a deep breath. "As I've already said, Jeramiah. Milly wrote to me," he began. "This was before she ever met you. Eventually, I invited her here." Conty bowed his head. "It was a mistake. While she was here, she, like you now, found out the truth."

"The truth?" said Stone. "What do you mean?"

Conty sighed. Jennifer left his side and went outside.

Conty and Stone watched her leave. Conty then turned to Stone, who was waiting for an explanation.

"She was walking through the rock pools one morning after she had breakfast," he began. "I should have stayed with her but she slipped out early one morning. Whilst walking she discovered August. He was sketching on the beach." Conty gazed affectionately down at his son. "It's strange really. August is normally scared to meet anyone because of his disfigurement, but he warmed immediately to Milly. That's when she found out."

Stone frowned. "Found out what, Abraham?"

Conty went to the desk by the window and took a sketchpad from the drawer. He flicked through the pad, found what he was looking for, and then handed it to Stone. "August was sketching this."

Stone took the pad. He stared at the picture – a sketch of the painting that he had seen in the Tate. Although in pencil, the subject matter was identical. It was a sketch of the painting 'Cleansed'. A mother held her disfigured child as she poured water over its head from a large urn.

Stone stared at the sketch for ages before saying anything. He scanned the paintings that lined the walls. He then turned back to Conty who nodded.

"But you painted this," Stone said.

Conty shook his head. "I can't paint, Jeramiah."

Stone's mouth fell open. "What are you telling me?"

Conty went to one of the windows and gazed out thoughtfully. "Milly knew immediately, of course. She knew by the quality of even the sketch that August had done them all."

"You mean all of it? The paintings in the Tate. A Blind Eye?"

"All of it," confirmed Conty.

"But I don't understand," said Stone. "This is... unbelievable. Why?"

"When August was born, Louise and I knew he was special, different from all the other children. More intense. We noticed just *how* different when he started to draw. Even as a small child, he could draw quite wonderful pictures beyond his years. In fact they were more than that, they were extraordinary.

"Over the years, art was something we had to consider seriously for August as a career. His talent made us realise he would need special tuition, as none of the schools we sent him to were capable of teaching him anything. So, we arranged for private tuition and took him abroad. We were patient with him. Soon there was nothing more anyone could teach him so we gave him free rein. As he got older, he got better. By the time he was fifteen he was painting exquisite works – masterpieces. We knew he would have a prosperous future and a fine career."

Conty turned to face Stone. He looked drawn, the grief all too evident. Even his powerful blue eyes were softer. "That was until the accident," he said sadly.

"After the accident, I didn't think he would ever pick up a brush again. I stayed in Spain with him. He loved it here and I hoped it would somehow inspire him. At first, it was impossible. He grieved for his mother terribly and refused to even look at art. I tried to get him out, take him back the places he had loved before, but it seemed hopeless. He refused to ever be seen in public. On top of that, his injuries needed constant attention. I sold some of his work to be able to pay for care. The disfigurement of his face was something I wondered if he would ever get over. He would cry constantly to have his mother back, to have his face back. He would never let anyone take his photograph, still doesn't. Sometimes he couldn't even bring himself to look in the mirror. I thought I'd lost him.

"With all this, there was still more my poor boy had to endure. I knew something else was wrong, something much more serious. I watched him constantly. I would look at him eat, listen carefully when he talked. I observed everything. I quickly became aware something was not right. I took him to a specialist in Madrid who confirmed he had some brain damage from the accident. The reason he hadn't painted again was because he couldn't. He had lost a great deal of his memory and the genius that was once there I feared lost."

Conty shook his head. "I was so angry. After all that had happened to this poor child, the one thing he loved was now impossible for him to do. The one thing I knew would help him come to terms with his mother's death and his disfigurement had been taken from him." Conty clenched his fists by his side. "I was so angry, Jeramiah. But, I am thankful for that anger now. It made me resolute in getting August to paint again." Conty held his fist up. "I just had to get him to paint."

Conty realised he was moving to anger and took a

deep breath. He ran his hand over his head. "I tried specialists in the beginning, but they didn't work. August was growing increasingly difficult and would not let anyone else help him. He wouldn't let anyone see him other than me and I knew that I wouldn't be able to get outside help. So, we did it together. Just the two of us."

Conty faced Stone. "Initially, I thought it would never happen. I placed brushes in his hand, but he refused to use them." Conty grinned. "He would throw the brushes everywhere. I swear I had to clean paint off my clothes every day. But, slowly, we got there. The experience was as good for me as it was for him. I blamed myself for what had happened. I was, after all, driving the car that day. But with my preoccupation to get August to paint again, I too came to terms with Louise's death. Of course it took time, but eventually August started to pick up the brushes. Slowly over time, there were signs it was working.

"More time and more care, it finally started to happen. August had found a place that he could be happy in again. We had a small apartment in the mountains. August had the seclusion he wanted and so he was content. And through his joy, came the work. And soon, the work became as magnificent as it once was. Painting was his therapy. 'Cleansed' was just one of the many pieces he did to understand what had happened to him. But there were happy works as well. Works that signified he was finally coming to terms with the past."

Conty went back to his son and put his hand on his head. "And I was so proud," he said, tears rolling down his face.

Stone stared at the floor, absorbing the information. His emotions were in turmoil. "Why did you pretend?" he asked softly.

Conty kept his gaze on his son. "To protect him," he replied. "I knew his work was phenomenal. I knew the paintings would one day be acclaimed. I spoke about this with August, but he didn't have the capacity to understand what I knew. He just wanted to paint. He couldn't and wouldn't be seen. He had no way of dealing with what his art could and would bring to him."

Stone was thoughtful for a moment. "But I don't understand. "What did you have to protect August from?"

"I knew soon after the accident that I was dying, Jeramiah. Before I did, I had to make sure August was able to paint again. And when he did, I knew that without me or anyone to take care of him, there was a possibility that he might be exploited. I couldn't ever let that happen. I had to make sure that after I was gone, August was protected from opportunists. As he didn't care about the financial side to his art or the fame, I decided *I* would be the artist. That way when I died, the world would think it was over. There would be no young boy they could go after, no one alive to exploit. I even changed our name. The family name is not Conty, it's Matherton. I erased our past. I had to make sure August would be safe."

Conty shrugged. "But none of it matters now. Last year August started having great pains in his head. I took him to a specialist where the tumour was discovered. It's inoperable. And now, at the age of twenty-five, August is dying."

Stone bowed his head.

Conty saw that Stone was moved. "Milly and I kept in touch. August was very fond of her and would write often. Milly chose to keep her knowledge a secret. She decided not to say anything. Not even to you."

Stone stared at the floor and shook his head.

"Please don't be angry with her, Jeramiah. If you're going to be angry with anyone, let it be me. I asked a lot of your wife. Something I will never forget."

"Were you going to tell me?" Stone asked.

"No," Conty replied honestly. "I also have to protect Jennifer. I wouldn't want the world finding out now. I fear if they did she would be hounded, her privacy taken from her. I don't want that to happen."

"You don't know it would be that way."

"I've seen what the media has done to others, what it's done to my friends. The way they hound them. Their vicious stories, their invasion of their lives. I won't risk that with Jennifer. I wouldn't have risked it with August."

"So I too keep my mouth shut, so you can make sure you go on conning the world and taking millions for work that you didn't even do? So you can go on manipulating people?"

Conty didn't respond. Instead he gave Stone a look that Stone knew he would never forget. The look stung Stone to the bone and all he could think to do was storm out of the room.

Once outside, Stone went to the edge of the cliff and looked out to sea. He was angry and confused. He couldn't understand why Milly hadn't said anything and was furious at Conty for entrusting Milly with such a responsibility. Now it seemed it was his turn. Snatching up a pebble, he hurled it out to sea. Then he felt a hand on his shoulder. He spun round to see Jennifer standing behind him.

"What does everyone do around here, just lie?" he asked angrily.

"Don't be angry, Jeramiah."

"Well, what do you expect?" he blasted. "It's just that it's rather a fuckin' lot to take in right now. I'm sorry if you think I'm being a little insensitive!"

"I don't think you're insensitive," said Jennifer, delicately. "I think you're angry because you're sad about all this."

"You're damn right! My wife kept secrets from me and none of you told me about her being here. You just strung me along hoping that I wouldn't find out about this charade."

"It wasn't like that."

"And you! Why didn't you tell me my wife had been here? All the time you kept it from me. All the time when we were..." Stone's voice trailed off. He was too angry to finish.

"I was going to tell you. I just had to be sure of your intentions, that's all."

"Oh, I see," replied Stone. "And what was last night all about? Were you just making *sure* of my intentions?"

The remark stung Jennifer. "Please, don't be angry."

"Why shouldn't I be? Conned by an old man who's made millions from art he didn't even paint."

"Now that's enough!" snapped Jennifer. "Haven't you learned anything?"

"*Learned?*" Stone said incredulously. "I've learned that we've all been conned. I've learned that the most famous artist in the world is actually a dying young man exploited by his own father. That's what I've *learned*."

Jennifer sighed. "My god. Is that really all you can see?"

Stone held his hands up. "What else is there, Jennifer?"

"There's a father who made sure that his son's art got the recognition it deserved. A father that devoted his whole damn life to a son that wouldn't be able to paint if it weren't for him. A father that devoted his life to protecting his son from a world August could never live in."

Stone stared in disbelief. "And you believe that?"

"Abraham spends all of his time with August. I witnessed Abraham become the artist August wanted to be, but couldn't. August would watch his father on television and read about him in the papers, as Abraham opened galleries showing August's work. He did it all for August. I've held Abraham in my arms as he's sobbed with the weight of his devotion for that boy. The weight of the lies, the sacrifice of his own life for his son's. Don't you see, Jeramiah? They are the same."

"But the money, Jennifer? The boats, the plane, the secluded island."

"What about the damn money? It's just stuff. Part of the charade. He gives most of it away. Are the paintings not worth it just because August signs them with his father's name? Of course they are. It's because of Abraham. Those are the facts, if you *want* to see them."

Stone sighed. "Then if those are the facts, people should know about them."

Jennifer closed her eyes in disbelief. "So you tell the world. Then what?"

"Then the truth comes out," Stone decided.

"Truth!" Jennifer shouted. "And what difference would it make except defy the wishes of two people who have a relationship far beyond most people's comprehension? How could anyone understand that, Jeramiah? And what difference would it really make anyway? What would happen if you told the world? Would everyone want their money back? Or would the paintings be worth more because of the almost unbelievable and moving story behind them." Jennifer's voice tremored but she was determined not to cry. "My god, I thought you were different, Jeramiah. Don't you see? It makes no difference. The only things you would damage are August's memory and his father's devotion. The truth is yours to decide what to do with, Jeramiah. I suggest you use it well."

Stone through his arms up. "And what do you expect me to do? I'm a journalist, Jennifer. I have to tell the truth."

Jennifer shook her head. "Is this what you really

believe, Jeramiah?"

Stone jabbed his chest with his finger. "I have a responsibility for God's sake!"

Jennifer stabbed her finger back at him. "You gave that up a long time ago, Jeramiah. Maybe once you cared. But I'm not sure about now."

Stone flushed with rage. "And what's that supposed to mean?"

"It means that if you write this one up then Abraham and August become just another couple of statistics on the end of your pen."

"Is that what you think?"

Tears welled in Jennifer's eyes. "I don't know, Jeramiah, you tell me. Is this the man that I was falling in love with?"

Stone just stared at Jennifer, and then bowed his head.

Jennifer put her hand on the side of his face. "No, you're not that man. At least I don't think you want to be. You're a good man, a good man that is upset. Not because Milly didn't tell you. Not because you think that Abraham has conned the world, but because you're upset for *him*. Truth Is, Jeramiah, I think you understand why Milly never told you. And I think you understand what Abraham thought he had to do for his son."

Stone rubbed his temple. "I'm not sure what I understand anymore. Least of all myself."

Jennifer went up to him and kissed him. "I think you do."

Stone gave her a weak grin. "What about us? Where do we fit in with all this mess? You're married for God's sake."

"No, I'm not, Jeramiah."

Stone was dumbfounded. "What?"

"It's all part of it, Jeramiah," Jennifer admitted. "I couldn't hurt that gentle man in there. Especially if I was married to him."

"I don't understand," said Stone. "What's all part of it?"

Jennifer sat down and covered her face with her hands. "Oh, God what a mess this all is." She sighed. "I never wanted to tell you like this."

Stone sat beside her. "I'm not sure it could get any messier, are you?" he asked.

Jennifer turned to face him. "After that time in Barcelona, the time in the gallery where I met Abraham."

Stone nodded.

"Well, he offered me a place to stay on the island. He was worried about me. Abraham knew that maybe if I was left alone again, I might end up harming myself." Jennifer shrugged. "Well, I had nowhere else to go, and you don't turn down an offer like that from someone as famous as Abraham Conty. Besides, I felt so safe around him. Anyway, in time I *did* get better. Abraham helped me to enjoy life again. He showed me a life that was worth living for. He told me about August pretty much from the start. I suppose he thought if I knew there was someone much worse off, it would help me appreciate life again." Jennifer took hold of Stone's hand. "It did, Jeramiah. I got well, ended up helping Abraham with *his* life. Most of his time was spent looking after August. It was getting too much for him, so I took care of the business side of things. I've been here ever since. Part of the charade."

"But why did you tell the world you were married?"

"To protect him."

"From what?"

Jennifer seemed momentarily afraid. "The media. You see, I was being watched. There was an Italian paparazzi apparently snooping around the mainland for some time, watching the island. It turned out he was monitoring the activity here; who came and went. I suppose he was trying to get a glimpse of a celebrity. Of Diana maybe, I don't know. I used to go to the mainland a lot..." Jennifer put her arms around herself as though suddenly chilled.

"He was watching me. Taking photographs, asking questions around the town. Well, one day he accosted me, started asking all sorts of questions. Who I was, what I was doing there. I didn't answer him, of course, but then he got rough. He started asking me horrible things. Was I a whore? Did Abraham pay me to go over to the island to have sex with him? It was awful."

"It was stupid of me, I know, but I wanted him out of the way. He threatened to come to the island and find out what was going on for himself. I was so frightened he might find out about August. I was worried my presence might hurt Abraham's reputation, so I lied, Jeramiah. I told him we had just got married." Jennifer couldn't help breaking into a wide grin.

"You should have seen the look on his face. Anyway, it worked. It took the emphasis off Abraham and the media suddenly wanted to know about Missus Conty instead. I told Abraham. He was angry at first but he soon forgave me. We thought one day when I left, we would just say that we separated. It seemed so easy at the time. You see, Abraham could never love anyone but Louise. All he's ever done is grieve her and devote his life to getting August well again. Through all that," she said, tearfully, "through all that, he found it in his heart to help me, to help Deklin. I owe him so much, Jeramiah."

She turned to Stone and took his hands. "I didn't mean to tell you this way. I never wanted to lie to you. Please forgive me. Please understand. I beg of you, please understand this."

Jennifer's eyes filled with tears. Stone took her face in his hands and kissed her. "I do understand," he said softly. "And there's nothing to forgive."

Jennifer closed her eyes. It was all she wanted to hear. "I should have told you," she cried.

Stone held her tight. "No, you shouldn't have. There was too much at stake."

Jennifer nodded. "I owe him so much, Jeramiah."

Stone kissed her forehead. "I know. I'm beginning to think I do too," he replied. "I'd better go and see him."

Stone went inside and found Conty at his son's bedside.

Stone stood by his side and looked down on August. "I'm sorry," he said. "I didn't mean to say the things I did. It's just been a lot to take in."

Conty beamed and put a hand on Stone's shoulder. "I understand, Jeramiah. I never wanted to put you through all this."

"Jennifer told me," admitted Stone. "About you not being married."

Conty smiled. "I thought she would. You know she's very fond of you, Jeramiah."

Stone was comforted that he knew about his affection for Jennifer. He stared at Conty, thoughtfully. "The photographs of all the celebrities in your library. The people that have been to the island, did they all know about August?"

Conty nodded. "Some."

"And none of them said anything?" Stone said, more to himself than Conty.

"You'd be surprised at the generosity of the human spirit," replied Conty.

"And Diana? She knew?"

"She loved August dearly. And he loved to paint her. She was instrumental in helping him come to terms with his disfigurement. People with pain in their lives can recognise it in others. Both had a bond with each other. Both felt the world didn't want them." Conty stroked his son's forehead. "And I suppose they didn't really want the world."

"My god," remarked Stone softly. "And no one knew of your past? No one investigated whether you had a son?"

"In the beginning, there was no need. It wasn't mentioned. People didn't question it. After we started making money from art sales, we bought our anonymity."

Stone reached down and put his hand on the side of August's face. He thought about the agonies that he had experienced in his young life.

Stone remembered the pictures he had seen at the Tate. It all made sense now. The anguish in the paintings. The pain. "That picture in the Tate," he said softly. "The one with the angel. Is that what August thinks you are? An angel that watches over him?"

Conty smiled. "I guess August just believes in them."

"And A Blind Eye? What does it mean?"

"That was me," said Conty. "Well, I mean the subject matter was my idea. August painted it for me. I felt as though I was drowning at times. The painting helped with the process.

"Process?" asked Stone.

"The guilt. The grief. You know about them, Jeramiah."

Stone didn't respond. He was struggling to hold himself together.

"He liked to paint here most of all," Conty remarked thoughtfully. "We had the studio built for him. He said it was like being at the edge of the world."

"How do you do it?" Stone asked. "How do you keep your faith with what this boy has had to endure?"

"You've seen his work, Jeramiah. How could I not

have faith when standing in front of one of his paintings?"

Stone felt a lump in his throat. Every word about every celebrity he had written about filled his head. Not good words, but bad. Horrible words and lines he knew when writing them would cause such pain. It was then, in that moment, that he felt so guilty, so humbled by the thin young man with shallow breathing before him; a young man that Stone felt almost unworthy to look upon.

Conty put his hand on Stone's shoulder. "You're a good man, Jeramiah. You should start believing that again."

Stone nodded wearily. He felt far from a good man. "How long has he got?" he asked, unable to take his eyes from Conty's son.

Conty lowered his gaze. "Not long now. The only thing keeping him alive is the machine. It's time to let him go."

"And you?" asked Stone, turning to face Conty.

Conty eyes narrowed. "My time here is nearly over too, Jeramiah."

"Jennifer knows, you know," said Stone sadly. "I didn't tell her. She knew already. She said she could sense something wrong."

Conty nodded. He winked at Stone. "But I have a feeling she's going to be all right."

Stone gazed into Conty's deep blue eyes and saw his reflection. "Why did you bring me here, Abraham? It was never for an interview, was it?"

"No, Jeramiah. It was never for an interview."

Stone shuffled nervously. "Then why?"

"You're here because I wanted to make sure you were safe," Conty said, seriously. "After Milly's death, I made it my business to follow your career. Through her correspondence I got to know you as well as I did her. I got you here to make sure that I had got it right. I had to make sure that I could trust you. You see..."

Conty stopped what he was saying. Jennifer walked in.

"Trust me?" Stone pressed him.

"I was going to tell you today, but things haven't exactly gone as I planned," Conty went on.

Stone took Conty by the arm. "Tell me what?"

"We have to go back to the villa," said Conty. "There's something I want you to see."

Stone was puzzled. He turned to Jennifer, who gave him a reassuring nod.

Conty went to Jennifer and kissed her on the cheek. "I'm going to take Jeramiah back to the villa."

Jennifer went to Stone's side. "I'll follow you down presently," she replied. "I'll call, Dek and let him know you're on your way."

Conty bent and kissed his son's forehead, then ushered Stone outside.

As they drove away from the studio, Stone wondered about the man sitting beside him and how fate had brought them together. He was nervous. By the look on Conty's face, whatever he had to show him seemed more important than anything he had told him so far.

FIFTEEN

As they made their way off the road and onto the beach, Deklin came out to meet them. Contrary to his usual happy demeanour, he looked concerned and hurried towards the Jeep.

Conty was quick to get out first. "It's all right, Deklin," he reassured him.

Stone got out of the Jeep. He felt nervous at meeting Deklin after their earlier encounter and felt compelled to make amends. "I'm sorry, Deklin. I didn't mean to speak to you the way I did before."

Deklin gave Stone a stern look, then smiled. "Yes, you did."

Stone beamed and shook Deklin's hand.

"It's time," said Conty. "It's time he knew it all."

Deklin nodded. "Very well, Abraham."

"Follow me, would you, Jeramiah?" said Conty.

Stone, flanked by Deklin, followed Conty into his

study. As they passed inside, Stone looked awkwardly at the portrait of his wife. Conty closed the door and asked Stone to sit down.

"Can I get you a drink, Jeramiah?" asked Deklin.

Stone shook his head, eager to know what this was all about.

Conty went to the drawer and took out the newspaper cuttings Stone had already seen. Conty noticed immediately that they had been tampered with. "So, you've seen these already?"

Stone nodded. "Yeah," he replied, sheepishly.

"It doesn't matter, Jeramiah. Just tell me what you think of them."

"Think? Nothing." Stone shrugged. "You obviously investigated my work and kept cuttings from my column."

Conty shuffled through Stone's weekly columns amassed since Stone started work with The Informer. "Did you notice anything strange about any of these articles?"

Stone didn't know where this was going. "I don't what you mean?"

"Did you notice anything similar between them all? A pattern?"

Stone frowned. "You mean having wrecked the careers of these people?"

"There is that, yes," admitted Conty. He glanced at Deklin. "But did you ever notice the similarities between any of these people?"

Stone was confused. "Is there one?"

Conty nodded. "Yes. I believe there is."

"I'm not following you, Abraham."

Conty held up one of the articles. "Michael Tanyard," he began, "Labour MP for North Lamington. Your article exposes Tanyard for having a homosexual affair with his secretary, Andrew Marsh. Since Tanyard is married, you argue that he is not fit for parliament on moral grounds."

Stone nodded. "It's true."

"Yes, it is," Conty agreed. "What is also true is that Michael Tanyard has been a close associate of a gentleman by the name of Omah Urabanhi."

Stone held his hands up. "If you say so."

"Omah Urabanhi is a millionaire businessman who runs the international cash and carry chain called 'Easy Stop'. Urabanhi was a major financial supporter of Tanyard's election campaign. In return, Tanyard has been openly supporting Urabanhi's application for a British passport."

Conty held up the next cutting. "Pannaup Patel, chief executive of Medpro, a large international pharmaceutical company. Following your article, investigators discovered Mister Patel's company was fraudulent because millions of pounds had not been declared to the Inland Revenue. It was also discovered that Mister Patel was making unsubstantiated claims about the medicines his company makes to boost the share price. As you know, Patel is now serving four years in prison."

Stone looked puzzled. "But this is all public knowledge. I don't know about the medical claims."

Conty held up the next article. "Kamran Surak, the well-known American financier. Your article said that Surak had been seen in a nightclub. He was conveniently photographed with ladies that turned out to be prostitutes, and members of his party were known to have been taking cocaine that night. A subsequent raid on Surak's home in Hampstead by the vice squad revealed two kilos of cocaine. The jury is still out on this one, as you know."

"Everything I wrote was true, and all my informants were substantiated by the police," defended Stone.

Conty held his hand up. "Did you know that Surak had bought a sizeable amount of shares in a company called Comtelemac?"

Stone gave his answer with a frown.

"The company makes motherboards and high-tech computer components. The share purchase meant Comtelemac would have forty-five percent of the company owned by Surak, with the rest being owned by a German merchant bank called Smitt-Ladel."

"So?" asked Stone.

"Since the arrest of Surak, his almost certain custodial sentence, and the company's bad publicity, meant shares in Comtelemac have crashed. The banks have lost a fortune and the company is sure to go into receivership."

Stone sighed. "Oh, I get it. So this is a lesson to show me how ruthless I've been and the lives I've ruined. Spare me the moral lesson, Abraham. We've been through all this. I wrote nothing but the truth."

"I'm not here to give you a lesson in morals or work ethics, Jeramiah. I want you to hear me out."

Stone looked at Deklin, who gave him a reassuring nod.

Conty held up yet another article. "Now to the more recent. Royston Shillingway, the popular Labour MP who recently shocked the country for having relations with a prostitute."

"Again, true," sighed Stone, growing tired of the cross-examination.

"What is also true, Jeramiah, is Shillingway was an outspoken critic of the monarchy. Because of his popularity, not only with the public, but also within Parliament, Shillingway was seen to be a real threat to the establishment and an influence in the monarchy's future. Indeed, he was predictably always the first parliamentary figure to pounce on the slightest misdemeanour committed by any member of the Royal Family. Transgressions that of course reinforced his argument concerning their legitimacy in a modern democracy. He was thought to be orchestrating a real challenge to Britain's political structure."

Stone looked bemused. "I'm sorry, I just don't get where this is going."

"Don't you see the link between all these people?"

"No, I don't," replied Stone. "Other than the fact that all these people are in positions of influence. But then, if they weren't, I wouldn't write about them, would I?"

"Of course you wouldn't," agreed Conty.

"Obviously, the first link to all of these people is *you*. The second is of the paper you work for, The Informer."

Stone frowned. "Yeah, so? Is that it?"

Conty's brow narrowed. "No, it's not. I think there's a third. I think you've been used, Jeramiah. I think you've been set up."

Stone rolled his eyes. "How so?"

"How did you come about all of this information about these people?" Conty asked, holding up the pile of Stone's articles.

"Leads come into the office," answered Stone. "Some are anonymous calls or a tip-off. Some come from leaks in high places. Some are passed from the top. Stories come from all different ways."

"Yes, but always from the top?" Conty enquired.

"Look, what is this?" asked Stone.

Conty leant forward. "Please, Jeramiah. I promise you I'm coming to the point. I said the top. Don't the leads come from the editor?"

Stone stared intently at Conty then let out a resigned sigh. "Yeah, a lot of the leads come from my editor."

Conty clasped his hands together, both forefingers resting under his bottom lip. "Precisely! The third link."

Stone folded his arms defensively. "What do you mean? I still don't get what you're trying to tell me."

"I think you've been preyed on," began Conty. "I think a good journalist who, for the past two years, has been struggling to come to terms with the death of his wife has been used because of that. You've been so angry, wanting to find some sense of justice in the world, that it blinded you to what was really going on around you."

"What the hell are you talking about, Abraham?"

"I think someone's been using your anger to get at all these people. I think you've been an unwitting accomplice to bringing down these people because of a much more serious and sinister agenda."

"What the hell are you talking about?" asked Stone, looking first at Conty then at Deklin for the answer.

"Look at the evidence, Jeramiah," urged Conty, holding the articles out towards him. "Every single one of these people has one thing in common. They're either a foreigner who has vested interests in this country from abroad, or outspoken critics of the monarchy, or the nation in general. Pannaup Patel is Muslim with huge British assets. Kamran Surak, again a Muslim with huge British assets. Michael Tanyard, the Labour MP trying to get a passport for the millionaire Omah Urabanhi. Smitt-Ladel, the German bank with a multi-million pound investment in Contelemac. This is just a handful. The list is very long."

Conty put the articles on the desk. "And you've helped to bring them all down. Don't you see?"

Conty's findings astonished Stone.

"Someone wanted these people brought down on purpose," Conty continued. "They set them up so you would go after them. The reason you went after them was always legitimate, conveniently overshadowing the real agenda. Now, if I'm right, then the people behind this are some sort of anti-foreign establishment or a group with a pro-British agenda and are extremely dangerous."

Stone laughed. "You've got to be kidding me? This is absurd!"

"No, I'm not kidding, Jeramiah. Thing is, if I'm right, they've gone further than you can possibly imagine."

Stone feigned a smile. He pretended Conty's story didn't spook him. "Who do you think is behind this? And why are you so worried about it all, Abraham?"

Conty sighed. "I don't know who they are, for sure. As to why I'm involved you'll soon see."

"Do you have any evidence of any of what you're saying?"

"Yes, I do."

Stone watched as Conty went to a portrait of Jennifer on the wall behind him. He carefully took the picture down, revealing the door of a small safe. Conty turned the combination switch a few times in opposite directions then opened the door, retrieving a large manila envelope. Conty glanced at Stone then reached inside. "Recognise this?" he asked.

Stone took the photographs while keeping his gaze fixed on Conty. After a moment, Stone looked at it. His mouth fell open. The photographs were similar to the ones he had received in the post a few days before arriving at the island; the same image of the white Fiat alongside the Mercedes taking the Princess of Wales and Dodi Fayed from the Ritz hotel in Paris. Stone stared at the outstretched arm of the passenger pointing a gun at the princess's car.

Stone couldn't believe it. "You," he exclaimed. "You sent me these? It was *you* all along?"

Conty nodded.

Stone stared at Conty in disbelief. "But... how?"

"I took the photographs," declared Deklin.

"You?" asked Stone, turning in Deklin's direction. "I don't understand." Stone turned back to Conty. "What the hell is going on?"

Conty moved away from the desk and sat directly in front of Stone. "Listen to me carefully, Jeramiah. Three weeks before Diana was killed, she came with Dodi to stay on the island for a few days. The visit was done in complete secrecy. Only them, me, and a handful of security staff knew they were here. Their relationship, as you know, created a tremendous amount of press attention and they simply needed a little time out of the spotlight. Diana asked me if would be all right if they came. While they were here, Diana told me her fears. She had received a warning by way of a letter."

"Warning?" asked Stone.

Conty nodded. "Diana explained she'd been feeling vulnerable. She couldn't readily explain why this was, but Diana felt she was in great danger nonetheless. She started to trust no one, not even her own security. The letter sent to her confirmed those feelings. Now, normally when corresponding with members of the Royal Family, you would write to the address of the royal residence where the letter would go through the normal screening process by the press office."

Stone nodded, familiar with the procedure.

"That way any unwanted mail, especially the regular amount of threats and sordid letters, are intercepted and never reach the hands of the targeted person. The only exceptions are if you know the Royal personally, in that case you have a specific address to send it. Diana received a letter mailed to this address so this letter went straight to her hands. The letter was anonymous, but very specific in its warning to her."

"What did it say?" asked Stone.

"The letter said quite simply that, while she was in Paris, an attempt would be made on her life."

Stone couldn't say anything. The only sound in the room was the amplified ticking of the clock in the adjacent hallway.

Conty waited a moment then proceeded. "The fact Diana was going to Paris was not exactly a secret to anyone, least of all the press. Her press office even made her itinerary available. But the letter writer remains a mystery. While it was, of course, a cause for concern, Diana decided not to show this letter or mention it to her security staff. Instead, she told me."

Conty paused for a moment is if pained by what he had to say next.

"Diana told me, because she wanted someone she trusted so that if something were to happen, it wouldn't be covered up. With what I knew about the letter, I could make sure of that. You see, Jeramiah, she was aware of a possible conspiracy against her. Diana knew she might be making waves in very high places because of her popularity and relationship with Dodi. I agreed to help, but insisted I do more than just harbour that piece of knowledge. If something *was* going to happen to her, I wanted to stop it, or at least prove her death was no accident."

Conty looked up at Deklin who standing in the doorway. "Deklin is an excellent photographer. He took all these photographs," he said, pointing at the pictures of famous faces.

Conty was coming to the hard part and ran his hand over the top of his head. His face looked weary, his eyes tired. "On the day of her death," he continued. "Deklin and I went to Paris. Deklin was to shadow the princess and take photographs of her movements as much as he was able to. We hired Deklin a motorbike so he could follow her, blend in with the photographers. Diana knew he would be there and what he was doing. I think, in a way, it gave her some reassurance." Conty paused and glanced at Deklin. "I think it's better Deklin tell you the rest."

Stone turned his chair to face Deklin. The unfolding story was captivating. He waited for the next instalment.

Deklin came forward. After a deep breath he began his account of events. "We knew, like the rest of the paparazzi that night, Diana would be eating with Dodi at the Paris Ritz. Me, along with the rest of the photographers, began our long vigil outside the hotel, waiting for them to come out."

"Where were you?" Stone asked Conty.

"Waiting at our hotel. I couldn't risk being recognised."

"We knew where Diana was going afterwards," Deklin went on. "She had plans to go back to Fayed's Paris home." Deklin took in a deep breath, preparing to recount the dreadful turn of events that followed.

"I had been taking photographs of the paparazzi and security going in and out of the Ritz all day, and was doing the same that night. I took hundreds of photographs in the hope something suspicious would be captured on camera if anything were to happen. Nothing did. I hung around with about eight other riders and their drivers. I was on my own, so they thought I was just another rider hanging about the square hoping to catch a glimpse of Diana. The paparazzi were just chatting; nothing seemed to be out of the ordinary. In fact, I remember wondering how they could do such a boring job. Just waiting for hours on end for a single photograph. But then..."

Deklin closed his eyes then opened them again. A watery film covered his pupils.

"But then it all changed. Just after midnight the paparazzi obviously saw some commotion coming from the lobby of the hotel. I heard one of the photographers shout, 'She's coming out.' I knew Diana would insist on going out the front because she knew I would be there."

Deklin took moment to wipe his eyes. "Oh God, that was the first mistake. If we'd only insisted she go out the back!"

Conty came to Deklin's side and put a hand on his

shoulder. "Do you want to go on?"

Deklin nodded his head and wiped his eyes. He took a deep breath and continued. "The paparazzi immediately mounted their bikes, getting their cameras ready. One or two drove around the back. They must have thought it was a decoy. It wasn't. Diana came out the front of the hotel and hurried into the car with Dodi. Two security officers flanked them." Deklin paused again. "God, it all happened in a flash. The car raced off and they all followed."

Deklin looked at Stone, eyes welling with tears again. "I couldn't get my bike started. The others raced off but I was left there. After about two minutes, I got it started and raced after them. I rode out of the Place Vendome onto the street where they had gone, expecting them to be way ahead of me, but as I rode into the street, there they all were. A lorry had pulled out in front of them, blocking their path. They were shouting at a woman driving the truck. It was pandemonium. The princess's car had raced off." Deklin paused for a breath. "That's when I saw it. I knew something was wrong. The situation just didn't seem right. You know, when you know something's not right?"

Stone nodded, remembering what his friend Robert Sumpter had told him about his version of events that night. "Saw what? Then what happened?"

"A white Fiat," Deklin continued. "It came out of a little side alley. A gap at the side of the truck allowed me to see it. The paparazzi didn't seem to notice it, they were too busy shouting and arguing with the woman, but I did. And I knew, Jeramiah. My god, I knew it was wrong."

"Then what?" urged Stone.

"I turned the bike around. There was another way out of the square. I knew where Diana would be heading and if I took another exit front the square, I could hopefully catch up with them on the Courts La Reine. And I did catch up." Deklin put his hand to his mouth.

"Take your time, Deklin," said Conty softly.

Deklin nodded, "I'm all right," he said, and took a deep breath.

"I managed to catch up and saw the two cars ahead of me. At first, I thought I was wrong and had overreacted. The white Fiat seemed to stay back from Diana's car." Deklin squinted at the wall as he recounted the events in his mind's eye. "It was so strange. We raced down that underpass. I mean we were really going fast, but everything seemed to be happening in slow motion. All of a sudden, the Fiat sped up. I don't know how, but I knew something dreadful was going to happen. So I raised my camera and pressed the shutter. I kept my finger pressed on it, holding the camera out in front of me, hoping to get something. I could see it all, as though each click of the shutter slowed the world down. The Fiat moved along the side of the car and the passenger leaned out and pointed the gun at Diana's car. You see, the rear window of Diana's car was open. I didn't know if I got any of it on film. I just kept my finger on the shutter. The driver or someone else in the car must have been shot because the car suddenly screeched on its brakes and went into a slide. The car hit the pillar and started to roll. The Fiat clipped the Mercedes as it passed."

Stone put his hands up to his face. "Jesus Christ!"

Deklin rubbed his eyes. "I managed to avoid the car and saw the paparazzi coming around the bend in my rear mirror. I should have stopped, I know, but I went after the Fiat. I was so angry! Just wanted to *get* them." Deklin bowed his head. "I lost them though. By the time I arrived back at the scene, well, you know the rest... God, I should have stopped to help," he murmured.

Stone absorbed what he had just heard. He felt sick. Looking up at Conty he said, "But she couldn't have been shot. There was an investigation."

Conty got up from his chair. "Exactly! Which is why we haven't been to the police. Whoever is behind this is certainly more powerful than the authorities. Powerful enough to cover it up."

The room was silent for a moment.

"You said there's a link?" asked Stone. "A link between all those people in my column? What has *Diana* got to do with all of them?"

"Because of the speculation that she was going to marry Dodi," Conty surmised. "He's a Muslim. If whoever killed her is motivated through racial hatred, then it all makes sense. She was a threat to the establishment. If not that, then it was because her popularity threatened the monarchy; overshadowed it. She was critical of it. Whoever had you go after all of those people in your column and whoever went after her are the same people. I'm sure of it, Jeramiah."

"Do you think there's a connection to the Royal Family?"

Conty shook his head. "No, Jeramiah, I don't."

"Then who?"

Conty glanced at Deklin then stared down at Stone. "The day Diana was coming to Paris; Deklin told you he took hundreds of photographs. He photographed people coming in and out of the hotel and in and around where Diana would go that evening. We studied all them. Until we found this..."

Conty reached into the manila envelope and produced another photograph. "I think you should look at it." He handed it to Stone.

Stone took the photograph carefully, not sure what to make of it. The picture seemed harmless enough – just four people sitting around a table outside what seemed like a bistro. He inspected the faces of the people sitting around the table. There he was!

"Becker?" he said, looking up at Conty.

Conty nodded. "Marcus Becker. *Now* is it becoming clearer? Marcus Becker in Paris. The day before the princess died."

Stone looked at the photograph again. Becker leaned across a table talking to the three other people around him. One of the people was a woman. Stone squinted at the black and white image more closely. He couldn't make out the faces of the other two men, but Becker and the woman were clearly visible.

"I'm sure I know her," he said almost to himself.

"Who is she?" asked Conty.

"I don't know," replied Stone, "but I know I've seen her somewhere be..." He paused. "Of course, that's it. She was one of the gas people."

"What do you mean?" quizzed Conty.

Stone looked up. "She and another man came to my house just before I came here. She was from the gas company. They said I had a leak."

Conty glanced at Deklin.

Stone stared blankly at them both.

"She was also the driver of the truck that pulled out in front of us that night," said Deklin.

Stone felt the blood drain form his face. "You're saying *Becker's* involved in all this?"

Conty nodded. "Now you're getting it. And who is the editor in charge of giving you all these leads?" he went on, holding Stone's articles in front of him again.

Stone just stared. "Oh my god, this can't be true."

"I'm afraid it is true," replied Conty.

"Why were these people in my house?" Stone said.

Conty sighed. "They must have known you were onto them."

Stone felt his mouth go dry. "Why didn't you just tell me this from the start?" he asked, getting to his feet. "Why not tell me when I got here?" Stone thought for a moment. "And why did you send me the photographs in the first place?" Then it dawned on him. "Oh, I get it. You wanted to know what I'd do. You wanted to know if I was involved in all this?"

Conty rolled his eyes. "Without fear of correcting your cynicism, we did need to know what you would do, yes, but we knew you weren't involved. I chose to send the photographs to you because you're a fine journalist, Jeramiah. One that was married to a friend of mine and one I knew I *could* trust."

Stone frowned. "But you sent me the damn note, so why the hell didn't you meet me?"

"Well, contrary to your rather angry display at thinking no one met you, someone did. A tramp by the name of Deklin."

Stone flashed round to Deklin. "You? The tramp?"

Stone remembered how he'd thought the tramp's face was covered in a thick, black layer of dirt.

"We had to see who would follow you to the meeting," Conty continued. "We had to know what interest the photographs generated."

"And was I followed?"

"You were. As yet, we don't know who by. A large man came to the warehouse just after you. He got the same angry reaction from Deklin as you did, then left."

"Jesus, so you put me in danger? They came to my home!"

"You would've been in no danger," corrected Conty, "if you had followed my instructions on the note. You were told not to tell anyone about the photographs. However, for you to be followed would indicate you did what I explicitly asked you not to. Deklin was to meet you, but because of the fact that you *did* show the photographs to someone else and were followed, meant we were forced to change plans and bring you here."

"Rachel," said Stone suddenly.

Conty frowned. "Who's Rachel?"

"She's my assistant at The Informer."

"You showed *her* the photographs?" asked Conty.

Stone nodded. "I left them with her… But she can't have anything to do with all this."

"You're sure of that?" Conty asked.

"Of course I'm sure."

"Does she have anything to do with Becker?"

"Well, no. No, I don't think so. I mean he's the editor. She has to work with him."

"But could she have showed the photographs to him?" pressed Conty.

"Maybe. But I told her not to."

"Did you show the photographs to anyone else or tell anyone else about them?" asked Conty urgently

"No, no one," replied Stone.

"Then the only way Becker found out you had a meeting or that you had the photographs is because this Rachel told him. If she really does have nothing to do with all this and innocently told Becker, then I believe she's in a great deal of danger, Jeramiah."

That comment reminded Stone of the missed call he had received from Rachel that morning.

"Jesus, my phone," he said, jumping up. "She phoned me this morning!" Stone raced out the room.

Conty and Deklin then ran after him, following him across the beach to his apartment. Inside, they saw him with a mobile phone to his ear.

"Sssh," he said, holding his hand up. "I'm checking the message she left."

After a moment, Stone looked at them both, face pale.

"What is it, Jeramiah?" asked Conty.

"She said that I must check my e-mail. She sounded frightened, told me that I must get safe. She said that I'm in great danger. That I can't go to the police."

All three men stood staring at each other. Then they looked at the laptop on the table.

"Do as she says," said Conty.

Stone nodded dumbly, and then went to the laptop. Deklin and Conty stood behind him as he turned it on. He went online; after entering his password, he was taken to his inbox.

There were several e-mails from but only one sent by Rachel. It was from her personal e-mail. Stone hit the mailbox icon.

Rachel's message blinked opened up.

Stoney,

I haven't got much time so I'm going to be brief. Becker is dead. They killed him. They're blaming me, but you know I didn't do it. They are looking for me and they will try to get to you too because of what you know. I've attached the file Becker kept on them.

Get safe! Do not go to the police, they have people working for them. Use this file, Stoney. Bring them down! I don't know what you can do but you must get somewhere safe. When I find somewhere to stay, I'll contact you.

This is my entire fault. I'm so sorry, Stoney. I told Becker about the photographs. Please forgive me. Please get safe!

R.

Below the message was an icon indicating a file attachment. Stone dragged the mouse pointer to it and clicked on it. Becker's file came up on the screen. All three of them started to read.

Although there was an endless amount of detailed information that he had compiled, Becker gave an overview of the secret society of which he was a member.

The Family, as its members knew the organisation affectionately, was born in the Thatcher years of government. Initially, it was just a small lunch club where Edward Murren and his friends, Captain Andrew Haines and Major Robin Rothmead, would meet once a month at Murren's mansion for good food, expensive wine, and patriotic deliberations on the state of the country they all held so dear. However, over time, it grew into a formidable society of men with unrivalled power and influence, in which they could exercise their grievances.

The glue bonding every member was the apparent disintegration of their country's identity and the endless tide of foreign invaders that did nothing more than exploit it. They were obsessively patriotic, disillusioned with the government of the day, finding it weak and liberal on home policy and guilty for the loss of British identity. More and more asylum seekers were being let into the country, meaning jobs, houses, and businesses were being threatened by what they considered foreign abuse of their land. At first it was just table talk, but Edward Murren saw an opportunity to actually do something about it.

The opportunity came in the 1979 general election. Margaret Thatcher was in the running for the political throne and seemed a more appropriate leader for the country they all served. As owner of the largest selling daily newspaper in the country, Murren put the wheels in motion and sought to make sure she was elected. The massive amount of aggressive support The Informer had given Thatcher's campaign paid off. On May fourth, she was elected and 'Thatcherism' was born. The new government, with its policy to adopt free economics, strong defence and, above all, nationalism, was a perfect backdrop for Murren's future plans.

The election of Thatcher made Murren and his followers appreciate the power they could wield in the country and, ultimately, bring about their warped aspirations for the nation. Murren became the powerhead. His media empire would be the weapon used to deliver the organisation's increasingly aggressive assault on all things foreign. They even decided to give themselves a name to represent their cause and so, The Family was born.

Thatcher's government was one that would bring radical change to Britain. With a seemingly invincible government and in indestructible Prime Minister, the tide turned and gathered momentum. With Murren's right-wing tabloid supporting a far right government, it caused resentment, especially among ethnic communities increasingly feeling isolated in a country they once called their own. Because of this, ethnic unrest was inevitable which suited Murren and his colleagues perfectly. Public opinion bought the propaganda Murren made sure got out – "The foreigners are the troublemakers. Let's put the Great back into Britain!"

Murren and his colleagues became increasingly powerful during the eighties under Thatcher's dark blue government. With their combined influence, The Family sought to pursue a wholly nationalistic alliance. Murren's wealth funded right-wing political organisations and militant socialist groups; indeed any group with a right-wing voice and a desire to cause disruption.

Allied to this, The Family secretly funded nationalist parties in Northern Ireland to help maintain sovereignty. In short, The Family looked after their own. Murren's media was the catalyst for making sure the country was intolerant of everything being taken by foreigners, unwittingly supported by the government he helped put in power.

Murren made it his business to have contacts everywhere. He even had lists of passport applications, especially wealthy businessmen applying for citizenship. These lists were very important to the organisation as they gave The Family sensitive information that it had to know in order to discredit them. Slowly but surely, The Family's pockets bulged from the people they had in them.

Throughout their networking, Murren and his colleagues made it their business to increase the capacity of the organisation by recruiting other members. Jeremy Luflin, Simon Losely, Ian Bailey, and Lewis Wright Smith came on board; powerful men with influence and one thing in common – love for their country.

Luflin worked as a Senior Immigration Officer at the Home Office. His influence in that position was essential in providing sensitive information about passport applications.

Ian Bailey was senior commander of the Metropolitan Police. Because of Bailey's position, The Family could embark on more daring criminal activities and, more importantly, get away with them.

Marcus Becker had been editor of The Informer through most of the Thatcher years and had strong right-wing views of his own. If Murren was going to successfully conduct his patriotic campaign through his media, it would be important to have an editor on his side. Initially Becker was invited to the lunch clubs and slowly exposed to its radical ideas.

Becker had been easier than they thought. He had his own ideas of things that could be done to make sure foreign influence was kept at bay. With Becker on board, The Family was now complete. Eight senior members with combined power and influence – a formidable force – formed the base of The Family.

By the time the 'New Labour' administration had come to power, The Family had a highly organised infrastructure with many operatives working for them. These members were almost always recruited from the forces or radical groups that The Family secretly funded. There were even some operatives who were retired police officers, brought in by

Commander Ian Bailey. The Family was now a powerful network serving to maintain British sovereignty at all costs. They were single and bloody-minded in this pursuit and would stop at nothing, now that they had the means and power to do so. In fact, The Family was now, quite literally, getting away with murder.

Princess Diana had just started a serious relationship with Dodi Fayed. The media even speculated on marriage. The Family took the speculation very seriously, seeing it as a potential catastrophe for the monarchy that could not be tolerated. Diana's popularity already cast a shadow over the monarchy and was potentially a huge embarrassment to the Queen who, above all else, Murren served passionately. Murren tried everything through the use of his paper to undermine the relationship. He sanctioned the aggressive and unrelenting media invasion in an attempt to bring ridicule to her and the ambiguous role she'd made for herself. His strategy didn't work. The more Murren tried to ostracise her from the public, the more they rallied around her. More radical measures would have to be taken.

The only remaining course of action for The Family was assassination. The organisation initially thought the idea to be madness. But Murren was determined and, after a Churchill-like speech at a half-yearly meeting, he convinced the rest of the members it was for the good of the country and could not be avoided. The ball was set in motion.

Murren knew only the most loyal of operatives needed for the job would be willing to carry out the assassination of one of the most famous and well-loved women in the world. Murren put his feelers out to the more radical of the fascist organisations he funded. Most he found to be too undisciplined to be reliable, but eventually, he came across an organisation known as the National Liberation Alliance.

The NLA was a small outfit with few members but a disciplined and well-managed fundamental group. The founding members of the NLA were a married couple called Nathan and Carla Green and their friend, Samuel Parker. In 1986, Nathan and Carla Green served eight years each for the attempted murder of a wealthy Asian businessman.

Murren found them to be exactly what The Family needed and capitalised on their racial hatred. Becker, however, made it clear in his file that he never liked the fact that Murren recruited them. In Becker's view, they were both unstable, liking the thrill of action as opposed to having any real dedication to the overall cause.

Despite Becker's objections and with the promise of great wealth and power, the founding members of the NLA were recruited and used in what the senior members always referred to thereafter as 'The Paris job'. Becker, because of his connections with the media, was asked to co-ordinate the assassination and take care of the logistical element of the job. Since Becker knew where Princess Diana would be, he was Murren's choice to run the show. The mission had been a success. However, it was not without complications.

Becker's file went into detail about how the assassination of the princess was originally meant to take place. Diana was to be followed from the Ritz in Paris to Fayed's Paris home, where she would be taken out. This did not happen. Nathan Green took matters in his own hands.

Becker gave details of the event in icy detail.

Samuel Parker drove the Fiat specifically bought for the assassination. As Green and Parker pursued the Mercedes from the Place Vendome, the story goes that Nathan saw that the rear window of the Mercedes was wound down. Immediately he asked Parker to speed up until he was alongside of Diana's car. Becker went on to say that the driver of the Mercedes suddenly saw Nathan aiming a gun and instinctively braked. Due to the weight of the bullet-proof vehicle, the speed it was travelling and the sudden use of the brakes, the driver lost control. The car skidded, hit the pillar of the underpass and turned over.

The accident turned out better than all expectations. Because Nathan didn't have to actually fire a shot, the whole event was put down to a tragic mistake. Becker noted his anger at the reaction of Murren towards this foolhardy action and was dumbfounded at the amount of praise Nathan had received from his boss.

Following the job, the car was taken to a breaker's yard near Versailles and crushed, never to be found. Samuel Parker was executed after it was found out that he was trying to flee the country.

Details of the attempted assassination of the princess was the last entry in Becker's file.

The file, in its entirety, was unbelievably detailed. There were lists of every operative who was a member of The Family, their addresses, and facts about the criminal association they had with the organisation. There were names of people who had been paid off and specific stocks owned, including ones that had been manipulated. There were particulars of classified information leaked from specified sources, fund managers that had acted for Murren and bank accounts of transactions from fraudulent companies. There were names of politicians that had been on the payroll, illegitimate companies set up to launder money, details of donations used to fund illegal and unscrupulous racist groups as well as names and addresses of councillors paid off for information concerning planning permission. Pages of facts about university placements that The Family had paid to have made accessible for white students. The list went on, evidence endless and truly damning. Becker had been meticulous in updating the file as if it were a diary.

Conty had been right about Stone's unwitting involvement. Every article he had written or followed up on since joining The Informer had been set up by Becker and the organisation. Most were lies. Prostitutes had been planted as well as cocaine, if necessary. Auditors and accountant firms funded by The Family had been used to make sure companies owned by overseas investors were set up to look fraudulent. In short, The Family was responsible for over a decade of criminal activity, all of which was meticulously catalogued.

Stone sat back and just stared at the screen. The pit of his stomach ached, his body trembling. "So that's how they did it," he said eventually. "That's why there was no investigation. They never even fired a shot. They got away with it."

Conty had to sit down. "No, they haven't," he managed. "Not now you've got this."

"They couldn't have killed Becker," said Stone. "This just can't be." He looked back at the file. "Edward Murren! I just can't believe it. I just can't." Stone turned to face Conty. "Becker can't be dead."

"Well, we'll soon find out," said Conty. He went to the television set and turned it on, flipping through the channels until he came to Sky News. "Must be something on the news."

All of them waited.

At first nothing was said. The newsreader reported a rail crash in northern Cyprus where thirty people had been killed after the train had derailed. He then went to a reviewed the day's football fixtures. Then he summarised the headlines.

They didn't have to wait long for the newscaster to tell them the latest concerning the death of The Informer's editor, Marcus Becker, murdered in the early hours of yesterday morning at a hotel near Heathrow. A picture of his suspected killer came up in the corner of the screen. The newscaster informed the world Rachel Martin was still at large.

Stone stared at Rachel's face. "Jesus Christ!"

"That's your friend?" asked Conty, putting a hand on Stone's shoulder.

Stone nodded. "Yeah. It's true, they've set her up."

"We have to think what to do," began Conty, turning the sound down on the TV. "We need to put our heads together and decide what to do next."

"I'll fix us a drink," said Deklin. "I think we need one."

As Deklin started to make his way to the bar, the door of Stone's apartment came flying open, smashing into the wall. They all jumped at the sudden crash, and then stared in horror at the doorway.

A large man held Jennifer in front of him. He was formidable, at least six foot five, his head shaved, dressed in a black pair of combat trousers and a black T-shirt clinging to his muscular frame. The giant held a gun to the side of Jennifer's head. Tears were streaming down her face. Slowly he moved her inside, not taking his eyes off the rest of them.

"Everyone back up to the end of the room," Kirns ordered. "Now!"

"Do as he says," cried Jennifer.

The others did as they were told.

"Don't hurt her," said Conty, holding his arms out as if to calm the man.

"Just do as I say!" Kirns demanded. "Back the fuck up!"

As soon as he thought the men were far enough back, Kirns pushed Jennifer towards them.

Stone took her into his arms. "Jesus, I know you," he said. "You're the guy that was sick on the plane!"

"Yeah, the one that followed you to Berrick Street," said Deklin.

Deklin's remark surprised Kirns. "Listen to me carefully," he said, addressing Conty directly. "You are Abraham Conty?"

Conty was surprisingly calm. "I am. And you are?"

"Don't worry who I am," said Kirns. "I'm going to ask you some questions and if you don't tell me the truth, I will kill you. Do you understand me, Abraham Conty?"

"I do."

Jennifer held Stone tighter.

"It's all right," said Conty. "We're going to get out of this. It's all right, I promise."

"I suggest you listen to your husband, Missus Conty," said Kirns. "It will save your life." He then turned his attention back to Conty. "Now, Abraham Conty. Remember, I want the truth."

Conty was unfazed by the intruder. The effect seemed to work on the others. He nodded.

"How many security guards are on the island?"

"Only two. They're on the east coast, at least an hour from here."

"Good," Kirns replied. "There are no others?"

"None, I promise."

"Do you have any panic alarms on the island? Any way you can alert the authorities?"

"No."

"Good. Is there anyone else on the island except the people present in this room?" Conty hesitated. "There's a maid and a gardener."

Kirns noticed the hesitation "Where are they?"

"The maid is in the villa next door," replied Conty, nodding to his right. "The gardener is fishing around the west of the island. It's his day off."

"Good for him. No one else?"

"No."

Kirns looked at them each in turn. He stared hard at Stone.

"What do you want?" asked Conty.

Kirns kept his eyes on Stone. "I've come for him," he replied, gesturing to Stone.

Conty stepped forward. "The Family sent you?"

Kirns eyes widened. "How do you know about them?"

"Well it's true, isn't it?" asked Conty "That's who you work for, The Family? Isn't that what you call yourselves? Who sent you? Edward Murren?"

Kirns was visibly shocked. "I'll ask you one more time," he said, aiming his gun at Conty. "How do you know about that information?"

"We know all about you," Conty came back angrily. "What you've done. What you are."

Kirns was losing patience. He pulled back the hammer on the pistol.

"Was it you in Paris?" Conty continued, defiantly. "I mean we know you didn't actually have to fire a shot. But it's you in that car, right?"

"How do you know about Paris?" asked Kirns. He felt awkward. He felt the beginning of a dull ache in his skull.

"Come here," he said to Stone.

Stone let go of Jennifer walked tentatively towards him. Kirns's face contorted with rage. Without warning, he grabbed Stone by the scruff and threw him down into the armchair.

"Don't you hurt him!" screamed Jennifer. "Leave him alone!"

"Start talking," ordered Kirns, and pressed the pistol painfully against Stone's temple. "How do you know all this?"

"Because I sent him the photographs," said Conty, coming forward. "That's why you're here? To get Stone because he had the photographs of you taking a shot at the princess? That's why The Family wants him dead, isn't it?" Conty moved nearer. "Well you're going to have to kill us all because we all know who you are now."

Kirns was flustered and confused. The ache in his head worsened. He felt smothered, bombarded by information these people shouldn't know.

"This is the last time I ask," he said, pressing the muzzle of the gun harder into Stone's temple. "Explain yourself!"

Conty held his hand out. "Okay, okay… I was a friend of Diana's. She was sent a warning that an attempt might be made on her life. This man," he pointed to Deklin, "followed the princess's car. He took the photographs. There you have it. Now, suppose you tell us who you are? In fact, let me guess? You're, Nathan, right?"

Kirns eyes widened. "Keep talking," he demanded.

"I sent the photographs to Stone. I brought him here to get him safe from the people responsible. I wanted him to start an investigation into her murder."

"How do you know about The Family?" he shouted. "How do you know all this?"

"We've got a file," said Stone painfully. Kirns pressed the muzzle harder still into his temple. "Rachel Martin sent it to me."

"What file?" Kirns shouted.

"Stop it, you're hurting him!" Jennifer screamed at him.

"What file?" winced Kirns, trying to ignore the pain spreading over the top of his head.

"From Marcus Becker," said Stone. "A file Becker kept on you all."

Kirns knew of the file, but couldn't understand how Stone had gotten it. His head swam with pain. "How did you get it?" he managed.

"She sent it by e-mail," replied Stone. "She got the file from Becker after you killed him and sent it to me. She's on the run. You must know this for God's sake. You set her up."

Kirns started to shake. He couldn't have heard what he just did and stared wildly at Stone as if any second he would push the muzzle of the gun right through the side of his head.

"What are you saying?" he screamed. "What are you telling me?"

"There, have a look for yourself!" shouted Stone,

the pain in his temple almost unbearable. "The laptop!"

Kirns took the gun away and pushed Stone back into the chair. He went to the laptop and turned it around. The rest watched his face contort as he read.

"You're lying," said Kirns, turning away.

Conty watched Kirns intently. Something was wrong. He quickly grabbed the remote and turned up the sound on the television. The timing was perfect. The newscaster was again giving an update on the Marcus Becker murder.

Kirns stared in disbelief, watching as a picture of his brother flashed up on the screen. Then Rachel Martin. Then the crime screen. The story switched to a picture of Commander Ian Bailey of the Metropolitan Police, who was investigating Marcus Becker's death. Finally, a picture of Edward Murren came on the screen. The newscaster read a written statement from Murren of how shocked and sorry he was over his editor's death and how his thoughts were with Becker's family.

This was too much. Kirns staggered back, falling against the table. The throbbing in his head had taken on a ferocious urgency and he winced as the scalding pain engulfed the top of his skull.

He clutched at his head and stared at the image of Murren on the screen. "No!"

Kirns's reaction stunned the others. He grabbed a chair from the dining table and threw it at the television. Glass shattered, spraying the room. The pain in his head reached its violent crescendo, sending the world into darkness. Kirns staggered back, wailing in agony as he did so.

As Kirns reeled back, Deklin went for it, diving at Kirns. Both men crashed to the ground. Deklin drew his fist back to punch him.

He was about to deliver the blow when Conty took hold of his arm. "Stop it!"

Deklin looked down to see Kirns out cold.

Jennifer went to Stone. She helped him up and inspected the side of his temple. Stone winced as she touched the soreness. "Are you okay?" she asked.

Stone nodded. "I'll live."

"What's going on, Jeramiah?" she asked. "What's this file you've all been talking about?"

"You'd better see for yourself." Stone motioned to the laptop.

Jennifer got up and started to read it.

"Get some rope," said Conty. "Quickly, Dek."

Deklin did as he was told while Conty gathered up Kirns's pistol.

"What happened?" asked Stone.

Conty shook his head. "I don't know."

"I can't believe this is all happening," said Stone. "This is a fuckin' nightmare."

"Well it *is* happening, Jeramiah," Conty assured him.

"Why do you think he reacted that way?"

"I don't know. But it has something to do with Becker. It was clear he had no idea he was dead, that's for sure."

"We'd better call the police," said Jennifer, as she finished reading Becker's file. "And we'd better do it right now."

Deklin came back into the room with rope. He handed to Conty.

"Give me a hand here, Dek."

The three men managed to get Kirns to the sofa and they tied his hands and feet. When they felt he was secured, they all looked down at their newly acquired prisoner.

"What now?" asked Deklin, giving voice to their mutual thoughts.

"We call the police," said Jennifer, again.

"Not yet," said Conty, and searched Kirns's rucksack. All he found was a change of clothes and some fruit. Conty checked Kirns's pockets. In one, there were some notes and a handful of loose change. In his back pocket, Conty discovered his passport.

"John Kirns," he said, reading the name out loud. "Dek, check the list of names on the file. See who he is?"

Deklin scanned the file. "It's not on there," he said, after a moment.

"So he's using another name," said Jennifer. "What does it matter? We have to go to the police."

"I want to see what he's got to say for himself first," replied Conty. "Deklin get some water, would you?"

Deklin did as asked and came back with a large jug

of cold water. Conty emptied the contents over Kirns. Almost immediately Kirns began to come around. He tried to focus on the world around him, but his vision was still blurry. His head still hurt but the intense pain had subsided.

Patiently, they waited for Kirns to fully regain consciousness. When he did, he stared up at the four faces. Then he remembered – his brother was dead.

Conty knelt by his side and looked into his eyes. "What's wrong with you?" he asked.

Kirns stared back at him.

"Are you ill?"

Still groggy, Kirns could only nod. "What are you going to do with me?" he asked.

"What made you react the way you did?" asked Conty, ignoring the question.

Kirns closed his eyes.

"You didn't know about Becker's death, did you?" asked Conty.

Conty had a thought. "Is your real name John Kirns?" he asked, holding up his passport. "Or is it really Nathan Green?"

Kirns grimaced. "It's Kirns. John Kirns."

"You're lying. There's no John Kirns mentioned on the file."

Kirns stared at the people around him. He didn't see much point in keeping quiet. Besides, these people were no longer the enemy. "My name wouldn't be in the file."

"Why would Marcus Becker omit your name from the list?" asked Conty.

"To protect me," replied Kirns, solemnly.

"Why?" asked Conty.

"Because... Because I'm his brother."

Conty frowned.

"Why are you even talking to him, Abraham?" asked Jennifer. "He's a murderer! He killed Diana!"

"I didn't," Kirns spat angrily, and immediately regretted it. His head thumped with pain.

"And you expect us to believe anything you say?" Jennifer shouted back. "The file says it all, you bastard. You're evil!"

"I tried to warn her," said Kirns, painfully.

"So it was you?" asked Conty. "You sent the letter warning her?"

Kirns nodded. "I tried to stop it."

Jennifer came forward, her face reddening. "But you didn't, did you?"

"You don't understand," said Kirns. "You don't know who you're dealing with."

"Why did your brother keep a file?" asked Conty.

Kirns sighed. "So he could use it against them if they ever turned on him. That way he had something on them. A way out."

"I see," said Conty. "And just what is it do you do for them, John? I don't believe you're a killer. So what *do* you do for The Family?"

Kirns sat up. "I haven't done any work for them for ages. I used to do surveillance work. Protection, that kind of thing." He looked up at Jennifer. "I don't do any killing."

"But you were going to," offered Conty. "That's why you're here, isn't it?"

"To protect my brother."

"From what?"

"My brother said Stone came to him with some photographs. He needed my help. If Stone started snooping around, then the organisation would be found out. I don't give a damn about the organisation, I never agreed with the Paris job, but I had to protect Marcus."

"Where is Rachel?" asked Stone.

Kirns shook his head. "I don't know. I don't even know who she is. Marcus never told me about her."

"But they've set her up," said Stone. "She didn't kill your brother, you know that. I've got the evidence. I've got to get hold of her." He moved toward the phone.

"I wouldn't do that if I were you," Kirns advised.

Stone stopped dialling. "Why the hell not?"

"If you try to contact her, they'll know you're alive and I've failed my mission. They'll send others. They'll keep sending others until they do get you; until you're dead. Believe it!"

"Why are you telling me this?"

"Because you've got the information to bring them down. If you're dead, my brother's file will do you no good. It will be for nothing. There is another way."

"Why the hell should I trust you?"

The whole time they'd been talking, Kirns had been working the rope on his hands. His training had given him much knowledge and proficiency at getting out of confinement and the rope around his wrists was crudely tied. Kirns gave a final tug and the rope fell away. He started to rub his wrists.

Deklin raised the pistol. "Stay where you are!" he shouted.

Kirns ignored the order, working on the rope around his ankles. Deklin came forward. "I said, stay where you are."

"I suggest you don't point that thing at me unless you intend to use it," Kirns recommended without looking him. He stood up.

Kirns raised his hand to Deklin. "Don't be silly," he said calmly. "I don't want to hurt you."

Deklin stopped and contemplated the warning.

Conty took hold of Deklin's arm. "Don't, Dek."

"How do I get off this island?"

"What are you going to do?" asked Conty.

Kirns looked at him. "You're safe," he said. "I won't hurt any of you. Just tell me how I can get back to the mainland. What transport have you got?"

"You're going after them, aren't you?" asked Conty.

Kirns didn't reply.

"Wait a minute," said Stone. "What about Rachel?"

"She's dead," snapped Kirns. "Now I suggest you play the same. You have the file. Use it!"

"I have to get her," said Stone, walking up to him. "You have to tell me where she is."

"And just what are going to do?" asked Kirns, facing him. "You don't know who you're dealing with. These people are killers. Even if she were alive, you can't help her now."

"Damn you," said Stone. "Take me with you!"

Kirns almost laughed. "Forget it."

"If they have her, where will she be?"

"Could be anywhere," replied Kirns. He then gestured for Deklin to hand the gun back to him. Deklin turned it over. "How do I get off this island?"

"I can get you off the island," said Conty, "but how far do you think you'd get with that?" He said, gesturing to the gun In Kirns's hand.

Kirns knew Conty had a point. He could dump the gun; the authorities would be monitoring the airport. "I'll take my chances," he said after a moment.

"If someone's life is in danger we have to help them, John," said Conty.

Kirns stared at Conty. "It's not my problem, I'm sorry."

"I can help you," suggested Conty.

"How?"

"I have my own plane. I could get you out of the country."

Kirns studied Conty.

"But Jeramiah goes with you."

"No," said Jennifer. "This is absurd. Just go to the police, Abraham, please." She went to Stone. "You can't do this. This is absurd."

"I have to, Jennifer," Stone replied. "I have to help her."

"She's right," said Kirns. "Just go to the police."

"No," replied Stone adamantly. "You know as well as I do I can't. Jesus, they have police working for them. No, I'm going with you."

"What do you think this is?" snapped Kirns. "She'll be dead, I know these people. They're professional. They clean up after themselves. You can't do anything now. Just use the file."

"But she might be alive. And as long as there's a chance, I want to take it. Take me with you. Take me to where she might be. That's all I ask. I'll use the file but need to get back."

Kirns stared at Stone incredulously. "You have no idea what you're up against. Listen to me. You've got a chance. They will think you're dead. Give yourself a break and get that file to someone you trust."

"Like you, I'll take my chances," said Stone.

"What happens if they find out you're alive? They'll get you and then what will you do? They'll carry on just like before. My brother's file will have been a waste of time."

"He's right, Jeramiah," said Jennifer. "Please listen to him."

"I'll e-mail the file to someone I can trust first. If

anything happens to me, then they can still be brought down. Now, I want this chance."

Kirns studied Stone for as moment then turned to Conty. "Why do you want to help me?"

"I don't. I want you to help me. I believe what you have told me. I don't believe you had anything to do with what happened in Paris. I don't even believe you wanted to come here. Given all that, maybe you could put your talents to good use and clean some of this ghastly mess up. Which I believe would be to our mutual satisfaction, would it not?"

Kirns eyed Conty suspiciously. He wasn't used to this much understanding from a man that knew nothing about him. "What can you do for me?"

"I can get you to the airport by Hele-Taxi. Then I can have my plane take you back to England. Straight through, no customs, no police. But like I said, Jeramiah goes with you."

Jennifer raised her arms up in disbelief. "Are you *trying* to get him killed?"

Conty took Jennifer by the shoulders. "Of course not. He'll be all right. I know what I'm doing. You have to trust me, Jennifer. You have to believe in me like never before."

"How do I know you won't have police waiting for me?" asked Kirns.

Conty turned to Kirns. "You don't. But I don't think you have anything to lose, do you, John?"

Kirns thought for a moment then gave Conty a wry smile. "Very well," he said, turning to Stone. "But I warn you, stay out of my way. You do as I say.

When I've taken you to where she might be held, that's it. I have my own agenda after that, and you certainly don't want to be anywhere near me when that starts. You understand me?"

Stone nodded.

"This is ridiculous!" said Jennifer, and stormed out of the apartment.

"I'll start making the arrangements," said Conty, then left.

"Why did they do it?" asked Stone. "Why did they kill Marcus?"

The question pained Kirns. "Because that's what they do. When people get sloppy, they kill them."

"What made you ever get involved?"

Kirns ignored the question. He had tried to answer it too many times.

"When does it stop?" Stone went on. "When does the killing end?"

Kirns faced Stone. "You still don't get it, do you? It doesn't stop."

Conty came back into the room. "It's done," he said. "The chopper will be here in an hour."

"I need to use a phone," said Kirns.

"Use this one." Conty pointed to the phone by the drinks bar.

Kirns dialled the number that he knew off by heart. After several rings the phone was answered.

"Yes," came the reply.

"It's Kirns."

"About time. We've been wondering where you were."

"Give me Murren."

"Wait a moment."

Kirns waited, listening to the gentle clicks of the call being transferred to Murren's home. The Family always used this procedure when receiving confidential calls. Operatives were to phone a special number linked to a secure switchboard. There, the call could be transferred to any senior member they wished to speak with. The call could never be intercepted or traced.

"John, it's Edward," came the leader's voice. "Where are you?"

Kirns thought he might be angry on hearing Murren's voice but instead was steely cool. In his mind, he pictured what he was going to do with the man that sanctioned his brother's death. For the time being it was enough.

"I'm still in Spain. I'm on my way back."

"Everything go to plan?"

"It's done."

"How?"

"The subject drowned."

"Excellent. Listen, John. I don't know how to tell you this. I've got some terrible news."

"What is it?" asked Kirns.

"We better wait until you come back."

"What is it?" asked Kirns again, wanting to hear it

from Murren's own lips, wanting to hear him lie.

"It's your brother, John. He's been murdered."

Kirns squeezed the receiver. The hate he felt for the man on the other end of the telephone was almost uncontrollable. Unintentionally, the inadvertent pause Kirns left was surprisingly effective.

"John? John, are you there?"

"Who?"

"It was one of his news team, a Rachel Martin. Do you know her?"

"No," replied Kirns.

"Apparently they were lovers. They were running away together. They must have argued. I think it was over money. She shot him, John. God, I'm so sorry. I wanted to tell you before you saw it on the news. I was so mad, John. I've had the whole organisation looking for her. We've got her now though. We've held her for you. You can have her, John. My gift."

As Kirns listened to Murren he closed his eyes and squeezed the receiver tighter.

"John, are you there? I'm so very sorry, John. I know how much you loved each other. Come home. The Family will take care of you now."

"When did this happen?"

"Yesterday morning," Murren went on, his voice trembling.

"Where is he? Where's Marcus?"

"He's at the morgue, John. I'll take you to see him myself. I'm so sorry. We couldn't get hold of you. We were waiting for your call."

"I'm on my way," said Kirns. "Where do we meet?"

"I can have you picked up at the airport, John."

"It's all right," replied Kirns. "I can be there this afternoon. I'll meet you at my brother's. You keep that woman for me."

"Yes of course, John, whatever you say. I'll be there. You'll have your revenge, I promise. I'll bring her to you. I'm so sorry, John. God, I loved him like a brother, you know that."

"I know you did, Edward," Kirns replied, and put the receiver down.

He stared down at the telephone, mind racing with hatred. Tears welled in his eyes.

"So she's alive?" asked Stone.

Kirns turned to face him. "Of course she isn't."

"But I heard you," said Stone. "You said for them to keep her for you."

Kirns sighed. "What the fuck do you think is going on here?"

"If they're trying to frame Rachel, then they'll eventually give her to the police."

"They *are* the police!" shouted Kirns angrily. He was still enraged by Murren's play-acting. "If they have her, then do you honestly think they'll let her go? She'll turn up dead. They'll make it look like suicide. She kills Marcus then she ends up killing herself. I know how they work. I told you, forget about the damn girl."

"No, I won't," Stone countered firmly.

"So be it," Kirns replied. "I'll take you to where she could be held, and then that's it. You're on your own from there." He glared at the phone and stormed out of Stone's apartment.

For a moment there was an uncomfortable silence. "You'd better get your things together, Jeramiah," said Conty. "The chopper will be here soon."

Stone nodded.

The first thing Stone did was save Becker's file to a floppy disk. He put the disk in his top pocket then packed the laptop away. He packed his holdall and looked around for anything he might've missed. As he came down the stairs, Jennifer stood in the doorway.

"Don't do this, Jeramiah," she said.

"I have to, Jennifer."

"Why do you have to? For God's sake, go to the police."

"I can't. You heard what Kirns said. You've read Becker's file."

"Then go to someone else. Abraham knows people you can go to. Important people. They'll help you."

"I know who I'll go to, but first I have to get Rachel."

"But you heard what Kirns said. She might not even be alive."

"I have to take that chance. Don't you understand? How can I just ignore her? I would never be able to live with myself knowing that I could have helped her."

"Why is she so important to you?"

"She's in trouble. I know her, Jennifer. I owe her. I got her into this mess in the first place. I have to help her." Stone paused. "And for the first time in a very long time, I want to do something for someone else for a change. I just want to do something good. Something right."

"And what if anything happens to you? What then? What about us, Jeramiah?"

Stone took Jennifer into his arms. "Nothing is going to happen to me, I promise." Stone held her tightly, hoping he could keep the promise.

SIXTEEN

As Stone came out of his apartment with Jennifer, the thumping sound of the helicopter could be heard in the distance.

"We'd better get going," said Conty. "We need to get to the landing pad in the north."

"Is Deklin coming?" asked Stone.

"No," replied Conty.

"I'll say goodbye then," said Stone, and headed for the villa. Deklin came out to greet him.

"Thank you for everything, Deklin."

Deklin shook Stone's hand. "You take care of yourself, Jeramiah. I'll be seeing you again."

Stone tried a smile, although in his heart of hearts he didn't share Deklin's confidence. "I'll hold you to that."

Before he went to the Jeep, Jennifer came to him. "I'm staying here too," she said. "I'm not very good at goodbyes."

Stone saw her sadness. "Don't worry," he said, taking her hand.

Jennifer barely held back the tears. "Now you listen to me. You take care. Don't do anything stupid."

Stone smiled. "I love—"

Jennifer put a finger to Stone's lips. "You tell me that when I see you again, you hear me?"

Stone took Jennifer's hand and kissed it. "Promise," he said, and then headed for the Jeep.

Conty and Kirns were already inside. As soon as Stone got in, Conty drove off. Stone watched out of the window, staring at Jennifer and wondering if he'd ever see her again.

An hour later, they were at the studio. The chopper had landed and was waiting for them, its blades gently turning. Conty immediately went inside to check on August.

He emerged after only a short time. "There'll be someone to meet you at the airport," he said to Stone. "They'll take you to the plane."

Kirns boarded the chopper.

"Is August all right?" asked Stone.

"He will be," said Conty. "His suffering is nearly over."

Stone stared at the great artist, overwhelmed with emotion. He knew Conty had had a profound effect on his life and at that moment contemplated whether he was doing the right thing.

Conty put both his hands on Stone's shoulders. "Everything is going to be all right, Jeramiah."

Stone's stared at Conty. "I'm not going to see you again, am I?"

"I want you to have something, Jeramiah," began Conty.

Stone stared at him.

"I have a painting I want you to have."

Stone shook his head. "I can't," he said.

"You will," said Conty adamantly. "It's one I've always wanted you to have. I'll send it to you. It will help." He paused. "It will help you… make the right choice."

Stone nodded.

"You'd better go," said Conty.

Stone stared at Conty, into blue eyes reflecting his sad self, and then the two men hugged. Stone held Conty as tightly as he had ever held anything in his life.

Conty then took Stone at arm's length in front of him. "You keep well, Jeramiah Stone," he said. His face glowed with the youth Stone remembered when he'd first seen him.

"And take good care of Jennifer for me." Conty grinned at him reassuringly. "Now, you'd better go."

Stone turned got into the chopper.

As it lifted off, Stone stared at Conty until he and the island were out of sight.

SEVENTEEN

As soon as the helicopter landed at Malaga airport, a smartly dressed airport representative from Iberian Airways met them both on the tarmac.

The representative led them to a car, and then drove them from the airport to the airfield. Both were then escorted through customs. The representative took their passports and personally checked them through. She then escorted them back to the car and onto Conty's awaiting Leer jet. A hostess waited by the steps and greeted them warmly. The pilot came back to see if they were comfortable and informed them that they would be taking off in fifteen minutes. The stewardess brought them drinks and a round each of cheese sandwiches with the crusts cut off. Stone found the hospitality absurd under the circumstances. He couldn't look at Kirns or at the reflection of himself in the window. He couldn't eat or drink and felt sick.

Kirns stared out of the window, going over in his

mind what he needed to do when he got to England.

Three hours later, they landed and were taken by a British Airways representative through customs. After that, the men were escorted outside where a chauffeured limousine waited for them. Driving away from the airport, Stone felt an overwhelming sense of danger. He put his hands together and interlocked his fingers to stop them shaking. *What the hell am I doing?* he thought.

As they drove down the terminal exit road, the driver asked where they would like to go.

Kirns squinted as he thought for a moment. "Head into the city," he told the driver. "And take the scenic route. Not the motorway."

The driver nodded obediently at Kirns through the rear view mirror.

After about an hour, and four miles from London, they came to a Happy Eater restaurant.

"Drop us off here," Kirns instructed.

The driver pulled into the car park and stopped the car.

"We won't be needing you anymore," he said, and got out. Stone was confused but did the same. The driver shrugged, but did as he was told. Kirns and Stone watched the limousine drive off.

Stone thought they might be stopping for food, but instead, Kirns led him into the car park, stopping by an old Ford Granada. Checking that no one was around, Kirns picked up a rock and smashed the small back window. He then put his hand inside and pulled up the lock. All the doors unlocked with a simultaneous clunk.

"Get in," Kirns ordered.

"We can't just steal it," said Stone, looking around to see if anyone had seen them.

Kirns shook his head. Stone tried his patience already. "Either you get in or you don't," he said. "Like I said, Stone, we do it my way or not at all."

"But we had a car. Why are we stealing one?"

"Because I have things to do first. Now get in!"

Stone reluctantly did as commanded.

Kirns went to work on the steering column, smashing the plastic ignition cover with his boot. He gathered up three wires and twisted them together. The car wheezed for a moment then fired up. Kirns slammed the car into gear and took off.

"Where are we going?" asked Stone.

"I need some things."

"Then where?"

"My brother's flat. They'll be waiting for me."

"Is it going to be dangerous?"

Kirns sighed.

"Why don't you just tell me where Rachel is? I mean, what if something happens to you? How will I reach her?"

"You won't," replied Kirns, effectively ending the conversation.

Forty minutes later they approached the outskirts of London. Kirns drove carefully, obeying the speed limits to avoid police attention.

Eventually he pulled up outside a small block of flats in Woolwich where he lived. Kirns knew no operatives would be waiting for him here as it was one place his brother had never divulged to the organisation.

"Wait here," he said, and ran into the apartment block.

Stone lit a cigarette, hand shaking as he held the lighter to the tip. He was scared. More scared than he had been in his whole life.

Kirns wasn't long and came out of the house with a large hold-all over his shoulder and carrying a black bag. He threw the bags in the back and then got in the front.

"What's all that?" asked Stone, looking at the ominous looking cargo.

Kirns said nothing. He started the car and drove off.

They drove for another half an hour until they came to a street with rows of expensive-looking apartments. Kirns stopped the car, reached into one of the bags, retrieved a pair of binoculars and then scanned the front of his brother's apartment building. Kirns then started the car up again and drove around to an adjacent street, along the back of the building. A hundred yards from Becker's flat, he brought the car to a stop and switched off the engine.

Kirns got out then sat in the back seat. Stone watched as he rested one of the bags on his lap and opened it. He gasped as Kirns took out pieces of a modern-looking automatic rifle.

"What the hell is that?" asked Stone, watching Kirns assemble the weapon.

"Heckler and Koch MP-five with silencer," replied Kirns casually.

"Jesus Christ! What are you going to do? You'll bring every police force in the country here."

"I said with silencer," Kirns reminded him. "This baby spits quieter than you do."

Stone's hands started to shake again. He was terrified. "Listen. What are you going to do? I mean, you're not..."

Kirns laugh cut him off. "You think I'm going to get a warm welcome in there? They're going to try and kill me."

"Then don't go in."

Kirns gave Stone a hopeless glance then continued working on the weapon. As soon as he had the automatic assembled, he got out and came around to the front of the car. Stone backed away as Kirns got in and sat next to him.

"Listen to me very carefully. People in there will try and kill me. I'm going to try and not let that happen, you understand?"

Stone nodded dumbly.

"You stay in the car. You don't get out. You understand that?"

Again, the dumb nod.

"If I'm not back in half an hour, you go. You get

somewhere safe, then contact someone trusted. And I mean *really* trusted."

"Okay," said Stone uneasily. For some strange reason, he was genuinely afraid for Kirns's safety. "Do you think Rachel's in there too?"

"No." Kirns sighed. "No, I don't. But if she's alive and they have her, I'll find out where she is."

"What about Murren?"

"I doubt he'll be here either," Kirns answered thoughtfully. "But wherever he is, his pets won't be far behind him."

"His pets?" frowned Stone.

Kirns didn't respond, instead he pulled the small semi-automatic's cocking lever back with a metallic snap. "Wait here." He got out of the car.

Kirns made his way to the back gate, waited a moment, then sprinted across his brother's back lawn towards the metal steps leading to the back door of the kitchen. Kirns felt surprisingly calm at this point. He had been scared before. Fleeing from the Iraqis, he'd been scared, at times even terrified, but not now. In fact, he was actually looking forward to getting the job done. For the first time in his life, he would have peace. Ordinarily, Kirns would worry about having an attack, especially in an environment such as he was now. But for some reason he thought an attack wouldn't happen.

As he was about to step on the first rung of the metal stairway leading up to the back of the flat, a man suddenly emerged. Kirns froze. He looked up to see the man light a cigarette. The man was armed, with a semi-automatic pistol tucked crudely in the back of his jeans.

Kirns waited patiently until the butt of the cigarette sailed over the railing and the man went back inside. Kirns slowly ascended the metal stairs. He came to the top and looked in through the kitchen window. The same man that had come outside was now sipping coffee. Kirns's appearance startled him.

Kirns smiled at him. The man came to the back door and opened it.

"I'm Kirns. You've been expecting me."

The man looked somewhat nervous. "Hang on a minute," he said.

Kirns waited.

"Carla," the operative shouted. "He's here!"

Kirns's heart raced at the mention of her name. One half of the psychotic duo. He just hoped the other half was here too.

Carla came through into the kitchen with a beaming smile on her face.

"John," she said, coming to shake his hand. "Good to see you."

Kirns grinned. She was good. "Hello, Carla," he said.

"John, I'd like you to meet Danny Blake." She gestured to the operative.

Kirns nodded at him. "Where's Murren?"

"He's on his way, John. Come in."

Kirns followed them both into the kitchen. As he

entered, he could smell fresh coffee.

"Better let Murren know John's here, Danny," said Carla. The operative nodded and left them in the kitchen.

"When did you get in?" asked Carla.

Kirns was impressed by her coolness. "Just now."

Carla frowned suspiciously. "We could have picked you up from the airport."

Kirns knew there would have been operatives at the airport anyway.

"Had some things to do first."

Carla nodded. "You want coffee?"

Kirns glanced at the fresh pot. "That would be good," he replied, finding Carla's niceties almost perverse.

Carla got a mug from the drainer. "I'm really sorry about your brother," she said, turning to face him. "We've got the bitch that did it though."

"Where is she?"

"Murren and Nathan are bringing her. She's all yours." She grinned.

"What happened?" asked Kirns.

Carla retrieved a pint of milk from the fridge. "Didn't Murren tell you?"

"He told me some," said Kirns. He wanted her to tell him; he wanted to hear Carla lie as well.

Carla stood the milk on the side. "Well, apparently Marcus and this Rachel Martin were lovers. We think they were running away somewhere together because they went to a hotel near Heathrow. They checked in real early in the morning. We don't know where they were heading. Well, apparently, the owner of the hotel heard them arguing, then a gunshot. We wouldn't have known who it was that shot him, if it weren't for the fact that she left her bag. She worked with Marcus and was the assistant to that piece of scum, Stone." She winked. "Nice job by the way. Anyway, Murren pulled out all the stops. You know one of the seniors, Ian Bailey?"

Kirns nodded.

"Well Murren had Bailey do everything to track her down. We found her trying to sneak back to her own flat. Stupid bitch."

Carla picked up the coffee pot from the stove. Kirns looked at it. Fate was on his side. Two shapes swam over the metallic surface and disappeared. There were two other operatives in the next room.

"Here," said Carla, handing Kirns his coffee. "After you." She gestured for him to go through to the sitting room. "I'll get some biscuits."

As Kirns was about to go through to the living room, Carla reached for the cupboard. She was quick, but Kirns was quicker. He threw his scalding coffee at her face and flung himself at the cupboard. He smashed the door shut, trapping Carla's hand. She screamed as the coffee burnt her. Kirns already had his MP5 out of the back of his jeans. He opened the cupboard and Carla fell to the floor. An automatic sat on the shelf by the tin of biscuits. He took the gun and tucked it in his jeans.

Carla held her face and whimpered. Kirns had to

be quick now. As he stepped towards her a hail of silenced bullets smashed into the arch separating the kitchen from the sitting room; the splintering of wood making more noise that the discharge of ammunition.

In those seconds, Kirns contemplated his options. In such a confined space as the kitchen, he was vulnerable. He made sure the MP5 was cocked then edged to the kitchen arch and swung out.

He entered the room already firing, sweeping the spitting MP5, so that he would hit everything along a horizontal path from left to right. He caught the first of the men in the midriff. Although the MP5 was silenced, the ferocity of the shot was almost surreal. The injured operative was thrown off his feet and back into the furniture.

The second man in the room had time to evade the attack. He leapt behind a leather sofa just as Kirns came into the room. Kirns aimed the spitting MP5 at the sofa knowing that it would be no protection. His gun jammed.

The man hiding behind the chair heard the click and knew. He sprang up, screaming like a lunatic, and started firing.

Kirns dove for cover but was caught in the top of the leg. He fell heavily, blood erupting from the wound.

The operative came round from the back of the sofa to finish him. Kirns pulled the automatic pistol from his jeans just as the man levelled his gun. Kirns fired, shooting him in the chest. The operative swayed on his feet like a doll, then fell back into the very sofa he had just taken refuge behind.

Kirns struggled to his feet. The tissue around the wound was already going into shock and his leg was going numb. His combats were already soaked with blood. Quickly he moved to the kitchen and grabbed a tea towel. He tore off a strip and tied off the flow of blood crudely above the wound.

Carla had got up in those seconds and was going for the door. Kirns grabbed her by the hair and pulled her to the floor. Carla screamed as she hit the ground. Kirns put the gun muzzle to her forehead.

"Where are they?" he demanded. "Where are Murren and Nathan?"

At first, Carla didn't answer. Kirns knew she didn't have what it took to keep quiet and pressed the muzzle harder into her forehead.

"At the house!" she squealed.

"What house?"

"Murren's."

"What was the plan?"

"We were to kill you then go there. Please, John, don't do this," she begged.

"Who's at the house?"

"I told you, Nathan and Murren."

"Who else?"

"I don't know, probably security."

"How many?"

"I don't know how many!" she screamed. "I promise!"

"Is the girl alive?"

"I don't know. She was when I left but they were going to kill her."

"On your feet," said Kirns, pulling her up.

Kirns took the flex from the telephone and tied Carla's hands behind her back. He took her by the hair and led her forward down the iron steps. As they crossed the garden, a horrified old woman next door watched the large man, blood covering the front of his trousers, march a woman with a burnt face and bound hands across the lawn. Kirns glared at her and she scuttled away.

As soon as they reached the car, Kirns roughly bundled Carla into the back. He opened the passenger door to find Stone staring at him. "Move over," he snapped.

Stone did as told. "What the fuck is going on?"

"In the back, in the holdall, is a roll of heavy-duty tape. Get it out," Kirns ordered, painfully.

Stone rummaged around in the back. He looked at Carla, who stared back at him. Her face was covered in large blisters. They both just stared at each other.

"You're alive!" Carla gasped.

"Yeah he's alive," said Kirns. "If you want to remain the same way, I suggest you shut your mouth."

Stone got the tape and handed it to Kirns who started to wrap the tape tightly above the wound in his leg. The steady stream of blood abated but Kirns knew it was bad.

Stone winced at the amount of blood. "Oh my god, you've got to get to a hospital. You're hurt bad."

"You'll have to drive," said Kirns. "Your friend may be alive. They're holding her at Murren's mansion. You drive, I'll direct you."

"But you need attention," said Stone.

Kirns glared at him. This was not the time and he was in no mood.

Stone's quickly started the car.

An hour later they reached the area where Murren lived. Kirns told Stone to park the car a couple of hundred yards before the mansion gates. As soon as they came to a stop, Kirns retrieved rucksack out of the back seat. He got a new clip for the MP5 and loaded it. After putting the rucksack over his shoulders, Kirns got out and dragged Carla out of the car.

"What are you going to do?" asked Stone.

"You stay here," said Kirns, checking the bindings on Carla's hands.

"What about Rachel?"

"If she's here, I'll get her. You know the routine. If I'm not back in half an hour, you get going."

"I can't just stay here," began Stone.

"You'll do as you're fuckin' told," Kirns reminded him. "You certainly don't want to go in there with me. Wait here!"

Kirns marched Carla right up to Murren's security gates. Putting his gun to Carla's temple, he stood them in front of the mounted camera. After a brief wait the camera whirred round and focused on Kirns and his hostage. Kirns made sure the automatic was clearly visible. After a brief wait the gates began to open.

Kirns walked Carla up the gravel drive to the house. As he did, two security guards ran from the side of the house. Both had automatic weapons levelled.

Kirns wasn't flustered and made sure that Carla shielded him. "Stay the fuck back or she dies!"

The front door of the house opened and Nathan stepped out. His face was ablaze with rage and he levelled a pistol at Kirns.

"Let her go, Kirns," he shouted. "You dare touch her!"

"Back up, Nathan, you know the drill," ordered Kirns.

"You're fuckin dead!" Nathan hissed, on seeing his wife's badly burnt face. "What has he done to you, baby? You're fuckin' dead!"

"Just do as he says, Nathan," Carla pleaded. "For God's sake, just do as he says! Don't do anything stupid, Nathan."

Kirns stopped. He turned Carla from right to left, making sure that whoever thought about firing on him knew they would probably hit Carla first.

"Where's Murren?" he asked.

"I'm here," said Murren, emerging in the doorway. "Just calm down, John."

"You killed my brother."

"How do you know that, John?"

"He's alive," shouted Carla. "Stone's alive!"

"That's right," said Kirns. "That's how I found out."

"What are you talking about, John?"

"You killed him. You killed Marcus. But he's going to have the last laugh, Murren. You see my brother kept a file on you, on everything you ever did. And now Stone has it. You're all finished."

Murren's eyes widened with rage. "Kill him!"

"No," shouted Nathan, but he was too late. The two operatives knew only one master and opened fire.

Carla took several rounds in the chest and belly. One of the rounds caught Kirns in the left shoulder. He swung the MP5 round with his good arm and fired back, hitting one of the guards in the guts. Kirns dived to the ground and fired again, this time where he knew Murren had been standing, but he ducked inside as soon as the firing started.

The other operative started to run back. Kirns fired but missed as he turned the corner of the house. Nathan ran for him now. Kirns got to his feet just as Nathan fired a volley of shots. Again, Kirns was struck in the left arm, just above the elbow. He slumped back, returning fire at the same time. Nathan dived, landing by the side of his wife's body. Kirns got up and ran to the side of the house.

Adrenaline kept the pain at bay. Kirns was not going to die like this. He was driven and would see this through no matter what. He crept along the side of the house and around the back where there was a large pool house and glass sunroom. Kirns ducked down by the side of a small pump house and reloaded the MP5. Reaching into his rucksack, Kirns withdrew three smoke grenades and a gas mask. *Just like the old days*, he thought. This is how he was trained, what he knew best. As soon as he heard the sound of his own deep breathing in the respirator he became Sergeant John D. Becker of Her Majesty's twenty-second SAS.

Kirns inched his way along the wall, and then stood when he came to one of the back windows of the house. Peering in, he saw two operatives in the doorway to the next room. They turned, wary, not knowing where the next assault would come from. Kirns knew he had the upper hand now. They were spooked and woefully unskilled at close-combat warfare.

Kirns readied himself. Standing with his back to the wall, he gathered two of the smoke grenades with his working arm and took a deep breath. Holding each grenade with his numbed arm, he pulled each pin on the grenades, smashed the window with his elbow, and threw them inside. They scooted across the kitchen floor, smoke filling every pocket of space. Kirns pulled the pin of a third grenade and kicked the door in.

As soon as he was inside, he threw the grenade into the adjacent room and started shooting. One of the operatives was so disorientated that Kirns actually bumped into him as he ran inside. The guard shouted something but the sentence was never finished. He was shot multiple times at close range, dead before he hit the floor.

Kirns stormed the next room and was somewhat disorientated himself by this time, the smoke making an almost impenetrable fog. Kirns started to run forward, when something hit him from the side with tremendous force. Kirns crashed to the ground. He heard a roar then rapid gunfire from someone hoping to hit something. Kirns levelled his gun at where he thought the shots had come from and fired.

A brief scream echoed, then silence.

Kirns got to his feet. He ran across the room, toward the scream, and found a man struggling with his breathing. Kirns put his gun to the man's face.

"Where are they?"

The man tried to speak but his mouth was full of blood. He coughed and spluttered, then died. Kirns cursed the man but heard more coughing coming from the adjacent room. He got up.

*

Stone had heard the commotion and gunfire and didn't know what to do. He couldn't call the police, but he couldn't just do nothing either. He went to the back of the car and opened the bag Kirns had left. In it was a Glock 9mm semi-automatic pistol. Stone picked up the weapon and examined it. He'd never held a gun before and played around with it for a moment. Stone touched one of the small levers just above the plastic handgrip, and the clip fell back into the bag, making him jump. Stone picked it up. There were bullets in it, so he knew it was loaded. He put the clip back in and snapped it shut.

From the movies he had watched, he was sure he had seen this type of gun before. At the end of the rectangular muzzle were two grips. Stone took the chamber in his thumb and forefinger and pulled. The chamber gave a little. He pulled it again, this time drawing it back until there was a click. The gun was now partially cocked. Something didn't look right, as the whole chamber was bearing over the gun. He examined the side of the gun and knew there must be something else he should do. He saw a button on the side of the stock and pressed it forward. The barrel suddenly snapped shut. The Glock was loaded.

Stone held the weapon in his hand. *You're not honestly thinking of going into that house?* he thought to himself. He leaned against the car. The lane he was in seemed eerily quiet now that the gunshots had stopped. Stone looked up the road to the house. Then he looked back at the other end of the road where there were bright lights – a way out – freedom.

Stone couldn't run away. Rachel was in there, he was sure of it. He had to go in, had to bring her out.

With a deep breath, Stone marched down the road, gun by his side. His heart banged against the inside of his chest. This wasn't like the movies. Not even the gun made him feel safe. As he walked up the road, the gates of the mansion drew nearer. Stone could sense death there and didn't even know if Kirns was still alive.

Whatever the reasons for Stone to head back, it was incredulous he didn't obey them. He came to the gates and stopped. The mansion was at the end of a long drive. Stone started to walk up the driveway, gravel crunching under his feet so loudly he knew he would bring the attention of every killer in the world. Stone froze when he saw the two bodies lying on the lawn. One was Carla. Stone walked past, her lifeless eyes staring up at the place she might have gone had she been a better human being. Blood soaked the front of her blouse. Stone realised that he just couldn't go through with it.

Conty Island filled Stone's thoughts. He felt so safe there, so incredibly protected. His thoughts went to Jennifer and Abraham. Stone wished that somehow he could be transported back to that sanctuary and away from the horror he now faced. He squeezed the gun by his side, contemplating possible actions.

"Like what you see?" asked Nathan. He put his gun muzzle to the back of Stone's head.

Stone dropped his gun and put his hands up, again just like he'd seen in the movies.

"That's my wife you're looking at," said Nathan.

Stone heard the venom in his captor's voice. "What are you going to do?"

"I'm going to kill you," whispered Nathan. "I'm going to do it real slow. You see what you've done? Take a good look before I do the same to you."

"Listen," began Stone.

"No, you listen," corrected Nathan. He pushed Stone forward towards the house. As they started up the flight of stone steps to the front door, Kirns came into view.

Nathan stopped, pulling Stone in front of him.

"Let him go, Nathan," Kirns ordered.

"You must be joking," mocked Nathan. "It's *you* that's going to do what *I* say. You killed my wife, you fuck!"

"And you killed my brother," said Kirns, aiming

his gun. "Looks like we're even."

Nathan pressed his pistol into the back of Stone's head. "Not quite. I like to be in front. You see, I don't really care about living if it isn't with her. But I can take dying a whole lot better knowing I've taken one more thing from you, Kirns."

Stone felt the muzzle of the gun press a little harder against his head, knowing Nathan would pull the trigger. He closed his eyes. This was it.

Kirns saw the chance and knew he had to take it. As Nathan prepared to pull the trigger, he stepped briefly to the side, giving Kirns the slightest of view of his body. Kirns fired once, catching Nathan in the shoulder. Nathan squealed and went to ground.

"Stone, get him!" shouted Kirns.

Stone turned to see Nathan writhing with pain on the ground. He watched dumbly as Nathan brought the pistol up. At first Stone thought he would aim it at him, but Nathan put the pistol to the side of his own head. Without a second thought, Stone dived on him, lunging for the gun.

Stone heard the gun go off and a bullet whine away. He picked himself up to see Nathan looking up at him.

Kirns rushed down the steps and pulled Stone up. He grabbed Nathan by the scruff and hauled him roughly to his feet.

"Jesus, look at you," said Stone. "You're hurt bad."

Kirns's left arm was covered in blood.

Stone followed Kirns, who hauled Nathan back into the house. "Did you hear me, John? You've got to get to hospital."

"Get the girl," ordered Kirns, as they entered the house. "It's safe. I've secured the rooms. She's down in the basement. Hurry!"

Stone sighed with relief. "Where's Murren?"

"In there," said Kirns, motioning his head to The Family meeting room. "Get Rachel, and then come back here. And be quick. You haven't got long."

"Where's the basement?"

"Down the hall to the right. You'll see some stairs. Hurry!"

Stone ran off down the hall. The house stank of cordite and smoke from the grenades still hung in the air, making his eyes water. Stone found the door under the stairs. He found a light switch and flicked it on. A dampness hung in the air and a foul smell wafted from the room below. Stone took a deep breath and descended the stairs.

The cellar was filled with racks of wine. The basement was vast, covering the dimensions of the house. Stone turned the corner and headed for another room. Kicking the door in, he stepped inside. Empty. Frustrated, he ran into different rooms, shouting Rachel's name; his voice resounding in the cellar. As he ran, he bumped into a rack of wine bottles that crashed to the floor.

"Rachel," he cried out. "Rachel!"

Stone ran to the end of a corridor the light had trouble illuminating. At the end was a door. Instead of stopping, he burst through into the room and fell sprawling into the gloom.

Stone lay for a moment as his eyes adjusted to the dimness. As they did, he saw a bundle of old clothes. At first, Stone paid them no attention. As he got to his feet, they moved.

Stone pulled back a large jacket and saw a face. Rachel. She was gagged and blindfolded, but she was alive.

Stone knelt. Carefully he removed the blindfold and got out his lighter so that he could see her better. Stone gasped at the sight of Rachel's dirty face and hair. She was covered in bruises and dried blood crusted the corner of her mouth.

Gently, Stone tapped the side of her cheek with the back of his hand. Rachel was alive, but as to her mental condition, he could only hope. He shook her and Rachel's eyes flickered opened. She stared up at him with a blank expression. Stone shook her again.

"Let me go," she moaned. Her eyes were dilated and she hadn't a clue that it was Stone. "Let me go, please."

"Rachel, it's me, Stoney. Rachel, you're safe."

Rachel still didn't appear to recognise him. "Hello, Stoney," she said dreamily.

She was obviously drugged and Stone inspected Rachel's arms. Two puncture marks tinged with bruises were above her vein. Stone held back the tears. He took her face in his hands. "Rachel," he shouted. "Listen to me. It's Stoney. You're safe now!"

Rachel's eyes found focus. She stared for a moment at him then tears formed. She then began to sob. Rachel clung to Stone as long as she could.

Stone kissed her and stroked the damp hair, away from her eyes. "Yes, it's me. You're safe. You're safe."

Rachel kept sobbing and Stone rocked her in his arms.

"I'm sorry. I'm so sorry," she cried.

*

They emerged from the cellar to find the smoke had all but cleared. It revealed a grim setting. Stone saw two bodies of the dead operatives lying in the library as he passed. He supported Rachel and walked her into the room Kirns had told him to go.

Kirns stood behind Nathan and Murren. Nathan was unconscious. Both were tied to chairs, both wore a necklace of grenades.

"You've got to help me," pleaded Murren. "For the love of God, don't let him do this!"

"What the fuck are you doing, John?" asked Stone, in disbelief.

Kirns swayed behind them, barely able to stand. Blood loss had turned his face ashen. By his side, he gripped a grenade.

"John," said Stone, holding up his hands, "there's been enough killing. I'm going to get help, John."

"Listen to me very carefully," began Kirns. "Take the information you have, Stone, and get out of here, get safe. You know what you have to do!"

"Don't listen to him," blasted Murren. "You've got to help us, for God's sake. You can't just leave us here with him. He's crazy!"

"You can't do this, John," Stone implored. "We've got to get you to a hospital."

"Too late for that," said Kirns wearily. He grinned. "You've got what you came for." He nodded to Rachel, who could barely stand up herself. "I've got what I came for. Now, get as far away as possible. I'll give you five minutes."

"What?" asked Stone. "What are you going to do?"

Kirns stood up straight. "Five minutes, Stone."

Stone just stared at him. "John?"

Kirns held up the grenade and pulled the pin. "Five minutes, damn you!"

Stone knew he could do no more. He lifted Rachel under his shoulder and struggled with her out of the house.

Kirns had lied. He gave them longer than five minutes. In fact, they had made it all the way back to the car before they heard the explosion.

Stone and Rachel slumped against the car. "Damn you, John," whispered Stone. "Damn you."

In the distance, police sirens.

*

Stone pulled up outside the large cottage and turned off the engine. He turned to check on Rachel who slept soundly. He stared back at the cottage, imagining what reception he would receive from its inhabitants.

Stone had contemplated waiting for the police at Murren's mansion, but he knew he could trust no one. Not until at he had spoken with the only person he knew he could. He pulled the blanket up around Rachel's neck, and then headed up the small path to the front door. He stopped and took a deep breath, then rang the bell.

After a short wait the door was opened. The man standing in the doorway froze when he saw his visitor.

Stone said nothing. He realised that he was a mess and wiped his face with his sleeve.

It was then that Shillingway recognised him. "You!"

"Who is it dear?" asked a female voice from inside.

For a moment Shillingway could say nothing.

"I know what I must look like," Stone began calmly. "That's because I've been to hell and back. I also know I'm the last person you want to see now as well, but I need your help like I've never needed anyone's help before."

"Royston, who is it?"

Shillingway ran a hand through his thick beard. He looked passed Stone at the tatty Ford Grenada.

"Please," said Stone.

Shillingway's eyes narrowed. "You better come in."

Stone sighed with relief. "I have a friend," he said, and ran back to the car.

Rachel reluctantly came round to Stone's shaking. Stone helped her out of the car and up to the house. By the time they entered, Shillingway's wife was standing by her husband's side. She gasped when she saw the pathetic sight in front of her. Her maternal instincts however, immediately took over and she went straight to Rachel.

"Royston, get me some blankets, and some water. My god, you poor child."

Shillingway did as he was told.

"I'm so very sorry for this intrusion," began Stone. "And thank you."

Mrs Shillingway sat Rachel on a sofa and put a pillow behind her back. "We need to get this girl to a hospital," she said, inspecting her patient.

Shillingway returned with a shot of brandy. Rachel took a sip. She smiled at Mrs Shillingway as the warmth trickled down her throat.

"What the hell's going on, Stone?" asked Shillingway.

Mrs Shillingway's eyes widened at the mention of the name. Her husband confirmed her realisation with a nod.

Stone felt awkward at Mrs Shillingway's reaction. "I know what you both must think of me, but I need your help. I have no one else to turn to."

Shillingway's face reddened. "Go on."

Stone reached into his jacket and retrieved the floppy disk. He held it up. "I think it's best I start from the beginning."

When Stone finished his story he waited as the Shillingways absorbed it. For a few anxious moments there was silence.

"And it's all on here?" asked Shillingway, taking the floppy from Stone.

"All there," replied Rachel, before Stone could.

Shillingway squeezed his wife's hand then stood up. He went to the telephone and picked up the receiver, his gaze very much on the reporter.

"You can't phone the police," said Stone, getting to his feet.

Shillingway took a deep breath and started dialling. "I'm not," he replied.

"Who then Royston?" asked his wife.

Before Shillingway could respond, his call was answered. "I wish to talk with the Home Secretary," he said in a low voice of authority. "This is Royston Shillingway. And it's a matter of the utmost importance that I speak to him right away."

EIGHTEEN

Stone walked the steps to his apartment. For the past month he had been living under virtual house arrest with Rachel as the investigations into The Family had been conducted. Now, the armed protection squad were gone. Arrests had been made and once again he and Rachel were able to get on with their lives after the police had deemed it safe.

Rachel was temporarily living with Stone. She had decided to move to her sister's in Australia in just a few weeks. Her mental state was still fragile and a fresh start in a new country was the therapy she would need to get on with her life. Both had left The Informer, as the paper was no more. It was a time of reflection and healing. But, for Stone, his thoughts were always with one person.

He walked into the living room where Rachel was having breakfast and watching the morning news. Arrests were still being made by police as they continued their investigations into associations of the organisation known as The Family.

"I've got some milk," said Stone, going into the kitchen.

"They've arrested another one," shouted Rachel.

Stone came back to the living room and listened to the news coverage. A London councillor had been taken into custody following allegations of bribes taken to refuse housing to ethnic minorities. He was said to have taken the bribes from The Family.

Stone sighed and went to leave. *And so it goes on*, he thought.

"What's that?" he asked, referring to a large package leaning against the wall.

"Courier came when you were out," replied Rachel, through a mouthful of cereal. "It's for you. There's a letter on the table that came with it."

Stone picked up the white envelope. There was no stamp or postmark.

"Who's it from?" he said, thoughtfully.

"Why don't you open it and find out?" replied Rachel.

Stone studied the envelope again then fingered the seal open.

Dear Jeramiah,

I guess you heard about Abraham. The world has lost a great artist. He went peacefully in his sleep and was buried by his studio so he can always look out to sea. I've sent the painting Abraham wanted you to have. I'm so sorry I haven't been in touch sooner. I have to see you. Please, could you meet me tomorrow? It's very important. I'll be there at 10 a.m.

Please come, Jeramiah.

Love, Jennifer.

Stone flipped the letter over and found an address of a cemetery in Suffolk.

He sat and stared at the invitation.

"What is it?" asked Rachel.

"He's dead," said Stone softly.

"Who?" asked Rachel, sitting and putting her arm around him.

Stone handed Rachel the letter. "Abraham."

Rachel read the letter and handed it back to him. "I'm so sorry, Stoney."

Stone sighed. "I guess she wants me to go to the funeral."

Rachel squeezed Stone's shoulders reassuringly. She knew all about the brief encounter with Jennifer and knew how much she had meant to him. "And you're going to go, right?"

"Yeah," Stone nodded. "I guess I will."

"I'm going to have a shower," Rachel said. She got up and left Stone with his thoughts.

Stone got up and went to the package he'd been sent. Once the wrappings were removed, he stood back to view the untitled picture he had first seen at the Tate. The painting was as beautiful as he remembered. As he knew now, August sat at his easel painting 'A Blind Eye'. To his left was the angel figure representing his father, serenely watching as his son painted the masterpiece. Whether the recent events had finally caught up or it was the sheer joy of the picture, Stone simply sank to his knees and wept in front of it.

*

The following morning, Stone took the train to Suffolk and read a copy of The Global on the way up. The front page was dedicated to the recent death of the greatest twentieth-century artist. Most of the other pages had been given to eulogies from famous friends. Photographs of his works were shown as well as speculation of their value now that Abraham Conty was dead.

Even as Stone read the news, the monetary value of his gift never occurred to him. He didn't care. All he could think about were Conty's final words to him. Conty was right. Stone was a different man, his life had indeed changed. Stone had even come to terms with Milly's death. He thought of her of course, but the grief was completed, her death finally accepted.

The train pulled in at the station and Stone made for the taxi rank. He gave the driver the address of the small cemetery and sat back for the short journey. He was saddened to be here for the funeral of his friend but also nervous about seeing Jennifer again. Stone had fallen in love with her on Conty Island and he wondered if that was still real.

Eventually the taxi drew up outside the cemetery. As Stone got out, he noticed another car parked outside. He assumed it to be Jennifer's. Instead of going into the church, he went around the back to the vast cemetery. There he saw Jennifer standing with Deklin. Both came to greet him.

"Hello, Jeramiah," said Jennifer.

Stone thought Jennifer was more beautiful than he had ever remembered. She wasn't wearing black like he had expected, instead she had on a white summer dress. She looked radiant.

"Hello, Jennifer," he said. They embraced. "Hello, Dek."

"Nice to see you again, Jeramiah." Deklin replied, with the trademark smile. "I'll wait in the car," he said, and took his leave.

"Thank you for coming, Jeramiah."

Stone smiled at her. "It's the least I can do."

"I've missed you so much."

"I've missed you too."

Stone kissed her.

"Walk with me?" she said.

Jennifer put her arm through Stone's and they walked along the path.

"How have you been?" she asked as they walked. "You look tired. You must have gone through hell?"

Stone shrugged. "Okay, I think." He smiled. "It was sad to hear about August."

Jennifer looked at the ground. "He went a week after you left." She looked up. "I've missed you, Jeramiah. I'm sorry I didn't try and reach you sooner, but I had to be there for Abraham."

Stone nodded. "I understand. Really I do."

"Did you like the painting Abraham left you?"

Stone beamed. "It's beautiful." He then bowed his head. "I'll miss him not being in the world anymore."

"Yeah, me too," replied Jennifer.

"What happened? How did he die?"

Jennifer took a deep breath. "Two days after August passed, by the studio." She tried not to cry. "He was just sitting in a chair overlooking the island. He passed away in his sleep."

Jennifer choked and Stone quickly put his arm around her.

"And what now?" asked Stone. "What about the estate?"

Jennifer shrugged. "I have to manage the works. Where they go and stuff. I don't want to stay on the island. I don't know what I shall do with it."

"What about the people that knew Abraham? Are they coming here?"

Jennifer shook her head. "No, it's just us. They think Abraham was buried at a private ceremony at the island. August was cremated. Abraham scattered his ashes on the wind at the very top of the island," she said thoughtfully. "It was what August wanted. He loved it there so much.

"Look Jeramiah, I've got something to tell you," she said nervously.

"What is it?"

Jennifer hesitated a moment, then came out with

it. "It seems that night we spent with each other on the island was more important than we thought... I'm pregnant, Jeramiah."

Stone was taken aback. "But I thought you...?"

"Well it seems I can." Jennifer grinned and placed his hand on her tummy.

At first Stone didn't know what to say. He just stared dumbly. "Oh, my god, I can't believe it."

"Are you happy, Jeramiah? Please tell me you are."

"Of course I'm happy," Stone laughed. Tears suddenly filled his eyes. "Oh God, yes, I'm so happy."

Jennifer put her hand on the side of his face. "Oh, my love, I'm so glad."

Stone clasped his hand against hers.

They walked a little further arm in arm until they came to the fresh gravesite.

"This is the village where Abraham was married," said Jennifer. "This is the place he always wanted to be buried. Alongside his wife. He was buried two days ago. Deklin and I came in secret." She smiled and let out a long sigh. "No more secrets now."

There were two graves. One was new, of course. Sunlight seemed to favour these graves above all others. Stone stepped in front of the headstone and read the simple and touching epitaph.

Here lies Abraham and Louise Matherton.
Together at peace.

Jennifer took him by the hand. "I love you," she said.

In that moment, Stone found it hard to say anything. He just held Jennifer's hand and knew he would never let it go.

EPILOGUE

Commander of the Metropolitan Police, Ian Bailey, was the first on MI5's list. They raided his home in the early hours of the morning and dragged him from his bed.

As soon as the wave of arrests started, word spread to the remaining heads of The Family. Captain Andrew Haines was found dead in his country home in Chichester, hanged with the cord from his housecoat.

Major George Rothmead was arrested at his home in Aldershot. He was having supper with his wife and family on the evening of the raid. Reportedly, he had calmly kissed each of his family members in turn and gone genially with the police.

Jeremy Luflin of the Home Office's Immigration Department was in Saudi Arabia when he was arrested. MI5 operatives working in conjunction with the Saudi authorities had turned up at a banquet that Luflin had been invited to by the Saudi government and arrested him there. He cried as the police took him away from the large dining hall, to the amazement of the other guests.

Lewis Wright-Smith of the solicitors, *Wright-Smith*, was found on the banks of the river Thames. He had taken a lethal cocktail of barbiturates and whiskey before drowning himself.

Simon Losely of *Losely Merchant Bank*, threw himself from the fourteenth floor of his offices in Los Angeles. A suicide note was found on him saying that he hadn't meant for things to turn out the way they did and was sorry.

Mitchell Seymour of *Seymour Financiers* was arrested at his home in Oxford. The police had to restrain his wife who had attempted to stab her husband with a kitchen knife after the police read out the charges.

Michael, Murren's butler, had hidden himself in the attic when the shooting had started at Murren's home on that fateful day. He turned himself over to the police but was later released as it was discovered he had no involvement with The Family. He later committed suicide.

Waves of arrests were made around the capital, as all mentioned in Becker's already infamous file were rounded up. Most came quietly because of surprise raids at known addresses. All except two operatives, loyal to the last. They had reportedly held themselves up and tried to shoot it out with the police. Marksmen killed both. In all, twenty-eight operatives had been arrested. All assets relating to The Family were frozen and properties seized.

After a week's search, the body of Samuel Parker was found near the banks of the River Rye in Surrey following the interrogation of the remaining senior members. Police confirmed publicly Parker was the driver of the Fiat Uno carrying Nathan Green, that infamous Paris day.

Robert Sumpter's family attended the photographer's funeral. Stone of course felt responsible for his friend's death, something he would have to live with for the rest of his life.

Marcus Becker was buried in his birth town of Maidstone, Kent. Only close family and relatives were at his funeral. Not a single employee of The Informer attended.

Stone felt he owed John Kirns and insisted the man who had saved his life be buried with full military honours. Given the evidence, and a great deal of political persuasion from Shillingway, the Home Office agreed and John Kirns was laid to rest as he might have wanted.

The Prime Minister went on national television to inform the public about the turn of events and to reassure the population that the government did not know about the secret society and were co-operating fully with the authorities to bring the remaining members of this 'evil' organisation to justice. An internal governmental investigation as to how this organisation went undetected was to follow.

The practices undertaken by all tabloids were now under review and legislation was expected to change the way tabloids and their journalists conducted their business.

Those framed by The Family, whose careers or businesses were ruined, were now under review and a statement would follow shortly. The government and

MI5 investigated councils across the country as well as all organisations or charities The Family had anything to do with. Given the comprehensive details left in Becker's file, the task was not as daunting as first thought. Three weeks after the explosion at Edward Murren's mansion, most of The Family and its associates were either under arrest or MI5 investigation.

Buckingham Palace also made a statement, outlining the Palace's full co-operation in any investigations and its insistence that it had nothing to do with the attempted assassination of the princess.

*

Abraham Conty's complete works were donated to Spain by his widow Jennifer and a new gallery to house them is being built on the island where the artist lived and died.

Jennifer Conty re-married Jeramiah Stone and now lives in Barcelona with their new daughter, April.

Deklin Owuzukabe married and now lives in Denmark. He is expecting his first child.

Rachel Martin moved to Sydney and works at an inner city primary school.

Printed in Great Britain
by Amazon